P9-DBZ-115

It reared, rising almost to the level of his throat, mandibles clacking in the air. He leaped aside, rolled, and came up with his shuk in front of him. The huraj settled back to the ground, then whipped around and started forward again. Hult had long enough to see Forlo swiping his own blade at the other one, keeping it at bay while he tried to circle to its flank. Then the black huraj came on again, clawed legs churning. He brought back his saber, spun it, then snapped it around as hard as he could, striking with the tip of the blade at the creature's neck. It was a powerful stroke, swift and well aimed, strong enough to take off the huraj's head. But it didn't.

Instead, his sword shattered.

TALADAS TRILOGY

Volume One
Blades of the Tiger

Volume Two
Trail of the Black Wyrm

Volume Three
Shadow of the Flame

Also by Chris Pierson

Bridges of Time
Spirit of the Wind
Dezra's Quest

Kingpriest Trilogy
Chosen of the Gods
Divine Hammer
Sacred Fire

TRAIL

TALADAS OF THE TRILOGY

BLACK WYRM

VOLUME TWO

CHRIS PIERSON

The Taladas Trilogy

TRAIL OF THE BLACK WYRM

©2006 Wizards of the Coast, Inc.

All characters in this book are fictitious. Any resemblance to actual persons, living or dead, is purely coincidental.

This book is protected under the copyright laws of the United States of America. Any reproduction or unauthorized use of the material or artwork contained herein is prohibited without the express written permission of Wizards of the Coast, Inc.

Published by Wizards of the Coast, Inc. DRAGONLANCE, WIZARDS OF THE COAST, and their respective logos are trademarks of Wizards of the Coast, Inc., in the U.S.A. and other countries.

Printed in the U.S.A.

The sale of this book without its cover has not been authorized by the publisher. If you purchased this book without a cover, you should be aware that neither the author nor the publisher has received payment for this "stripped book."

Cover art by Matt Stawicki
First Printing: April 2006
Library of Congress Catalog Card Number: 2005928125

9 8 7 6 5 4 3 2 1

ISBN-10: 0-7869-3979-6
ISBN-13: 978-0-7869-3979-4
620-95461740-001-EN

U.S., CANADA,   EUROPEAN HEADQUARTERS
ASIA, PACIFIC, & LATIN AMERICA   Hasbro UK Ltd
Wizards of the Coast, Inc.   Caswell Way
P.O. Box 707   Newport, Gwent NP9 0YH
Renton, WA 98057-0707   GREAT BRITAIN
+1-800-324-6496   Save this address for your records.

Visit our web site at www.wizards.com

FOR MICHAEL.
BET YOU DIDN'T SEE THAT COMING.

Prologue

THE TEMPLE OF AKH-TAZI, NERON

She awoke to darkness, to silence. She awoke to it every morning—if morning it was. It could be the middle of the night. There was no way to know.

Light came twice every day: the cold, white glimmer of magic, shining from the hall when her captors brought her food. That was it. With this light, she had defined the boundaries of her cell. It was small, three paces on a side, with a high ceiling that caused every cough, every groan, to echo horribly. Its walls and floor were dark stone, graven with images she did not recognize—awful images. Eagles with serpents' heads. Men with the heads of hunting cats. Corpses with their chests flayed open. She tried not to look at them when the light came, but it was hard. They were all around and never seemed to be in the same place twice.

There was a bed, reeds stretched over a wooden frame, with a blanket of some woven plant fiber that itched horribly. There was a clay pot for waste. There was nothing else.

She had yet to see her captors. The food simply appeared; the scraps vanished. The waste pot was emptied, replaced by a fresh one. She could sense them when the door opened—mocking eyes in the shadows—but they did not reveal themselves.

Essana Forlo, Baroness of Coldhope, had never felt so desolate in her life.

Sleep brought terror, dark dreams she could barely remember when she woke. The glisten of black scales, the creak of leathery wings, the chanting of many growling voices. Shadows that walked like men, whose touch was like knives of ice. The dreams had no coherence, made no sense. She tried to untangle them, but they frayed, fell apart. Every time. She wept with frustration.

Where in the Abyss was she?

The door opened. Cold light spilled in. No one there. Food came. It was almost always the same meal: a roasted game bird of some sort, the skin crackling, the meat succulent. A porridge of something close to mashed turnip. A mound of little, round fruits, red-fleshed and sour. A cup of bitter, steaming tea that must be drugged. There was plenty of it . . . which was good, for she had another to feed, growing inside her. Her son, by her husband, Barreth—Barreth, who had left to fight a battle both of them knew he couldn't survive. He must be dead now, slaughtered by barbarians. How long until their son was born? Three months? Four? It was impossible to tell; time in this place meant nothing.

After the door slammed shut, she wolfed her food. It could have tasted like ashes, and she would have gobbled it down—her unborn child made her hungry beyond reasoning—but it was delicious. That only made her imprisonment worse, somehow. Still, she needed the food for strength. Today she would try to escape.

It had taken a long time to make the decision, longer still to find the courage. But Essana knew there was no hope if she stayed here. What her captors had in mind, she didn't know . . . but she had to get out. So she decided as she sat in the dark, stuffing porridge in her mouth, that she would leave her cell the next chance she got.

And if they caught her? If they killed her?

She didn't care anymore.

She was still half awake when the door opened again, well after supper. She hadn't drunk the drugged tea today; had poured it into the waste pot instead. She feigned grogginess, moaning as the light spilled in. The platter holding the scraps of her meal quivered, then rose off the floor. So did the waste pot. Nothing held them up; they simply floated into the air and slid out of the room. She bit her lip, gathered her strength, tensed herself to follow. She would have a second, maybe two, to heave her pregnant body out the door. The door would probably crush her if it shut on her. Had to be quick.

Wait . . . wait . . . now.

Something appeared in the doorway, just as she was leaping forward: a shape. It was tall, maybe seven feet, slender, and not human. The thing was an abomination: its flesh a mottled mess of moss green and ruddy brown; its hands three-fingered, with long, slender talons; its head a bulbous, hairless orb with dead-white eyes and four writhing tentacles where its mouth should be. A stink rose from it, like skunk spray mixed with rotting fish. It burned her nose, made her eyes water. It wore a filthy gray cassock, cinched with rope, like a monk's habit.

Essana let out a near-voiceless scream and fell back. The thing watched her, its gaze devoid of emotion. Its tentacles twitched, moving as if each had a mind of its own. When it spoke, it made no sound: the words simply formed in her mind, toneless and scratchy.

We know what you were going to do. If you try, this will be your fate.

An image blazed in her mind, as clear as if she were seeing it with open eyes. Essana beheld herself from above. She was naked, chained to the floor of this very cell, her body a ruin. Her arms were broken; so were her legs. Her eyes were hollow pits. Her tongue was gone. But her belly was large, round and hard: the baby, almost ready to emerge. And she knew what she'd suspected since she first awoke here:

Her captors cared nothing for her. They wanted only the child.

"Why?" she screamed. "What are you going to do with him?"

The tentacled horror stared at her without emotion. More words came.

Do nothing to thwart us, and you will not suffer. Betray us, and you will know pain, for the rest of your life. Soon the Brethren will send for you.

Essana stared at the wretched creature, hate boiling inside her. She wanted to crush it, smash its awful, glistening head against the wall until it cracked open. But she held herself in check, backed against the wall, slid down to the floor. The creature watched her a moment longer, then vanished into the shadows. A clean waste pot glided into the room and settled to the floor. The door rumbled shut.

Darkness again. Essana sat in the gloom, shaking. In time, sleep came—and with it new dreams, of tentacles and blank, white eyes.

———◆—✖—◆———

She woke. She slept. Inside her, the new life grew.

Essana lay on the bed, her hand on her belly. She knew the baby was still alive, but sometimes, in the stillness, she prayed the gods would claim him. It would be easier if she miscarried . . . but she did not. For many years, she and Barreth had struggled to conceive a child. Now her body would not give it up.

"They won't have you," she whispered. "I will not give you to those . . . those. . . ."

Creatures. Things.

She was lying there, aching, when the door opened again. A figure stood framed against the light. She shrank back against the wall, then realized it wasn't the monster that had confronted her before. This was a man, clad in a dark cloak, a deep hood drawn low over his face. He watched her from the doorway, framed by the light.

"Who . . ." she croaked.

"I am called the Keeper," he replied. His voice was strange, with a thick, rasping quality. It was the voice of a strangled man, or one whose throat has been cut.

Essana swallowed painfully. "What do you want with me? With the child?"

"You will learn the answers," said the Keeper, "if you come with me."

"And if I refuse?"

His head tilted, his shoulders shaking. The man was laughing—not mockery, but genuine mirth.

"Spirited," he said. "I knew one like you, once. Before I came to this place. But you cannot refuse—you will come of your own accord, or . . . by their command."

He stepped aside. There was movement behind him. Two of the things came in. One was green and brown, the other fish-belly grey. They stared at her, unfeeling, tentacles waving. Essana felt a prickling in her mind, like a name she wanted to remember, but couldn't. She put a hand to her forehead. The feeling grew, became a thought.

Get up.

Her eyes locked on the creatures. They are doing this to me, she thought. I must resist.

Stand.

She bunched her hands into fists. She bit her tongue. She thought of songs, memories, making love to Barreth. She fought the command, but the suggestion kept growing in her mind, growing so strong her legs burned to move.

STAND.

It was too much. Groaning, she swung her legs off the bed and lurched to her feet. Tears of frustration crawled down her cheeks.

5

"Gods damn you," she growled, her teeth grinding.

The Keeper had watched it all happen, not saying a word. Now he raised a hand. "Enough," he murmured. "Leave us."

The creatures glanced at him, and at once their minds were gone from Essana's. She nearly collapsed as they withdrew from the cell. She staggered against the wall, glowering at the cloaked figure.

"What are they?" she asked.

"They are called yaggol," he replied. "An ancient race. They built this temple. Once they ruled a mighty empire, but now they serve the Brethren."

Essana wiped her face with the back of her hand. "And who do you serve?"

"You will see. Now come."

She still wanted to tell him to rot in the Abyss, but the thought of the yaggol compelling her again sickened her. Defeated, she gestured for him to lead on.

He did, and she followed. The yaggol walked behind, silent. The Keeper strode down the cramped stone passage, his black cloak billowing behind him. They came to a stairway, leading up. The Keeper climbed, and Essana and the yaggol followed. He never glanced back.

Scents came to her: fresh air. Trees. Strange flowers. She heard wind through leaves. She glimpsed moonlight, red and silver, upon the stone. They emerged into an open courtyard, at night, a clear sky above: Solis and Lunis and stars. The plaza was ringed with pillars of black stone, crumbling and vine-throttled, some broken, some toppled. The floor was stone as well, huge blocks between which grew white flowers surrounded by blue-glowing fireflies. Beyond, on three sides, stood dense walls of jungle. The trees were huge, rising high above. Strange animals called from within. The air sweltered, humid and hot even at night.

She knew where she was now—Neron, the southernmost reaches of Taladas. A thousand miles from home.

Despair clawed at her—even if someone were looking, how could they ever find her? How would they even start?

On the fourth side of the courtyard rose a tall, stepped pyramid, a ziggurat hewn of the same black rock as everything else. A broad, steep stair rose up the pyramid's side, awful gargoyles of animal-men perched on each step. More cloaked figures loomed at the top.

"The Brethren await," said the Keeper, and he walked on. Essana glanced at the yaggol, who stared back. She followed him.

The stairs were hard going, especially in her condition. She moved slowly, using her hands to brace herself against the steps above. Not far from the top she faltered, slipping. The Keeper reached down and caught her wrist before she could fall. His grip was firm but gentle. He helped her the rest of the way up.

There were five more like him atop the ziggurat. All wore cloaks. They watched from the shadows of their hoods as the Keeper led her forward. There was an altar, old and worn, with grinning skulls carved on its sides. Dried blood crusted its top. Essana froze at the sight.

The Keeper glanced at her. "Do not fear, lady. That is not for you."

A mad impulse came to her, then—she should turn and run. Throw herself down the stairs. The fall would almost certainly kill her. It would definitely kill the baby. But when she looked behind, the yaggol were there, watching. They saw what was in her mind. She wouldn't be able to take two steps before they seized control of her again. She hated them, more than anything she'd ever hated in her life.

Another of the cloaked figures exchanged hushed words with the Keeper, then turned toward her. She felt her knees buckle. This one had no humanity left in him; there was only malice, and burning zeal. She could feel his evil gaze, and it made her shudder.

"You have questions," he said. "You will have answers

soon. I am the Master; the Keeper you already know. The others are the Watcher, the Speaker, the Teacher, and the Slayer. We are the Faceless Brethren."

As one, the six figures cast back their hoods, and Essana let out a gasp of horror. What they revealed weren't faces at all, but leering skulls, the flesh stripped away by blade and flame to lay bare the bone beneath. Black tongues worked behind long teeth. Bloodshot eyes glistened in their sockets. They had been human once; now they were something else. Essana tasted bile. She wanted to look away but realized she couldn't.

"You wish to know who we are," said the Master, the tendons of his jaw working. "We are heralds, disciples. We prepare for the return of a great power—one who once slept, but is now awoken."

A shriek pierced the night: a furious, skirling cry that awakened a memory buried deep in her. She looked up, and saw it—the vision from her nightmares.

The black dragon.

It slid between the stars, long and sinuous, almost invisible. Its wings eclipsed the moons as it swept over the trees. Its scales glittered. Its eyes were coals of burning red. Venom dripped from its fangs. In its claws it held two things: the limp, dark-skinned form of a person, and a statue carved of dark stone.

A statue she knew too well.

A moan escaped Essana's lips, and she fell painfully to her knees. Barreth had brought the statue to the castle of Coldhope, their home, several months ago. It was said to be an ancient relic from the lost empire of Aurim—worth a small fortune to the right people. They'd both hated the thing, but had kept it, hoping to sell it to sages in the city of Kristophan. They had hidden it beneath the castle, out of sight.

Not long after, the elf had come. Shedara had been seeking the statue for months. She called it the Hooded One and told them its tale: hewn in the image of Maladar, a mad sorcerer-king who once ruled Aurim, it was said to house his spirit, trapped within. The Hooded One was dangerous beyond reckoning, and Shedara had come to see that it was destroyed. But before they could do anything about it, Barreth had been drawn away, to fight the Uigan barbarians as they crossed the straits of Tiderun. He rode out, giving the statue into Shedara's keeping.

Then Essana's memories ended, and her nightmares began. The dragon had come for her. It and other fiends—little, shadowy creatures that killed with knives that spilled no blood—overran Coldhope. They brought her here. And they also brought the Hooded One.

The dragon circled the pyramid . . . once, twice . . . then spread its wings and swooped down. It set down the statue, and dropped the other shape onto the altar. Looking closer, Essana saw it was an elf—small, naked save for a loincloth of woven leaves and a necklace of red and yellow stones. His face was painted with white lines, and his head was shaved, save for a tight, black knot of hair at the crown of his head. He was battered, blood leaking from his nose. He groaned, blinking, then saw the Brethren and cried out, trying to rise.

He couldn't: his legs wouldn't work. The dragon had broken his back.

The great wyrm settled on the far end of the roof, tucking in its wings and lowering its head. Its eyes fixed on Essana as the largest of the Brethren strode toward the altar. In his hand he held a long, sickle-bladed knife. Essana knew he was the one called the Slayer. The elf's struggles grew more frantic.

The Faceless turned toward the statue, and Essana saw that it had changed. When she'd last seen it, it had been shrouded; now, somehow, its stone cowl had fallen back to reveal a ruined, fleshless face, much like the Brethren's. One of them, the Speaker, raised his hands to it and intoned in a deep, mellifluous voice.

"Hail, the Faceless Emperor! Maladar an-Desh, lord of wizards, reaver of cities, sleeper within the stone!"

"Hail, the Faceless!" echoed the Brethren.

"We give you the blood of the innocent. Let his life sustain yours until the time of your return."

The elf's shrieks were not in a language Essana knew, but she understood nonetheless. He called to his ancestors, to the gods. The Slayer seized the knot of his hair, jerked his head back, and with the practiced movement of a butcher, cut his throat.

The cries ended in an awful drowning sound. The elf's struggles ceased. Blood flowed thick. The Slayer put away his knife and produced a bowl, made from an empty skull. He held it under the killing wound until it was full to the brim. Then he walked to the Hooded One, raised it in salute, and poured the blood at the statue's feet.

"Blood for the Faceless!" he shouted.

"Blood!" the Brethren repeated.

The Master seized Essana by the shoulders, dragging her to her feet. Roughly he thrust her forward, toward the statue. She stumbled again, light-headed with shock.

"Be careful!" said the Keeper. "The child must not be harmed."

The Master waved him off, then strode forward and hauled Essana up before the Hooded One. "Behold, sleeper!" he called. "Behold your vessel, and know your time is nigh. The child will come, as the Watcher proclaimed. The child will come, and be yours."

Essana looked up at the Master, horror robbing her of speech. He stared down at her, and though his face was incapable of emotion, his eyes burned with scorn. The last piece of the puzzle fell into place. She knew why the dragon had brought her here. Why they wanted her son.

"Yes, my dear," rasped the Master. "You see, don't you? Maladar's spirit stirs. It longs to quit its prison of stone.

But it cannot. Not yet. He needs flesh to house him. The Faceless seeks a body."

Finally, it was too much. The sheer awfulness of it overwhelmed her. With a despairing sigh, Essana Forlo collapsed.

Chapter

1

COLDHOPE, THE IMPERIAL LEAGUE

The wind whipped in off the Tiderun, raising foamy caps on the surface of the water. It was a chill breeze, the first sign of the coming autumn. Gulls fought it, flapping hard to try to get out to sea but barely moving at all. No ships plied the waves. Surf exploded against the rocky shore, sending tall billows of spray streaming inland.

Barreth Forlo faced the wind and the spray and cared about neither. He leaned against the rail of the balcony known as the Northwatch, the largest overlook of Coldhope Keep. This place had been his home, once, but it no longer felt like it. The castle had not fallen—was still intact, in truth. But it had been overthrown, by an enemy no walls could stop. They had come, in secret and in silence, and they had taken away all he had left to care for in this world.

And he had no idea what to do about it.

It was because of the statue, the damned Aurish statue. He cursed the day the Hooded One had fallen into his possession. He cursed Harlad, the pirate—dead now, with his crew, amid the isles of Mislaxa's Necklace—who had given the artifact to him, as ransom for violating Coldhope's waters. Most of all, though, he cursed himself, for not dumping the gods-be-cursed thing into the sea when he found out how evil it was. He'd been greedy—had seen only the gold the statue would bring among the scholars of the capital—and now he paid for his avarice.

He beat his fist against the balustrade, skinned a knuckle, stuck a stinging finger in his mouth. The tang of blood washed over his tongue. He barely tasted it. He was lost in memory, reliving the days just past. It seemed a lifetime since he'd ridden out of Coldhope. He'd gone to fight the Uigan, a barbarian horde who had gathered under a mighty prince and ridden south for plunder. They had crossed the Tiderun—a shallow gap between their lands and his—when the three moons brought the tides so low that the waters fled. They were thousands strong. His men had numbered a few hundred. Not one of them had thought they had a chance.

And yet, by a miracle, they had persevered. A mighty wave, conjured by magic, had come raging down the Run and swept most of the horde away. Though many good men had died in the fighting—including Forlo's best friend, the minotaur Grath—the Imperial League's defenders had prevailed. The Uigan were broken, and their leader, a warrior who could take the form of a steppe-tiger, was slain. Against all expectation, Forlo had hurried home from the battlefield victorious—only to find utter defeat awaiting him.

It was clear to him now: the fight against the Uigan had been a ruse, nothing more—a distraction to pull Coldhope's warriors away. When they were gone, the shadow-fiends had struck. Twisted, wicked creatures that once had been living kender, the shadows had overrun the keep, killed its few defenders, and taken three things beyond price:

The statue. His wife. His unborn son.

He'd returned six days ago, dust-caked and road-weary. He'd come on foot, his horse slain by the shadows upon the road. And he hadn't come alone. He turned now, to look back over his shoulder.

Hult stood still, watching him without seeming to. A youth of not yet twenty summers, he had been the Uigan prince's protector. It had been his duty to avenge his fallen master on the battlefield. And yet, he had not done that duty. Forlo still didn't know why. They didn't speak each other's language. But Hult hadn't been far from him since that day, and he stayed close now, trying not to look directly at the sea. The water had devoured his people, on the verge of their greatest victory. Forlo could sense the boy's fear, his hatred of the heaving waves. He understood; there were things he feared and hated too.

Six days. He still didn't know where his family was. Or where to begin looking.

"I won't learn anything here," he muttered to himself. "I don't know how I'll find them again, but the answer isn't in Coldhope."

Hult said nothing. He seldom did, and then only in the strange, harsh tongue of the Uigan. He simply stood, one hand on the hilt of his saber, the curved blade his people called a shuk. His tanned face betrayed no emotion. The lone braid he wore atop his head—the rest of his scalp was bald—flapped like a pennant in the wind.

"We have to go," Forlo insisted. "We've got to leave this castle. There are places we can seek help, people who can give us answers. Somewhere. We'll find them. We must pick up the trail, somehow."

Hult said nothing. Forlo grunted, turned to cast one last look out to sea, then turned his back on the waters and strode down the Northwatch to an open doorway into the keep. Quietly, the Uigan followed.

Coldhope was dark within, the shutters closed against the gale, except for one that banged ceaselessly, off in the servants' wing. Forlo had lit only a handful of lamps and candles, keeping a lone fire on the hearth of the greatroom. Darkness gnawed at the vaulted ceiling; the banners and weapons and animal heads upon the halls stood dark and foreboding. Once, this had been a vibrant place, alive. Now it felt like a tomb. Forlo knew he could not spend a seventh day within its walls.

For all the stillness and gloom, though, the greatroom wasn't empty. A lone figure, a woman, sat at the far end of a long banquet table in its midst. She sat with her head bowed, an empty wine cup before her. There was something else, too: something on which she focused all her attention, so strongly she didn't hear Forlo and Hult approach. Only when they were a few paces from her did Shedara of Armach look up.

The elf was tired and haggard, her face so pale it looked almost blue. Streaks of white ran through her coppery hair, a strange sight in one whose people stayed young for centuries. Those marks were new, signs of struggle against darkness and despair. Shedara had been at Coldhope when the shadows came; they had cornered her in the master bedchamber, where she had tried in vain to keep them from grabbing Essana. She had barely slept since then. Now she met Forlo's gaze, and her shoulders slumped. Dejected, she tossed the object she had been studying down onto the table. It landed with a thud, knocking the cup over.

It was large and round, the size of a buckler, the color of polished obsidian. It was harder than iron, glistening in the firelight. A scale from the hide of a black dragon, the only token left from the raid on Coldhope. Shedara had barely let it out of her possession, these past six days: she was magi after all, and had spent all her energy trying to divine something—anything—about it.

"I give up," she said. "Dragons are magical creatures. I can't see anything, no matter how hard I look."

Forlo nodded, reaching out to touch her shoulder. "Thank you for trying."

"There has to be something," she said, shaking him off. She refused to be comforted. "Some way to find out where the statue went."

Forlo drew back as if she'd stung him. Anger flashed through him—how dare she worry first about the statue when his wife was missing?—but it quickly passed. Shedara's people had sent her to find the Hooded One. She'd followed its trail halfway across Taladas, only to lose it. Of course it would be first in her thoughts.

He heard a scrape and glanced back to see that Hult had drawn his shuk halfway out of its sheath. He shook his head, gesturing for the barbarian to back down. Not for the first time, he wondered why Hult chose to protect the man who had slain his master. The Uigan were certainly a strange folk.

At the same time, Shedara had also pushed back from the table, reaching to her belt for one of her many knives. Now she, too, relaxed.

"Tell him if he ever draws that sword the whole way, I'll put a blade in his eye," she muttered.

"I could tell him you love him dearly and wish to wed him next Springrise," Forlo said. "He'd understand it just as well."

Shedara chuckled, then laughed out loud. Hult's face darkened, but he made no move, said no word. He simply glowered at the elf as she wiped a tear from her cheek. When she was done, she looked up at Forlo, her eyes narrowed.

"We're leaving, aren't we?" she asked.

"Yes."

"Where are we bound?"

Forlo shrugged. "First, we should find the soldiers who survived the battle. They should be done hunting down the last of the horde by now. After that . . . Kristophan, I think. We might find answers there. Or perhaps your people, in Armach-nesti, if they'll have us."

She considered this. "It would be . . . difficult. Humans aren't welcome in our woods. There are laws against their presence. But a lot's changed, these past months, so maybe they'll make an exception. Maybe. When do we leave?"

"Today. As soon as we can." Forlo glanced around, then shook his head. "I can't look at this place anymore. I need a road beneath my feet."

"Suits me," Shedara said. "I'm ready now, if we travel light. We don't need to carry much."

Forlo nodded. "It's settled, then. Let's gather what we can carry from the pantries, and we'll be gone before the sun starts to fall."

An hour later, they stepped out the front door of the manor into the courtyard. Forlo looked to the stables and felt a pang of regret: there had been a few old horses left at Coldhope, but the shadows had killed them too. They'd have to travel on foot, at least until they caught up with his men.

The sky had turned gray, and a fine rain had begun to fall. The raindrops pinged on his helmet as he made his way across the bailey. With Hult's help, he lifted the bar from the inside of the gates and pulled them open. Finally, swallowing, he turned and looked back at the keep. It looked cold, forlorn, dead. The last time he'd left Coldhope, he'd thought he would never see the place again . . . but he'd been wrong.

This time, though, he was sure.

"Forlo," whispered Shedara on his left.

He stiffened. Something in her voice wasn't right. A tightness. A heartbeat later, he heard the ring of her daggers leaving their sheaths—and then the hiss of Hult drawing his saber. He whirled, clapping a hand to his sword.

Beyond the gates stood a crowd of dark shapes . . . half a dozen at least. They were small, less than four feet from head to foot, and as insubstantial as mist. Blackness sloughed off them in waves, caught the wind, and writhed away. Each held two hooked blades, one in either hand. It was impossible, at this distance, to see their faces, aside from the glint of hungry, hateful eyes.

Rage exploded inside Forlo at the sight of them: the shadow-fiends, the things that had been kender, once, but now were ruined, murderous monsters. They had taken his Essana, his Starlight. He jerked his blade from its scabbard.

The sky had grown darker, taking on the color of slate. The rain fell in fat drops, turning the courtyard to mud. The three of them stared at the shadow-fiends. The shadow-fiends stared back. Time stretched.

"What in Hith's Cauldron are they doing?" Forlo growled. "Why are they still here?"

"I think they're after me," Shedara replied. "Their masters must know that I used the statue, that I forced the Hooded One to summon the wave. The dragon probably told them."

Forlo's lips pursed. "Then they may know where Essana is. We should try to take one alive. Question it."

"And how do you propose to do that, exactly?"

He glanced at her, his mouth opening to reply, then realized he didn't know. They could not be subdued, and they would never surrender. "Don't you know any spells to capture them?" he asked.

"No more than you do," Shedara answered. "Let's just concentrate on surviving, shall we?"

Hult had been listening to their conversation, annoyance creasing his brow. Now he stepped forward, sword raised, and yelled something at the shadows.

"Yagrut!"

The word was in the Uigan tongue, so Forlo didn't understand, but he got the idea. He'd been a soldier most of his life, and knew profanity when he heard it. So, apparently, did the shadows. They fell back at first, surprised by the barbarian's challenge, then started creeping forward. Their blades twirled in their hands, weaving silently through the air.

Six. Two each. Forlo thought they could handle those odds. He'd never seen Shedara fight, but she seemed to know what she was doing. And Hult was capable enough with his saber. Six shouldn't be much of a problem.

And then there were twelve.

The second wave seemed to come out of nowhere, seeping out of the darkening rain curtain. They glided forward, just behind their fellows. A dozen, now.

"Khot," Forlo swore.

Shedara nodded, her face grim. "Make a circle," she murmured. "If those things outflank us, we're dead."

We're dead anyway was the first thought that came to Forlo's mind. He thrust it aside, forced himself not to believe the worst. He couldn't afford to fail now, not after all he'd been through. Not with what he still had to do.

"Hurry," Shedara said. The shadows were nearly upon them.

Forlo grabbed Hult's arm, pulled him to them. The barbarian looked confused, but only for a moment. Forlo and Shedara stood back-to-back, and he joined them. Together they formed a triangle in the mouth of the courtyard, blades extended before them. The creatures hesitated, studying this new tactic—but not for long.

The first wave broke over the three of them, sweeping around on either side. Forlo, Shedara, and Hult met them with their blades, sword and shuk and knives slashing through the rain. Two of the creatures died in that first rush. A third parried Forlo's sword with one of its sickles then snapped the second around, aiming for his eyes. Forlo jerked his head back, the wind of the weapon's passing making him blink. His throat tightened: he had seen what those knives did when they struck flesh. There never was any blood from the wounds they cut—but they were more lethal than any mortal blade.

Yelling an Imperial battlecry, he reversed his blade's arc, slicing high, then spinning low at the last moment. The feint worked: the shadow moved to block where it thought the sword would come and screamed when steel sliced through its midsection. The blade went right through without even slowing—it was like dueling the wind. A streamer of shadowstuff trailed in the sword's wake, then the whole wretched creature unraveled before Forlo's eyes, blowing away like so much black smoke.

The rain worsened. The sky grew darker still. The remaining three shadows from the first wave fell back, letting their fellows step up. Then they came on all at once, swarming around Hult, Shedara, and Forlo. Shadow-knives danced, met blades of steel, and glanced away. Hult's shuk found one fiend, tearing it apart. Forlo grazed another, and darkness leaked from it like blood, though it didn't die. The shadows ringed them round, darted in then back again, like striking serpents. They came from two directions at once, or from three. A sickle caught Shedara across her left wrist, and she gasped, her dagger dropping from a hand gone white and nerveless. Her flesh parted like a pair of lips, black at the edges. It looked, to Forlo's eyes, like frostbite. The wound didn't bleed.

"Help me!" she cried, her voice cracking with the pain.

Forlo and Hult both moved at the same time, their swords leaping toward the shadows before the elf. Forlo's found its mark, jabbing right through one of the fiends' faces. It shrieked—the sound was like the cry of an injured child, trapped at the bottom of a deep tunnel—and collapsed into inky shreds. Hult missed, his target shrinking away. His move bought Shedara time, though, and she dropped her second knife and drew a shortsword from her belt. She brought it around in a looping arc that clove through the neck of another shadow. The head came free, turning to smoke as it toppled off its shoulders. The creature's body did the same.

Six left. It was too many, and Forlo knew it: the three of them were tiring, and the fiends were not. The shadow-creatures blocked killing blows with ease. They coordinated their attacks, moving as if one mind controlled them. If anything, they were getting faster. Hult grunted in pain as a sickle scored his side, ripping through his leather vest to open a gash across his ribs. The edges of the wound shriveled, turning black. It was bad, Forlo could see, but it could have been worse: it had just missed his vitals. Another inch deeper, and he might be dead.

Forlo cut down another shadow. Shedara did too. Hult barely held his own, weakening with every breath. His blade moved sluggishly. Forlo wondered if the wound had been deep enough, after all. Was the barbarian slowly dying? If he went down, they would have to leave him and fight on alone. If he or Shedara fell as well, it would be all over in an instant.

Hot pain creased his thigh, then turned chill . . . then colder still, until it seemed to burn again. He felt his knee buckle, willed his leg not to give way, and barely kept from stumbling. Furiously he flailed with his sword, driving off the shadow that had cut him while he got his balance back. Shedara saw his trouble and helped him force the fiend back. The pain was incredible . . . and now they were all hurt, with four shadows left.

Too many.

He didn't glance at his wound, didn't want to see his own flesh puckered and dark and bloodless. He made a low, animal sound—the closest he could come to speech, with agony lancing straight up his leg, right into his spine. He stumbled, nearly fell, and righted himself—just in time to dodge a blur-quick sickle that sought to tear open his throat.

And six more shadows appeared out of the gloom.

The sky was as dark as a moonless night. The rain pounded. Their enemies faded in the murk, hard to see. The ground turned to sludge, stuck to their boots, weighed them down. The shadows surrounded them, fighting on, quicker every moment. The shadows would never tire—but Hult was breathing hard now, and Shedara moaned from the pain in her wrist. Forlo's sword seemed like it was made of lead; he couldn't feel anything below his knee. A shadow dived at him from the side; he turned to catch the blow with his shield, and missed. One of its sickles ripped through his stomach, cutting deep. A blossom of pain unfurled in his gut. With a bellow of defeat, he crashed down into the muck.

"No!" Shedara cried.

She tried to turn toward him, but a shadow stepped between them. A second slid in to block Hult. The barbarian raised his shuk high, brought it down, clove the fiend in two. Another took its place. Cursing, Hult fell back, pressing his back against Shedara. They left Forlo lying there, at the shadows' mercy. They had little choice.

A shadow loomed over Forlo. He could see its face now, hidden beneath its hood: a death mask of gray, shriveled flesh stretched taut over bone. It leered at him, its eyes pools of black, as he raised his sword abjectly, to defend himself. He couldn't get back up. The pain and nausea of his wound were too great. The shadow held its sickles poised, like a scorpion's stingers.

No, damn it! he thought. Not like this. Not like this!

The sickles came down, lightning quick, one-two. He got his sword in the way, somehow. The force of the blows made his whole arm ache. The blade got even heavier. It fell from his hand, landed awkwardly on his chest, and rolled into the mud. The shadow's grin widened. He spat at the thing, swallowing the urge to look away, to close his eyes. Barreth Forlo had sworn, long ago, to meet death face-to-face.

He glimpsed the arrow, in the corner of his vision, without realizing what it was at first. It was diving down, darting through the rain without a sound. The shadow never knew: one moment it was drawing back its knives to finish him, and the next it was screaming and ripping apart, the shaft plunging into the back of its neck. The arrow tore right through it, struck the ground a hand's breadth from Forlo, and stuck there in the mud, quivering. It was fletched with black feathers, its nock carved into the image of a snarling dragon.

"Where did that come from?" he murmured.

He heard Hult and Shedara, still fighting, off to his right. He reached for his sword, managed to pick it up, and started to rise—then collapsed, the agony too great to endure any more. With one last, vile oath, he slipped into darkness.

Chapter

2

COLDHOPE, THE IMPERIAL LEAGUE

Hult saw Forlo fall and didn't know what to do. One moment, the man's shoulder was pressed to his; the next he was gone, sprawled in the mud, torn by the shadows' knives. His armor did nothing to stop the black blades—it split like cloth. He did not bleed, but the wound ran deep. Hult risked a glance toward Forlo, saw him still fighting on his back, holding off the creature that stooped over him for the killing blow.

Had it been Chovuk, he wouldn't have hesitated. Years and training had honed his instincts when it came to his old master. He would have leaped to the man's defense, even if it meant his own death. He would have thrown himself on his enemies' weapons, if it meant winning his master a chance to survive. He had been a tenach, a protector: that was his role. His life for Chovuk Boyla's.

But Chovuk was gone now, slain at the disastrous battle of the Tiderun. Forlo had killed him in fair combat. Hult had been duty-bound to avenge his master, had had the opportunity to kill the man easily . . . but he hadn't. He was still working out why. Perhaps it was because Chovuk was no longer Chovuk when he died. He had given himself over to evil and sorcery, in exchange for power. The Boyla would have spent anything—even his own people—to earn glory. That was not the way a prince should behave, and now that Chovuk was dead, Hult could admit to himself that he had no longer loved his master, at the end.

Forlo was a different matter: Hult had sworn no oaths to him. He still, in his darkest thoughts, entertained the notion of killing him, eventually. But he felt ill to see him go down, and licked his lips as the shadows closed in.

Shedara snapped something at him, over her shoulder. He didn't know her language, but he understood her tone. Don't you dare go after him. If the two of us part now, we're dead.

Even so, he nearly left her anyway. Just as he was tensing to leap, though, the shadows took the choice away from him. One appeared between him and Forlo, and he killed it with a furious blow of his saber. Then a second took its place, and it was all he could do to block the flicking blows of its sickle. His side was numb where another creature's blade had gotten through. He forgot about Forlo, his back pressed hard against the elf's. They both fought for their lives. His shuk moved sluggishly, clumsily: weariness and pain were slowing him down. The shadows, meanwhile, were speeding up. It was only a matter of time.

He prayed to his people's god. Jijin, Horse-father, give me some luck. Get me out of this, and I will slaughter goats in your honor. I will spill their blood and burn their fat on an altar for you. . . .

He heard the sound of the arrows a heartbeat before he saw them. He'd heard those same shafts fly before; he'd watched them kill men. He'd even been shot by them once, himself, in what seemed like another man's life now. They dropped out of the mist like Jijin's own lightning bolts . . . one, two, three. Each had its own target, and each found it, slicing through shadow-stuff and tearing fiends to ribbons that vanished into the gloom. They slammed into the ground and stuck: three arrows, black-fletched and dragon-carved, each a killing shot.

He fought on, killing two more shadows, then exhaustion caught up with him. The pain in his side was growing too great. All the strength went out of his legs, and he sat down hard. The taste of bile bit at the back of his throat. I may die here, he thought helplessly. And there is nothing I can do to stop my death.

Forlo wasn't moving anymore. He had either passed out or died. Hult couldn't tell which. Shedara stayed on her feet, swaying a little, her wounded wrist pressed beneath her other arm. Her face was dead white as she cut down another fiend; then another volley descended and destroyed the last remaining pair. She looked at the arrows quivering in the muck, then sheathed her sword and drew a throwing dagger. Hult wanted to tell her that he recognized the archer, their unseen savior, but even if they'd known each other's tongues, he no longer had the breath to do more than grunt. He slowed his breathing, focused, tried to get his wind back. He would need it soon, if things went wrong. He had no idea what the next few moments would bring.

The rain suddenly slacked off. The sky brightened, from charcoal black to a dull, unhappy gray. As the darkness lifted, Hult beheld a figure at the edge of the woods, nearly two hundred paces from Coldhope. The figure was tall and slender, all bones and corded muscle. It had long, braided hair that Hult knew was dyed fire-red, and though it was too far to see, Hult knew his face was also painted with crimson stripes. The newcomer wore buckskin leggings and boots, leather armbands, and a breastplate made of a giant insect's shell. In his hand was a bow of layered horn and wood, which was even taller than he was. It had been said that no one north of the Tiderun was better with such a weapon, and Hult believed it. He'd seen this one shoot.

"Eldako," he wheezed.

Shedara shot him an incredulous look—you know

him?—then turned back to face the distant figure. The archer started walking forward, his long strides devouring the rain-sodden turf. He moved easily, but Shedara was tense, shifting the knife to hold it by the blade. Her brow furrowed as she studied the archer—then, when he had come halfway to her, her eyebrows shot up. She knew what he was now, despite his appearance. Eldako's tribe called themselves hosk'i imou merkitsa, the people of the ancient land, but most knew them as wild elves.

Hult got some strength back and heaved himself back to his feet. He raised his shuk to Eldako, who lifted his bow in reply. Neither smiled. Eldako never smiled, not that Hult had seen, and Hult . . . well, in truth he feared Eldako. The merkitsa elves had tried to kill him and Chovuk once, before the Boyla convinced them to aid him in his war against the southlands instead. The aid they provided had consisted of Eldako, and nothing else. That was measure enough of how deadly this elf was.

Somehow, Hult managed to find his voice. Someone had to say something before the merkitsa got in range of Shedara's knives, and Eldako spoke only a little more often than he smiled.

"Hail, son of Tho-ket," he called. "We thank you for your aid."

"It is freely given, son of Holar," answered Eldako. "Tell your friend to drop her blade, or I will feather the hand that holds it."

Hult shook his head. "We do not understand each other's words."

"Ah."

Eldako stopped, then nodded to Shedara and spoke something in his own language. It was a strange tongue, the sounds like birdsong and flowing water. Hult shuddered: the last time he'd heard it had been in the Dreaming Green, when he'd been a prisoner of the merkitsa.

Shedara blinked, her mouth opening. Eldako regarded

her coolly. After a moment, she regained enough of her wits to reply. What she spoke was not the same dialect—the sounds were softer, almost slurred—but even Hult could tell it was close enough for them to understand each other. Eldako cocked his head, concentrating on pulling meaning from the words, then replied. He pointed to Hult, then to himself, then to the north. When he was done, Shedara looked at Hult for a moment, then shrugged and put her dagger away.

Eldako started walking again.

"What did you tell her?" Hult called.

"The truth," the wild elf replied. "That I was part of your master's horde. That I went to war with him. That I escaped the flood that killed the Uigan and have been tracking survivors since."

Hult stiffened. "Survivors? Of my people? How many have you found?"

"One, now."

Hope, quickly kindled, snuffed out just as fast. Hult slumped, then looked to his left and gasped. In the strangeness of the past few moments, he'd forgotten about Forlo. Now he turned and hurried to where the man lay. Shedara followed. The wound across Forlo's belly was terrible, the flesh split open without so much as a drop of red showing, but when Hult touched his throat, the life-beat felt strong. Forlo was breathing. Hult nodded to Shedara, trying to look encouraging.

Eldako joined them. He touched Hult's shoulder. "Let me see his wounds."

"We are all hurt," Hult replied. "Look at mine instead."

He took off his vest and lifted his arm, cringing. The gash in his side blazed white-hot. Eldako knelt, rubbed his chin as he studied the cut, then quickly reached out and pressed its edge. What felt like cold flames erupted in Hult's body. He jerked back, hissing, and shot a glare at the wild elf.

"I apologize," said Eldako. "I had to do that."

"You could have warned me," Hult grumbled.

"Then you wouldn't have let me."

Hult shrugged. That much was true.

"The wound will kill you," said Eldako evenly. "It may take days, but the venom already burns in your blood. The other will last hours, at best."

Hult followed his gaze, feeling queasy as his eyes settled on Forlo. "How do you know this?"

"I have seen this sort of wound before. My people fought monsters like the ones you faced, during the Second Destruction. They were larger, and some took the form of dragons, but they were much the same. They came out of great rents in the earth. I was young then, but I watched many of my kin die by their poison." A ripple of emotion passed over Eldako's face, before he regained his former sternness.

"Then is there nothing to be done?" Hult asked. He could feel his heart beating, and knew that with every pulse, the venom worked its way deeper and deeper into his body. When it reached his heart, it would kill him.

Eldako shook his head. "There is always something to be done. The wounds can be treated, but we must be quick. Help me bring this one back into the castle. If we don't act immediately, he will fade beyond all hope."

Hult considered this advice—but only for a moment. He nodded. Eldako turned to Shedara and explained in her language, too. He studied her injured arm, and her eyes widened when he told her that it, too, would prove fatal sooner or later. He pointed to the castle. She nodded.

Together, they lifted Forlo's body and carried him back into Coldhope.

Hult got a fire going on the hearth, and Shedara fetched water while Eldako stripped off Forlo's armor. The wounds seemed to fester, but gave off no stink of rot. Forlo's face, normally a deep tan, had grown so pale that it had become translucent, with small, blue veins showing through. His black beard, frosted with gray, seemed to turn whiter with every shuddering breath he drew.

"He is nearly gone," the wild elf declared, feeling again for the life-beat. "It will be a near thing, even with my help."

Hult hovered near. "Help him. You must do what you can."

"He slaughtered your people," Eldako noted, one eyebrow rising.

"Even so. He is a good man."

Eldako nodded, though he clearly didn't understand Hult's motives. Hult didn't blame him—he didn't, either. Vengeance was the way of the Uigan, as it was of the merkitsa. But if Forlo died, Hult knew, he would be alone in a dangerous place, with only elves for company. And he owed the man, as well. Forlo could have had him killed after the battle, but hadn't. That counted for something.

The wild elf shrugged off a leather bag he wore at his hip. He pulled out bundles of dried herbs, several clay phials, and a small holy sign: the twin teardrops of Mislaxa, carved of dragon-horn. Shedara brought the water, several bowls, and a mortar and pestle, then stood nearby to watch.

"You are a Mislaxan?" Hult asked, staring at the teardrops. "You never mentioned it."

"I am trained in the healing arts," Eldako replied, not looking up as he sorted his medicines, picking some dried leaves here, a pinch of mold there. One by one, he dropped them into one of the bowls. "All royalty are, among the merkitsa. But Chovuk Boyla needed me for my archery, not my healing. Now, let us share our tales, son of Holar. How did you survive the flood at the Lost Road?"

He set to work then, grinding and mixing a poultice. With a few words in Elvish—which he had to repeat so she could understand his accent—he gave a bowl of leaves and powdered roots to Shedara, who soaked them in water and took them to the fire to make a tea. She moved with the same confidence as Eldako, knowing exactly what she was doing. Hult watched the elves, feeling helpless—his own training at this sort of thing consisted of birthing foals and knowing where to cut to give a wounded man a quick death—then sat down and began to speak.

He told of Chovuk's madness, in the moments after the great wave devoured his people, robbing him of victory in one terrible moment. He told how his master, having changed his skin into that of a steppe-tiger, abandoned the fight to seek the commander of the enemy. They had found him—Forlo—in a broken stub of a tower overlooking the battlefield. The enemies had faced off, and in that moment Chovuk's magic failed him, leaving him naked and weak before his foe. He fought anyway, and Forlo killed him in the end. Hult told how he and Forlo had formed their strange partnership, rather than crossing swords themselves.

"Why did you join with him?" Eldako asked, not looking up. "Is it the way of your people that the servants of a slain lord belong to his slayer?"

Hult shook his head. "No. I should have killed him. It would have been the honorable thing."

"Then why didn't you?"

Hult gave no answer. Eldako's eyes flicked up, took in the troubled look on the young barbarian's face, then returned to his work.

"And so you came here and found her," he finished. "You were leaving when the shadows attacked."

"Yes. And we would have died, without your aid."

Eldako kept grinding and mashing and mixing. "You still may."

Shedara brought the tea, poured it in cups, took one for herself. Hult took another, drank . . . and nearly spat it out again. It was the sourest thing he'd ever tasted. It made his cheeks hurt when he swallowed.

"What's in this?" he sputtered.

"Dragonwort," Eldako said. "Crone's Cowl. Dew of Morgash. It will fight the poison, keep it from moving deeper into your blood . . . if it hasn't already gone too far. Drink."

Shedara sipped hers and, after steeling himself, Hult took another drink. After a few swallows, his tongue started to go numb—certainly Jijin's mercy at work—and his fingertips began to tingle. Eldako continued to make the poultice, pausing now and then to inspect Forlo's wounds. The injuries were worsening, black threads spreading outward, under his skin. A high, reedy note cut through the sound of the man's breathing. Hult knew that sound: it was the noise the elders made just before they departed for the halls of the ancestors.

"And you?" Hult asked. "I thought you'd drowned in the Run. How did you survive?"

"I felt the wave coming," Eldako replied. "I sensed magic and the rumbling beneath my feet. So I climbed as fast as I could. Even then, I almost didn't make it. The wave came, and when I looked down . . . all I saw was foam and flotsam, and men and horses drowning, just below my feet. It was one of the most terrible sights I have ever beheld . . . that much life destroyed in an instant. . . ."

He stopped, his eyes far away, lost in grim memory. Then he shook his head and got back to work. "I climbed and climbed, fleeing into the woods. I watched the end of the battle, saw the soldiers burn the Uigan bodies. I searched for survivors, as I have told you . . . but there was no one. His men"—he nodded at Forlo—"combed the woods and killed them, one by one. They tried to take me, too, but my woodcraft and my bow saved me.

"After a few nights, I spied on the soldiers' camp and heard them say their commander had ridden east, to this place . . . and that one of your people had gone with them. I chose to follow and see who it was. I thought it might be one of the Tegins. I did not expect it to be you."

"You know their tongue as well?" Hult asked.

Eldako's eyes glinted. "I know many tongues, son of Holar. I know the speech of the Snow-folk of Panak, the Abaqua ogres, and the Glass Sailors of the Shining Lands. We elves live long, and have much time to study such things. Lady Shedara, I am sure, can speak many languages of the south." He reached to his medicine pouch, pulled out a cracked leather strap, and handed it to Hult. "Put this between his teeth, then hold him down. What I am about to do will hurt him very much."

Hult took the strap, eyeing Eldako. The wild elf had barely spoken three words to him in their long ride to battle at the Run. Now he never seemed to stop talking. There were many questions he still wanted to ask, but now was not the time. Turning back to Forlo, he eased the man's jaw open and slid the strap into his mouth. Forlo coughed twice, trying to spit the leather back out, then his breathing settled. Hult looked up at Eldako, who was scooping two fingers' worth of reddish-brown paste out of the mortar. Their eyes met, and the wild elf nodded. Hult grabbed Forlo's shoulders. Eldako spoke a few words to Shedara, and she held Forlo's ankles.

Licking his lips, Eldako reached down and spread the paste onto Forlo's wounded thigh. At once, Forlo made a bestial, howling sound, muted by the strap as his teeth ground into it. His back arched. He fought and bucked like a stallion near a mare in heat. One of his feet got loose and kicked at the air several times before Shedara caught hold of it.

"Hold him!" Eldako snapped. "I have to do that again!"

Hult and Shedara held on. It was all they could do to keep Forlo in place: he fought them like a madman. He scratched and clawed at Hult's arms, even drew blood, but

Hult held on while Eldako took a second handful of salve and spread it on the gash in his belly. Forlo roared, flecks of spit flying. Then, with a final whimper, he fell still again. Hult and Shedara let go, panting. Forlo's chest rose and fell, very slightly: it was the only sign that he was still alive.

Eldako put a pad of moss over the wound then bound it with linen. He leaned close, listening to Forlo's breathing. He laid a hand on Forlo's throat, checking his life-beat.

"He will live, I think," he said with a sigh. "He will sleep for a while. The bandages should be changed, at dawn and at dusk. If his fever worsens, we must make him drink the dragonwort tea."

He repeated the instructions to Shedara in Elvish. She nodded.

Eldako eased the strap from between Forlo's teeth. "Now," he said, scooping more salve from the mortar, "come here, both of you. It is your turn."

The pain was incredible, like a thousand wasps had burrowed into his side and all started stinging at once. Hult bit down so hard on the strap, he thought his teeth would crack. He screamed and raged; he shoved Eldako away; he grabbed a chair and smashed it against the wall. But as long as the poultice clung to his wound, the burning continued. Finally he sat down on a bench, put his head between his knees, and let the pain wash over him. In what seemed like a hundred years, the agony began to fade.

Shedara bore her suffering a little better because her wound wasn't as great. When the salve was in, she drew a dagger and focused on stabbing the table, again and again. Splinters flew. Tears leaked down her cheeks. Finally she, too, grew still again.

"I will . . . never . . . let them hurt me . . . again," Hult gasped, tasting bile.

Eldako bandaged them both. "Wise," was all he said.

They told him the rest of the tale, and with the wild elf to translate, learned a bit about each other. Shedara spoke of the statue, the Hooded One, and the sorcerer's spirit trapped within. She told of Forlo's wife, Essana, and the child she carried. She explained about the shadows, the black dragon, and the scale it had left behind—their one clue to where the dragon had gone.

"I've tried all my spells," she said. "I can learn nothing more."

Eldako rubbed his chin. "Hmmm," he said. "Might I see this scale?"

Shedara looked at Hult, who shrugged. Eldako was trustworthy, as far as he knew. She reached into her pouch and produced the scale. It glistened in the pale daylight that streamed through the greatroom's high windows. Eldako took it, turning it over in his hands, slowly.

"Do you know it?" Hult asked.

Eldako shook his head. "I have only seen a few dragons in my life, and this does not come from any of them. I cannot tell you anything about it."

Shedara's shoulders slumped. She took the scale back.

"But there is one who might. The Wyrm-namer."

Shedara started, looking at Eldako in amazement. Hult glanced from one to the other, confused. After a moment, Shedara began to laugh.

"The Namer is a myth," she scoffed. "My people have searched for him since the Great Destruction, but never found him."

"Then they did not look in the right places," Eldako replied.

"Are you saying you've seen him?"

"No. But I know those who have."

"Please!" Hult cried, holding up a hand. The conversation was confusing, with Eldako saying everything twice—once for Shedara, and once for him. Hult looked at both of them, imploring. "Just who is this Wyrm-namer?"

"A bedtime story," Shedara muttered.

"An ancient dragon," Eldako corrected. "A silver. He dwells far to the north, hidden in the wastes of Panak. It is said he knows the name of every dragon alive. If anyone can tell us where the scale came from, it will be him."

Shedara snorted, rolling her eyes.

Eldako turned a cold eye on her. "I would be pleased to hear your alternative, my lady."

There was a silence. Hult coughed. "Who knows where this Wyrm-namer dwells, then?" he asked.

"The Snow-folk," Eldako declared. "I lived among them for a time, during the Godless Night, and they often spoke of him. They call him Ukamiak, the silver sage. They could show—"

He stopped then, eyes widening and nostrils flaring. His whole body grew taut and tense. He reached across his body and drew his long, slender sword. Shedara was on her feet a heartbeat later, a dagger dropping from her sleeve into her uninjured hand. Hult rose and drew his shuk as well. His side blazed as he pulled the blade from its scabbard.

"What is it?" he hissed.

"Trouble," Eldako replied. "Many men, in the courtyard. No—not men. Minotaurs."

Shedara swore under her breath. Hult did the same. There could be only one answer to who these newcomers were: soldiers of the Imperial League. They would not take kindly to finding a Uigan and two elves here in Coldhope. Hult could hear, now, what the elves' keen ears had detected before him: the tromp of feet outside, the rattle of mail, voices calling to one another in the bull-men's guttural tongue. He cast about, trying to think what to do.

Then the door slammed open, and the minotaurs came charging in.

Chapter

3

Coldhope, The Imperial League

Forlo roused from dreams of slithering scales and rushing wind, to the crash of splintering wood and pounding feet. Someone shouted something in a deep and booming voice, but he was still too groggy to make out words. Pain and nausea gripped him, though not as strongly as when the shadows brought him down. He opened his eyes. Gray light burned his sight, and it was a struggle to focus.

He was in Coldhope again. The greathall—lying, it seemed, on the banquet table. Shapes moved around him, three of them. Shedara and Hult, and a third. A strange-looking elf with long, braided hair and the garb of a savage—a merkitsa of the northern woods, beyond the steppes. They were not looking at him; their eyes were turned toward the door.

Groaning, Forlo lifted his head and saw the minotaurs.

There were eight of them: none shorter than seven and a half feet tall, massively built, encased in steel armor and bristling with axes and swords and huge, flanged maces. Their long horns gleamed wickedly, banded with bronze and ivory rings. Their lips pulled back into fang-filled snarls. Their eyes were yellow and red, cruel. Forlo had had a minotaur friend, Grath. Grath had been jovial, warm-tempered. These bull-men, however, were clearly killers, born and bred. They were the League's shock troops and craved only battle. He knew—he'd commanded minotaurs like this in battle, against the undead hordes of Thenol.

They will kill us, he thought. They'll gut us and stake our heads for the crows. If they carried crossbows, we'd be dead already.

"Easy, now," he murmured in Elvish, not daring to take his eyes of the bull-men. "No rash moves. We can't handle this many—not in the state we're in."

The others heard him and looked down, surprised. Forlo struggled to sit up, the pain in his belly running through him like sheets of fire. Hult grabbed him, helped him rise. The strange elf—he must have been the archer who'd saved their lives—said something, reaching out to stop him, but Hult warned him away with a word in the Uigan tongue. Forlo almost blacked out, but struggled to his feet. He looked at the minotaurs, glaring at them from across the room. They watched him, their red eyes narrow.

"Shedara. Weapons away," he said. "Tell the others."

Slowly, carefully, Shedara sheathed her dagger then showed her empty hands. The merkitsa did the same, saying something in Uigan to Hult, who frowned and followed suit. Forlo looked down to inspect the bandages on his leg and stomach. Whatever treated his wounds, it felt like it was working: his injuries throbbed but also tingled a little. Magic? Probably. He wondered who had tended him. He suspected the wild elf.

Warily, Forlo faced the minotaurs. His hand went to his side, found his scabbard empty. He glanced at Hult, whose eyes flicked back to the table. Looking, Forlo saw his sword resting near where he'd lain. Forlo met the boy's gaze: while they didn't understand each other's speech, they were both warriors, and he knew Hult understood. If things go wrong, his look said, I'll need that blade quickly. Hult nodded.

All right.

Forlo stepped forward, limping on his injured leg. "All is well, friends," he said. "We do not wish for trouble. All we want is to be left in peace."

One of the minotaurs moved ahead of the others. His breastplate was etched with crossed spears, marking him as an officer. He raised a huge, spiked hammer, then brought it down on an ornately carved, teak chair. It shattered, sending pieces flying every which way. Forlo gritted his teeth, remembering how he and Essana had searched for just such a chair, haggled over the price, and proudly brought it home to this room, but he held his temper.

"We are the Fourth Legion," rumbled the bull-man. His fur was a deep, rust color, patched with cream on the snout and forearms. He hefted his maul like it was a willow-switch. "We will say how we will leave you . . . if we leave you at all."

Forlo knew this act well enough. He'd lived among minotaurs most of his life. They tried to act as fearsome as possible, as early as possible in any encounter, to intimidate those they spoke to. If you backed down, if you let them scare you, they won the upper hand. These ones did scare him a little, but he refused to show fear. He nudged a broken chair leg with his foot, kicked it away.

"I know you're the Fourth, soldier," he said. "I recognize your colors. And you should know that I am Barreth Forlo, lord of this manor, and a marshal of the Sixth Legion. I don't think it will go over well with your captain if he learns you broke down my door, then started smashing furniture and threatening me and my guests."

The minotaur blinked. He hadn't expected to be spoken to this way, clearly. After a few moments, though, his eyes narrowed, and one corner of his lip curled into a sneer. He hawked and spat at Forlo's feet.

"That to you, and the Sixth!" he barked. Behind him, the other minotaurs chuckled. "Your threats are empty. Our captain would laugh to hear them! We are glad to make your acquaintance, Barreth Forlo, lord of the manor—for we have come here not to honor you, but to bring you to Kristophan in chains!"

"What?" Shedara blurted.

Forlo risked a glance at the others. Hult and Shedara were confused, but his third companion seemed to understand. The wild elf's fingers twitched near the hilt of his sword. He wanted a fight but held back. For now. Forlo could tell he would draw steel and leap to battle in an instant, when the need came.

He turned back to the minotaurs. "In irons? That's preposterous! Who are you? Who is your commander?"

"I am Brosh, lieutenant of the Blood Horn Company," declared the bull-man with an arrogant toss of his huge, horned head. "I report to Marshal Omat of the Fourth. And I place you under arrest, lord, for deserting your post after the Battle of the Lost Road."

"I didn't desert," Forlo replied. He didn't have time for this, not from minotaurs such as those he'd led in the wars. "I left my men under the command of Captain Culos. You can ask him. I came back here to find my wife."

"Enough!" thundered Brosh, pointing his hammer at Hult and the wild elf. "If you are no traitor, why do you keep company with Uigan and elven scum?"

The merkitsa drew his sword again.

"No man speaks to me that way," the wild elf snapped. "Much less cattle."

Forlo shut his eyes, blowing a long breath out his nose. Great.

A couple of the minotaurs barked approving laughs at the elf's brazenness, but Brosh silenced them with a look. He stepped forward; against all better judgment, Forlo didn't edge back. He knew better than to show weakness now.

"What pretty hair you have, elf," the bull-man sneered. "Your scalp will look fine, hanging from my battle-standard."

"And wine will taste all the sweeter when I drink it from your horn," Eldako snapped back.

"Shut up, damn it," Shedara muttered.

It was too late, though: Brosh's nostrils flared wide with rage. He pawed the ground, his hands twisting around the thick haft of his hammer. The wild elf held his sword firmly in reply, shifting onto the balls of his feet. It was said the merkitsa fought like dancers, even more graceful then the civilized elves of Armach. But graceful or not, he'd be just as dead if the mallet found his skull. Snorting, Brosh strode forward.

Forlo had tried reasoning. That hadn't worked. So there wasn't much else to do. He shouted to Hult, who grabbed up his sword and tossed it into Forlo's waiting hand. Shedara was even quicker, though: as he was bringing his blade around, she reached to her belt, plucked a throwing knife from its sheath, and side-armed it at Brosh.

The minotaur, whose eyes were fixed on the merkitsa, didn't see the dagger coming until it was too late. The blade pierced the base of his jaw, driving deep into his neck. Brosh stopped, baring a snarl full of sharp fangs, then took a single, shaky step before dropping his hammer and crashing headlong to the floor. He lay still, his spine severed clean through.

"Khot," swore one of the minotaurs.

Forlo, for one, agreed. He looked at Brosh, then at Shedara, and gave her an appreciative nod. Then it was the wild elf's turn. With a shrill cry, he sprang at the remaining bull-men, sword raised high. It caught them flat-flooted; they stumbled back, still stunned by how suddenly their commander had fallen.

The companions had the advantage, but only for the moment. The remaining minotaurs spread out to meet them, recovering from the momentary surprise. They started their axes moving, spinning them in wide, whistling arcs that never stopped. There was no parrying

weapons like those; you could either dodge or lose an arm
. . . or a head.

"A good throw," said the wild elf, as Shedara drew her
sword.

"Thanks," she answered, then over her shoulder said,
"Barreth, this is Eldako of the Dreaming Green. He's a
friend of Hult's. Eldako, Barreth Forlo."

"You saved my life," Forlo said.

The merkitsa raised an eyebrow. "Twice. You may yet
have the chance to repay me."

"We can't hold this room," Forlo said in a low voice.
"Better if we try a fighting withdrawal, to the upper
levels."

Shedara shook her head. "We'll be trapped up there."

"We're already trapped down here," he replied. "Better
to keep things confined to close quarters."

"Hmm," she said. "Good point."

"We will hold them," the wild elf said firmly. "Shedara
and I. You and Hult should flee first. Your injuries would
otherwise slow us down."

Forlo wanted to argue with Eldako, but he couldn't deny
the pain in his leg and gut. He couldn't fight well in this
state—and neither could Hult. The elves would be better
off if they didn't have to worry about their welfare.

"How long can you give us?" he asked.

"As long as we can manage," Shedara said, spinning her
sword in lazy circles. "A few minutes, at least."

With a swiftness that startled even Forlo, Eldako
launched himself at the minotaurs. He hit them spinning,
his sword snapping around once, twice. Red ribbons flew
from one of the bull-men, his throat and stomach sliced
open with lethal precision. A heavy axe clattered to the
floor, and the minotaur crashed to his knees. Eldako glided
around the creature, and his sword whipped down, raking
across the back of its neck. The minotaur's head came halfway off, and he collapsed.

"Mother of Astar," Shedara murmured. "He's good."

Then she joined in, ducking under a whistling axe, spinning so a second clanged behind her, then tucking into a roll that carried her right past her target. She came out of it on the minotaur's off side, a little behind. As he was turning to face her, her sword slipped up and in, piercing chainmail and sliding between his ribs. He staggered, grasping at the wound, and she jerked the sword out and leaped away. Clots of blood blew out his nose, and he fell bellowing onto his side.

"Go!" she yelled to Forlo and Hult. "Get out of here while you can!"

Forlo limped away, grabbing Hult and hauling him away from the fight. The Uigan protested, shouting in his language, but Forlo half-dragged the barbarian to the door before looking back. Eldako finished another minotaur just then, feinting high with his sword then dropping low and kicking him hard in the side of his knee. There was a crack, then a roar of pain, and the wild elf's blade went up and into the bull-man's gaping mouth, then jerked out and away just as fast.

Just like that, four minotaurs lay on the floor, dead or dying or too badly hurt to matter. But there were still four left, and they regrouped into a tighter knot—discipline taking over where sheer force had failed. Eldako sensed the change in tactics and stepped back again, his sword pointed at them. Blood dripped from its tip.

One of the bull-men turned and yelled. There was commotion outside, feet pounding up Coldhope's steps. Brosh had brought more men. A lot more, from the sound.

"Now we're in real trouble," Shedara said.

Forlo tarried in the doorway, watching as one of the bull-men swung a heavy mace at Eldako. The cudgel missed the wild elf by less than a hand's breadth, but it didn't seem to perturb him; he snapped his sword around in reply, and it bit into his attacker's arm, all the way to the bone. The minotaur's fingers went limp, and the mace flew from his grasp, smashed into the wall, and tore a tapestry from its mountings. The hanging fell in a tangled heap, and Eldako spun about, his foot rising and catching the bull-man full in the face.

Shedara glanced back and saw Forlo and Hult still staring at the fight. Her face turned furious. "What are you doing?" she snapped, then turned in time to evade a whirling hatchet. "Upstairs! Now! Don't wait for us!"

A fresh spike of pain drove into Forlo's gut. He grunted, pressing his hand against his wound as he doubled over. Now it was Hult's turn to drag him away, jabbering in Uigan and shoving him down the hall. Forlo staggered away from the din of battle, deeper into Coldhope's heart.

Up and up they went, higher and higher, toward the topmost floors of the keep. The pain in his stomach got worse. White and black spots exploded in front of his eyes. Every breath felt like sucking in razors. Still they lurched on, and the clamor of fighting died away behind them. Forlo wondered if it was because the elves had finally retreated or because they were both dead.

He found out when they reached the third landing, where a doorway led to a hall, which led in turn to Forlo's bedchamber. Where the black dragon had taken Essana. Hult was pale and breathing hard, his face pinched with pain. Forlo caught a glimpse of himself in a silver mirror, and felt horror claw at him. His face was green. Behind, he heard running feet, and he turned, sword rising, to see the elves pounding up after them.

"They're coming," Shedara said. "More and more of them. I cast a spell to grease the stairs, which should slow them down, but . . . there's no going back that way."

"Well, we can't go any higher," Forlo replied, leaning hard against a wall. "There's just the tower up there, and that's a prison."

Shedara made a sour face. "I know. You kept me there, remember?"

"So what do we do now?" Eldako asked. "Where do we go?"

"The bedchamber door is strong," Forlo said. "And it bolts from the inside. It will take a while for them to chop their way through."

The bull-men's bellowing was getting closer. Horned shadows played on the wall of the stairway. They were out of time; they needed more.

"All right," Shedara said, pointing at the bedchamber. "Let's go."

They ran inside. The bed was still in disarray from when Forlo had risen, early that morning. He'd slept poorly, haunted by dreams of his wife . . . suffering . . . dying. He'd expected never to see the room again.

The minotaurs reached the landing. Hult's strength finally gave out, and he collapsed against the bed. Forlo sagged to the ground as well, cramps wracking him. Shedara called to Eldako, who ran to help her bolt the doors shut. They were heavy, dark oak, bound with brass and carved with images of the keep, with its five spires. Shedara laid a hand on them, shutting her eyes and murmuring. Eldako stepped back, giving her a wide berth. His people used magic as well.

The bull-men hit the doors hard, even as she was uttering the spell. The wood jumped beneath her hand, and she nearly lost control of the moon-power that coursed through her—but she kept her calm, kept hold of the magic. They hit it again and again, with the dull, hacking sound of heavy steel blades biting into oak. Sweat poured down Shedara's face. Beside her, Eldako slipped in and thrust his slender sword through the gap between the doors. From the other side came the shriek of metal punching through metal then a grunt of pain. The assault relented, if only for a moment.

It was enough. She finished the spell, and the magic passed out through her hands, into the wood. Forlo saw the magic, a silvery lattice that spread through the doors, binding them to the frame, the floor, each other. The mesh of magic turned rigid, like thick cables of steel, holding them fast. Shedara stumbled back, breathing hard, and nearly fell. Eldako caught her, kept her on her feet.

"Thanks," she said, stepping away. She shook her head to clear it. "Good fighting back there."

The merkitsa shrugged, as if it were nothing at all. "You as well."

Outside, the bull-men attacked again. Axes fell against the door, slowly chewing through. Shedara stepped back, shaking her head.

"They'll break through eventually," she said. "It'll take time, but the magic won't do anything if they hack all the wood away."

Hult struggled to rise, breathing hard. He was soaked with sweat, and his bandages had slipped. Eldako went to him, helped him sit down on the bed, and inspected his wounds, muttering in Elvish. Shedara, meanwhile, went to the window. Forlo followed. It was open a crack, looking out on the rain-gray sky and the angry sea below. Forlo knew what she could see, for he'd seen the same sight every morning he'd dwelt at Coldhope: a long drop, hundreds of feet down to sharp rocks and churning surf. There was no way anyone could survive such a fall.

"Interesting," Shedara murmured.

The minotaurs kept chopping and pounding, yelling curses, alternately demanding their surrender and promising to tear them apart. Forlo couldn't help but grin at how poorly the two ideas meshed. Shedara glanced nervously toward the door.

"This one cannot run anymore," Eldako said, looking up from Hult. The boy looked more than half-dead, his eyes glazed with pain. "We appear to be trapped."

An axe tip pierced the doors, then was withdrawn for another blow.

Shedara laughed. "Bet you're thinking twice about having saved us earlier on."

Hult asked a question, wheezing for breath. It didn't need any translation. What are we going to do?

"I have an idea," Shedara said, "but first, you're all going to have to swear to trust me."

Eldako repeated her words in Uigan. Hult looked reluctant but nodded. The wild elf looked back at Shedara, his eyes gleaming. She turned to Forlo as the doors shook again. An ominous crack snapped across the room.

Forlo's eyes narrowed. "What do you have in mind?"

"We're going to jump."

They all stared at her. They looked at the window. They stared at her again. There was another snapping sound from the doors, and a twang like a broken lute string. The binding spell was starting to give way. The minotaurs outside raised a vicious cheer.

"Jump?" Forlo asked. "Out the window?"

"I know a spell," Shedara explained. "It will make us fall slowly. Like leaves. We won't be hurt."

Hult leaned forward anxiously, his face troubled. Eldako spoke in Uigan. The barbarian's eyes went wide. He shook his head, drawing back, and jabbered something. He bit the heel of his hand—a ward against evil, no doubt. Shedara rolled her eyes.

"If any of you has a better idea," she said, "say something now, before the gentlemen with the axes join us."

The doors were slowly giving way, they could all hear the smashing sounds. Hult looked at Forlo, then back at Shedara. His mouth firming into a line, he tried again to stand. He succeeded this time, but he was shaky, and could

47

barely raise his shuk. Even so, he turned away from the elves and started toward the door.

"For the black moon's sake!" Shedara shouted at his back. "That way is certain death!"

"That is his intent," said Eldako. "I know his people. They do not trust sorcery. He would rather die with his blade in his hand."

Shedara shook her head then looked to Forlo. "We don't have time for this," she said.

Forlo's eyes flicked to the window. If they leaped from the window, the minotaurs would think them lost on the rocks below. And if their bodies weren't found . . . well, the relentless, crashing surf would explain that, wouldn't it? But he sympathized with Hult. It was difficult to trust her magic enough to leap out the window.

"This spell," he said. "You're sure it will work?"

She met his gaze, unsmiling. "My spells always work."

There it was. Forlo sighed, then looked at Eldako. "Tell him this," he said, nodding at Hult. "I'm staying with him. If he chooses to die, we'll die together. Or he can jump, and I'll follow."

The door trembled, cracked again.

The merkitsa spoke in Uigan. Hult stiffened, then looked back at them, aghast. Forlo raised his chin, challenging him with a look, and stepped away from the window. Shedara nodded, beckoning to Eldako.

"Come here," she murmured. "Leave him."

The wild elf wasn't convinced, but gave her the benefit of the doubt. Together they pushed the shutters open. Wind blew in, billowing the curtains, bringing cold, slicing rain with it. Eldako looked down, licked his lips, then heaved a sigh.

"I will trust you," Forlo heard him whisper. "The Abyss take you if you're wrong."

Shedara began to recite the words of the spell, which skittered like lizards through Forlo's brain. He felt the moons' power flow into her, cool and clean. She gestured, shaping the magic.

Forlo kept his gaze on Hult, refusing to look away. He put everything he could into that stare, silently telling the young barbarian that both their lives were now in his hands. He hoped he'd guessed right about the boy, that the strange, protective urge he felt toward Forlo would be strong enough to overcome his pride. Hult stared back, stubborn, angry . . . but nervous too.

"Stay," Forlo said, "or go. Choose."

The door cracked. It began to come apart. The minotaurs cheered again, raucous, thirsting for blood.

The magic burned bright, flaring all around Shedara. She caught it, then reached out and touched Eldako's forehead. He shuddered as power flowed into him.

"Go," she said.

He frowned. "But you—"

"Now!"

He jerked back, surprised by the shrillness of her cry. Then, sheathing his sword, he stepped up onto the windowsill. Forlo turned to watch. The wild elf's braids blew wildly behind him. Murmuring a prayer to his people's gods, he leaped out into nothingness . . .

. . . and fell . . .

. . . and stopped. He hung in the air, buoyed by the wind, and for a moment Forlo worried he might actually blow back into the room. Then the gust slacked off, however, and Eldako began to float slowly downward. The last thing Forlo saw before he disappeared from sight were his eyes, which were wide with wonder.

He glanced back again at Hult. The Uigan remained where he stood, but now he was staring at the window. He looked away sharply, his face reddening. Shedara shook her head, annoyed.

"Last chance," she said and cast the spell again—first on herself, then a second time, on Forlo. When it was done, she stepped onto the sill, starting to hoist herself up.

Hult looked at Forlo. Forlo looked at Hult. The barbarian's eyes filled with venom. Then he stepped forward. "Tak!" he called, raising a hand.

Wait.

Shedara looked back and couldn't conceal her smile. Hult was furious, but she didn't care. He started walking toward the window, every step seeming to pain him. With a sigh of relief, Forlo followed.

The minotaurs bellowed triumphantly. Forlo turned and saw the blade of an axe lodged between two boards. It rocked back and forth, then jerked out of sight again, leaving an inch-wide, splinter-fringed hole. More of the magical bonds broke, showering sparks onto the rugs.

"Hurry up," Forlo said.

"Stay still," Shedara said. She tried to sound calm, but her voice broke. She was afraid. So was Hult. So, now that he thought of it, was Forlo.

The power was slow now—faint, sluggish. She pulled it in anyway, focused her will into speaking the words. She slapped her hand against Hult's chest, driving the magic into him. His eyes widened as it suffused his body. Then the elf hurled herself out into the rain, into the nothingness and over the waves below. She dipped, and the spell caught her. She began to float down.

"Come on!" she shouted.

Hult wavered, glancing back. With a grimace, he pulled himself up onto the sill. He stood there, watching her . . .

. . . and didn't move. At the last moment, his courage failed him, and he balked.

"Jump, you fool!" Forlo yelled.

"Come on!" Shedara screamed.

He didn't. He couldn't. He watched, helpless, as the elves sank down, out of sight. When he turned back to face Forlo, his cheeks were wet with more than just the rain, and his eyes burned with terror and regret.

The pain in Forlo's stomach redoubled. He thought he'd been clever, weighing the Uigan's duty against his pride, never thinking there might be another factor. Hult was terrified.

Of course, Forlo thought. He fears the sea. How could I forget?

There was a thunderous smash, and the last of the binding spell gave way, taking the door with it. It burst to smoldering pieces. The minotaurs boiled into the room, a sea of horns and blades, surging through the shattered timber.

Forlo glanced at the window one more time. So close. They'd almost gotten away. But he might as well have been trying to reach the moon. He could never get to it before the bull-men caught him.

Khot, he thought, and turned to face them.

Chapter

4

The Tiderun Shore,
The Imperial League

As she dropped, Shedara saw Hult climb up onto the sill and balk at jumping. She heard Forlo shout, then fall silent. She saw the minotaurs seize the young Uigan and haul him back into the keep. She heard the sounds of fighting, but the wind and rain snatched most of it away, as she floated farther and farther down the side of the keep. Cursing, Shedara turned and dived after Eldako, tucking in her arms and lowering her head to arrow down toward him.

As she drew near, Eldako shouted something, pointing up past her. A bull-man had appeared in the window. He had a crossbow and was aiming it at them through the rain. Eldako grabbed and strung his bow, reached for his arrows, and nocked. The minotaur loosed. Shedara twisted in midair, and a bolt struck one of her packs and stuck there. She turned deathly pale, and a cold feeling passed over her. Another inch to the left, and the quarrel would have taken her in the heart.

Eldako pulled, aimed, let fly. The minotaur wasn't expecting the falling elves to shoot back, and didn't see the arrow coming. It hit him square in the left eye, and he stood erect for a moment, stunned, then collapsed, hanging halfway out the window. The crossbow dropped from his hands and smashed against the rocks. Eldako readied another arrow, but no more bull-men appeared. Shedara dived again, caught up with him, grabbed his arm so they fell together.

"We have to get them back!" she yelled in his ear, above the rain.

He nodded, then looked below, at the mass of broken rocks and churning foam. He slung his bow over his shoulder again.

"Later," he said.

The wind swirled and gusted, tugging them this way and that. They were helpless against it: the magic buoyed them but didn't let them steer their flight. The best they could do was angle their bodies to shift direction a little, but even that didn't help much. They fell past the jagged, rocky cliff, dotted with scrub and bird dung, rainwater coursing in runnels down its side. Nothing to grab there, no way to arrest their fall. They had to find some place safe to land.

Shedara scanned the rocks, looking for one that was large and flat and level and not very far out to sea. The tide was still somewhat low in the daytime, as the silver and red moons were nearly full at night. That meant there were places that were sheltered from the worst of the battering surf—but not many, and most were jumbles of scree that would slide out from underneath them when they landed.

"There!" Eldako shouted, a finger stabbing down and to the right. "That one!"

Shedara looked and saw a slab of water-darkened rock, maybe twenty feet long and eight feet wide, not quite flat but sloping down slightly, toward the water. She made a face. It wasn't ideal, but it was better than anything she'd spotted—and they were running out of time. They were still falling, leaf-slow. She met his eyes—pale and strange, the color of glaciers—and nodded once, firmly.

They dived for it.

The wind fought them, tugging and shoving this way

and that. One moment, it threatened to blow them out to sea, then it shifted and nearly smashed them against the rock. Then it got under them, and it seemed they might sail forever through the air, never coming down. But the spell would only last so long. Shedara could feel its power fading, its edges starting to fray.

Eldako must have felt it too, for he angled himself down even more sharply, dragging her with him. They plummeted, descending like arrows toward the stone, which loomed closer and closer. Shedara had the sick premonition of it smeared with her blood. She tried to pull up, but Eldako shook his head. The merkitsa was fearless. He shouted something she couldn't hear.

Then the wind caught her, and jerked her away from him. She flailed, tried to grab him again, but he was already too far away. A wave broke nearby, drenching Shedara in spray.

She looked down, and the rock loomed, and she couldn't worry about Eldako anymore. She spread her arms like wings to slow her descent. It worked, to a point: when she struck the stone, there was a lot of pain, but no snapping bones, no hot lances through any of her joints to herald a sprain. She rolled, then stopped herself at the edge of the rock, battered and breathing hard.

Eldako landed a moment later, hitting the stone even harder than she had, his arrows scattering from his quiver. The landing drove the wind from him with a loud grunt, stunning him. He began to slide, down toward the dark water. Shedara heaved herself up and, shoulders and elbows burning, hurled herself at him, catching his wrist with her uninjured hand. She slid a few inches with him, then managed to get one foot wedged into a crack, stopping them both.

The waves boomed, driving away all thought as they pounded the nearby rocks. Sea-spray and rain fell upon them. Coldhope Keep was above them somewhere, but all Shedara could see was the shoulder of the cliff, blocking out all else. She dragged Eldako closer to the bluff, into a hollow beneath the rock, carved out by surf. The minotaurs, looking down, would never see them here. With luck, they would assume the two elves had fallen to their deaths. Finally safe within the shallow cave, she collapsed and let the world slip away for a while.

✦━━━✖━━━✦

Eldako shook her awake. "Get up. The tide is coming in."

She opened her eyes, sat up, felt her head spin. She hurt all over, but it was just scrapes and bruises. A large, green crab was studying her foot; she nudged it away, then looked out of the cave.

The rain had stopped; the sky had cleared a little. It was late afternoon, the clouds glowing gold on their western fringes. The wind had died down too, and the vicious surf with it, thank Astar. The water had risen quite a bit; the slab they'd landed on was half submerged, and the edge of the Run was nearly to the cave's mouth. At high tide, the spot where they lay would be well under water.

"Are you hurt?" Shedara asked.

"Yes," Eldako replied with a serious look. "All over. You?"

She laughed at that. "No worse than you are. Nothing that needs healing. Even my wrist's feeling better, though that slop you put on it got washed away."

She raised the hand the shadows had injured, earlier that day—gods, was it still the same day? It felt like years, not hours, had passed. Her fingers opened and closed slowly. There was a white scar where the awful black wound had been. The wild elf's herb-magic had worked well.

Eldako was inspecting his quiver. He'd lost most of his arrows in the fall, and had only three left. He shook his head, annoyed.

"My bow is intact, and that's what matters," he said, his expression still impassive "I can make new arrows without much trouble, but a proper merkitsa strongbow takes months to craft."

Grimacing at the aches that ran through his body, he got the rest of the way to his feet.

"We've got to get out of here," he said. "Back up the cliff, away from the water."

"We need to get Hult and Forlo back," Shedara said.

"I agree," he answered. "Let us see what is possible. Come."

He strode out of the cave, clambering up on a barnacle-crusted stone to stare up the cliff face. It was nearly vertical, even bowed outward in places, with no clear paths to the top. There was a harbor village a few miles from here—Shedara had seen it on her way to Coldhope—but there was no way they could walk there across the rocks before the tide made the going impossible. Their options were few.

"We have to go up that way," Shedara said, shading her eyes. She looked up, leaning back. "I have a climbing spell to help, but just one. And I can make us invisible too. But that's all I've got left for today."

"You use the spell," he said. "I have climbed without magic all my life . . . and I wouldn't trust that arm to hold your weight yet."

She nodded, flexing her stiff fingers again. She scrutinized the cliff a while longer. Then she spoke a few words, making passes with her hands as she drew in the moons' power. The air seemed to shimmer, just for the blinking of an eye, then she blew out a long breath.

"Ready," she said.

They walked to the cliff's edge, to a place where the stone hung low over the water. He boosted her up—she was still remarkably light, the falling spell still clinging to her—and she pressed her hands flat against the rock. They stuck there, and she pulled herself up the rest of the way, clinging to the stone like a spider. She scrambled a few feet higher, then glanced back, waiting for him.

He studied the rock a moment, looking for outcrops and cracks. With a quick jump, he caught hold of a narrow lip of stone and hung from it, swinging slightly. He looked up at Shedara. She grinned down at him, already impressed. She was a climber, too—during the Godless Night, when the moons and magic were gone from the world, she'd had to do it without the spider spell—and she could tell he knew what he was doing. She went up a bit farther, feeling Eldako's eyes on her, then turned to watch him pull himself up after her. He found another handhold then another, and soon his feet found purchase on the stone as well.

Shedara decided she liked the merkitsa. She climbed onward, the rising tide receding beneath her.

✦━━━◆◆━━━✦

It took more than an hour, but finally she reached the top: a wooded promontory nearly a mile east of the keep. The wind had blown them farther than she'd thought while they were falling. Eldako came up a while later, and she caught his hand and pulled him up onto level ground again. He lay there a moment, on the carpet of pine needles, while he gathered his strength.

"The minotaurs are still there," Shedara reported. "All around Coldhope. Looks like at least five hundred of them."

Eldako groaned. Shedara sat beside him and gazed up at the boughs, swaying in the breeze, and listened to the creak of the trees. It was cool, autumn coming. Sunset soon.

"Do you still have the strength to make us invisible?" he asked.

"Barely . . . but yes."

He drew a deep breath, held it, then let it out and rose slowly to his feet. "We'll go scouting at dusk," he said.

"They'll be changing their guards and concentrating on their supper. It would be foolhardy for us to attack, but we can move among them and use our eyes."

"That's what I thought," she said, smiling. "I have the feeling they took Forlo alive and he may still be here, but Hult—"

"Don't speak it," Eldako interrupted. "Bad luck."

He stretched, working the aches out of his muscles. Shedara did the same. She could feel the weariness, deep within her. It had been a hard day; she would sleep well tonight.

"I am ready," he said. "Cast the spell."

She stood before him, chanting her incantation. The air rippled. Her fingers danced, her left hand no longer hindered at all. Her wound had healed. Then the air around her surged again, tingling like the moments before a storm, and the world became, for an instant, as clear as crystal. She could see through Eldako, through the trees, through the ground beneath him. The wild elf caught his breath, surprised—and then everything snapped back to the way it had been before, solid and opaque.

"You will be able to see me," she said, in answer to his unspoken question. "And I can see you too . . . but no one else. Just remember—stay quiet. The magic doesn't make us silent. And don't attack anyone, or you'll break the spell."

"I understand," he whispered.

They looked to the west. There was a gap between cloud and horizon, the red sun peeking through, touching the distant hills. Eldako took a moment to secure his gear, making sure his remaining arrows didn't rattle. Shedara did the same, securing her sword in its scabbard. When she looked up, she caught him watching her intently.

"You are like a merkitsa woman," he said. "They fight alongside the men. The Uigan do not. It is good to be with a woman again."

That caught her off guard. She felt her face flush.

"Forthright, aren't you?" she asked, looking away. "Come on. Let's see what we can see."

The forest ended half a mile from Coldhope, giving way to rocky grassland with a few fields nearby—fields whose serfs had fled with the barley still unreaped, fearing that the Uigan horde would soon overrun the area. The grain gave them cover, but they had to move carefully, or the bull-men would see the movement and investigate. No one came for them, though, and soon they were outside the keep's walls again, crouching in a ditch and peering over the edge. The minotaurs had lit fires all around Coldhope but had put up no tents. They were bivouacking, not camping, and would be moving out in the morning.

Shedara's estimate seemed about right, up close. Half a thousand of the bull-men, with some humans thrown in as well. Banners of black and gold, emblazoned with various regimental emblems, fluttered in the breeze. The minotaurs were doing what all soldiers did when not fighting or marching: they were eating, sparring, gambling, singing, and drinking copiously. A few stood guard with crossbows and spears, but even they were busy guzzling from wine-skins. Clearly, they didn't expect any trouble.

"Give me twenty of my people," Eldako murmured. "Twenty strong bows and hands to pull them. I could leave this lot in tatters."

"I could say the same of the Silvanaes," Shedara whispered back. "But they're not here, either. What can we do with just the two of us?"

They kept studying the camp. "I think I see where they're keeping the prisoners," Eldako said after a while, pointing toward a thicker knot in the crowd.

Fifty or so bull-men were gathered together, watching something the elves couldn't see. They shouted in the minotaur tongue, and every now and then broke out in bursts of laughter. Swords and fists lashed the air.

"It must be Forlo and Hult," Shedara whispered with a

scowl. "The bastards are making sport of them. Come on."

They stole forward together, making no sound at all. The last two hundred yards to the bivouac were wide open—without the invisibility spells, even a drunk watchman would have spied them. As it was, though, they crossed the distance and slipped past the sentries without any trouble. From there, it was easy going: the noise of the bullmen was enough that they didn't even have to move very quietly, and the sentries were so widely spread out that the two elves got past all of them with ease. Only once, when a minotaur suddenly rose from where he sat and stumbled directly into their path, did they almost give themselves away. Eldako nearly slammed into the bull-man, but pulled up quickly, gliding around him like smoke.

The knot of shouting, laughing minotaurs was harder to negotiate. There was no way to get through the pack to see what was in its midst. Fortunately, there was a tree nearby: an old, gnarled ash with overhanging branches. Eldako climbed it with ease, barely shaking its branches as he rose. The bull-men noticed nothing. Shedara came up behind him, the spider spell still lingering, and they clung to its upper limbs, looking down.

Hult was in the midst of the pack. A leather thong tied his ankle to a stake, which was hammered into the ground. He had a dagger in his hand—a minotaur blade, not his Uigan knife—and was facing two snarling black dogs. A third lay in the dust, a pool of blood spreading from its pierced throat. One of the hounds darted forward, its powerful jaws snapping; Hult slashed and missed, but a kick sent the dog yelping back to its mate. The minotaurs cheered; silver changed hands.

"And they call my people barbarians," Eldako sneered.

"They're not all like this," said Shedara. "Forlo's friend Grath—"

Just then the other dog came on, and this time Hult couldn't fend it off. The beast's jaws clamped down on his calf, and he yelled in pain. The bull-men laughed as he pounded on the animal's head and shoulders. Finally he stabbed the dagger down into the base of its skull, and the animal went limp with a whimper, bringing a new round of whoops from the minotaurs. Hult rose, bleeding, and turned to face the last dog.

"Stop this! Stop this at once!"

Everyone—the minotaurs, Shedara and Eldako, even Hult—turned toward the voice. A black-furred bull-man in plate armor strode forward, hefting a massive morning star. He wore an officer's badge, and the others parted to let him through.

"What is this?" the officer thundered. "Tormenting a prisoner? Are you lot citizens of the League, or savages like him? Call off that beast at once!"

The final dog was just tensing to leap when a blond bull-man with a scarred face whistled. The animal looked back at him, and he spoke a sharp word. Head lowered, the dog slunk to his side.

"Now," said the officer, "whose idea was this?"

The minotaurs glanced at one another, then moved away from the dog's owner. Glowering death at the others, he took a step toward the officer. "Beg pardon, Captain," he declared. "We gave you the traitor Forlo. We didn't think you cared about this one."

The black minotaur was silent a moment, then lunged forward and struck the blond warrior with a mailed fist. The minotaur went down hard. The others fell silent.

"Use some sense, Marn!" said the captain. "This one's valuable. Think of the price they'll pay at the Arena for a real, live Uigan warrior to fight on the sands!"

The minotaurs muttered. A few jeered. Hult looked confused, holding his dagger ready. The blond minotaur, Marn, got up from where he'd fallen, blood trickling from his snout. "Sorry, Captain," he said. "Reckon I wasn't thinking clear."

"You can lay silver on that," said the captain. "Now take that blade away from the barbarian and put some irons on him. Then get some rest, the lot of you! We march at dawn to meet up again with Marshal Omat and the main force. After that it's back to the capital—and anyone who slacks because they're tired is in for a flogging! Understand?"

The bull-men muttered agreement and withdrew. Two brought forward long poles with metal prongs on the end and used them to pin Hult to the ground. A third got the dagger away from him. The minotaurs clapped heavy shackles to his ankles and wrists, then led him away. Shedara watched them go, feeling murderous.

She looked over at Eldako. His face was cold.

"Come on," he said. "There's nothing we can do for them. Not now, anyway. At least we know they're still alive, and where the cattle are taking them."

She glared at the minotaurs a while longer before sighing. "All right. Let's go."

Away from the bivouac again, back in the woods, Shedara let the invisibility spell lapse. She fell to her knees, exhausted, then leaned back against the trunk of a pine tree. Eldako crouched beside her, looking back toward the fire-glow from Coldhope. For a long time, neither of them spoke.

"We have the scale," he said at last. "We could go on to the Wyrm-namer without them."

She blew out a long, slow breath. "The thought has occurred to me," she said. "The statue's what really matters . . . finding the dragon, and stopping Maladar. Not Forlo or Hult—or you or me, for that matter."

Eldako nodded, saying nothing for a time. "But they are your friends."

"Yes," she said. "Well, Forlo is, anyway. I have to try and rescue them."

"Then I will stay and help. We can't rescue them ourselves, though," Eldako declared. "No matter how good a fighter you are. We need help, like you said—particularly if we have to free them from this Kristophan place."

Shedara scooped up a handful of pine needles. "Well, then," she said. "There's only one place to go."

"Where?"

She looked at the needles in her grasp then tilted her hand and let them fall, bit by bit, back to the ground. "Armach," she said. "My home . . . or what remains of it."

Chapter

5

Akh-tazi, Neron

The baby was growing. She could feel it. On the worst days, she wished it would stop: that her "troubled" womb—as the physics had called it when she was younger, when she and Barreth had failed repeatedly to make a child—would do what it had always done and reject the life it held. Then there would be bleeding, and grief, and loss . . . but the Brethren would be foiled. They would not have her son. She prayed to Mislaxa sometimes, but no answer came.

There were alternatives. Essana was not yet ready to consider them.

The darkness was her constant companion. Days passed when she saw not another living soul, and most times it was worse when she did. The yaggol came to inspect her, to study the progress of her pregnancy. When she fought them, tried to escape their clammy, grasping hands, their minds entered hers and froze her in place until they were done. She wept when it was over, every time.

Twice the Faceless came: always the same one, the one who called himself the Keeper. He was surprisingly calm, even gentle, and never did a thing to harm her. She could feel his power, though—the black-moon magic seething within him. He could burn her to ashes with a word or strip the flesh from her bones . . . that knowledge alone was enough to still her.

Both times, he brought her to the same place, to the altar on the rooftop. There they joined the rest of the Brethren— all who were at the temple, anyway. Once, the Teacher was absent; the others, all were there. The Master would look her up and down, noting the growth of the child—the vessel—and then the dragon would appear, bearing the statue and another elf.

She asked the Keeper about the elves. He told her they were a tribe native to Neron, called the cha'asii. They were ancient enemies of the yaggol, and once had been their slaves. That had been thousands of years ago, before some long-forgotten calamity . . . war, disaster, plague . . . had toppled the jungle kingdoms. Since then, cha'asii and yaggol had fought a savage war across the breadth of Neron, erupting into open, bloody battle every century or so.

When they first came to the temple, many years ago, the Brethren had found use for both of the jungle's races. The yaggol were willing allies and servants, and bowed to dark gods. Akh-tazi, to whom the temple was holy, was said to be the same deity as Hith, the lord of deceit. As for the cha'asii, who worshipped the spirits of nature and rejected the Brethren's overtures . . . they still had their uses.

The second time, the ritual was the same as the first. The Brethren pulled back their hoods to reveal their horrible, disfigured faces. The dragon laid the elf—a woman this time, broken and pale with terror—upon the altar. The Master hailed the Hooded One, and his disciples replied in kind. Then the Slayer cut the cha'asii's throat, gathered the blood, and poured it at the statue's feet. When it was done, they gave the elf's body to the dragon, which devoured it in two swift bites, then lifted the statue in its talons and bore it away again into the night. After that, the Keeper brought Essana back to her cell and left her there, with only her memories of the elf-woman's dying screams for company.

The third time was different. The victim—a silver-maned elder, with bright feathers and beads of amber and jade strung into his hair—did not struggle, nor did he cry for help. He simply stared at the Brethren with a strange expression. It wasn't fear or hatred; it might have been pity. Perhaps even a hint of mockery. He spoke in a strange language, like the song of birds; Essana didn't understand the words. Whatever he said, however, angered the Master so much that he took the Slayer's knife and cut the elf himself. The cha'asii made no reply, only lay back, let out a breath, and died.

The Brethren's faces, fleshless as they were, could show no emotion. Yet the Master's bloodshot eyes, when he turned to face the others, seemed to blaze with rage. His hands trembled.

Essana's heart lurched when he said, "Bring her."

The Keeper hesitated. "It is not time. She is not ready. The child—"

"Is grown enough. I will say when she is ready, Brother. Or do you forget your place?" The Master's words dripped with venom.

"No, my lord," said the Keeper, his own voice edged with frost.

"Then bring her. Now."

Reluctantly, it seemed, the Keeper took Essana's arm. She resisted, but his fingers gripped her fast, finding a nerve that sent bolts of lightning shooting up through her shoulder to her spine. She gasped, her knees buckling as he led her toward the altar.

The Master was even less gentle, wrenching her from the Keeper's grasp then ordering him back. Furious, he pushed her to her knees before the Hooded One, then seized her hair and jerked her head back, making her look at the statue. The knife was still in his hand, dripping with blood. Bile burned Essana's throat.

But the Master's thirst for murder had been slaked, for the time being. Instead, he gave the blade a swift flick, slitting open her shift to expose the growing roundness of her belly. The flesh there was taut, distended. Inside, she felt the baby kick.

Mislaxa, she prayed, oh, hand-who-heals, I beg you . . . take my son.

"Blood for you, Faceless One," spoke the Master. "Blood for Maladar, the Sleeping King."

Turning the sickle, he wiped it on Essana's stomach. It left a long, dark streak of the dead elf's blood. It trickled down her skin, sickeningly warm. It soaked her clothing, staining it crimson. Then, with a sudden, rushing sensation, as if the whole world were dropping away, she felt a presence flood her mind. It was not cold and emotionless, like the yaggol, but hot and filled with fury. This presence burned with hate, with rage, with hunger for the life within her.

Maladar.

I will have the child, said the Faceless Emperor. *I will claim him, and be born again into the world. I will grow, and in his flesh I will conquer. I will raise a new land, from the ashes of the old.*

The world faded before her eyes, and another place revealed itself. She saw a sea of molten stone, roiling beneath a smoke-heavy sky. Red lightning smote distant, black peaks. Islands of glass floated upon the magma, moving in slow, spinning circles around a column of fire at its midst. The fire rose high into the hazy air, a mile and more. It was white at its core, slender and straight—but it was not just fire. It held a shape, hidden within. There were windows, buttresses, turrets. It was a tower, built of flame.

Chaldar, she thought. She had heard the tales; every child in the League did. The Chaldar, the Burning Spire, was said to stand at the heart of Hith's Cauldron, the great, fiery wound where the gods had split the earth, and laid low the empire of Aurim in the Great Destruction. The tower, the stories said, had arisen in the spot where Aurim's capital once stood. None had entered it and returned to tell what lurked within, but there were many rumors. Some said the ghosts of the Aurish dead haunted it, others that demons from the Abyss walked its burning halls. Others claimed it was empty, waiting for its true lord to come. No one knew, but Essana thought she sensed something in her vision . . . something watching her. She quailed before those unseen eyes.

I will rule, said Maladar. *My realm, reborn.*

The sea began to churn. As she watched, new islands arose, pillars of obsidian that pushed up from the churning lava. Flickering red, they rose higher and higher, and she saw now that they were not just columns but buildings . . . shining, black buildings in an antique style. A city.

His city.

"No," she moaned. "Not with my son. You will not."

Laughter filled her head. The Flaming Spire erupted, hurling tendrils of fire across the sky. It poured down like rain, burning as it fell. It washed over her, scorching her skin, roasting flesh, charring bone. It ran down her throat, into her lungs. Her hair became a torch. Her eyes boiled.

She screamed.

<hr />

"She wakes."

Essana ached all over. She tried to roll away from the voice. She couldn't move her arms and could barely feel her legs. She tried to groan, but all that escaped her mouth was a noiseless sigh.

Hands touched her roughly. They gripped her wrist, pinching down to the bone, then ground into her throat, probing for the life-beat. Then they drew back. She drew a breath . . . and all at once, out of nowhere, a hand slapped her—hard—across the face.

Her eyes flew open. She cried out. The Master stood over her, glaring from the depths of his hood. All she could see was light shining off the moistness of his eyes.

"There, sweet one," he hissed. "You tried to escape from us, didn't you? Crawled inside your mind, so far even the yaggol couldn't reach. But it couldn't last, not forever. We are not made to hide like that for long."

He struck her again, across the other cheek. His leather glove stung her. She tasted blood.

"Enough!" said another voice. "She is awake. Leave it."

The Keeper grabbed the Master's hand as it rose to deliver another blow. The Master whirled, glaring. "I could kill you where you stand!" he grated. "Do you forget yourself, Brother?"

"Do you?" the Keeper replied, not flinching. "Every time you harm her, you endanger the child. Will you explain to Maladar if it dies?"

The Master was silent. There was hate between him and the Keeper, deep and abiding. A history there. Essana wondered what it was.

"You will go too far one day," said the Master.

"Of course. We all will."

The Master stayed still for a moment longer, then turned and stormed away. Essana heard a door open, then boom shut. The Keeper looked down at her. He examined her, his hands gentle. Not like the Master's. The Master had a warrior's hands. The Keeper's were those of a healer. Essana shut her eyes and let him touch her belly, to feel the life beneath.

"The child is healthy," he said after a time. "All is well."

She laughed bitterly. "Oh? I should be happy?"

He drew back, startled by her rancor, then turned away.

She heard the whisper of his robes as he moved to another part of the room. He returned with a steaming cup that smelled of bitter herbs. He put it to her lips.

"Drink," he bade. "It will help."

She sipped, nearly spitting it out. The tea tasted awful, like it came from a well where something had died. The flavor lingered long after she forced the mouthful down.

"H-horrible," she gagged.

The Keeper nodded. He watched her, his eyes glistening beneath his cowl.

As she lay there, Essana felt her strength return, the throbbing pain in her head subside. She pushed herself up, looked around. The room was one she hadn't been in before, more comfortable than her cell, but not much. The same black stone. Lanterns on the walls, glass orbs filled with what looked like glowing centipedes. They scuttled around and around their prisons, casting eerie, blue-green light. She lay on a divan padded with velvet. A small fire burned in a brazier nearby, with a kettle over it, giving off the same acrid stink as the tea. There was a table, laid out with strange metal instruments, and numerous crystal jars of herbs, powders, and oils. Books bound in leather the color of dried blood lined a shelf opposite the door. A map hung on the wall, of a land she didn't recognize. A land far from Coldhope, to be sure. It was a large island, triangular, and its longest coast—in the southwest—was jagged and broken. Off its eastern shore were numerous smaller islets. Mountains formed a spine down its center; forest covered its southern half; ice its northernmost edge.

The place tickled at her mind. She had seen this island before, in studies when she was a child. Where was it?

"You had a vision," said the Keeper, drawing her gaze away from the map. These were his chambers, she was certain. The home of a scholar and a surgeon of sorts. "When the Master brought you before the Hooded One."

She saw no reason to lie. "I did. Then I blacked out. How long?"

"Two days. You had a fever. You would have died, but. . . ."

"But you took care of me."

Again, the Keeper said nothing.

"The vision," she said. "I saw the Chaldar and Hith's Cauldron. I saw *him*. He spoke, and a city rose from the flaming sea. A city of shadow and fire."

The Keeper stiffened, then controlled himself and gazed down upon her. "This city . . . did it look like the old paintings? Images of Aurim?"

"Yes. Is that it? Does he mean to raise the old empire from the ruins of the Destruction?"

The Keeper shook his head. "I don't know. But you should not speak of this to anyone. Not even the Master. If he asks about the vision, it is best if you tell him you remember nothing."

"And if he uses the yaggol? If he tells them to drag it from my mind?"

"He already has. They couldn't bring it forth."

Essana shuddered, thinking of the creatures' cold, twitching tentacles, touching her while she lay unconscious. She could see their empty eyes in her mind, feel their spindly fingers on her. Gooseflesh rose on her arms.

The Keeper watched her silently.

"Why are you doing this?" she asked. "Why did you take me?"

He shrugged. "We needed the child. You were with the statue. The fact you were pregnant spared you, or Gloomwing and his shadow-servants would have killed you with the others. We need the unborn son of a human, a boy of noble birth. It is prophesied. When the dragon saw you, he knew you were the one. . . ."

"My son. You're going to give him to this Faceless Emperor."

"Yes."

"Why?"

He studied her, steepling his fingers. "Do you truly wish to know?"

"I do."

"Very well," he said, his eyes glistening. "You know as well as I that there is plenty of trouble in Taladas. There has been, for many years, but it is growing steadily worse. You have seen it—earthquakes that topple cities. Restless barbarians razing their neighbors' lands. Riots, banditry, and seemingly endless war. Fire and blood. We have seen this spreading trouble, even in the Rainwards."

Essana caught her breath, glancing again at the map. Of course—the Rainward Isles! A cold, mist-shrouded place, off the northeastern shore of Taladas. It was the one piece of Old Aurim that had survived the Destruction nearly intact . . . at least, it was not blasted to wasteland like the rest. Great kingdoms had risen there in the years since: warlike realms that fought one another constantly. They were lands of legend in the League, too far to trade with or invade.

"You come from there?" she asked. "All of you?"

The Keeper nodded. "I lived my life before in a kingdom called Suluk. I was a healer . . . a physic, not a Mislaxan. This was during the Godless Night, when the Mislaxans had no power. I met the Master then, and the others. We saw what had befallen the world since Aurim fell, and we knew Taladas could never recover. Things would only get worse. The land is dying, killing its people by stages. In five hundred years, in a thousand, who is to say what will remain?

"The Master was the one who first learned of Maladar, and the Hooded One. It was his decision to form the Brethren . . . to scar ourselves and seek the statue. He read prophecies, and made some of his own. We traveled here, to Neron, so we could work in secret, away from the eyes of our people. We searched long and hard for the Hooded One, ranging across the Aurish wastes, even into the Cauldron itself, but we found nothing. Still, we never lost hope.

"In time, the Hooded One was found, but not by us. Word came to us that the minotaurs had located it in the ruins, and brought it back to their empire in the west. Your empire. So we set plans in motion, to throw their League into chaos by shattering their capital, then threatening it with a barbarian horde from the north. The Teacher was our envoy. He goaded the Uigan to war, seduced their prince, their Boyla, with promises of power. And meanwhile, the Slayer went forth to find the statue itself. He tracked it across the continent, from one owner to the next, killing as he went. He even murdered the Voice of the Silvanaes elves, in Armach.

"For a time, the Slayer lost the trail. But we knew, once the Uigan came south, that Maladar would surface again. Some fool would be seduced by the power of the Faceless Emperor, and use it against the barbarians. We were right."

"Shedara," Essana murmured.

"Yes, the elf," agreed the Keeper. "She invoked his power and summoned the wave that destroyed the Uigan. And, in so doing, she revealed herself, and drew the Slayer to her. To you. And now . . . now we have all we need, at last. All that remains is for the child to be born. When he is, Maladar will claim him, and the Sleeping King will be free of his prison at last."

"And he'll raise Aurim from the burning sea," she said, her voice now no more than a whisper.

The Keeper paused then inclined his head. "Just so, if your vision holds true. He will bring peace to these troubled lands. Order will return to Taladas, for the first time since the rain of death fell upon this world. Maladar will bring new life to the fallen empire, and reign over all. Even, perhaps, the fabled lands across the sea."

Essana studied the Keeper. There was something peculiar about this man: a hesitation she hadn't sensed in the others. The Keeper was worried about her. He had been a healer; it was his task to keep her and the baby alive and healthy. And in doing so he had grown attached to her.

"You should rest," he said. "You are better, but you still aren't well."

Weakly, she held up a hand. "First, tell me one more thing."

"What?"

"What about me?" Essana asked. "What will happen to me, when my child becomes lord of all Taladas?"

He stared at her, silent. He knew the answer, she sensed, but didn't want to speak it.

Then he didn't have to. The door opened. One of the other Brethren came in, flanked by two yaggol. "Keeper," he said.

The Keeper turned, looked across the room. "Teacher. What is it?"

"The Master wishes to speak with you, at once."

Another silence fell. The Keeper glanced at Essana. She watched him, wondering if he would answer her question. He didn't, which meant once her son came into the world, she would leave it. If she were still around to witness the Faceless Emperor's return, it would be as a ghost only, lost and striving between worlds.

The Keeper left the room, left her alone. She lay there, bound to the bed by magic, and staring into the darkness, thinking. She began to sob, and only stopped when sleep claimed her.

Chapter

6

Kristophan, The Imperial League

Forlo dreamed again, though he did not want to.

Dreams had troubled his sleep ever since Hawk-bluff, his last battle as marshal of the Sixth Legion, long before he ever heard of the Hooded One. He woke every night, his whole body tingling, his heart thundering against his ribs. It used to be he dreamed of that final clash, against the undead hordes of the mad Thenolite bishop, Ondelos . . . but the battle never reached its ending, never came to the point when he and the bishop met. Only shortly before he rode to meet the Uigan horde did he learn what was truly at work: Shedara told him that a spell was buried deep within his mind, blocking his memory of that day. But the magic was slipping, and that caused the nameless terrors that left him sweat-soaked and shivering in the dim hours before dawn. Together, they had entered his dreams and discovered what had truly happened at Hawkbluff.

He had killed children. Dozens of them.

They weren't real children, he'd told himself. Bishop Ondelos had murdered them, then raised them again as blood-hungering ghouls to protect him in his temple. They would have torn Forlo to pieces, if he hadn't cut them down . . . but that made it no easier, hewing through their ranks, watching them pull down and slaughter his men.

Children.

His friend, Grath—dead now, at the Lost Road—had paid a wizard to ensorcel him so he couldn't remember that day. It had been a mistake, but a well-meaning one. Knowing was terrible, but it was still better than the dreams.

Since the day Shedara lifted the spell, not a single night had passed when he had woken screaming—even after the shadow-fiends took Essana.

Now, though . . . now the nightmares had returned, different and yet the same. Even as this new one began, he knew how the dream would end. They always ended this way now. There was no way he could stop it.

The setting of his visions had changed—it was no longer the temple of Hith in Hawkbluff. He was in a stairway, running up the midst of a tower. He had never seen the place before, though there was something familiar about it. The tower was unpleasant to look at, all carven black stone, its walls hewn into ridges, like the ribs of some enormous serpent. Coils of smoke hung in the air, rising from iron braziers. It stank of brimstone, hot metal, and . . . faintly . . . the sweetness of burning flesh. A constant, rumbling roar battered his ears.

In the dream he was climbing, moving up the steps with sword in hand, alone. He didn't know what lay behind him, but he didn't look either. He was afraid to see what might be following him. Something terrible had happened . . . was happening . . . here.

A flickering, red glow shone down from above. He'd seen enough villages razed to recognize that gleam: something was burning, well beyond control. The air grew warm, stifling. Sweat sprung from his pores. He kept climbing, his mouth dry, and as he rounded the curve of the stairway, he saw the source of the light.

It was a window, tall and crowned with a pointed arch. Sheets of flame ran up the pane, bathing the other side of the glass. He stopped, staring: the tower's lower reaches must be on fire! But that wasn't possible. The place was solid rock. What stone could burn like that? Raising his sword, he crept toward the window, through waves of eye-watering heat, and peered outside.

For a time, all he could see was fire. Its warmth seared his face, and he could smell his beard scorching, but he couldn't look away. Then, like curtains, the flames parted, and he gazed out in his dream at a true nightmare.

All around the tower was a sea of molten rock, glowing red and golden about islets of black stone. Jagged mountains rose in the distance, wreathed in haze. Crimson lightning shattered one of the peaks as he watched. Looking upon it, he knew this was Hith's Cauldron, the Wound of the World, which no living man had crossed. Which meant the tower had to be . . .

"You are in the Chaldar."

Forlo whirled, his eyes wide. His blade whipped around, and would have taken off the head of the one who spoke, had he stood a little closer. The man was cloaked, head to foot, in blue satin. A deep hood hid his face. A wizard. Forlo could almost smell the man's magic through the miasma. He brought his sword back around, pointed it at the shadowed cowl.

"Who are you?" he asked.

The man's head tilted. "I had hoped you would guess. We have met before, though we have never seen each other."

"Speak plainly," Forlo said, moving his blade an inch closer to the man. "I've never had patience for riddles."

"Yet the riddles are your own," the man replied.

He reached out, quick as a striking scorpion, and seized Forlo's weapon. His hand wrapped around its blade—which should have cost him his fingers, but the razor-sharp steel did not cut his flesh. With a vicious yank, he pulled it from Forlo's hand and cast it, clattering, back down the stairs.

"This is your dream," he said. "Your mind makes it."

Though he was disarmed, Forlo refused to back down. He glared at the wizard. "Then I can make you show your face."

"Yes. If you wish to see it."

Forlo drew the dagger from his belt.

"Ah," said the man. "You're as stubborn as I suspected. Very well."

With that, he reached up, took hold of his hood, and drew it back. Forlo stared, the knife falling from his hand. It hit the stairs with a bone-jarring clash.

The face Forlo beheld was his own . . . not as it was, but as he remembered it. Younger. Beardless. The dark hair still full and thick, the skin unlined, unscarred. But there was something different, too, and he soon realized what it was: the eyes. His eyes were hazel. This man's were deep blue.

Essana's shade.

A sound escaped him, one he knew well. It was the grunt of a man who'd taken a spear through the gut.

The familiarity that had been nagging at him throughout the dream became clear now. He'd seen this man in his nightmares of Hawkbluff, although in those dreams, this one had been only a child. It had always been the last thing he saw, the final horror before waking.

His unborn son, grown to manhood.

The man smiled. It was Essana's smile, not his. He shuddered.

Then, as quickly as he'd grabbed the sword, he reached out and shoved Forlo. The blow drove the wind from Forlo's lungs as he stumbled back, back—into the window. Forlo cried out, feeling the glass break, hot shards slashing his flesh. He flailed, trying to hold on, but could not. For an instant, he teetered on the sill.

"Farewell, Father," said the man.

And Forlo fell, out into the flames. He screamed, and fire rushed down his throat. The agony was unbearable. The surface of the molten sea rushed up toward him. . . .

"Easy, now. Easy."

Forlo's eyes opened. Spears of golden light stabbed his brain. He could only sense simple things: an ache in his stomach, where the shadow-fiends had wounded him; the rasping ring of someone sharpening a sword; an awful sourness in his mouth, like something had crawled inside and died. He tried to speak, but his tongue was too heavy, like a slab of meat in his mouth.

"Rest," said the voice again. He knew that voice, but couldn't think from where. "You nearly didn't make it, Barreth. If the fever had lasted another day, your brains would have boiled in your skull."

Wincing, he forced his eyes to focus. The glare that had blinded him condensed to a single, dim candle flame. All around him were shadows, swathing a small, windowless room of red-brown stone. He lay upon a canvas cot. There was a thick, wooden door, bound and barred with iron. A prison cell? Where was he?

Then the one who had spoken leaned over him, and Forlo's heart froze. The owner of the voice was an aged minotaur, his brown coat frosted with gray that ran to white around his muzzle. His left hand was missing, a three-tined steel claw in its place. His right eye was milky-white, surrounded by gnarled flesh.

"Vuldak," Forlo groaned, sitting up. "You're still alive. . . ."

He'd known Vuldak in his youth. When he became an officer in the imperial legions, the minotaurs had forced him to prove his worth as a warrior. It was a normal rite of passage among the bull-men for their leaders to demonstrate their mettle upon the sands of Kristophan's gladiatorial arena. Forlo had fought on those sands, some twenty years ago, and had come to know Vuldak well. The one-handed minotaur had been a physician, closing cuts, setting broken bones, and easing the passing of gladiators too badly hurt to survive. Vuldak had been old even then, and Forlo would have bet a fortune he was long dead.

He was still trying to sit up when a wave of nausea clenched his insides. He collapsed, then rolled on his side and tried to vomit. His stomach was empty, however, so he could only heave until he lay light-headed and weak, a rope of spit hanging from his lips.

"I said easy, didn't I?" Vuldak asked, wiping Forlo's mouth with a rag. "You were cut up bad. You need to regain your strength before the trials."

Forlo regarded him blearily. "Trials? Where are we?"

"Kristophan," the old bull-man said. "The arena, of course. Would I be anywhere else?"

Forlo blinked, trying to piece things together. Flashes of memory, barely more than shadows, played through his mind: the greathall of the keep, and a savage-looking elf. The window of his bedchamber. A camp of imperial soldiers, in black and gold. A bed of straw in a cart, jouncing as it rumbled along a road. And now . . . this place.

"What am I doing here?" he wondered.

Vuldak shook his head and held a bowl of water to Forlo's lips. "Drink," he said. Forlo drank. "You've been arrested, Barreth. Treason, deserting your command. You're at the arena, awaiting trial. Your barbarian friend is here, too."

"Hult?" Forlo asked. He looked left and right. "Where is he?"

"Chained in the lower dungeons. He's fierce, that one," the old minotaur said, chuckling. "Grabbed a guard's club and nearly beat him to death with it when they tried to part the two of you. He owes you his life—they would have killed him there, but they had orders not to. Rekhaz wants the two of you brought before His Imperial Majesty together."

Forlo slumped. "Rekhaz is emperor now?"

Vuldak sighed. "Yes, to my sorrow," he replied. "And he's not happy, my friend. Not happy with you at all."

Minotaur justice was not known for its clemency, though the bull-men always strove to be fair, in their way. Those accused of a crime were allowed to plead their case, but only the wealthy could afford to pay tribunes to argue for them against the state. Most, particularly humans dwelling within the League, had to defend themselves. The council of magistrates usually consisted of a number of high-ranking officers: never fewer than three, sometimes as many as eleven, depending on the crime. Though famed for their cruelty in battle, the minotaurs did not torture their captives, nor did they coerce them into lying after they swore to tell the truth. Such unfairness was for dishonorable races, not the chosen people of Sargas. And even for those convicted of the greatest crimes—even regicides—there were ways to escape sentencing.

There were always options.

Forlo thought about this as he waited in an antechamber off the Hall of Laws. Heavy iron chains bound his ankles and wrists, and half a dozen bull-men with crossbows watched him as he stared at the tall, bronze doors that led to the court, the imperial axe-and-horns etched into their surface. Beyond, low voices murmured.

Hult squatted nearby, his stubbled head bowed, his face dark with anger. The minotaurs had docked his long braid, and he bore dark bruises over half his body. They'd brought him in here, half an hour ago, bellowing and raining blows on their backs with his bare fists. They'd had to knock him half unconscious with their cudgels to subdue him. Now he sulked, wiping at the trickle of blood that leaked from his nose and glowering at the world.

He's better off here than I'd be among his people, Forlo thought, and knew it was true. Minotaurs were harsh, but the Uigan killed foreigners for the sport of it. Chovuk's horde had sacked two towns, Malton and Rudil, and the tales told by survivors were gruesome.

Vuldak tried to inspect Hult's wounds, but the barbarian snarled and lashed out with his chains, earning him another thump from one of the guards. The physic turned to Forlo instead.

"You have no chance," he said. "Be sure of that. Rekhaz wants your head even more than he wanted the throne, I think."

Forlo nodded. The emperor—who had won his crown by slaying his chief rivals in battle—had little use for him now. Forlo had been a favorite of Ambeoutin, the previous emperor, who had died with all his heirs when an earthquake destroyed half of Kristophan, including the imperial palace. Rekhaz had disliked him for that favoritism and had become an enemy when Forlo resigned his commission after Hawkbluff. Forlo had made things worse by refusing to help Rekhaz in his campaign for the throne, then—when the danger of the Uigan became clear—begging for troops to aid in the empire's defense. Rekhaz had given him just one cohort of humans, trusting Forlo would die in the fighting. As that hadn't happened, the new emperor now wanted to settle matters for good.

He pictured the imperial executioner—a monstrous bull-man with red eyes—honing the blade of his great-axe on a spinning grindstone. He could almost hear the shriek of the steel, feel the heat of the sparks showering from its edge. Soon enough, if Rekhaz had his way, that edge would cleave through his neck. After that, they would coat his head with pitch and stake it before the gates of Kristophan, and give his body to the dogs. That was minotaur justice.

But there was another way. Another option.

He heard footsteps, then the bronze doors clicked and

swung wide. Three minotaurs entered: a pair of soldiers, clad in full imperial regalia and the black-and-gold of the Fourth, with a bailiff in gray robes. The bailiff looked at Forlo, his eyes dark.

"Barreth Forlo, once lord of Coldhope Holding," he proclaimed, "you are called to answer the charges of desertion and treason against the Imperial League and its sovereign, Emperor Rekhaz the Fierce. Come forward. The savage as well."

Forlo took a deep breath and let it out. Vuldak leaned close, one last time. "I would say farewell, my friend," the old physic said, "but that seems unlikely."

"True," Forlo said. "But I can say it to you. Fair wind at your back, my friend."

"And a full mug before you," Vuldak replied. The old soldiers' good-bye. Vuldak turned and left, while Hult's guards prodded and shoved him forward.

Together they entered the Hall of Laws, a broad room of gleaming green serpentine, thirty feet high, with a vaulted ceiling painted to show Sargas, the Horned God, with a broadsword in either hand. One gleamed in sunlight; the other dripped with blood. Hewn bodies and severed heads lay piled around the god's feet. On either wall of the Hall, arrow-slit windows cast stark lines of sunlight across the floor. At the far end was a dais with nine steps, atop which stood a long bench of blood-red stone. Behind the bench sat seven minotaurs in robes of rich, scarlet brocade. All but one wore masks of brass and silver, crafted to hide their identities. Forlo recognized three of them, anyway: Lord Mettar, Lord Omat, Lord Skai . . . marshals in the legions, the Seventh and Fourth and First. Rivals, all, who had resented the fact that he, a human, had commanded the Sixth. They would be against him, and he had no doubt the three other magistrates had been chosen for the same reason. This was a kender court—only for show. Again he heard the whetstone on the headsman's axe.

The magistrate in the center wore no mask. He rose from his seat as Forlo and Hult approached, a white-furred giant nearly nine feet tall, clad in gilded plate armor beneath his robes. A golden crown, spiked with dragon's teeth, sat upon his brow, and rings of platinum and ivory adorned his long, curving horns. His nostrils flared as Forlo drew near.

"Hail, Rekhaz, Emperor of the Imperial League and the Conquered Lands," declared the bailiff, "and protector of the lands beyond the Run."

Forlo snorted; he couldn't help it. The honorific was preposterous, after what had happened to Malton and Rudil, after Rekhaz's failure to protect against the Uigan. The minotaurs had no lands beyond the Run anymore. Rekhaz didn't find it funny, however, and his eyes brimmed with fury. At a nod from him, one of the guards grabbed Forlo and threw him to the floor. Hult snarled, but they clouted him with their clubs and he fell as well.

"You dare mock me?" thundered Rekhaz. "You, who threw aside the chance to serve your empire? Who abandoned your men after battle to skulk back to your keep? Who consorts with one of the very wretches you swore to fight?"

Forlo looked up at the emperor and said nothing. He let his gaze speak for him, and it seemed to do the trick. Rekhaz's expression grew even more fearsome. Barreth Forlo had loathed many in his day—Thenolite fanatics, murderous bandits, opportunistic officers, soldiers who betrayed their comrades—but he'd never felt the revulsion that boiled inside him now.

With effort, he struggled to his feet.

"Hult is no wretch," he declared. "He chose not to kill me when he had the chance. There is more nobility in him than in all the lords I see arrayed before me."

The magistrates growled and sputtered, uttering curses and pounding on the bench. Rekhaz's massive hands clenched into fists, each the size of a man's head. "You will not speak that way to this august assembly," he said.

"I'll speak however I choose," Forlo replied, shrugging. "It makes no difference. There's nothing I can say to sway you to my favor, and I know it. So hear this, Rekhaz—you keep me from my purpose. My wife and son are missing, abducted. The time I spend here is time I should be searching for them. Time I will never get back, thanks to you. If the gods are just, there will be a reckoning for it. And as to your august assembly . . . and your precious crown. . . ."

He paused, smiling a serpent's smile, and spat on the floor.

The magistrates surged to their feet, raging, shaking their fists. One of the guards tried to seize Forlo again, but he turned and glared so ferociously that the warrior rocked back on his heels, then raised his spear to strike. Rekhaz raised a hand before he could attack, however, staying him.

"You have always been too bold for your own good, Barreth," said the emperor. His words were glittering ice, his anger drained of all heat, and all the more dangerous for it. "You are right, though—you will not be found innocent. When this trial is done, you and your new friend will be morsels for the crows. But I will hear no more threats or insults from you."

Forlo spat again. The magistrates snorted, looking to their leader.

"As you will," Rekhaz declared. "If that is your answer, we will skip to the sentencing."

"No," Forlo said. "You won't. I invoke my right, as a citizen of the League, to answer for my crimes upon the sands."

The magistrates fell still.

"The sands?" Rekhaz asked. "You would fight as a gladiator?"

"It is my right," Forlo answered. "And Hult will fight beside me. Let our swords declare our innocence, or the blades of our enemies our guilt."

It was an ancient custom, one the minotaurs held with

reverence above all others. Any citizen could choose to fight for his freedom in the arena, if he was willing to give up his right to trial. Rekhaz stared, stunned, and Forlo laughed out loud.

"Had you forgotten, Your Majesty?" he asked. "These are the laws of your realm. Will you follow them or cast them aside?"

Rekhaz's eyes narrowed. He quivered with rage, his fangs tightly clenched. "Very well," he said. "The sands it is. It matters little—your blood will flow just as red there as on the block."

He gestured, and the guards took hold of Forlo and Hult. Forlo's eyes locked with the emperor's one last time, defiant, before they dragged him from the Hall of Laws.

Chapter

7

THE MARINERS' CREST, ARMACH-NESTI

We are being watched," Eldako said.

He leaned against the base of a moss-bearded pillar, one of more than fifty atop the ridge. Atop each column stood a statue of an elf: these were the original fifty sea captains who had brought the Silvanaes people to Taladas, nearly twenty-five centuries ago. Moss half-covered them now, and birds nested in the crooks of their necks and the folds of their cloaks. The beacons that had shone beside them had gone out. The only thing that lit them now was the red glow of Lunis, rising above the wooded hills.

Armach, the elf-home, was in trouble. Shedara had known this since the night on which she had last tried to communicate with Thalaniya, the Voice of the Stars, who ruled her people—and found, when she cast the speaking spell, only her queen's corpse, slain by the same shadow-fiends who had stolen the Hooded One. From that day, she had known Armach would not be the same as before, but she had not tasted the reality until now. The sight of the First Mariners, dark on their perches, made her eyes sting and her throat tighten.

And yet, some things didn't change. Even though dire

times had befallen the Silvanaes, they still kept watch over their borders. Even now, they kept outsiders from entering. She could sense the same thing Eldako did: unseen eyes, sighting along half-drawn arrows. Ready to kill, should the intruders prove not to be of pure elf blood.

"How many?" she murmured, not looking around. She didn't want to act suspicious. It would be bad to get shot by an over-watchful sentinel in her own homeland.

Eldako glanced up at the stars. Ribbons of cloud stretched across the sky. "Six, perhaps more, deeper in the trees. They're quite good at hiding themselves."

The unspoken words: for civilized folk. No doubt, the elves of the Tamire could conceal themselves in their woodlands with skill even beyond this. At least, Eldako seemed to think they could. Shedara allowed that he might be right about this: she had only counted four watchers.

"Push your hair back from your ears," she whispered. "Make sure they can see their shape."

Eldako raised an eyebrow, as if wondering what kind of lunatic would think he was human, but he did as she bade, casually pushing his red locks—chestnut brown at the roots—back to reveal the sharp points of his ears.

"There are many shadows in these woods," he said. "A great many, and some very close. They have overrun the Silvanaes."

"I know."

"What aid will your people be able to give us?"

Shedara shook her head. She'd been wondering the same thing. The Silvanaes were fighting for their own survival; why would they help her save two humans?

Because they had to. If the Hooded One was to be destroyed, if the shadows were to be stopped, they had to help. She only hoped she could make them agree. Not for the first time, she cursed Hult's reluctance to leap out Coldhope's window. That one moment's hesitation had cost them.

A shrill noise rang out: a keening cry that was half

eagle's shriek, half horse's whinny. She turned to gaze across the valley, the autumn-bronzed leaves dark under the red moon, and a smile touched her lips. There, skimming low over the treetops, was a winged shape, a creature with the golden head and foreclaws of a bird of prey, and the hindquarters of a white stallion.

"Tan-amat," Eldako said in his native tongue, and bowed his head in reverence. "The Uigan hunted them out in the Tamire long ago."

"Not here," Shedara said, watching the great sky-steed, the hippogriff, approach.

The creature skirled again, then swept up and over the ridge, trailing a storm of red and golden leaves. Banking sharply, he spread his wings wide and landed at a trot, not ten paces away. He came to a halt, eyeing her shyly, then walked forward, bowing his head to nuzzle her. The hippogriff cooed as she stroked his feathers.

"I know, Falasta," she said. "I know. It is hard for us all. But you must do this. It will help."

The hippogriff looked up at her, his great yellow eyes glittering, full of intelligence. His hooves stamped the turf as he turned to stare at Eldako. The wild elf closed his eyes, touching his lips with both hands.

"I greet you, Noble One," he spoke.

Falasta cocked his head, then glanced back at Shedara. *Should I trust this one?* he asked without speaking. *Or tear his heart out?*

Shedara smiled again. "He is a friend. He is elf-kind— not heerikil. Will you bear us both?"

The sky-steed considered this, then lowered his head again, wings spreading wide and low. A gesture of agreement. Eldako watched, his painted face blank. Shedara wondered, as she stroked Falasta's powerful neck, if the merkitsa had ever flown before.

"My brother," she asked, then hesitated, biting her lip. "Does he . . . does he live?"

She dreaded the answer. Quivris had been warden-protector of Armach. There was every reason, given what had befallen the Voice, to believe he had died with her. But the hippogriff bobbed his head, and Shedara felt her heart lift for the first time since Coldhope—and not just because Quivris was her kin. Her brother knew of the statue, and of Maladar the Faceless. He knew the danger. He, of all people, would understand what was at stake.

"Can you take us to him?" she asked.

Falasta nodded again. Shedara almost wept with relief. She looked to Eldako, who pushed away from the pillar. His arrows rattled in his near-empty quiver. There hadn't been time to make new ones during the long, hard trek from Coldhope. There'd barely been time for sleep. Now, she hoped, they would find both . . . and friendly faces, besides. Her smile broadened at the promise of seeing Quivris again. Soon, soon.

As she climbed onto Falasta's back, the watching elf-wardens withdrew, melting away into the forest. The sky-steed would never allow an enemy of the Silvanaes to ride him. Eldako mounted up behind, taking care not to touch her. She glanced back, shaking her head.

"This is no time for modesty," she said. "If you don't hold on, you'll get blown off."

He hesitated, then nodded. She noticed his lips: they were pinched tight, whiter than usual. So he *hadn't* flown before. She managed to keep her satisfaction from showing as he slipped his arms around her waist. His grip was firm, strong. Shedara felt her face flush at the thoughts that flashed through her head.

The sky-steed looked back, one huge eye gleaming, and let out a whickering cough. Shedara nodded, patting his neck again.

"Ready, my dear," she said. "Let's go."

Coming around, the hippogriff broke into a canter, then a gallop, the pillars of the Mariners flashing past. Ahead, the crest ended at a jagged cliff, dropping sharply away to pines and talus a hundred feet below. Eldako saw it, and his grip tightened; Shedara only smiled as Falasta hurtled closer and closer to the precipice, gaining speed with every stride, then leaped into nothingness.

Golden wings spread wide, catching the night wind. They dipped a little, then rose, up and over the trees, banking to the south and away over the whispering leaves of Armach.

It was nearly morning when they landed, the sky purple and beginning to swallow the stars. Solis's thin crescent hung over the hills to the east. The sea stretched out before them, dark waves breaking against tall, white cliffs. The wind carried the smell of salt, richer than at the Run. This was true ocean, which did not empty at moonrise.

The woods stood dark, still. Ominous. The Silvanaes had never been a raucous people, preferring to live in peace among the trees. Besides the spires of New Silvanost, which the elves had built in vain hope of recapturing the glory of their homeland across the sea, nothing they built rose above the canopy of leaves. Their homes were hidden among the woods and valleys and brooks. But to Shedara's eye, a deeper quiet had fallen over Armach. The darkness here was greater, the shadows thicker. The fiends, the twisted things that once had been kender, had conquered these parts, not far from where the Voice had held court. From the feel of the place, they still ruled. Falasta hadn't made a sound in nearly an hour.

Of course Quivris would be here somewhere. Her brother would be in the thick of the fight against their enemies, not hiding where it was safe. He was that kind of leader. She glanced over her shoulder and saw Eldako behind her, pale but composed. He deliberately was not looking down. She didn't blame him: the first time she'd ridden a sky-steed, she'd shut her eyes for most of the flight.

Falasta wheeled, gliding up over a hilltop and down into a ravine pierced by a silver ribbon of a stream. Large, white rocks lined the water's edges; the hippogriff arrowed toward one of these, spreading his wings to slow his descent. He landed, hooves clattering, then leaped as momentum carried him past it, and landed on the floor of the woods. Branches whipped by; Shedara and Eldako had to duck to keep from getting lashed in the face. Spruce needles flew. Finally, the sky-steed came to a halt beside the stream. In the distance, a waterfall murmured.

Shedara swung off the hippogriff's back and hopped down onto the grass. She drew her sword and a dagger as Eldako dismounted behind her.

"Where is this brother of yours?" the wild elf whispered. He slid his own blade from its scabbard, eyeing the trees. He had dwelt in the Dreaming Green, to the north of the Tamire, for much of his life. He was woods-crafty, and immediately he could sense a wrongness in this place.

"He'll come," Shedara said. She looked to Falasta and nodded. "Go. I will call if I need you."

The sky-steed stared at her with his golden eyes, pawing the turf, then vaulted into the air without a sound. In a flurry of wings, the creature was gone, rising into the brightening sky. Shedara watched as he winged away above the branches, then heard Eldako draw a sudden breath and looked down again.

The shadows had come.

There were a dozen of them—no, fourteen, lurking among the trees. They would have been invisible in full darkness, but in the gray mist of dawn they stood out just enough to see. Their curved knives looked like talons at the ends of their sleeves. She swallowed, glancing over at Eldako. A furious look creased his face, and she read his suspicions with ease: the hippogriff had betrayed them, had delivered them right into their enemies' hands. She wondered, with a cold feeling, if that could be true. If the ones who stole the Hooded One could corrupt the innocent kender, surely they could turn one of the Silvanaes' noble sky-steeds as well.

Suddenly there was movement behind them, figures dropping out of the trees, brown-and-gold cloaks—dyed to mimic the patterns of the autumn leaves—billowing as they fell. There were eight in all, and every one had a longbow. No sooner had they landed than each drew his arrow and loosed. Eight arrows flew, and eight shadows shrieked, shredding into nothingness as the shafts found their marks.

Undaunted, the remaining shadows charged. The golden-cloaked warriors dropped their bows and drew swords, striding forward to meet them. Eldako joined the newcomers, and after a moment's hesitation, so did Shedara. Between them, they cut the last of the fiends to howling pieces.

When it was done, the leader of their rescuers pointed silently, and four of his men broke off from the group, fetching their bows and spreading out into the woods. The others gathered around Shedara and Eldako. Hoods and cloth masks concealed their faces. It didn't matter; it took only a moment's study before Shedara rushed to embrace the leader. She knew him too well to be fooled by any mask.

"Brother," she said, relief sweeping through her. "I've never been so happy to see someone in my life!"

"You will not be happy, for long," he responded, and pulled off the mask.

Shedara made a strangled sound at the sight of Quivris's face. He had been beautiful before, with the perfectly pointed features and almond eyes of their kind. Now, however, the whole right side of his face was a ruin. Long, jagged scars had torn from his jawline to his forehead; his eye was gone, an empty, lidless hollow in its place. The ear had been torn off, leaving a gnarled lump behind. A few shallower cuts also marred his left side, which was not as bad as the right.

"The shadows did it," he said. "I nearly died. Some would say I should have, since the Voice didn't survive."

Shedara could only gape. Words would not come. It was Quivris who broke the silence again.

"And what of your quest, sister?" he asked. "I cannot think you succeeded, if the fiends still haunt Armach. Yet you are back."

"My quest . . ." Shedara murmured, still stunned.

"The statue. Is it destroyed?"

She flinched at the tone of his voice, the accusation there. If she'd found the Hooded One sooner, none of this might have happened. Lady Thalaniya might still be alive, the shadows would not have taken over the woods . . . and her brother would not be maimed, disfigured for life. She looked down, her face coloring, and said nothing.

"I see," Quivris went on. "Then you've come to declare your failure."

"We are here for no such reason," Eldako said, stepping forward. An arrow thudded into the ground in front of him, and he stopped, glaring at the elf who had shot it. "We came to seek your help."

"And who are you to speak with such scorn?" Quivris asked, arching an eyebrow. "A merkitsa, by your dress. Where did my sister find you?"

"He saved my life," Shedara answered. "He is helping us search for the Hooded One."

Quivris eyed Eldako for a long moment. Eldako stared back, neither threatening nor afraid. His eyes glittered. Finally, Quivris turned back to Shedara. "Us? I only see two of you. Are there others?"

"There were," Shedara replied. "Two humans. But we've lost them. That's why we need you."

Quivris paused, his brow furrowing. That humans were involved certainly troubled him. As he was opening his mouth to speak again, though, one of the scouts strode out of the mist, right up to him, and leaned close to whisper in Quivris's ear. Shedara watched the color drain from her brother's face.

"Truly?" he whispered. The scout nodded, and he turned back to Shedara. "We must leave. There are more shadows nearby. Hundreds of them, coming this way. I'll hear your tale, sister—but you'll have to tell it on the move."

※——※——※

She could hear the fiends behind her: the rustle of cloaks, the whisper of small feet through the brush, the raspy breathing. When she turned to look, however, there was nothing there. The shadows stayed out of sight, hidden in the forest gloom, and the group struggled to keep ahead of them. The woods thickened as they went, climbing up a hill-shoulder dusted with fallen leaves. Humans would have slipped and fallen, or run headlong into a gully or bramble-thicket, but the elves had no trouble at all. Neither, apparently, did the shadows, whose pursuit never seemed to flag.

Shedara told her story as they ran, from the moment she last left Armach on the trail of the Hooded One. She told how twice she had nearly found the artifact—once among the dwarves of the Steamwalls, then again aboard a pirate ship on the Run—but both times it had already eluded her. She spoke of how the shadows had shown up, too, and slaughtered both dwarves and pirates. She'd finally tracked down the statue at Coldhope, but Forlo had caught her trying to abscond with it. She told about the Uigan horde, and how the shadows had stolen the statue while the battle raged—how Forlo and Hult had saved her, then been taken captive by the minotaurs.

She told it all, leaving out one thing: she never mentioned that she had invoked the Hooded One's magic, coercing

Maladar into summoning the great wave that destroyed the Uigan. Shedara hated keeping secrets from her brother, but the shame of having awoken the Faceless Emperor was too great. It was partly her fault the shadows had finally managed to steal the statue.

Quivris listened, never speaking, never even looking at her. When she reached the end of the tale, he was quiet for a long while. They reached a narrow, rock-walled canyon, through which roared a river that was mostly white foam. A bridge of woven vines stretched from one side to the other. A pair of elves took positions at either side, arrows nocked, watching. The rest started across, one by one. It was full daylight now, the morning already an hour old.

When it came their turn, Eldako went first then Quivris gestured for Shedara to cross. She shook her head. "Not until you say you'll help us," she said.

"Then you'll wait a long time," he replied, stepping onto the bridge.

Shedara stared incredulously at his back as he made his way across the chasm. Finally, when he was on the other side, she shook her head and went after him. It was a long way, and the bridge seemed to sway wildly with each shift of the breeze, but finally she stepped back onto solid ground. She gave herself a moment to compose herself, then turned to glare at Quivris.

"We came all this way!" she exclaimed. "You're the only chance we have—"

A noise from the far side cut her short. She turned and looked back across the canyon. The shadows were pouring out of the trees, swarming toward the bridge. The two elf guards rained arrows upon them, killing one after another, but it hardly thinned their number. Finally, the elves turned and ran.

"What happens now?" Eldako wondered.

A grim smile curled Quivris's lips. "Watch."

One of the elves bolted across the bridge, but the other one had stopped, jerking his sword from its scabbard. He brought it down hard on the vines, hewing through one after another. The bridge lurched, then finally gave way. The last elf turned, sheathing his blade again, and one of the archers across the chasm fired an arrow, trailing a rope. The arrow arced over an overhanging branch, then fell near the last elf's feet. Without hesitating, he grabbed it and leaped out over the canyon, just before the flood of shadows could reach him. He swung, leaning into the arc, while several elves hauled on the other end of the rope. When he reached the end of the swing, he let go, flying through the air to land on the safe side of the gap.

Eldako raised his eyebrows, nodding as the elves reeled in the rope. "Impressive."

"Thank you," said Quivris. "We've become quite resourceful."

The shadows on the far side snarled and waved their sickles, to no avail. There was no way for them to cross. The elves loosed a few more arrows at them, then the whole group melted away into the forest again. Quivris never once looked at his sister.

<hr />

It was nearly noon when they came to their destination: a fallen broadwood tree, which rolled aside when Quivris knocked on it. Behind it gaped the narrow mouth of a cave. Several more Silvanaes were already inside, among barrels of food and water and boxes of arrows. Shedara and Eldako followed the rest of the party into the cavern. No one spoke. When they were all inside, the trunk rolled back into place, covering the entrance with a muffled thump. Darkness surrounded them; it took Shedara's elf-sight a moment to adjust. The warm shapes of the Silvanaes swam out of the blackness.

"Stop right there," she snapped, grabbing Quivris's shoulder as he started to turn away. "What's the matter with you? Why won't you help us?"

He rounded on her, shoving her hand away. "With what? I have sixty elves at my command. Sixty! The rest are dead or scattered. It's all I can do to keep the shadows from destroying our land completely . . . and you come here, asking us to rescue humans?"

Shedara's mouth dropped open. She felt as though he'd struck her. She looked around as the elves removed their masks. They were tired, hungry, weak. Many had grievous wounds, like her brother's. A beaten people. She stumbled back, bumped into the cave's wall. The stone was cold against her back.

"Only sixty. I didn't know," she said.

Quivris smiled bitterly. "No. You didn't."

"Then the shadows. . . ."

"Have already won the war. More arrive every day, and they take more of the forest from us. We can't keep up . . . and attrition will finish us soon." Quivris sighed. "Sister, I'm sorry. I am at my wit's end. I can do nothing for you."

He shook his head and started to walk away.

"What if, together, we can stop the shadows?"

Shedara blinked, turning to stare at the one who had spoken. So did her brother. Eldako stood with arms folded, his head cocked back. The cave grew silent, even the other elves becoming still. All eyes were on the merkitsa now.

"What do you mean?" Quivris asked.

"We know they were kender once," Eldako said. "And the kender's home is in the valleys of Marak. Whatever is breeding these shadows must be happening there."

Shedara stepped forward, understanding. "Yes, we'll go to Marak," she said. "We'll find out what's happened to the kender and try to stop it."

"If I give you what you want," Quivris said.

She spread her hands. "It's what *you* want too. If Maladar is freed, none of this will matter. The shadows are nothing compared to what he can do to Armach."

Quivris shook his head.

"Brother," Shedara said, "you said it yourself, just now—you have no hope. Eldako and I are offering to give you some. You claim you can't afford to give us what you need . . . but the truth is, you can't afford not to."

He scowled at her. She smiled. He looked at her a long time.

Chapter

8

KRISTOPHAN, THE IMPERIAL LEAGUE

Hult awoke to the rattling of keys outside his cell door. He didn't try to rise, but lay still, pretending to be asleep. His mind was on escape; it had been since the minotaurs captured him. He had tried several times, to no good. He wasn't going to let that stop him from trying again, though.

He had been in this strange place for somewhere between two and three weeks. Without windows in his cell, it was hard to know for sure. He already knew the fate that awaited him and Forlo. They had brought the two of them back, to the Arena shortly after their trial. They had shown him the sands beneath the massive, looming stands, the racks of weapons, the gladiators and caged monsters who fought there. It was a pit fight—most of the tribes of the Tamire had such contests, where criminals fought and rivals settled disputes. This pit just happened to be many times larger than the largest Uigan village. It could have held all of Chovuk's horde, several times over.

He understood, now, the folly of the Boyla's ambition. Chovuk had doomed his people the day he decided to cross the Run. Even if they had won at the Lost Road, what then? They would have pushed deeper into the League, and eventually met their deaths on the long spears of fifty thousand minotaurs. No rider, in his bloodlust, could ever have imagined there were this many bull-men in the world. It seemed a cruel joke, as if Jijin were a trickster-god instead of a warrior.

The door swung open, and two minotaurs entered. They held man-catchers, and they used them without hesitation, slamming the weapons against Hult's stomach and legs as he sprang from where he lay. Both poles hit him hard, then the pincers on the end closed around him. The bull-men yanked him off his feet, and he hit the ground hard, with a rattle of chains. One of the bull-men said something in their harsh language, and both laughed. They were mocking him, and why not? He was a fool. All the Uigan were fools—even their prince.

A third came into the cell while he struggled against the man-catchers. This one had a massive, iron-studded cudgel in one hand, and a ring of keys in another. He stood over Hult and growled something, raising the club to make his meaning clear. Stop it, or I will crush your skull.

Hult lay still. There were times to fight, but this wasn't one of them. Wait for the opportunity, Chovuk had taught him. Be like the skrit, who hides in his shell until the time is right. Until prey is close. Then sting, and sting, and sting until it is dead.

He only hoped he would have the chance to sting before this was over.

The jailer used his keys to unlock Hult's chains, then clamped manacles around his wrists and ankles. Hult ground his teeth: weeks had passed since he'd spent more than a few moments without chains on him. He hated it. He hated them. Most of all, though, he despised himself.

He could have prevented this. He could have jumped with the elves. He and Forlo were here because he had hesitated, out of fear. Because he was a coward. He'd doomed them both because he couldn't face the sea.

They jerked him to his feet, pushed him out the door. He stumbled as the man-catchers released him. They laughed. Red mist began to gather in front of his eyes; he fought it back. This was no time for rage, not yet. They brought him down a tight, stone tunnel, then up a flight of stairs. As he climbed, he heard roaring from above: tens of thousands of voices shouting. He thought of the horde, now drowned by the waters of the Run: it was the same noise the riders of the Tamire had made as they swept down into Malton, to burn and pillage. The voices were shouting for blood.

His blood. The skin on his arm rose into bumps.

A curving hallway waited at the top of the stairs, all gleaming white marble, lined with bull-headed statues. There was sunlight beyond, and from that way the cheering got louder, and he heard the stamping of feet. More guards met him, bearing pole-axes, their armor gleaming. They surrounded him, brought him forward, leaving the jailer and his men behind. That made him angry: he wouldn't get the chance to snap their necks, as he had dreamed at night in his cell. He knew that, whatever happened to him, he wouldn't be going down into the prison again.

Forlo stood at the end of the corridor, surrounded by another group of crossbowmen. He was clad in his armor, but had no helm or weapon. All part of the game. Hult himself was naked, but for a cloth covering his loins. They had taken his garments, just as they'd cut his braid. Dishonor after dishonor. And they called him a barbarian.

Forlo couldn't look him in the eye as he approached. Hult wanted to tell the man that it wasn't his fault. It's mine, he thought again. If only I'd jumped. . . .

Through an archway lay the sands, the pit. The light was bright, a cloudless autumn morning. The air was warm and still. Dust hung in the air like ghosts. The guards said something, then shoved him forward, prodding and jabbing with the butts of their weapons. He went, Forlo walking beside him. The other man tripped, nearly fell. The bull-men laughed some more.

Out on the sands, the sun stabbed his eyes. He squinted through the glare, baring his teeth, walking blind for a while. Gradually, everything went from white back to normal. He and Forlo were halfway across the arena floor, a perfect circle a hundred paces across, shimmering in the heat. It burned the soles of his feet. Around its edges stood minotaur guards in plumed helmets, armed with crossbows. High above, bull-men filled the stands all around him. There were so many that Hult didn't even try to guess at the number: some dressed in finery, others in the garb of common workers. Some waved banners. Some blew war horns or pounded drums. All were shouting, the noise like the din of a thunderstorm. It was like a vision of the Abyss, from the elders' tales: horned demons presiding over brutal torments. Hult shuddered, his stomach clenching.

The guards did not stop at the center of the circle, as he thought they would; instead, they brought Forlo and Hult all the way to the far side, beneath a gallery covered with a canopy of gold and crimson silk. Wealthy minotaurs sat on chairs along its length, and in its midst, robed and crowned, was the one they called emperor. Rekhaz was his name. Forlo sneered at the sight of him and said a vile word.

"Khot."

The emperor smiled, rising from his seat. A hush fell over the arena as he stepped forward. The guards shoved Forlo and Hult down on their knees, hitting them hard with the butts of their axes. The red mist began to gather again. Hult forced himself to be calm, to concentrate, listening to the emperor's words. He didn't understand them now, but he forced himself to remember. Later, he would know their meaning.

"Barreth Forlo, lord of Coldhope, once marshal of the Imperial Armies," Rekhaz declared, his deep voice filling the arena, "you are guilty of high treason against the League and of deserting your command without leave. You have chosen to answer for these crimes upon these sands. Here the justice of Sargas will be done, and your blood will answer for your sins.

"As for your barbarian friend, he is an enemy of the empire. His life was forfeit the moment he was caught. He will fight beside you, at the whim of the throne. His fate is already chosen: whether you prevail or not, he will be slain. You fight for yourself alone."

"What?" Forlo asked, glaring up at the emperor. "That isn't the law . . . any prisoner who survives the arena must be freed!"

Rekhaz smiled, cruel and condescending. "Any citizen of the League," he said. "Barbarians from far lands have no rights here. This savage sealed his fate the day he rode howling across the Run with his misbegotten brothers. This is my ruling, Lord Forlo. It is final. If you speak again, I will make the guards cut out your tongue."

Forlo fell silent. His eyes were daggers, glinting in the sun. The emperor raised his hands.

"The empire watches your doom," he said. "The mercy of Sargas will judge you. Go now, and die if he wills it."

The throngs in the stands cheered, the noise so loud that it left Hult's ears ringing like funeral bells. The guards prodded them to their feet, marched them back toward the center of the ring. As they walked, a young minotaur sprinted from the arena's edge, planted two blades point-first in the sands, and bolted away again. Hult saw them and nodded: Forlo's blade and his own shuk. They would fight with their own weapons, at least.

Forlo's face was red, his nostrils wide. Hult knew the rage was threatening to claim him too. He wanted to tell the man about Chovuk's lessons, about the patient, deadly skrit . . . but he couldn't, so he just kept walking.

The cheers grew even louder as they reached the sands'

midst. The guards withdrew, leaving them alone. Forlo lifted his blade, and Hult took up his saber as well. Its worn grip felt right in his hand, its weight familiar and comforting. He gave it a few practice spins, working out the stiffness in his joints. Forlo did the same, then turned and said something. Hult didn't know the words, but he understood the look in the man's eyes.

"No," he said. "I am the one who should be sorry."

Forlo didn't understand. There was no way to explain. Then, after a moment, the opportunity passed. At the highest reaches of the arena, trumpeters raised silver horns and blew a fanfare that stilled the crowd. The echoes of the blare gave way to silence. The minotaurs leaned forward, craning their necks as they looked toward a broad, bronze door on the south side of the ring.

Hult and Forlo watched the door open, revealing iron bars. Beyond, in the shadows, something stirred. Whatever it was, it wasn't human. Hult licked his lips, his shuk weaving in slow loops before him. A dim clank sounded from the portcullis; with a squealing groan, it started to rise.

The things that waited behind the gates scuttled out so quickly, it set Hult back a pace. They were massive, wormlike creatures, each ten feet long and as wide across as a man's trunk, covered in shells like banded mail, one deep blue and the other oily black. They had more legs than he could count—it seemed like hundreds, each ending in a wickedly curved hook that dug into the sand as they darted forward, throwing up plumes behind. Pincers like scytheblades gnashed around their chittering mouths; their eyes were like faceted jewels, as black as an ogre's heart.

"Horax!" Forlo yelled, moving back a step as the beasts scurried toward them.

Hult glanced at him in surprise, recognizing the name: his own people called these creatures hurajai, which in the Uigan tongue meant "cutters of bone." They dwelt in caves in the hills and mountains, coming out at night to prey on the herds. Their armor was too thick for arrows to pierce; a man had to hew at them with steel to kill them. But the hurajai he had seen hadn't been this big: none was much longer than a man was tall. These were almost twice that size. Either they were mightier in the southern lands, or the bull-men bred them especially, like dogs, to use in their pit-fights.

They moved like flowing water, weaving this way and that, making awful wet hissing sounds as they came. The crowd leaped to its feet, roaring, banging on cymbals, and waving banners. The commotion was spellbinding, and Hult had to force himself not to look up at them as a huraj—the black one, rainbows writhing in the reflections of its shell—shot straight at him.

It reared, rising almost to the level of his throat, mandibles clacking in the air. He leaped aside, rolled, and came up with his shuk in front of him. The huraj settled back to the ground, then whipped around and started forward again. Hult had long enough to see Forlo swiping his own blade at the other one, keeping it at bay while he tried to circle to its flank. Then the black huraj came on again, clawed legs churning. He brought back his saber, spun it, then snapped it around as hard as he could, striking with the tip of the blade at the creature's neck. It was a powerful stroke, swift and well aimed, strong enough to take off the huraj's head. But it didn't.

Instead, his sword shattered.

Hult had had the shuk since he was ten summers old. His father had given it to him, shortly before he died. He'd learned to fight with it, had carried it when he ventured into Panak on the hunt that would make him a man, had laid it at Chovuk's feet—and thrown it aside when Chovuk died, only to have Forlo return it in a gesture of goodwill. It was the one thing he had left of his homeland. It had never failed him. But the moment it struck the huraj, the blade made a horrible sound and broke into glittering shards, which rained down upon the sands. He was left holding a jagged stump, shorter than his forearm.

He stared at the broken weapon in disbelief, and the moment nearly cost him his life. The blow had knocked the huraj aside, but the creature quickly swung around again, pincers snapping. Hult twisted aside, barking a curse, and felt a hot line of pain in the side of his neck as one of the mandibles sliced through his flesh. Blood sprayed, and for a panicked moment he thought he had been slain, but then he realized it wasn't enough blood. He batted the huraj with the edge of his hand, painfully. It was like striking solid steel. The creature flopped away, and Hult danced back, what remained of his shuk at the ready.

He heard the laughter: the crowd, hooting and jeering, mocking him. He glanced around, understanding; the minotaurs had broken his blade, not him. They'd scored it, leaving it intact but so weak that it would snap the moment he hit anything. He cursed again. He wanted to jam the broken end of his shuk, his birthright, in the foul emperor's eye. He wanted to bathe in bull-man blood.

Another metallic snap rang out to his right. "Khot!" Forlo swore again.

Hult didn't have to look to know: now both of them were unarmed, and the hurajai were still unhurt. He lashed out with his foot, kicking his opponent and flipping the creature halfway over. As it writhed and flopped, trying to right itself, he lashed out with his broken blade. It struck the creature's armor, but didn't penetrate; instead it ground along the plates with a spine-jarring squeal, snipping off three legs, which lay twitching on the ground, oozing something that looked sickeningly like butter.

The huraj tried for him again. Hult leaped over the creature, stumbled, and dropped the hilt of his sword. The crowd laughed louder still.

He was casting about, searching for what was left of his saber, when Forlo let out a shrill cry. Hult glanced over and grimaced: the blue huraj had latched its pincers around the man's right wrist and was sawing with them, back and forth. If he hadn't been wearing armor, it would have cut off his hand in an instant; instead, it was grinding links of chainmail into his flesh. Blood darkened Forlo's glove, and he shook his swordarm wildly, trying to throw off the creature. He started beating on its chitinous head with his left fist. He might as well have been punching solid iron.

A hiss brought Hult's eye back to his own huraj, just as it was scuttling toward him once more. He flexed his hands. Either he won the fight now, in this pass, or he was dead. He crouched low, watching, waiting. The huraj rose up to strike.

He was quicker. With desperate speed, he reached out with both hands and grabbed it just below its head. Pincers snapped in midair, close enough to his face that he smelled the bitter tang of acid from its mouth and felt burning drops of the acid hit his skin. He hissed and spat right back. Then, probing, he got his fingers around the plate that covered its head and began to pry.

The huraj screamed, its tail thrashing, throwing up great fans of sand. Clawed legs dug into his arms, ripping bloody furrows in his skin. Hult ignored the pain, concentrating on ripping the creature's head off. It wasn't easy: the edges of the shell were sharp and cut into his fingers. The carapace clung fiercely to the pink flesh beneath, but bit by bit, it began to work free. The monster bucked and thrashed, wrenching him left and right; he moved with the pressure, bracing himself and yanking again whenever it stopped. The muscles of his arms, his neck, and his back stood taut and trembling. The red mist settled over him, and this time he didn't will it away. He bellowed a booming, wordless shout—and then, with a hideous ripping sound, the shell came free.

White slime was everywhere, covering him. The huraj slipped out of his grasp, the shell-plate dangling from the side of its head. It fell to the ground and thrashed some more, trying to escape. His teeth bared in a feral grin, Hult ran after the creature, raised his foot, and stomped on its naked, oozing head.

The huraj's screams stopped at once. Its back continued to twitch and squirm, but it was only reflex. The beast was dead. Hult hurt all over. But there was still another creature left. He turned and saw it was still latched around Forlo's wrist. It had driven the man to his knees, with blood darkening the sand all around him. But he fought it still, hitting it again and again, trying vainly to break free.

Hult ran to him. The remains of Forlo's sword lay half-buried in the sand; he grabbed it up, the hilt unfamiliar in his hand, and tried to stab the huraj between the plates on its side. He missed, hitting only shell.

Forlo was extremely pale. His chainmail was torn, hanging. The huraj's mandibles were grinding against bone now. Hult met Forlo's gaze, then nodded toward the creature's jaws. The other man nodded back, understanding.

Together, they grabbed the pincers—Forlo seizing one half with his free hand, Hult the other with both of his own. For good measure, Hult planted his foot against the creature's neck. Pulling hard, they eased the pressure off Forlo's arm, then pulled the pincers wider and wider apart. Forlo wriggled free, and the mandibles came together again with a snap.

Hult felt something like a tug, but didn't think anything was wrong until he glanced down and saw two fingers lying in the dust. He looked at his left hand in shock: it was covered in blood, his first and middle fingers gone at the first knuckle. He gaped, amazed—and the huraj's mandibles closed around his ankle.

The crowd was jumping up and down, excited for the kill. Hult howled as the monster began to slice through his leg. In fury, he slammed the stub of Forlo's sword into the creature's eye, turning the orb into a jellied ruin. The huraj squealed but held on, intent on ripping off his foot.

Forlo yelled, grabbing the pincers again. But he didn't have much strength anymore. Neither did Hult. They grunted and strained, and black ghosts danced in front of Hult's eyes as his consciousness began to fray. He struggled against the pain, but it was too much. He had only moments left. The huraj was going to cripple him . . . and then he would die, for the bull-men's twisted pleasure.

Jijin, he prayed. Not now. I have much still to do.

A wind passed his ear. There was a solid sound, a *chunk*. The huraj tensed . . . then let go with a gurgle, an arrow thrumming at the top of its neck, between two plates. An arrow with black fletching, and a nock carved like a dragon's head.

Hult looked up, into the stands. He saw Eldako there. He thought: how?

Then he saw the rest.

Chapter

9

KRISTOPHAN, THE IMPERIAL LEAGUE

The spell will be impregnable for two hours," Nalaran explained. "Then it will begin to weaken. After that, the moment you strike a blow against anyone, the magic will fail."

Shedara nodded—she already knew this—and glanced at Eldako to make sure he understood. The merkitsa's face was pinched, his eyes narrow. He didn't like the idea of trusting magic, particularly from a wizard he didn't know. Shedara knew Nalaran, though. He had been Armach's greatest archmage, before doom fell upon the kingdom. His magic had served the Voice—but it hadn't saved the Voice, or many other Silvanaes, and Eldako had confessed that failure worried him. To be honest, it had worried Shedara as well.

But Quivris had told her that Nalaran hadn't been with Thalaniya when the shadows attacked. The survivors had found him a week later, hiding in the wilds, hungry and exhausted. Since then, the wizard had proven his worth again and again. Quivris swore on his sword that Nalaran was reliable.

Besides, there weren't many ways to infiltrate a minotaur city without being noticed, if you were an elf. And they were running out of time.

They had traveled west through the woods, avoiding the shadows, until they came to the shore: Eldako, Shedara, Quivris, Nalaran, and thirty other elves, half of those who dwelt in Quivris's secret caves. There, in a sheltered, rocky cove, they had found three small boats, left there in case the Silvanaes had to flee Armach. They took one of them up the coast, nearly a hundred leagues, moving at night and finding places to hide during the day. This, and a few judicious spells to make the vessel invisible, let them slip past the formidable minotaur navy and make landfall a few leagues south of what remained of Kristophan.

Shedara knew the fabled city of the bull-men well: its tremendous sprawl of white marble, once home to half a million people. Its bustling markets sold goods from all over Taladas, its thriving harbor used to be a forest of masts flying sails of every color imaginable, and the streets of Kristophan were packed with humans and minotaurs, all jostling and bumping to get somewhere else. What she hadn't yet seen, however, was that half of that grand metropolis was gone, smashed to rubble and sunk beneath the sea by an earthquake earlier that year. The emperor's palace, the grand halls of the senate, and the mighty temples to Sargas, Jolith, and Zai were all gone, swallowed by the great rift that had opened beneath the city. Its walls ended in jagged stubs atop cliffs of raw, rough stone. Mourning-fires still burned in great, bronze bowls atop the jagged islands where Kristophan's northern half had been. They would keep burning for years to come.

Now the League was recovering. A new throne had been made. A new emperor sat upon it, a warlord unloved by the people: Rekhaz. Soldiers were everywhere. It would make things even more difficult than they imagined.

They hid in a grotto along the seashore, four miles from the city. The moons were not in the same phase now, so their shelter stayed dry even in high tide. Nalaran went into the city alone, hidden by magic, to find out what he could.

He was gone a long time, long enough for both Quivris and Shedara to worry. But he returned, his face pale and grim, and told them what he'd discovered: Forlo and Hult were being held at the gladiatorial arena. They were to fight for their freedom—or, rather, Forlo's; Hult's life was forfeit either way. It would happen tomorrow.

Shedara saw the grim look on Eldako's face and knew hers held the same expression. "We're out of options," she said. "Now we have to act."

"We can't take them from the arena!" Quivris protested. "There'll be thousands of minotaurs there. There'll be hundreds of guards!"

Shedara shook her head. "You promised to do this, Brother. Are you afraid to keep your word?"

Quivris fell silent, fuming: she had challenged him in front of his men. Shaking his head, he turned and walked away. Shedara closed her eyes, her mouth pinching with pain. She and Quivris had been friends as well as close siblings, but things had changed. Grief and need were driving a wedge between them. Their kinship would remain, but it would never be the same.

She opened her eyes and saw Eldako looking at her— then his eyes shifted away, as if he believed she might think he just happened to be glancing in her direction for a moment. She knew better. She could feel the wild elf's stare, even when she wasn't looking at him. In truth, she wasn't sure she minded.

They made a plan. It was risky. Quivris insisted it wouldn't work: it relied too much on sorcery, and he was a warrior. Those who couldn't use the Art would never trust it, not fully. Eldako felt even worse about relying on magic—from the look on his face, he might have taken a bite of an unripe ishka-fruit. But both Shedara and Nalaran were confident that, if fortune smiled on them, they could rescue Forlo and Hult from the sands. And there was no time to devise anything better. They went ahead, the mages staying up all night to study their spells while the rest of the elves found what sleep they could. An hour before dawn, they gathered in the mouth of the grotto, and Nalaran cast the seeming spell upon them.

"Once the magic is gone," he explained, weaving his hands before Eldako and the Silvanaes, "it will not come back. You also will keep your own voice, and will not sound like one of them, a minotaur, so do not speak. Try not to stray too close to anyone who looks like a priest or a sorcerer, either. They might see through the guise, if they're looking for trickery."

Quivris scowled. "But other than all that, don't worry."

"Brother . . ." Shedara warned.

Smiling slightly, Nalaran turned to Shedara and cast the spell. Though she understood the words he spoke, they still seemed to crawl like beetles across her mind. The air shimmered, and for a heartbeat every hair on her body stood erect—and then, with a rushing sensation that made her feel like her head was suddenly full of blood, her body changed. She grew almost two feet. Coarse, gray fur sprouted from limbs that writhed with iron-hard muscle. Her neck thickened, her face lengthened, and long horns burst from her forehead. She swayed on her feet, dizzy from the change, and shut her eyes to steady herself. When she opened them again, her heart lurched with instinctive alarm before reason slowed it down again. She was surrounded by minotaurs: huge, hulking brutes of many different colors, some in armor, others in the short robes commoners wore in Kristophan. Every single elf in the cave had changed shape—except Nalaran himself, who now leaned against the stone wall, looking at once pleased with himself and extremely frail. He wouldn't be going with them; he had other things to do.

Shedara's gaze roved across the group, seeking out Eldako. There he was, rusty brown and battle-worn, a scar running from his snout to his left ear. He had a wide-eyed look on his face that made her want to laugh. She stifled the urge: she knew the merkitsa's pride.

Another minotaur, a towering, black-furred beast in segmented mail, stepped onto a stone outcrop and faced the rest. Quivris.

"You know the plan," Quivris said. In other, less grave circumstances his elf voice would have seemed hilarious, coming from that sharp-toothed snout. "Get into the arena. Find your places. Wait for Eldako to fire the first shot. Then move."

The minotaurs all nodded. And that was it. A few minutes later, they began to leave the cave—gradually, in ones and twos and threes. They split up, moving into the city, making their way to the arena. Shedara was one of the last to go, with Eldako. Quivris had already left, without a word to her. That hurt, but she thrust her feelings aside.

"Do you think this will really work?" the wild elf whispered as they walked along the dusty, cobbled road toward the haze of Kristophan.

She shrugged. "We have to make it work. No other choice, really."

A few minutes later, they met up with a larger group of bull-men and fell in with them. After that, they no longer spoke. When they'd passed through the city gates—where minotaurs and men alike were thronging—they made their way to the arena. Shedara felt at home, untroubled by the danger. This wasn't the first time she'd entered Kristophan this way. Seeming spells were a primary tool of a moon-thief, second only to invisibility as a means of infiltration.

Eldako, however, was clearly overwhelmed. He was trying not to stare at the looming marble buildings, towering on either side of him. Born and bred in the Dreaming Green, he had never seen a place like this. Shedara recalled her own awe, the first time she came to the metropolis—and *she* had seen paintings of it beforehand.

She'd tried to describe it for Eldako, but that could accomplish only so much. Words were one thing; being crammed into crowded streets with thousands more people than dwelt in the largest merkitsa village was another. To his credit, though, Eldako stayed calm amid the press of bodies, the noise, the stink.

The arena towered before them, huge, its fortified walls ringed with colorful banners and statues of minotaur heroes. Everyone was making their way toward it, and Shedara and Eldako followed the river of bodies until they reached the broad plaza surrounding the stadium. Then they broke away from the crowd and found a nearby street lined with taverns. The reek of the city was worse there, and became almost unbearable when they ducked behind one of the alehouses into an alley. Garbage was everywhere; a dog lay dead, swarming with flies.

"Welcome to the city," she murmured, flashing a crooked smile.

Eldako shook his head, trying to blink away the stench's sting. "I am trying to think of meadows and streams. I am trying to think of leaves. . . ."

Fortunately, they didn't have to wait long. The back door of a taproom swung open, and a pair of minotaur soldiers came staggering out, half-drunk and needing to piss. Shedara eyed their garb: it matched the armor worn by the archers who kept watch over the sands. This was where they came to drink, a run-down place called the Shivered Spar. It was a dive, but it had good ale, and didn't water its wine. She'd known a few of the archers would be indulging when they should be on duty: not all minotaurs prized honor equally. Some had appetites.

The bull-men weren't completely inebriated, but they were tipsy enough that they didn't realize they weren't alone until it was too late. Eldako stepped toward them, swift as a panther, and crushed one archer's throat with a swift chop from the side of his hand. The soldier dropped to his knees, choking and clutching, and Eldako drew a knife from his belt and plunged it into his neck, just behind his jaw. A jet of blood pierced the air, and the minotaur fell forward with a grunt.

The second minotaur was too shocked to react. Wits numbed by beer, he stared as his partner collapsed—a moment too long. Shedara flicked her wrist, drawing a dagger and throwing it with a single motion. It hit the bull-man in the eye, and the creature died without ever realizing what was going on. She slid in, catching him so his mail didn't clatter as he fell, and eased his dead weight to the ground.

She felt the seeming spell waver, strained by the violence they'd just committed, and held her breath. It had been less than two hours since Nalaran cast it, though, and in the end it held. She breathed again.

Glancing around, they yanked their blades from the dead bull-men, sheathed them, and stripped off their armor. In moments they wore the archers' breastplates, bracers, and greaves. Shedara also took their bows and arrows, but Eldako kept his own. No one would notice. With luck no one would see anything but the armor and his horns. They dragged the corpses down the alley, next to the dead dog, kicked a few rats away, and heaped trash on them. Then, hearts thundering, they made themselves walk out of the alley again and turned back toward the arena.

They got in with no trouble. The size of the place amazed Eldako. There were nearly as many minotaurs in its stands as there had been riders in Chovuk's whole, vast horde—and the seats were still only three-quarters full. Silently, they chose an empty post around the edges of the sands. Eldako strung his bow, nocked an arrow, and waited.

An hour passed. The seeming spell grew weaker. It would hold out for a day or more, but they were past being able to hold it if they committed violence. From now on, they would get one chance to fight, and then they would be elves again.

The plan could never work. But it had to.

Every now and then, Shedara caught sight of one of the others. A few had also taken positions around the edge of the ring. Others were in the stands. Quivris stood near the emperor's box. Some she couldn't pick out from among the crowd, though; she wondered if any had been caught. If they had, they were dead by now. She knew well enough that an elf spy would simply be killed on the spot. She'd seen it happen. She'd lost friends that way.

She was still lost in those grim memories when brass trumpets blew. All eyes turned toward the arena's great doors as they shuddered open, and she caught her breath. A band of guards escorted Forlo and Hult out onto the sands and made them kneel before the emperor's gallery while Rekhaz pronounced their sentence. Shedara stared, trembling with anger. Forlo looked all right, though Hult had had a rough time of it. He was battered and bruised, stripped to his clout, and his braid was gone. Eldako sucked on his teeth when he saw that, rumbling deep in his throat. He knew the Uigan's ways, knew what an insult that was.

A runner brought the captives' swords, planted them in the sands in the middle of the ring. Hult and Forlo took them up. The trumpets blew again. Shedara held her breath, her hands clenched into fists, and held still as the long, gnashing worms—she knew them as horaxes, though Eldako muttered a slightly different word—came skittering across the sands.

Eldako kept his fingers tense against his bowstring as he watched the fight, ready to draw and loose at any time. But he didn't shoot, even when both swords broke. Shedara held her ground as well, as much as she wanted to leap into the fray and help. It wasn't time—and besides, she had seen Hult and Forlo fight. They were both more than capable . . . she hoped.

Soon she was proven right. Hult killed one of the horaxes with his bare hands, ripping its armor off and stomping it to death. He ran to help Forlo, who was being gnawed on by the other beast. Together, they pulled free. Then Hult screamed, and even from halfway across the arena Shedara saw his fingers fall onto the sands. The minotaurs, rapt with bloodlust, cheered so loudly her ears rang. Eldako shut his eyes, his lips tight against his fangs. Shedara knew he was thinking of the Green, keeping his calm. The horax's mandibles locked around Hult's ankle. He screamed and fell. Forlo tried to help but couldn't pry the pincers loose.

Eldako had told Shedara there was no better archer in Northern Hosk than he. She wasn't sure if this was just boasting, but as he brought up his bow and sighted along the arrow, she prayed to Astar. The merkitsa's face turned blank, all emotion draining away. There was only him and the arrow and his target. Lost in that serenity, he exhaled and loosed.

The shaft flashed through the air. It hit the horax and killed it instantly. And the spell lifted. He was a merkitsa again, the stolen armor hanging loose on his body.

A heartbeat later, there were elves everywhere—or so it must have seemed to the bull-men, as startled guards and commoners alike drew blades and bowstrings and attacked those near them. Fifty minotaurs died in the time it took to draw two breaths. Chaos followed.

Eldako nocked arrow after arrow—he'd had time to make new ones on the journey to Kristophan—and loosed them at the minotaur archers. A half dozen of the Silvanaes joined him. Between them, they made short work of the guards, picking them off before they could do more than launch a few weak shots at Forlo and Hult. Two of the Silvanaes fell as well, one run through with a spear and the other with an arrow in his throat. Eldako leaped down onto the sands and aimed his bow up into the crowd. There were armored guards up there too; he started shooting them, one by one.

The Silvanaes were outnumbered by thousands of enemies twice their size. The plan should have failed. Against an arena full of minotaurs, thirty-three elves should have had no chance. But it wasn't a fair fight, either. The elves didn't drop their bull-man forms all at once, but gradually, slowly enough to let the thought sink in, all over the arena: any minotaur might actually be an elf in disguise. The bull-men started eyeing one another suspiciously, not sure who might draw a blade and attack next. Masses pressed anxiously toward the exits.

As for Shedara herself, she didn't move yet, didn't raise her bow. She waited, holding her minotaur form. It pained her to watch her people die, but she had a role to play in this, and fighting wasn't her job . . . not yet, anyway. She kept back, clutched her arm, and pretended to be hurt while bedlam erupted all around her.

At last, Quivris made his move. The warden of Armach had held his form long enough to push right up to the imperial box, appearing to the confused bull-men to be one of Rekhaz's personal retinue. Now he drew his sword and thrust it through the breast of one of the emperor's courtiers, then whipped it around and extended it toward Rekhaz before anyone knew it was happening. As he did, his form dissolved into the scarred elf, the brother Shedara no longer knew.

The emperor stared at him, his eyes narrow with fury. The tip of Quivris's sword hung, perfectly still, a hand's breadth from his throat. Elven steel glistened in the sunlight, the dead courtier's blood running along its edge. Quivris's blade was enchanted, one of the finest in Armach, an heirloom from the old kingdom across the sea. It could cut through stone as if it were water. Rekhaz didn't seem to care, didn't seem in the least afraid. Shedara watched as his gaze shifted from the blade to her brother, and his lips curled back to reveal his pointed teeth.

Rekhaz laughed, reaching for his own weapon, and Quivris stabbed at him. But he was no longer there—with an agility Shedara never would have expected from one so huge, he twisted aside, and the sword only grazed his shoulder. Bright blood sprayed the imperial box, and a hush fell over the arena.

The emperor had been bloodied.

Now Rekhaz was on the attack himself, whipping a jeweled, broad-bladed sword from his scabbard, batting Quivris's blade away, then leaping back and grabbing a battle axe from the huddled corpse of one of his guards, a warrior who'd taken one of Eldako's arrows through his forehead. He waved the surviving courtiers away, grinning as though he enjoyed himself. All eyes in the arena were now on the battle between Quivris and the minotaur emperor.

Rekhaz hurled himself at the warden of Armach, bringing the weapons down and across, an attack that ought to have carved any foe into pieces. But Quivris was nimble too, throwing himself backward, then spinning his sword in a tight arc that lopped off the axe's head, sent it spinning out onto the sands. Rekhaz's eyes flicked after it, then he pounded Quivris in the side of the head with the broken haft.

Shedara saw her brother reel, saw him stagger, and yearned to go to him. He was going to die up there. Rekhaz was a master swordsman. But she had a duty. Without her, the plan would fail. It could survive the loss of Quivris— maybe—but if she shirked, all this would be for nothing. And they would probably all be killed. So she stayed where she was, sick at heart, and kept waiting.

Quivris spat blood and tried to regain his balance. Rekhaz sneered, dropping the broken axe and shifting his sword to a two-handed grip. He swung it at the elf's neck, but Quivris ducked again, and the blow missed. He came up again, parried another cut, then swept his foot around and kicked the minotaur—hard—in the side of the knee. There was a crunch, and Rekhaz howled, stumbling sideways.

The ancient elven blade snapped around, its swing reversing in the blink of an eye. It struck flesh, just above the emperor's wrists. More blood flowed, and the jeweled sword clattered to the floor of the imperial box . . . with Rekhaz's hands still gripping it.

Rekhaz bellowed in agony. All around the arena, minotaurs cried out in outrage as he fell to one knee, staring in disbelief at the stumps of his arms. Quivris didn't hesitate, stepping in to lay the edge of his sword against the emperor's throat.

"Be still!" he shouted, even as nearby minotaurs pressed close. "If anyone makes a move toward me, your new emperor loses his head too!"

It worked. The other guards and courtiers, many of whom had been shoving toward him, all froze. Rekhaz's eyes burned with rage as he glared up at the elf who'd bested him. Quivris smiled a glittering smile.

"You know I'll do it, don't you, Your Majesty?" he asked. "And I'll enjoy it, too. So stay where you are, or I'll start with your horns."

Rekhaz glowered, but did not rise.

"You'll never escape," he rumbled through gritted teeth. "You'll die before you can leave this city. Your head will be on a spike before the city gates by nightfall. And then my armies will crush your kingdom and make ashes of its forests."

Quivris shrugged. His kingdom had already fallen. Then he raised his voice so that it carried across the arena. "People of the League! Your emperor is our hostage! If you don't want another interregnum, stand down!"

It was enough: all eyes, spectator and guard alike, were locked on the imperial box. No one noticed a lone minotaur archer step forward, onto the sands—no one but Eldako, who was watching for it. It was Shedara's turn: now she ran toward the center of the ring, where Forlo and Hult stood, dumbstruck and bleeding, by the remains of the horaxes. She shed her minotaur form as she ran, and smiled as she saw the stunned recognition on the gladiators' faces.

She didn't see the second archer, one she'd thought to be dead, rise to his knees and take aim at her—not until Eldako shouted for her to get down. She threw herself into the dust, felt the wind of the shaft passing overhead, then twisted in time to see Eldako pull and loose. The archer clapped a hand to his chest, where a dragon-nocked arrow appeared, then pitched back onto the ground.

"No one else interferes!" Shedara shouted, rising from the ground. "Not if you want your emperor left alive!"

Nobody moved.

Shedara ran the rest of the way to Forlo and Hult. "Hello again," she said. "Didn't think we'd leave you to this rabble, did you?"

"But . . ." said Forlo. "How? Where—?"

"Explanations later," she said. "We're still in a lot of trouble. Take off your armor."

"What?" Forlo asked.

"No questions. Take it off. Now."

He stripped, shedding plates and chainmail until he wore only the padding underneath.

"It's all about weight," Shedara said. "I can only carry so much, and all that steel's more than I can handle."

"Oh," Forlo said, unbuckling his greaves. "I see—wait, carry?"

"Hold still."

She spared quick glances at Eldako and her brother. Then she began to gesture, drawing in the moons' power. The magic swelled around her as she spoke words to shape it. The air surrounding her body began to glow a soft, golden color. Another guard lurched forward. Eldako put an arrow in his eye. The glow around Shedara grew, and she raised her voice to a shout—then grabbed both Forlo's and Hult's arms at once. There was a flash and a sound like ice breaking on a frozen lake, and then everything vanished.

* * *

When the world returned, they were no longer in the arena—but they were still in Kristophan, in a courtyard several blocks away. Shedara handed her shortsword to Forlo, and one of her long, fighting daggers to Hult. Then she drew a pair of slim knives and looked around. The plaza was deserted, a little square with a garden and bubbling fountain in its midst. She nodded toward a shadowy colonnade.

"Hide," she whispered. "Quickly."

"What happens now?" Forlo asked.

"We wait," she said. "The others will be along."

He looked dubious, but did as she asked.

The plan was for everyone to hold their positions until she and the others vanished. Then they were to get to the sands by the imperial box, make their way out together with Rekhaz as hostage, and find Shedara. It was mad, a desperate plan. She wondered how many more of her people would die. She wondered if any of them would make it. If half an hour passed without any sign, she was to continue without them. She wasn't sure if she could do that, just leave Quivris and Eldako and the rest.

Forlo asked questions. She gave answers while inspecting their wounds, explaining who the elves were and telling how they'd convinced Quivris to help. Hult's ankle was in bad shape—he wouldn't be able to travel without help. Forlo's face darkened when she mentioned their promise to stop the shadows, but he didn't contest her decisions. After that, they stayed quiet, listening to the tumult from the direction of the arena—there would be rioting in the city tonight, no matter what happened. There would be death.

Half an hour came and went. Shedara blinked back tears. Motioning for the others to stay put, she crept to the mouth of the alley, moving from shadow to shadow, and peered into the street.

Half a dozen soldiers were standing there, crossbows raised, pointing back toward the arena. She turned to look down the dusty street, and had to bite her tongue to keep from crying out when she saw them: her people, stopped in their tracks. Eldako was still with them—and so was Rekhaz, Quivris still holding a sword to his throat.

Shedara swore under her breath, then turned and waved to Forlo. He crept forward. Hult tried to follow, but his injured leg wouldn't let him. Forlo stopped next to her, saw the crossbowmen, and nodded. He raised two fingers, pointed, then slashed his hand sideways.

She wasn't completely sure what that meant, but all right. "Now," she murmured.

They bolted from the courtyard's mouth. She threw one of her knives as she ran, and it hit the nearest minotaur in the stomach. He howled, his crossbow clattering to the ground, then went down. He bumped the bull-man next to him as he fell.

Then Forlo was upon them, yelling a war-cry in the minotaur tongue. That startled them, and two turned to face him. He cut them down. Shedara, meanwhile, pounced on another, who dropped his arbalest and was reaching for a spiked mace when her knife opened his throat. He crumpled.

Two minotaurs remained. One shot at the elves. Shedara heard a voice shout in pain—and then arrows answered, from Eldako and the other Silvanaes. The last of the crossbowmen collapsed.

The elves came forward, arrows nocked, looking around for more signs of trouble. Shedara tried to get her throwing knife back, but the blade was bent, so she left it in the minotaur's body. She turned to the Silvanaes, counted them, and felt sick to her stomach. There were only nineteen.

"So few," Shedara said. "The others. . . ."

"Are dead," Quivris replied. "Eleven lives lost, to spare two."

She shook her head. "Brother, I'm sorry."

He said nothing.

"What about him?" Forlo asked. "Do you need him anymore?"

Everyone looked at Rekhaz. He wasn't in the plan, once they were clear of the city.

"We mean to release you, Your Majesty," said Quivris. "But you must swear not to take any action against Armach, or you will not go free."

The emperor was silent a moment. Then, his lip curling, he spat in Quivris's face.

"I take no oaths for elves," he said.

Quivris nodded, wiping his eye. He stepped back, turned, and handed Forlo his sword.

Rekhaz's eyes widened. He whirled and tried to run, sending two elves flying. It wasn't enough; he hadn't taken three steps before Eldako and four others put arrows in him: two in his left knee, one in his right, and two more in his back. With a roar, the emperor slammed into the marble wall of a building and crashed to the ground.

Forlo stepped forward, weighing the elven blade in his hand. "What do you think, Rekhaz?" he asked. "Would you rather suffer or die fast?"

The emperor glared at him, his face contorted with agony. Blood leaked from his snout. "To the Abyss with you, traitor," he hissed.

Forlo didn't reply. He stared at Rekhaz a long time. Then, his eyes as cold as a corpse's, he stabbed him through the chest.

And twisted the blade.

Chapter

10

Kristophan, The Imperial League

Bastard.

You used me. I was retired. I'd earned it. But you wanted my help, so you pulled me back in when I had no choice.

You were in charge of the League's armies. Its defense was your responsibility. But you were too busy chasing the crown, and you wanted to punish me. You could have dispatched whole legions to fight the Uigan, but you gave me only a handful of men. We should have died that day. You wanted us to die. Once you had my oath, my name supporting you, you threw me to the wolves.

And when it was done, when I had the temerity to survive, you had me arrested. Had me brought here. Would have beheaded me, if I hadn't demanded to fight on the sands. And when you did let me fight, you made sure my sword would break. You did everything short of cutting my throat yourself.

Coward.

My wife is out there. My unborn son is out there. The statue too. I should be looking for them, not here, nearly getting ripped apart by horaxes while you drink wine and laugh. My family is in danger, and I'm here for your petty vengeance, your power games. And it's your fault. If they die, it's your fault.

You *bastard*. . . .

"Barreth," murmured Shedara, touching his arm. "That's enough."

But it wasn't. It never would be. Forlo worked the blade back and forth, left and right, carving flesh, snapping ribs. He felt its tip grind against the cobblestones beneath Rekhaz's body. The emperor had long since stopped moving, quit writhing and choking, fallen still. Forlo kept twisting the blade. There was so much blood, more than he'd thought a body could hold. The emperor was big, nearly nine feet tall, though he seemed smaller now that he lay broken in the street. Forlo wrenched the blade, more violently than ever.

"Barreth!"

Shedara was in front of him now, grabbing his hands, shaking him. He blinked, looking up at her, wondering, why are you here? Where am I? What is happening?

He remembered only dimly. One moment he'd been trying to free Hult while the last horax worked at sawing off the barbarian's foot. Then there were arrows, and elves everywhere, and a minotaur who turned into Shedara as it ran toward them across the sands.

And now he was a regicide. A traitor to the League, a villain forever. No hope ever of returning to his old life, to Coldhope. If the bull-men caught him, they would cut off his hands and feet, tear out his tongue, blind him, and hang what remained in a cage for the crows and anyone who could throw a rock.

It was worth it, though. Rekhaz was dead. He'd died unarmored, unarmed, helpless. A dishonorable ending, early in his reign. The history books would record him merely as a footnote. The old proverb was right—revenge was as sweet and deep as autumn wine.

He yanked the blade free and handed it back to the elf who'd given it to him, the leader with the gruesomely scarred face. Then, for good measure, he kicked the emperor's corpse—hard—in the head. There was a crack, and a wetter thump beneath it.

"Enough," said the elven leader disapprovingly. "We must get moving. Nalaran will be looking for us."

"Not to mention half the Imperial Army," added Shedara. "In fact, here's some now."

They turned and looked down the avenue. A detachment of soldiers had emerged from a side street into a square with a garden of pear trees. They had stopped now and were staring at the elves, as if not truly believing their quarry was right in front of them. It was only a moment, though, before their officers barked an order and they lunged forward, spears leveled.

The elves needed only a moment. Raising their bows, they launched a volley into the charging minotaurs. Half the bull-men went down; the rest kept coming. Eldako loosed three arrows in what seemed like a single breath. Two soldiers fell.

"Treason! They've murdered the emperor! Attack—"

The merkitsa's third shaft found the officer, silencing his cries in a gurgle.

A couple of soldiers shot crossbows. One of the Silvanaes made an unpleasant coughing sound, his head snapping back with a quarrel in his cheek. He hit the ground hard and stayed there.

"Get moving!" said the elves' leader. "We'll all die here if we linger and fight! Go!"

They went. Forlo grabbed Hult; so did Eldako. The Uigan was barely conscious, his face gray with pain. His wounded leg was a red mess, the foot twisted at an awkward angle. Still, Hult stayed conscious, hopping with every other step on his good leg. He grunted with pain.

They left Rekhaz lying dead and mutilated in the middle of the road.

Some ways ahead, the street suddenly stopped. Forlo knew what it was: he'd surveyed the damage the quake had done to Kristophan, the last time he'd been to the city. The whole northern half was gone. In its place yawned a chasm, broken stone cliffs littered with chunks of white masonry, all the way down to the water. The street they were on—called Bortold's Way, after the realm's fourth emperor—ran straight up to the abyss and rose onto a bridge that had once spanned a much narrower gully dividing the city in two. Now half the bridge was gone, swallowed by earth and sea; the other half remained, flanked by statues of the marshals who'd led Bortold's armies, ending in a jagged stump high above the raging water.

We have to turn, Forlo thought. We have to find a side street. We'll be trapped if we don't. Won't we?

Shedara chanted words that entered his brain. She touched him. A strange sensation ran through his body, like he'd just swallowed something with many tickling legs. He shuddered. What spell had she cast on him?

She turned to Hult, laid her hand on him as well. "Trust me this time," she said. "Will you?"

Bleary as he was, the barbarian managed a smile.

Several soldiers emerged from an alley before them. The Silvanaes ran them down without breaking pace, swords dancing as they drove through their midst. Another of the elves fell. The rest kept going. Forlo hewed at the minotaurs as best he could with Shedara's shortsword—then he got a better look at them, caught a glimpse of the colors they wore: crimson and blue. The Sixth. His men, once . . . but never again.

Bile soured his throat.

Shedara moved from elf to elf, first Eldako, then the leader, then the rest. She worked the same spell, over and over, finishing with herself as they reached the bridge. Forlo glanced over his shoulder: the street was packed with soldiers, in every legionary color. They were furious. Their emperor was dead. But Forlo would jump into the maw of the sea before he let the bull-men take him again.

"Keep moving!" cried Shedara. "The spell doesn't last forever."

Forlo blinked. Keep moving? But there was nowhere to go, except. . . .

The elves backed up, away from the soldiers, shooting arrow after arrow to keep their pursuers at bay. They were on the bridge now, moving closer and closer to its end. Seaspray soaked them.

"Sargas's horns!" Forlo yelled. "What are you doing?"

"Escaping," Eldako replied. "Don't be afraid."

Oh, Forlo thought, all right. Backed up on a dead end, caught between half the Imperial Army and a two-hundred-dred-foot drop to sharp rocks and violent water. What's to be afraid of?

Some part of his mind knew the elves were disappearing over the edge of the broken bridge, but common sense refused to let him believe it. Still, there was no question that, when he finally reached the fractured stone lip, there were considerably fewer Silvanaes still with them. He looked at Shedara.

"What in the name—?" he began, and saw the last of the elves climb off the bridge. Among them was their leader, the scarred one whose sword Forlo had used to murder the emperor. They just stopped shooting their bows, turned, and stepped into the void where half of Kristophan had died.

He looked at Shedara. She gave him a wink and nodded down toward the water. Forlo glanced over, expecting to see no sign of the Silvanes—or maybe a couple of their bodies, smashed to ruin on the stones. Instead, he started in amazement: they were scuttling, with unsettling speed, down the sheer face of the cliff. To his eyes, they looked less like elves than strange lizards . . . or spiders. At the bottom, a small boat waited. Waves surged and boiled all around it, but it stayed improbably still. The air around it shimmered, like a road at midsummer.

Magic, he thought, his stomach clenching.

Crossbow bolts soared over their heads. One hit the tip of the bridge and spun away with a *ping*. Eldako shrugged off Hult, letting the Uigan lean his full weight against Forlo, then raised his bow and started shooting back. He was fast. Four crossbowmen fell, pierced. The soldiers' advance faltered. But there were far too many for one archer to hold off for long.

"Go!" the wild elf yelled. "I'll stall them!"

Shedara turned to Forlo, grabbed her sword from his hand, took Hult's weight off him too. "Jump," she said. "Catch the edge as you fall. The spell will help you. Climb down the cliff after the others. Take Hult, and help him."

"You've got to be joking!" Forlo shouted. "I can't—"

Shedara pushed him. He stumbled backward, unable to stop himself, and fell over the edge, dragging Hult with him. He yelled and lashed out, grabbing for the bridge as she'd told him. His hands slapped the end of the stone and scrabbled, but knew it wasn't enough. He didn't have a grip. He waited to drop, to watch the bridge rise swiftly away from him as he plummeted to his death. . . .

He didn't. He stuck.

Shock gave way to pain as the rest of his body swung down, jerking his arms in their sockets. His injured wrist felt like it had been dipped in burning oil—but his hands were bonded fast to the bridge, while his feet dangled free. Looking up, he saw Shedara peering down at him, Hult slumped against her shoulder.

"Quit messing around," she told him. "No time. Swing your legs up—they'll stick, too."

He did and they did. He was clinging to the underside of Bortold's Bridge! And now Shedara was helping Hult down, lowering the barbarian so he could grab the stones himself. His injured leg hung limp as he pulled himself, three-limbed, down beside Forlo.

"What about you?" Forlo asked Shedara.

"We'll be along," she said. "You were the last out at Coldhope, and it didn't work out so well. Let's try this instead. Now go, before things get really bad. Climb!"

He did as she bade, scurrying along the bridge to where it met the cliffside. Glancing up—no, it was down, and his head spun—he saw the Silvanaes moving swiftly to the waiting boat. Their escape. He looked at Hult.

"You first," he said. "I'll be right behind you."

Another time, the Uigan might have argued, but he was pale and glassy-eyed, and obeyed without question. He moved with surprising speed, feet-first down the sheer rock face. Forlo licked his lips, listening to the minotaurs shouting and the song of Eldako's bowstring above, then scurried after, head-first.

It was, without question, the single strangest, most disorienting thing he'd ever done in his life. As he went, he watched the Silvanaes reach the bottom, where the surf had darkened the rocks and spray erupted just below them. The ship moved to meet them, completely ignoring both wind and wave, and one by one they let go of the cliff, dropping lightly on its deck. An elf mage stood at the tiller, his white robes whipped by the wind. He pointed up past them, and a bolt of silver lightning sprang from his fingertip, sizzling past Forlo to strike the tip of Bortold's Bridge. The stone exploded with a deafening crack, raining down into the rift as fine gravel. It peppered Forlo's back, stinging him. Then he saw Shedara and Eldako, clambering down the cliff fifty feet above him. He laughed at the madness of it all, his ears ringing from the thunderclap.

Then the water was beneath him, and the ship's deck, too. He let go, as the elves had done, and hit the deck hard, falling on his side and rolling to a halt. Hult landed on top of him. He lay there, gasping, while the elves hurried about, grabbing oars. Shedara and Eldako came down last.

"That's all of us," she answered the wizard's questioning look.

"Cast the last spell, Nalaran," said the scarred elf.

The wizard nodded, looking tired. His powers were spent. Still, he managed to speak a few spidery words. Shedara joined him, lending what remained of her own strength to his. The air around the boat glowed golden, and Forlo understood: this was the same magic that had gotten them out of the arena, only much more powerful. He gritted his teeth, waiting for it to take hold.

The golden aura turned sun-bright. The cliffs above them vanished. The world dropped away.

※―――※※―――※

Three days later, the elven boat was bobbing quietly in a little inlet that was little more than a hook-shaped notch, carved into bluffs that bristled with thick brush and spruce trees. Its hull bumped softly against the stone, on waves much calmer than in Kristophan's chasm. Sunlight slanted through branches overhead, throwing bright slashes across cliffs, ship, and sea.

It had been a hard chase. There were no better mariners in Taladas than the minotaurs, and no navy greater than the League's. Its warships—huge, hulking dreadnoughts and swift, deadly cutters—had spilled out of Kristophan's harbor the moment trouble began, and the mariners knew of the emperor's death before most land-dwellers, thanks to a system of beacons and mirrors set upon towers all along the waterfront. Nalaran's spell had given the elves a head start, putting them a quarter mile from the nearest of the bull-men's vessels, but it had stood out on the open water, and the lookouts spotted it right away.

The next six hours had been a test of the elves' skill as sailors, and they let the sails out full and tacked again and again to keep them fully winded. Shedara and the mage, Nalaran, spent the whole time hunched in the stern, alternately resting and studying their spellbooks, trying to get back their strength while the boat skipped over the waves. Forlo kept near the bow, with Hult and Eldako, who tended their wounds as they swapped tales. Hult finally passed out.

Listening to Eldako's account, Forlo glanced up every now and then to peer past the boat's scrambling crew and swinging boom. There were three ships after them, flying black and gold sails emblazoned with the Horns of Sargas. Sometimes they came dangerously close, near enough to count heads on their decks—more than a hundred minotaur mariners in all. The elves' vessel always managed to dart ahead, but the minotaurs gained steadily as time passed.

One of the cutters got close enough to fire its ballistae. The heavy bolts hit the water a few yards aft of the elves and a bit to starboard. The bull-men shouted, working to adjust their aim. Quivris, the elves' leader, snapped quick, fierce orders, and the elves obeyed without hesitation, hauling on ropes and bringing the foresail around, forcing the boat to jibe. It seemed to stop for a breath, then swung violently to port, the boom flying from one side to the other so hard that the whole thing nearly capsized. Then it caught the wind and was off in a different direction, even faster than before. The ballistae fired a second time, but the shots came nowhere near, and the minotaurs dropped behind again, cursing. Forlo yelled with the exhilaration of it, but the Silvanaes stayed silent, attending to their work, their bows at hand if they needed them.

Or when.

Evening came on. Solis rose full, turning the sea from dusk's fire to molten platinum. The coast slid by, capes and coves and lighthouses that shone with white brilliance. Later, as word of Rekhaz's death spread, those same beacons would turn red to report the news to ships at sea. For now, though, most of the League still believed it had a living ruler, and that the winter would bring peace after a difficult year.

It was nearly midnight when Nalaran finally snapped his book shut. The wizard was frail, shivering as he pulled himself to his feet. Shedara, looking pale and weary herself, rose to support him as he walked back to stand before Quivris.

The elves' leader met his gaze, his one good eye glinting like steel. "Do you have it?"

Nalaran nodded, not speaking.

"We'll have one good chance," Shedara said. "Then we'll be spent till morning."

The elves nodded. They didn't have until morning. At the rate they were gaining, the minotaurs would catch them an hour before dawn—maybe sooner if the wind went bad. A hundred mariners, against about twenty. The minotaurs would kill everyone aboard, and burn the elves' boat to the waterline.

"Get it right, then," Quivris said and went back to his work.

Nalaran nodded, turning to Shedara. "Hold me steady."

He faced backward, gazing across the gleaming water at the dark shapes of their pursuers—two of the ships lay a hundred yards back, the third lagging farther behind. Shedara rested a hand on the wizard's shoulder, helping him move with the rocking of the deck. He shut his eyes and began to chant, pulling the magic in, weaving it between delicate fingers that never stopped dancing. This went on for nearly a minute, the elf's voice fading to a croaking breath by the end. He raised his hands in a grand, sweeping motion . . . then slumped in Shedara's arms. She caught him and eased him down onto the deck.

Forlo rose, looking around. So did Eldako. All was silent, except for the rushing of water and the creak of the rigging.

A new sound rose, a faint susurrus, like a voice speaking a language made of sibilants. Forlo felt a pressure against his face, saw Eldako's long braids begin to move, and couldn't help but grin. The wind was rising!

In moments the noise had grown from a whisper to a scream, howling gusts slamming into the boat from behind. The sails snapped tauter than ever, and the elves drew them down and in, angling them to catch the full force of the gale. Forlo crouched, suddenly afraid the bluster would knock him overboard. Eldako hunkered beside him, and Shedara and Nalaran came to join them, while the Silvanaes toiled to keep the ship thundering onward. It leaped from wave to wave, nearly taking flight as the magical gusts propelled it. Behind them, the minotaur ships, without the same magic wind, dropped away into the distance.

By morning, when the spell finally faltered and gave out, their pursuers were nowhere to be seen. The elven boat continued on natural wind alone, hugging as close to the coast as it could as the sky brightened above. They were far south of Kristophan now, in waters dotted with islets like stone knives, and nothing but wilderness on the shore. Eldako climbed the mainmast to look behind them but saw no sails besides the occasional fishing boat, miles off shore.

At midday they reached the notch, and Quivris guided the ship in. They moored there, posting watchers among the trees to keep an eye out for the bull-men. Most of a day passed before they saw them: the three cutters who had led the chase and two more behind. They sailed right past the elves' hiding place, and when they were over the horizon the Silvanaes finally began to relax. Some even laughed a little.

Not Quivris, though. He stayed grim and quiet. Though Forlo could see that he and Shedara were kin, neither went near the other. Forlo didn't interfere, but offered his thanks to the elflord, who nodded politely in reply. Day drifted into night, then back to day again. Hult awoke at last, still ashen-faced from his injuries, but looking better every hour. They rested. They recovered.

Finally, on the third day since leaving Kristophan, Quivris called his men back down to the boat and turned to

Forlo and Hult. "Good elves died to save the two of you," he said. "My sister believes it was worth it."

But you have your doubts, Forlo thought. Don't you?

"We chase the Hooded One," he said instead. "Anything to rid the world of that thing is worthwhile."

Quivris raised an eyebrow but did not reply. He looked at Hult, then Eldako. Never Shedara. "You must go north, to Panak, to seek this Wyrm-namer, this sage of dragons. My sister can sail. Can any of you?"

"I can," Forlo offered. He'd gone out on the Run in a little skiff many times, and even spent some time aboard the ships of the navy. Long ago it was, another life. "I can teach the others. Can you offer us a boat?"

"This boat," answered the elf. "We will sail back to Armach, and there my people and I will leave you. There are still many shadows to fight in our woods. And perhaps there shall be minotaurs soon, as well."

Forlo bowed his head, unsure what to say. The League might invade Armach in the spring, if it didn't fall into another civil war first. The bull-men and the Silvanaes had lived in peace beside each other for centuries. Now that was wrecked, perhaps for good. The minotaurs would not soon forget that it was an elven blade that slew their emperor.

"We'll do something about the shadows," Eldako said. "We will go to Marak and learn what happened to the kender . . . and put a stop to it, if we can."

"As long as it doesn't draw us too far from our main quarry," Forlo added. "The statue must be found, if any of this sacrifice is to matter."

Quivris said nothing, only looked away, to the south. Forlo understood his mind. He'd seen his own home overrun by the shadow-fiends. He held his tongue.

Nalaran came forward and kissed Shedara's cheeks. "Her Majesty would be proud of your service," he said. "You go into danger unbidden. You could abandon your path, and few would blame you."

"I would blame myself," she replied. "I lost the Hooded One, after all. It seems only right that I find it again."

The mage nodded, then turned to Hult. "You do not understand my words, rider of the Tamire," he said. "You understand little that has been said to you, since you left your people. Let that now be changed. Accept this gift."

From the folds of his snowy robes, Nalaran produced an amulet on a silver chain. It was made of green stone, jade, in the shape of an open book. It spun this way and that.

"A charm of Gilona," he explained. "When you wear it, you will be able to speak the tongues of those near you, and you will understand their speech."

Forlo's eyebrows rose. He watched as the young Uigan frowned, then reached out to touch the pendant. He looked questioningly at Nalaran. The mage nodded, encouragingly, and Hult flushed and bowed his head. With a smile, Nalaran slipped the chain over and around his neck. Hult blinked, his brow furrowing, then looked around at the others.

"What has happened to me?" he asked.

Forlo couldn't help himself. He laughed, for the first time since before the battle at the Run. "You're one of us now, my friend," he said.

Hult started, his eyes widening. He could understand. He glanced at Nalaran, who nodded, then stared at Forlo for a long while. Finally his face changed, smoothing and brightening to frame a smile. And then he, too, began to laugh.

Chapter

11

AKH-TAZI, NERON

Weeks passed. Maybe months. Essana didn't know. She never saw the sun. She saw the sky only when the Brethren brought her up to the roof of the ancient pyramid to witness another sacrifice. They killed so many of the cha'asii that she lost count. She saw the dying elves always, awake and in sleep: their pleading gazes, their faces suddenly wrenching as the knife bit, then smoothing until they almost looked as if they were asleep, curled at the feet of the Hooded One. They came to her in her dreams, rising from the bloody stone to stare at her, the gashes in their throats gaping right down to the bone. Though they never spoke, she heard their voices just the same.

You. We died because of you.

It wasn't a fair thought, not really. She didn't wield the blade that spilled out their lives. The Slayer killed them; the Master commanded it. The rest of the Brethren condoned it. She was as much a victim as the cha'asii themselves. But that didn't keep the elves' shades from appearing whenever she shut her eyes. It didn't stay their vengeance.

They were right, in a way: she had the power to stop this, to put an end to this . . . at least for a while. In time, she was sure, the Brethren would find another woman to take her place, another unborn child to desecrate in the name of their mutilated ghost-king. But she could do something for herself, and for her son. She could free them both.

If she died.

The hardest part was thinking about it the first time. After that, things were easier. The notion became almost welcome, liberating. It was the one way she could fight back. She lay in her cell, in the stillness, and trembled at the notion, forcing herself to accept it. She began to make plans.

She didn't have many options, she knew—and she couldn't let on what she had in mind. If the yaggol sensed her plans, if the Brethren learned what she intended to do, they would chain her up . . . or worse. So she kept her thoughts inside, only daring to think about the terrible idea in the quiet watches, between meals and sacrifices. It was her secret—and it gave her, for the first time since she'd come to this place, a sense of power.

I will show you, she thought, envisioning the Faceless. How they would rage when they found her dead! How furious they would be, when all the suffering they had caused came to nothing! How the Master's eyes would burn when he learned how powerless he truly was!

So she made up her mind. It was no longer a question of if, but when . . . and how. As to the first, it had to be soon: every time she touched the swell of her belly, it had grown larger; every kick inside her was stronger than the one before. It wouldn't be much longer now. Weeks. The moment her water broke, it would be too late.

How was more difficult. They gave her no knives with her meals, not even dull ones. The only time there was something to leap from was when she was on top of the temple, surrounded by the Brethren and the yaggol. She had no belt, nothing that would serve as a rope—not even enough clothing to tear strips off and make a noose from. There was nothing she could use to kill herself.

She thought about it for days. She prayed, truly prayed, for the first time in her life. She begged the gods for an answer. They gave her none. Either they didn't hear her or they weren't listening. She stopped praying again.

And then, after what seemed like forever, her chance came.

One morning—afternoon? night?—the yaggol left her food. It was bland gruel made from some root she didn't know; some small, bitter but edible shoots, and a piece of dry, tasteless fish, with a cup of awful-tasting herbal tea to wash it down. The plate and cup and spoon were brittle clay—she'd already tried breaking one, to see if the shards might be of use, but it had crumbled. She ate listlessly, picking at the food.

And in the fish, she found a bone.

At first, she set it aside without thinking. Two bites later, however, she stopped and stared at it again: a little white shard, barely half the length of her little finger, threads of meat still clinging to one end. It was perfect. She grabbed it, then stared at it, turning it this way and that. Yes. It would work.

She wasted no time. The longer she thought about it, the less likely she would be to carry through. Shutting her eyes, she put the bone in her mouth, then let it slide to the back, the top of her throat. It stayed there, balanced on her tongue.

Forgive me, my son, she thought. I must do this. I must spare you.

As hard as she could, she inhaled.

It was horrible: the pain, the helplessness, the knowledge that she had done this to herself, no one would save her, and she didn't want to be saved. The bone went half-way down her windpipe and lodged there, jabbing into flesh, as sharp as a razor. She began to choke, clawing at her burning throat, trying to cough out the bone . . . all her reflexes trying to betray her, make her live. Air

142

wouldn't come. She lay back, thrashing, making terrible, wet sounds.

Death wouldn't take long. She'd seen a man die that way once, at a banquet in Kristophan. He had choked on a piece of crabshell, about the same size as the fish bone. He'd died in minutes, his face purple, his eyes bulging.

I've done it, she thought, white spots exploding in front of her eyes. She wanted to laugh, but couldn't do anything but gag and whoop. I've done it!

The world began to dwindle, like she was viewing it from deep under water. She heard the awful hacking noises her body made as it tried to work the bone loose. Her face felt as if it were on fire. She couldn't feel her hands or feet at all.

The cell door rumbled open.

Essana saw black robes and running feet: one of the Faceless, the Keeper. You're too late, she thought, with a demented kind of glee. She even managed a ghastly smile as he bent over her. Too late. I've beaten you, you son of—

"No," he said and grabbed her. His grip was very strong. He turned her, clutching her beneath the arms, and squeezed her, sharp and hard, below her breastbone. "Not like this. You can't die like this."

Yes, she thought, with immense satisfaction. I can. . . .

He squeezed again, so hard it was a wonder her ribs didn't crack. Something erupted inside of her, and suddenly, horribly, she retched. The bone flew free, hit the floor in front of her. Air flooded her lungs, cold and clean. She screamed, anger and frustration exploding in her mind, making a red mist in front of her eyes. The Keeper held her up, kept her steady. She groaned, furious, beaten. Then her head drooped forward, and blackness came crashing down.

She woke to a pounding headache, eyes that stung like they'd been doused in vinegar, and a ferocious searing sensation in her throat. That she awoke at all made her moan with despair. She opened her eyes, and saw she was in the same room she'd been brought to after her vision of the Chaldar. The Keeper was with her.

She knew it was him not by his face—which, of course, was nothing but ruin, like all the Brethren—but by the look in his eyes. Of all the Faceless, he was the only one who ever showed concern. He was watching her that way now, sitting by her bedside with one hand upon the hard roundness of her stomach. She drew breath to speak, and was rewarded with a flash of blazing agony that set her coughing—which only made the pain worse. The Keeper laid his other hand on her forehead, his touch gentle.

Who are you? she wondered between waves of pain.

"You are brave, Essana of Coldhope," he whispered. "Not many would have attempted what you did."

She swallowed, winced, and tried to speak again. "I . . . failed."

"Not for want of trying. The yaggol sensed your pain and summoned me. If they hadn't, you and the child would be beyond our reach now. It was a near thing, even as it was. But you will live."

Essana shut her eyes. "And my . . . son?"

"That was nearer still. Only my magic saved him. The trauma brought you to the edge of miscarriage."

She lay silent and still. A tear slipped from her eye, running down her face. The Keeper wiped it away.

"Listen to me, Essana," he said. "The others do not know. They believe it was an accident. The yaggol who fed you have been killed for their mistake. I will not tell them the truth."

She opened her eyes again. It was amazing, the compassion his ravaged face could convey. Essana shook her head. "Why?"

144

He bowed his head and was silent a while.

Anger, frustration, grief—it seemed all these things were warring inside him. Essana, watched, fascinated. Were there limits to cruelty, beyond which even this self-mutilated fanatic would not go? Perhaps she could use this weakness in his character. He was half turned against the Master as it was; perhaps she could play on his sympathies, make him split from the Brethren. Get him to help her.

"Keeper . . ." she began.

"That is not my name!" he snapped. He put a hand to his forehead, touched bone, and pulled it back with a disgusted sound. He turned away. "Hand Who Heals," he murmured, "give me strength. . . ."

She started, her eyes widening. He had invoked Mislaxa, the healing goddess. "Who are you?"

He turned and looked at her, his bloodshot eyes shining. He looked around, then ran his tongue over his bare teeth and leaned close. His voice came as barely more than a breath.

"Essana," he said, "you must never speak of this. You must not think about it. If the yaggol sense the truth, they will tell the others. I will be caught, and all I have striven for, all I have sacrificed, will be for nothing. Can I trust you, Lady?"

"What?" she asked.

"Can I trust you?"

She stiffened at the anguish in his voice. A chill ran through her, and it was a moment before she could find the words. "You can."

He took a deep breath, then let it out as a sigh, a sound of relief. "I am a spy, working for the kings of the Rainward Isles. They knew of the Faceless, and sent me to infiltrate their ranks, to watch and report on their doings. I won the Brethren's trust and became one of their number . . . but I do not hold with their cause."

Essana stared at him, her heart pounding. Shame seemed to hang about him like a physical shape, a black cloud in which he huddled, miserable. This creature had been living among soulless men for . . . she had no idea how long. Years, certainly. Decades? He had aided them in their plots, watched them slaughter the elves to slake Maladar's thirst . . . watched over her and her child, knowing full well what they planned. He had torn off his own *face* to become one of them. Gods, how could he endure such things? How did he keep himself hidden? How was he not mad with guilt?

"Tell me your name," she croaked.

"No," he replied. "It's best you don't know it. Less chance you will make a mistake. We are too close to the end to be sloppy." He sighed again. "That's why I saved you, and the child, when it would have been more merciful to let you both die."

"What do you mean?"

"I will tell you again: the others must never suspect this. Yes?"

Essana nodded. They locked gazes. Finally he shrugged.

"Not all the Rainward Kings believe the Brethren to be a threat," he said. "They demand proof before they will act against them. You are that proof, Essana. If you died, all I have done here . . . all the innocent blood spilled, all the suffering the shadows have caused in the west . . . it would be for nothing!

"I tell you this, Lady—the Faceless will not have you, nor your child, as long as I have breath in me. I will keep you alive and unharmed. And when the time is right, when I know all I must know, I'll take you from this place. We will escape into the jungle, you and I. We will go to the Rainwards, to Suluk, and you will unite the kings against the Brethren. Together, we'll turn the battle against the Master and the rest! We will see Maladar's statue destroyed, and the Faceless—"

He stopped, suddenly. His voice had been rising with fervor as he spoke. Now he looked around, his posture that of a hunted animal. Essana reached out, slowly, and touched his hand. It felt thin and bony within its glove; she wondered if the flesh was gone from it as well. She squeezed his hand anyway, in spite of the disgust that welled up in her, and he turned to look at her in surprise.

"I will help you," she said.

The relief in his eyes almost broke her heart. "You don't know how hard it has been, bearing this burden alone," he said. "Not to be able to tell anyone. . . ."

His voice broke, trailing away.

"What . . . what do I do?" Essana asked.

"What you did before," he said. "Return to your cell. Sleep. Eat. Watch the sacrifices. And wait. When the time is right, I'll come to you. Have faith, Essana of Coldhope— have faith, and we will survive this. Together."

Chapter

12

WHITE-STORM SHORE, LOWER PANAK

The wind froze the blood. There weren't enough furs aboard the elven ship to protect them from its force. It clawed and gnawed through gaps in their garments, stealing the warmth from their bodies as it swept in off the leaden sea. Hult, standing at the prow, watched for submerged islands of ice—there were many here, in the far north, the children of Mother Winter by his people's legends. The islands lay hidden, ready to rip gashes in the bellies of ships. They were killers. Everything was, up here at the world's end.

He shuddered. He'd kept his mind off their destination most of the long way here. First recovering from his wounds—his hand still stung where the huraj had severed his fingers—then learning to sail the boat, under Forlo's guidance, he'd managed to concentrate his thoughts elsewhere. Now he had tales to tell too, thanks to the jade charm Nalaran had given him. It was strange, suddenly understanding every word the others said—and being understood by them, just as well. It was like waking up one morning and discovering he could talk to his tribe's horses. He'd gotten used to the maddening barrier between them.

But now the barrier was gone, and they'd each taken turns telling their stories. He'd held parts of his back, of course—mostly to protect the honor of Chovuk Boyla—and he was sure the others did the same, but it was good to know some things, in any case. Good to be free, too, of the land of the bull-men.

Now, though . . . now there was no more denying where they were bound, for they were nearly there. To their right, the green-black of evergreen woods and browns of autumn-parched grasslands had yielded to gray and white, snow-dusted rocks, dotted with rusty moss and pale lichen. The distant mountains had dropped away. Haze hung in the distance, colorless and frigid. Three weeks they'd sailed, up past the Tiderun's mouth and the western coast of the Tamire, to the land of snow and death.

Panak.

He'd been here before . . . only a handful of years ago, though it seemed another lifetime. He and his friends had journeyed up north, from his tribe's summer grazing grounds, to prove themselves men. White Sky, his clan, did this by hunting snow-drakes, dragons who dwelt in the Panak and sometimes came down to prey upon the horses and cattle of the Uigan. He and his friends had found their quarry, a whole pack of the creatures, nested in a snowbound valley among the badlands. They had made the kills they needed, with bow and sword and spear, then taken trophies from the bodies, already boasting of their deeds—tales that grew more preposterous with every telling. But on the way back. . . .

No. He would not think about it. Not now, not here. Bad luck. He turned his attention back to the water, to the blue and green hunks of death bobbing there.

"To the right!" he called then shook his head and corrected himself. "No, starboard. Starboard ten degrees!"

"Starboard, aye!" shouted Forlo from the helm. With a creaking of timbers, the boat shifted its course, turning toward the shore and swinging around a nasty berg. It swung back again when they were done and carried on its course.

A presence close to Hult drew his glance. Eldako was quiet. Eldako also knew this place; Hult could tell it. Since they'd passed into the frozen expanses of the northlands, since the weather had turned bitter and the wind grown teeth, the merkitsa had prowled the deck, watching the shore for some sign only he would recognize. Now he stood at the rail, leaning out over the water, his eyes narrow. The cold didn't seem to bother him at all. His arms were still bare, his face uncovered. Hult tried not to resent that as his teeth chattered miserably.

"What is it?" Hult asked. "What do you see?"

Eldako gave no sign of hearing. He leaned out a little farther, so that Hult took half a step toward him, ready to grab him if he toppled over the gunwale. The wild elf raised a hand to shade his eyes, then turned and focused his stare aftward. His braids whipped on the wind; seeing them fly, Hult put a hand to his own head, felt the short hair growing all over. He'd decided not to regrow his braid, the mark of a Uigan warrior. For good or bad, that part of his life was past.

"Another mile!" Eldako shouted. "It is close."

"Where are we?" Hult asked.

The merkitsa pointed off the bow. "The shores yonder belong to the Ice People. We must seek them out. Any farther, and we are in truly dangerous waters. Killer whales in the sea and snow-apes on the shore . . . and worse."

Hult swallowed, trying to stifle old memories. Evil times. "How do you know?" he asked. "Those rocks on the horizon look no different from the ones here. It's all just snow."

"And the Tamire is all just steppe," Eldako replied. "And the Dreaming Green all trees. But there are ways of telling, rider of the plains. You know the signs, if you know what to look for. There." He nodded toward the coast. "On that outcrop. Do you see?"

Hult looked shoreward. There, on a pinnacle of stone crusted with the dung of seabirds, stood a crude idol. It was made of large rocks, each half the height of a person, one piled on top of another to form the simple likeness of a man, more than twenty feet tall, facing out to sea. Nests bristled on each of its shoulders and between its feet. Its head was featureless, save for a pair of round, painted eyes, white rimmed with black.

A small, horrified sound escaped Hult's lips, and he stepped back. Eldako didn't appear to notice; his eyes remained fixed on the pinnacle. "They call these idols Ningasuk. The Patient Folk. They watch the borders of their land. The Ice People believe their ancestors' ghosts gather around them to dance on winter nights. I have seen strange lights about them, in my travels beyond . . . Hult? What is wrong?"

Hult could only stare, his eyes wide, his face pale. The idol's eyes seemed to bore right through him. Taking another step back, he stumbled over a coiled rope and fell to one knee. His eyes never left the idol, the Ningasuk, as it slid past them and behind. Another loomed up ahead, just around a bend in the shoreline. Its gaze pierced him too.

No, he thought. Not here. Not again.

He remembered the Patient Folk. He had seen them before.

The blizzard blew up out of nothing: one moment, it seemed, the skies were brilliant blue. The next, they crowded with menacing black clouds, and a gale was raging, and the snow came down so thick they could barely see each other. Hult and his friends, men now, drake-slayers, descended from the jubilation of a successful hunt—the necklaces of dragon claws and teeth, freshly cut from their kills, glistening proudly over their coats—into quiet awe at what vengeance the winds of Panak had unleashed upon them. It had been a good hunt, with no troubles, but now the frozen lands seemed determined to collect their due.

They found the cave as night came on and made a smoky peat fire and roasted strips of dragon flesh over the flames. They laughed and told their exaggerated tales, as their fathers and longfathers had done before them. Their mirth held up for two days of the wind's relentless howl, the endless rattle of snow against the blankets they'd hung over the cave's mouth.

And then a new sound rose, and the mirth died.

It began as a low groan, the noise a wounded animal might make . . . or a man. It seemed to come from just outside the cave, only a short distance away. Yamur, the eldest of their group, called out to the noise, mockingly.

"Whoever cries at our doorstep," he shouted, "enter or go away! Do not stay and weep when we are resting here!"

They laughed at that, but their humor had colored, soured: it was now the uncertain laughter of fear. None of them wanted to admit it, but the hunters of White Sky all felt like frightened boys, huddled as the elders told dark tales around the tribe's speaking-fire. The groaning didn't stop. If anything, it got louder, more insistent. It was inarticulate, but Hult would have sworn there were words buried deep within the sound—inarticulate words full of pain and suffering . . . and hate.

Finally, as the night grew colder, the noise grew into a scream. There was no more mistaking it—whatever was outside the cave was no animal.

"One of us must go," said Ushim, Hult's best friend and the group's leader. "If someone is in need, we cannot leave him to die."

They sat there, in the flickering firelight, for what felt like hours. None of them spoke, nor did they look at one another. Finally, Hult shook his head with a sigh.

"Let it be me, then," he said. "I will see."

"No," blustered Yamur. "You are only four-and-ten summers. I will go."

And with that, he had stepped out of the cave, letting the flap swing shut behind him. They never saw him again—only heard his scream, and saw the blood when they went to search. Just blood, and a great deal of it: no flesh, no bones. No sign of what had killed Yamur.

Two more nights they crouched in the cave, listening to the shrieking voices outside their cave. Each wept, when he thought the others were not looking. On the second night, Chag, one of the younger warriors, went out of his mind, drew his shuk, and charged out into the snow. Later they found his arm, torn off and broken . . . and again, the blood, but nothing more. After that, the rest decided to set out when dawn came, afraid that if they stayed, they would all die, one by one, like the others.

When they left the cave in the morning, a statue of a man, made of piled stones, was waiting in the snow, its white eyes glaring at them. Either someone had built the idol during the storm, or the snow had been too thick for them to see it when first they came here. Nor was the statue unadorned—two human ears dangled from its arms. Yamur's and Chag's.

They fled from the statue, running south through the blizzard, insane with terror.

And their foe gave chase.

Hult never saw what stalked them, except for two pale eyes gleaming through the snow, glimpsed over his shoulder as they fled. The unseen pursuer claimed all but two of the others, lastly Hult's friend Ushim, who had lagged behind. Hult saw Ushim stumble and fall, and paused in his flight to help him up, but unseen hands yanked his friend into the murk of the snowfall, and Ushim was gone with a strangled cry that Hult would never forget.

Finally, after Jijin alone knew how long, the storm broke, leaving no sign of their ghostly pursuer. The three Uigan left alive were all crazed and exhausted. They did not speak of the wraith that had chased them, or their lost friends, or anything else, the rest of the way home—another week of walking, leaving the snowy wastes behind. When they spotted their village again at last, the riders already gathering to see how few of their boys had returned from the disastrous hunt, the survivors each swore a solemn oath, before ancestors and gods alike.

They would never again return to Panak.

For Lachar and Kaligai, the other two, the oath was fulfilled: both had been among the warriors lost at the Tiderun, one drowned, the other cut down by Forlo's men.

But Hult . . . Hult had lived. And now he was back again, an oath-breaker . . . and the Ningasuk were waiting.

"Hult. Can you hear me?"

He blinked, shaking his head as the memories flowed away. The faces of his dead friends would haunt his dreams tonight, he was sure. He hoped that was all that would haunt the night.

Shedara crouched over him, a hand resting on his forehead. He was sitting down, his back against the gunwale. Forlo and Eldako were elsewhere; he glanced down the deck and saw the two working the rigging, bringing down the sails. The boat had stopped. They were moored. Time to go ashore.

"What's wrong?" Shedara asked, leaning in to peer into his eyes. He started to look away, but she grabbed his chin and held his head still while she looked him over. She held up her hand before his eyes. "You went down like someone cut your legs out from under you. Look at my fingers—are they blurry? Do you hear bells?"

"No," he said, shrugging her off. "I am well. Only . . . bad memories."

"About the last time you were up here?" she asked. He'd told them the tale—all but the part where he'd been as frightened as a child, the whole time the snow wraith stalked them. They'd probably guessed that, anyway. "You were looking at the Ningasuk when you collapsed. It made you remember, didn't it?"

He made a face, grabbing the rail to pull himself back to his feet. She was clever, the elf. Those clear green eyes could see right into his mind. He scowled, turning to gaze out across the water. "It is not the first one I have seen."

They had dropped anchor in shallow water, just south of a little peninsula that made a sheltered bay and kept the worst of the icebergs away. The cliffs were forbidding, but there were ways up them; he spotted three that even Forlo could climb. At the top, of course, was one of the idols, with its staring white eyes. The idol seemed to be looking straight at Hult, and he felt his knees begin to buckle again. He leaned against the gunwale to bear himself up. Shedara put a steadying hand on his shoulder, and he jerked away, throwing it off.

"I am well!" he snapped.

She left him without another word, going to help the others with the sails. Hult stared down at his hands, what was left of them. His mangled left hand still looked strange. The missing fingers itched. He made an angry face. Among the Uigan riders, missing fingers and toes were common—some of the fiercest warriors were short hands, or parts of arms. It came with living by the sword—but it hurt no less. His people were gone, his home and lord. Now he was losing bits of himself.

He chuckled ruefully at the thought. What shall I leave in Panak when we are done? he wondered. A thumb? A foot?

My soul?

The thought came unbidden, and drew his eyes up to the Ningasuk again. He swallowed, his mouth suddenly dry, and turned to assist the others. Soon they had finished with the sails and were readying a little rowboat to go ashore. They would leave the vessel here, trusting the weather and the natives not to harm it. There wasn't much else to do about it.

The dinghy bumped down into the water. Eldako let down a rope ladder while Forlo and Shedara gathered their gear and threw it down. They had food and water and more furs for sleeping. They had rope and arrows. They had their blades. Hult checked his own, a straight-edged weapon the elves had let him have. Forlo wore its twin. The sword was good, well balanced and not too heavy, but no less strange a weapon to hold, after so long wielding his shuk.

"It looks like snow," said Eldako, peering north and west. "A storm is coming. I do not think it will be too bad, though."

"The one I was caught in didn't look bad either," Hult said. He let the words lie there.

No one spoke for a while. Then Shedara laughed. "Well, we're a cheery bunch, aren't we? We'll have to keep an eye on the storm—but weathering it out here on the water doesn't seem any more promising than doing it on land, does it?"

They shook their heads.

"All right, then," she went on, throwing a leg over the railing and hooking it around the rope ladder. She clambered down out of sight.

Eldako followed, casting a last glance at the dark clouds massed over the ocean. Then Forlo, his armor rattling; one of the Silvanaes had managed to recover his mail, somehow, during the flight from Kristophan.

When they were gone, Hult stood alone on the deck, his gaze drifting back up to the Ningasuk. The stone statue loomed atop its perch, its eyes seeming to peer both into the distance and directly through him at the same time. Among the creaking wood and lapping waves, he heard his friends' death-cries echo in the distance. Yamur, Chag, Ushim, and the rest calling out to him, warning him.

Stay away. Turn back. Do not break your oath, Brother.

Watch over me, Jijin, he prayed. Then he climbed over the gunwale and started down the ladder.

The first snowflakes started falling when they were halfway up the cliff. It was as easy a climb as Hult had guessed. Centuries of ice and seawater had left the rock pitted and cracked, and for him and the elves it was almost as easy to scale as it was to walk on level ground. Forlo had a harder time of it, and his progress slowed them down some. But Hult had to admire his determination. The man could have been a Uigan himself.

The wind picked up, began to roar. The snow turned hard, sleety, hissing against the cliffs. Waves rose and burst against the rocks, drenching them with frigid spray. They kept climbing, faster now, heedless of the danger of slipping. All of them had seen enough winters to know that weather like this might leave the rocks sheeted with ice—and quickly, too.

When Eldako reached the top, ahead of the rest, the sky was nearly black, the sleet driving so hard it hurt to look anywhere but in the same direction the wind was blowing. Forlo slipped, and Shedara and Hult—both climbing behind him—had to grab him to keep him from falling. He hung there a moment, breathing hard and muttering minotaur curses, then hauled himself up. Eldako dragged him over the edge, then did the same for the other two.

Lightning lit the clouds. Thunder boomed a heartbeat later. They all flinched. "It may be worse than I thought," Eldako allowed.

"Do you think so?" Shedara asked, her mouth a lipless slash.

Forlo rolled his eyes. "What do we do now?"

For a moment, none of them answered, looking around, trying to see through the gathering gloom. Then Shedara caught her breath and froze, looking inland, away from the storm.

"Maybe we should ask them," she said.

Hult turned to look—then drew his sword. Beside him, Forlo did the same, letting his packs fall to the rocky ground. Shedara produced a throwing knife out of nowhere and held it poised. Only Eldako kept his hands empty, raising them slowly away from his body.

They were outnumbered, by a great margin. More than twenty shapes, indistinct in the gathering darkness, stood at the top of a snow-capped rise, gazing down at them. They were men, but covered in so many skins and furs that they seemed more ogrish than human. Scarves covered the lower halves of their faces, bone masks wrapped the upper, and thick felt hats adorned the tops of their heads. Most gripped long spears with barbed heads, ready for hurling. A couple had bows. One, in the middle, had a cudgel of stone, and a headdress made from a white wolf's pelt, the snarling head covering his own.

Ice People.

Hult's sword wavered in his hand; he didn't want to raise it, but with that many harpoons pointed at him, he couldn't bring himself to put it down either. Not yet.

"Eldako?" he murmured.

"Lower your blades," the wild elf replied, his own voice barely audible above the wind. He nodded toward the club-wielder in his headdress. "These are Amaruik, the clan of the Spirit Wolf. They are friendly."

"Really?" Forlo asked. "Those spears don't look very welcoming."

"We are in their lands, my friend," Eldako said evenly. "How would you like it if strangers suddenly appeared in your home, bearing arms?"

Shedara made her knife disappear as easily as she'd produced it in the first place. She held out her hands like Eldako. "Tell them we're friendly too," she said. "Say that we seek shelter from the storm."

Eldako did so, raising his voice so all could hear. Hult was surprised: the jade amulet made the Ice People's tongue as clear as any other. He listened as Eldako explained that they'd sailed north, seeking aid, and had come ashore to escape the blizzard. He named each of them, himself last of all. He did not mention the Wyrm-namer.

When he was done, the Ice People remained still, as if he'd said nothing. The wind gusted and howled, picking up with startling swiftness. Plumes of snow swept up, streaming away behind the spearmen. Finally, the leader of the Ice People reached up and pulled down his scarf, revealing half of a plump, nut-brown face with a wispy black beard. He smiled, baring yellow teeth.

"We know who you are, son of Tho-ket!" he called. "Though you have not walked among us since the time of our fathers' fathers. Our memories are long, though. We remember He-Who-Shoots-the-Pale-Worm. You were our friend then, and remain so. I, Angusuk Wolf-slayer, say so. But your companions must be rid of their long-knives, if we are to trust them as we do you."

Eldako bowed his head. "I will ask them, Wolf-slayer."

Hult sheathed his sword even as the wild elf turned to speak. Forlo did the same, reluctantly. Slowly, they both raised their hands.

"Good!" called Angusuk. He raised his cudgel and shouted at his people. "Weapons down, all of you! These are friends."

The Ice People obeyed, spears lowering and bow-strings relaxing. Thunder boomed again, directly overhead. Lightning tore the sky.

Angusuk shouted laughter, whooping at the weather. "The spirits sound their drums for you, son of Tho-ket!" he yelled. "This is an ill storm. We must take you from here at once, before it worsens. Tonight you will spend at the courtesy of the Wolf-clan—and you will tell us your tale, and why your coming has haunted our dreams. Come."

Chapter

13

THE DRIFTING SEA, LOWER PANAK

Angusuk was the chief hunter of his clan. He was big, taller even than Eldako, and surprisingly fast, running easily over the snows on shoes of woven sinew. All his people were thus clad, while Shedara and Forlo and Hult had to struggle, their feet breaking through the crust and making them stumble with nearly every step. Before long, the storm overtook them completely, blackening the sky and cloaking everything in a gray haze. Shedara could barely make out the Ice People: shapeless, almost ghostly forms in the gloom. They sprinted forward, then waited for the others to catch up, again and again.

We would have died here without their help, Shedara thought. Even Eldako couldn't have done enough to help us. We would have died, and our bodies would have stayed buried until spring.

They went on for hours, across wastes that never seemed to change. No trees, no rocks, no rivers—just waves of snowy ridges, sweeping on for miles, dotted by the occasional Patient One, the crude statues looming like angry giants out of the dark. How Angusuk and his people knew which way was which, especially in the storm, Shedara had no idea— but on they ran, never hesitating to get their bearings.

Finally, one of the travelers collapsed. It was Hult, his leg giving out, still smarting from the horax's jaws in the arena. He staggered, then fell forward in the snow and could not rise again. Forlo turned him over and slapped his face to keep him conscious. The Uigan was very pale, his eyes glassy.

"We've got to stop!" Forlo called. "He can't keep this pace anymore. None of us can." He was ashen and bleary, his beard crusted with ice.

Angusuk loomed out of the snow so suddenly that a knife dropped reflexively into Shedara's hand. He caught the motion and stared at her, his face invisible behind scarf and mask. Flushing, she put the blade away.

Eldako explained to Angusuk what had happened, in their stuttering language. Shedara watched the two speak, using gestures as much as words to convey what they meant. Angusuk kept shaking his head, pointing onward. Eldako gestured at Hult, making a slashing motion with the edge of his hand. Angusuk shook his head and pointed again. Eldako looked away, his lips pursed.

"What's going on?" Shedara asked.

"He says we cannot stop now," Eldako replied. "It is only another two leagues to their village."

"Hult can't walk two more leagues!" Forlo protested. "I'm not sure I can, for that matter. Not in this." He waved his arms at the blizzard all around him.

"I thought the Ice People knew ways to survive," Shedara said. "The stories say they can dig shelters out of the snow to weather storms."

Eldako made a face, then took her arm and drew her away from the others. "It's not the storm Angusuk fears," he whispered. "There are . . . creatures out here, he says. Evil things. They hunt in the blizzards."

"Like the one that hunted Hult and his friends?" Shedara asked.

He nodded. "The Ice People call them Uitayuik, They

Whose Eyes Are Open. They believe they're the ghosts of men who died in storms like these. They build the Patient Folk to placate them, to keep them away from the villages, but out here we are vulnerable. The Uitayuik cannot be harmed by mortal weapons."

"What about magic?" Shedara asked.

"Perhaps. But it would take a powerful shaman, and there are none among Angusuk's party. And . . . I am sorry, but I do not think your powers would be enough."

She glanced away, into the gloom. She thought she could sense movement out there—a shape where there should be none. And were those two glowing eyes, staring at them through the driving snow? She blinked, running a hand down her face, and when she looked again, the shape was gone.

"Great," she said. "So how do we get Hult moving again? He's spent."

"The Ice People will carry him. Here they come now."

She turned and Angusuk was standing now with three more of his people. They had laid their spears down on the snow and were lashing a seal-skin blanket between them, making a simple sled. Angusuk came over to the elves while they worked and spoke with Eldako again. There was more pointing, more gesturing, then the wild elf nodded, and the two of them put hands on each other's shoulders and touched their foreheads together. Angusuk jogged back to his people to help them finish the sled.

"They can build others for the rest of us, if need be," Eldako explained. "Though it will take time . . . and we shouldn't tarry here any longer."

Shedara thought of the shape she'd glimpsed. She could still feel it, out there—a sensation of hunger, loss, and loneliness, like a black well inside her. The Eyes were watching them, envious of their warmth.

"You sense something too," she murmured.

"I think we all do," Eldako replied. "Even Forlo, though he knows little of the wilds. The sorrow of the Uitayuik runs deep, and so does their hate."

Her eyes widened. "Their? There are more than one of them out there?"

"I have seen at least three. But I think there may be more."

"Why do they wait?" she pressed. "They could slaughter us all, if Hult's tale is true."

Eldako glanced away, into the storm. "Who is to say? Perhaps they like to toy with their prey. Perhaps they feed off fear. Not even the Ice People know . . . but the longer we stay out here, the more likely they will fall upon us."

He nodded into the murk, and Shedara gasped. There, unmistakably, were two sets of glowing eyes. They floated in silence, their gaze even colder than the wind. She took a step back, her hand dropping to her sword, then forced herself to let go of the hilt. If the Uitayuik fed off fear, the only hope was to make sure they stayed hungry. It wasn't easy, but she made herself walk away, back toward the others. Eldako followed. She felt those frigid eyes on her, black thoughts behind them.

Carefully, the Ice People lifted Hult onto their sled. Forlo stayed nearby, refusing to leave the Uigan's side. Forlo's face was as white as a corpse's, and he had drawn his own sword.

"I saw one of them," he said, pointing into the dimness with the blade. "It was watching us . . . then it was gone."

Shedara nodded. She told him what Eldako had said, what they, too, had seen. They both looked at the merkitsa, who was speaking again with Angusuk, hands flying as he talked. She turned back to Forlo and nodded at his sword.

"Put that away," she said. "Hult's friends' blades were no good against the Eyes. Our only hope is not to be afraid . . . or not so afraid that they come for us."

Forlo thought it over, then sighed, sliding his weapon

back into its scabbard. "Sure," he said. "Don't be afraid of the murderous ghosts we can't fight and can barely see. Easy."

Shedara laughed. The sound drew looks from the Ice People, their faces unreadable behind their masks. She flushed. A moment later, Eldako came back to them, crunching through the shin-deep snow.

"We're ready to move," he said. "Angusuk's men will pull the sled. As for the Uitayuik—"

"Oh, don't worry," Forlo said, his mouth twisting. "We're not afraid of them at all."

Shedara coughed, covering her mouth to hide the fact she was laughing again. Eldako regarded them both, curious, then turned and called out to Angusuk. "Akpattok!"

So they picked up their pace, Hult lying dazed upon the sled as it scraped through the snow. Shedara and Forlo stayed near him, leaning on each other to keep upright. Behind, invisible but palpable nonetheless, the Eyes pursued.

They had gone four miles when the screaming began. Off to their right, lost in the driving snow, one of the Ice People let out a horrible, strangled cry that rose and rose, going on for longer than seemed possible, then breaking off suddenly. Hearing it, Hult roused on the sled, his eyes white.

"Ushim!" he called, lost in memory. "Chag!" He was back with his friends again, watching them die, one by one. The Uigan fumbled for his sword, struggling to rise. The Ice People pulling the sled stumbled; one fell.

Off to the left rose another shriek, which soon trailed into a gurgle.

"It has begun," Eldako said. "I think we are out of time."

"I hadn't noticed," Shedara shot back.

Forlo pointed at Angusuk. "Ask him what we do!"

Eldako did. Angusuk barked something back, then hefted his club, calling the rest of his people to him. In the distance, another pain-wracked cry rose above the wind.

"What did he say?" Shedara yelled.

"We run."

"That's it?" Forlo demanded. "That's his strategy? Run?"

"No," Eldako replied. "There's something else."

"What?" asked Shedara.

"Pray."

The Ice People converged on Angusuk. Several were missing. Men screeched, out in the storm. Dark shapes moved through the gloom, and white eyes gleamed, then vanished again. Forlo dragged Hult to his feet: the Uigan was incoherent with terror, but understood what they had to do. He found new strength—the same strength, no doubt, he'd drawn on when he fled the Eyes years ago—and bolted off, through storm and snow. The others went with him, Angusuk falling into the lead, guiding them through the blizzard. Shedara glanced over her shoulder and saw them: the glowing eyes, yes, but something else—the shadowy forms of men, gliding over the drifts, their feet never touching the ground. Terror flashed in her brain, and she jerked her sword and a dagger from their sheaths. They were useless now, but the feel of the hilts in her hands calmed her enough to keep her going, to drive out thoughts of what the ghosts might do to them.

They ran on. The Eyes shouted louder, the words incoherent but their meaning unmistakable: outrage that living things were out in their storm. Their bellowing was so loud, it seemed to be inside Shedara's mind. She fought the urge to look back, afraid of what she might see. She envisioned withered faces, flesh peeled back by frost. She imagined long teeth and grasping, sharp-nailed hands. She thought she could feel them, right behind her, clutching at her back. . . .

And then there was something in front of them, a new shape looming out of the snowfall. The Ice People stopped running, so quickly that Hult slammed into one of them from behind. Forlo tripped, stumbled to his knees. Shedara twisted, avoiding a collision with Angusuk, and came to a halt with both blades extended before her. The new shape stood still, a man-sized shadow atop a jutting stone.

"They're all around us!" Hult cried, lurching back to his feet. "Yamur! Don't go out there!"

"Be still!" snapped Eldako. "That is no Eye."

"What, then?" Forlo demanded.

"Tulukaruk," spoke Angusuk in a voice that held no fear. "Ata matau pulumik."

The other Ice People spoke the same words, lowering their spears. Shedara looked behind them and felt her breath stolen away. The Uitayuik were close enough to see now—half a dozen dry, blackened corpses in ragged furs, their ears and noses gone, needle-like fangs jutting from slack mouths, clawed fingertips opening and closing on the air. Just as she'd imagined.

Their eyes shone like distant stars, the unhealthy white of snow-glare. They bawled and moaned and barked . . . but came no further. Something held them back, like chains weighing them down. They leaned forward, their hands snatching, but they couldn't take another step. Their anger and rage surged.

"Kan ingulut assarnuik," croaked the voice of the shadow blocking their way. "Auluru samak ukarvuit vanga!"

In that moment, the storm itself seemed to falter, and Shedara felt something familiar: power, coursing through the air, throbbing around the shadow-shape. The words were not in any tongue she knew, but they were magic nonetheless. Golden light flickered around the shape, driving the snow away. The wind's howl subsided to a murmur. Even the biting cold abated.

The light fell upon the shadow, and revealed a man: small, stooped, and impossibly old, bare-chested in the storm, his wrinkled flesh creased with patterns of glistening scars. His long white hair and beard were woven with talons and teeth and small blue stones. He leaned upon a long staff, capped with the horns of a white dragon. The golden radiance pulsed around him as he smiled a toothless grin.

"U vanga-vanga!" the ancient wizard crowed. "Samak utu vanga!"

Shedara leaned close to Eldako. "What's happening?"

"He is a makau," the wild elf replied. "The clan's Eldest, its sorcerer. The Ice People revere their magi."

"And the words?" Forlo asked.

"To the north-wind, the north-wind. Vanish upon the north-wind. . . ."

The Eyes raised their voices as one, a chorus of ghastly howls that made Shedara want to throw down her weapons and cover her ears. Hult did just that, sobbing at the unholy din. But the old man, the makau, did not falter. His childlike grin only broadened as he lowered his stick to point it, one-handed, at the bellowing dead men. Then he made a low, growling noise, so deep it could be felt more than heard. A second tone rose above it, high and whistling, like some mad piper. The muscles in the makau's scrawny neck twitched and writhed as he sang with two voices at once—and the golden light poured from his staff, warm as it flowed past Shedara and the others, onward to engulf the Uitayuik.

The makau's power tore them apart, burning the leathery flesh from their bones, turning it to soot, laying bare their skeletons. Then the bones themselves charred, blackened, and collapsed into heaps of ash that streamed away upon the wind. Only the eyes remained, glowing motes in the storm—and then they flickered and went out, like candle flames snuffed by the wind. When the golden light abated, all that remained of the Eyes were smears of gray in the snow.

The old man lowered his staff. Shedara thought the spell might have drained him, and took a step toward him in case he began to collapse, but he caught her gaze with his own—his eyes weirdly young-looking, black and sparkling—and shook his head, smiling once more. Satisfied, the makau turned and hobbled away.

The storm resumed abruptly, slamming into them again with its full fury. Forlo and Hult were both dumbfounded. Shedara looked to Eldako, who was busy chattering with Angusuk. "What next?" she asked, interrupting.

"We go on," Eldako replied. "We are safe now, thanks to Tulukaruk. He goes ahead, to make ready for our coming. Ahead lies Kitaglu, their village, and the way to the Wyrmnamer."

They started off again, Angusuk and his people leading the way. Eldako and Shedara started to follow, then stopped at the sound of Forlo's voice.

"Hult?"

Shedara paused, turning to see. The Uigan had walked back, to stand before the stains where the Eyes had been. Now he bent down and scooped up a handful of ash and snow. He held it in his hand, staring at what remained of the Uitayuik. His lips moved, but the howling wind snatched the sound away.

Forlo started to approach him, but Eldako caught his arm. "No," the wild elf said. "Leave this moment for him. For his memories."

Shedara bowed her head, thinking of all she had lost. Her queen, her home, the brother she knew would never speak to her again. Her eyes stinging, she forced herself to say farewell to all of them. Only the Hooded One remained. Only her quest mattered now. Hult, she knew, was saying good-bye not only to the friends the Eyes had killed, years ago, but to his own people, drowned by the Tiderun. She looked at Forlo, and saw understanding written on his face as well. They were all three homeless now, their pasts gone forever.

Hult whispered a while, then shut his eyes and cast the ashes into the wind. They vanished at once, borne away by the storm. He turned and strode through the snow after the Ice People. Icy tracks glistened on his cheeks.

The others let him pass, then silently followed after.

Chapter

14

KITAGLU, LOWER PANAK

Eldako said the village was not as he remembered it. This was not a surprise; a hundred years had passed since he'd last visited the lands of the Ice People—perhaps longer. It baffled Forlo to think of this, as it usually did when elves spoke of their age: to know that both the merkitsa and Shedara had been alive long before his own grandfather was born was difficult to grasp. To think they might still be alive, and unchanged, when he was long dead was even harder.

All the people the wild elf had known in Panak were dead now, as were most of their offspring. Some of the grandchildren were elders. Kitaglu seemed to have shrunk in that time, he said, as they entered the village. The gathering of huts, dug into hard-packed snow and frozen earth and covered over with seal skin, seemed almost absurdly few, a fragile thing amid the blizzard's blustering wrath. Hard times had visited Panak.

Angusuk had told him about the hard times during their trek. The Dread Winter, and the Godless Night after it, had been hard on the Ice People. Entire clans had perished. The Fox were gone, and so were the Orca. The Elk were scattered, many of them living with other tribes now. The

Spirit Wolf had nearly succumbed as well, but long and hard struggle had kept them alive. Forlo listened to Eldako translate the tale in a half-baffled haze: he knew nothing of these strange folk or what other clans might lurk out on the wastes. He had never expected, even in a life mostly spent far from home, to come to these lands.

Slowly, the people of Kitaglu were beginning to recover, but there were still only about two dozen family huts, gathered in a hollow that gave meager shelter from the hungering wind. Ragged white pelts flapped on long poles; others had been stripped away, blown the gods knew where by the storm. The yakuk, the tall tribal totem carved from dragonbone to resemble a snarling wolf's head, leaned precariously, on the verge of falling. The outdoor peat fires had all gone out. A handful of older boys came out to greet them, their faces muffled and masked. They took the warriors' spears, then sprinted off toward their tents.

Angusuk took a moment to speak with his men and take a count of how many the Eyes had claimed. Seven were missing, and Forlo knew they were gone forever. If the Uitayuik hadn't gotten them, the storm certainly would. Seven men dead, to bring them here. Eldako counseled them all to lay their hands over their mouths, the Ice People's sign for mourning; everyone but Hult, who was too dazed to think properly, did so immediately. Seeing this, Angusuk nodded. Though his face remained covered, the sorrow in the gesture was unmistakable.

"Come," he said. "Tulukaruk awaits in the anho-ti."

They followed him. Forlo asked what an anho-ti was. In response, Eldako pointed at a long hut ribbed with whalebone that stuck out of the top, like crisscrossed fangs. Snow-pack covered the hut, dyed with blue and violet symbols, spirals and jagged lines, faded and blurred by the storm's passing. Nine wolf tails hung before it—three white, three black, and three rusty with what had to be dried blood. There was no mistaking the portent: a sorcerer dwelt within.

The makau of the Spirit Wolf, eldest of the clan.

Angusuk stopped before the anho-ti. Ruddy light spilled out around the edges of the flap, along with curls of pungent smoke that vanished on the wind. Forlo felt the others tense: there was warmth in the hut, and they yearned for it. But before they could take a step closer, Eldako raised his hand.

"We must lay down our weapons," the wild elf said, shrugging off his bow and laying it upon a skin in the snow. He did the same with his sword and hunting knife. "None can bear arms in the presence of the makau."

Forlo was a soldier and loath to lay down his arms to any who didn't command him, but there were limits to military stubbornness. The Ice People clearly wished them no harm, or they would have simply left them out in the storm to die. Besides, he sensed his sword wouldn't be much use against the makau, so he drew it and set it down with Eldako's weapons. Numbed by cold and by their ordeal with the Uitayuik, Hult did the same.

Shedara had blades secreted all over her, however; Forlo counted eight, in all, when she finally stopped producing weapons. He gave her a hard look, and she rolled her eyes, pulled a stiletto from her boot, and laid it with the rest. Nine.

"That's all," she said, folding her arms. "Or would you like to search me?"

That was enough to satisfy Angusuk. He stepped aside, holding open the flap. A yellow-brown haze billowed out, and the wind ripped it apart. The hunter waved them in with a felt-wrapped hand, and so they went, back into warmth, and light . . . and low, watchful growling.

"Khot," Forlo swore, reaching for where his sword had been. He put a hand out to keep Shedara back. Hult did the same at exactly the same moment.

Three large creatures lay within the smoky hut. At first, Forlo thought they were wolves—larger than any he'd ever seen, with dead white fur and ice-blue eyes—but then he realized he was wrong. There was something half human about the beasts' faces, and their forelegs ended not in paws, but in stubby hands. Something about them made him think of Chovuk, in the tiger-shape he had worn just before their duel at the Run; glancing sideways, he could tell from Hult's pallor that the same thought had crossed the mind of the Uigan.

The half-wolves rose from the floor of the anho-ti, baring teeth like knives, their ears flattening back at the sight of strangers. Looking at them, Forlo realized there was something else strange about the creatures: he could see through them, just a little. Not just man-wolves, then, but ghost-man-wolves. Cold hung about them like a cloud.

"What in Nuvis' name . . ." Shedara breathed.

"Amaguik," Eldako whispered. "Spirit-wolves. Do not move. Their bite will turn your blood to ice."

Forlo stared at the beasts; the look of them alone seemed enough to draw the last of the warmth out of his body. Freezing mist puffed out of their snarling mouths. Head lowered, one of them sniffed the air, then took a step toward the tent flap.

"Suka, lie!" snapped Angusuk behind them. "Pachak, Pamir—be still!"

The spirit-wolves obeyed immediately, settling back down, their heads lowering to the tent's earthen floor. Angusuk let the flap close, then took off his mask, scarf, and hood. He was older than Forlo had expected, gray in his wispy beard, with a bald patch on his head. A scar ran the length of his nose, either from battle or some ritual disfigurement—both seemed equally possible. His eyes were dark, framed with wrinkles. He smiled, gesturing toward the fire.

"Go on," he bade. "The Amaguik will not trouble you. The makau awaits."

"So I do, Master of the Hunt, so I do," crowed a voice from the far side of the anho-ti.

The words startled Forlo, for they were in the language of the League; unlike Angusuk, Eldako did not need to translate them. The wild elf and Shedara were also taken aback. Only Hult, who understood everything thanks to Nalaran's amulet, didn't react with surprise.

Eldako led the way past the spirit-wolves. Forlo and Hult eyed them suspiciously as they crept past. But the creatures looked bored, no longer even meeting their gaze.

As they drew nearer to the fire, the heat of it was almost painful. Smoke watered their eyes. Heaps of skins lay around the flames; on the highest pile, wrapped in a blanket of white fur, was Tulukaruk. He looked even smaller and frailer than he had out on the wastes, when he cast the spell to destroy the Eyes; he was a wizened husk of a man with skin the color of old wood. Tulukaruk raised a hand in greeting, his fingers as thin and frail as bird bones. His dragon-horned staff leaned against the tent's wall behind him. This, and the tingling Forlo felt just looking at him, spoke of the makau's power. Shedara bowed her head, recognizing an archmage every bit as mighty as Nalaran.

Eldako steepled his fingertips before him, a sign of respect. "We greet you, Eldest. We owe you a great debt for saving us from the Uitayuik."

"It is not I you should thank," said Tulukaruk, "but the men whose families now wail in their tents, who went west to meet you and did not return."

"We weep for them, makau," Eldako replied. "And we shall pray for their spirits when this meeting is done. Your people have risked much and suffered greatly to bring us here."

The creases in Tulukaruk's face deepened. "We have." The makau's eyes glittered as they fell upon Forlo. "You are surprised I know the southern tongue. We have much lore, we elders. I can understand the hawk's cry and the wolf's howl. I can speak the languages of men just as well. I would have you all know what I must say."

Forlo bowed his head. "Thank you," he said.

"Not so swift!" Tulukaruk said, favoring them with a smile that boasted mostly bare gums: Forlo doubted the old man had more than six teeth. "The way ahead is dark for you. Are you not the one whose child was stolen?"

Forlo blinked, astonished, but said nothing.

"Yes," the makau continued. "The child, and the woman who carries him. Your beloved Starlight. Yes. And you, Shedara of the shadow-haunted wood, you seek the statue, the one whose hood has fallen. I know this. I have dreamed it, here in my tent." He gestured to the spirit-wolves, who looked back at him with glittering gazes. "The Amaguik sing to me of your tale while I sleep, for they can travel far beyond the winds when they will it. I know of your people's doom, Hult, son of Holar. I know you abandoned your master, in the end—and I know that you all will know fresh grief before this journey is done. Most of all you, Eldako, Prince of the Green—though what form this woe might take, I do not know."

The tent fell silent, save for the dull roar of the storm outside. Forlo shivered, and Shedara and Hult were both pale. Eldako looked even more unsettled, and he lowered his eyes to stare into the fire. Seeing that the merkitsa wasn't likely to speak again soon, Forlo coughed and cleared his throat.

"Then you also know why we're here," he said. "You know what we seek."

Tulukaruk smiled his toothless smile, which made him look disturbingly like the oldest infant in the world. "Ukamiak! The silver sage, the namer of dragons. Yes, yes, I know. That is why I sent Angusuk and his warriors to find you. For no man has sought the Namer since the ancient days, before the First Destruction. No man has dared. Yet you have come, at great need. Much rides on your shoulders—perhaps more than any of you know. Have you the scale?"

Forlo nodded. He shrugged off his pack, opened it, and rooted inside. He pulled out a bundle of cloth, and unfolded it to reveal the plate of glittering black. Head bowed, he laid it at the makau's feet. He heard movement behind him and glanced back to see that the spirit-wolves had risen again and were staring at the scale as well. Shuddering, he forced himself to turn his back on the Amaguik.

"It is as the spirits sang, then," Tulukaruk said, gazing at his own reflection in the scale's surface. "Ukani nau gut-apang, my wolves called it."

"A shard of broken night," murmured Angusuk.

"And so it is," the makau declared and looked up again. "Go, Angusuk. Tell the families of those who are lost that their kin have not died in vain. The Namer shall be awakened. Ukamiak shall speak again."

Steepling his fingers, Angusuk pulled on his mask then walked back past the Amaguik and out of the tent. The wind's screaming grew momentarily louder, then muffled again as the flap swung closed. Tulukaruk stared into the flickering fire, his eyes narrow.

"Will you show us the way, Eldest?" asked Eldako. "Will you tell us where the silver sage sleeps?"

Tulukaruk looked up. Again, the childlike smile. "No, brother merkitsa. That is something I do not know."

The others looked at him, troubled. "What?" Hult blurted—the first word he'd spoken since the Eyes disappeared. "But you must—"

"Must?" Tulukaruk interrupted, his voice suddenly as sharp and forceful as a spearhead. His expression grew fierce, his eyes like shards of flint. "Do not speak to a makau of *must*, child of the steppes."

Hult scowled but fell silent, chastened—and a little afraid, if Forlo read his expression right.

"Then what?" Shedara asked. "Who can tell us?"

Slowly, Tulukaruk's smile returned. "The same who tell me," he said and shrugged off his blanket to reveal his bare chest, webbed with scars. "I do not know the road you must take . . . but the spirits do."

With that he rose and went to fetch his staff.

The makau's chanting began low and soft, a rhythmic wheeze that wasn't words at all—only breathing. Tulukaruk stood before the fire, head bowed low, white hair spilling forward to hide it. The flames guttered and danced as if a wind blew upon them, though the air in the anho-tii was still and stifling. The dragon-horn staff in Tulukaruk's hand bobbed with his voice, rapping the ground again and again, strings of beads and teeth rattling against its shaft. The air seemed to darken at the hut's edges, while brightening around him. Bit by bit, so slowly Forlo didn't notice it at first, the ruddy color leeched out of the firelight, turning it gray. The flames did the same—before he knew it they had gone from golden to dead white. Their heat faded as well, and the cold of Panak seeped into the tent.

Outside, the storm roared.

The others watched, rapt, silent. This was not magic as it was practiced outside the snow-wastes—not even on the Tamire, among Hult's people. This was primal, frightening. The language Tulukaruk spoke wasn't the same, the gestures he made were strange. The energies that flowed through the anho-ti were different, more dangerous. Shedara, in particular, watched with wide eyes. Her people's wizards, even Nalaran, wielded power that, when unleashed, could rage like a mighty thunderstorm, whose thunderbolts might shatter towers of solid stone. What the makau tapped was a hurricane that could blast entire cities from the face of Krynn. It was sorcery, chaos, blood-magic; it had nothing to do with the power of the moons. If it went wrong, it would kill not just them, but everyone in Kitaglu. Forlo felt terror gnaw at his guts, and had to will himself not to jump up and flee out into the blizzard, just to get away from this terrible magic.

Tulukaruk's song grew louder with every breath, now not just a breath but a song with words, uttered in a deep, growling drone. His feet shuffled, his body swayed; sweat glistened on his wrinkled, many-scarred body. His free hand rose, scattering gray dust over the flames. The motes caught and leaped up in a billow of sparks. The fire shimmered, then turned blue, draining the last vestiges of warmth from the hut. Shadows swallowed everything more than a pace from the fire.

Hult whispered something, too soft to make out, but Forlo guessed it was a prayer. The Uigan little trusted even their own sorcerers; with someone like the makau, it went against all his instincts to hold still, not to flee or find some weapon to use against the old man. His hands were clenched into fists, the knuckles yellow-white with pressure. Even Eldako sat quiet, subdued, his face lost in thought.

Tulukaruk's voice grew deeper, lower still. The staff struck the ground twice for every beat: one-two, one-two. His hair rose in snakelike strands, floating about his head as though it were under water. He sprinkled more of the powder, and the flames leaped in reply, blazing violet now. A second voice, high and whistling, rose from the makau's throat, as before. The eeriness of it raised bumps on Forlo's arms. It warbled higher and higher, building into a shrill, hurtful sound; then, abruptly, it stopped, and Tulukaruk threw his head back at last, looking up at them.

But it was not Tulukaruk they saw. The shriveled, toothless old man was gone, and in his place was something that wasn't even human. Its eyes glowed like blue stars, their pupils the thinnest of slits. Mouth and nose had changed into a snout full of long, sharp teeth. His ears had lengthened, and hair had burst from his brown, wrinkled skin: pure white fur, the color of frost. Only his hands didn't transform, only they remained human, still gripping his staff.

In the darkness of the hut, the spirit-wolves howled. Hult let out a yell, then stumbled backward, reaching for where his sword would have been if he hadn't given it up outside the anho-ti. Shedara raised her hands, fingers tensing, ready to cast a spell of her own to escape, if necessary. Eldako stared, not breathing. From the neck up, Tulukaruk had become the image of a white wolf.

Forlo understood now. Tulukaruk communed with the spirits by becoming one of them, an Amaguik. And the three creatures, the spectral beasts who shared the makau's tent? Had they been sorcerers once, too? Were they Tulukaruk's predecessors, and would he become one as well, when his life finally ended?

The spirit-wolf swept its heavy gaze over his four visitors. Its lip curled, eyes flaring wide. When it spoke, the words did not come from its lips; they simply resonated in Forlo's head.

WHO DISTURBS MY SLEEP? it asked.

Forlo and the others exchanged glances in the stillness. The tent was growing colder by the moment; soon it would be just as frigid as outside, where the blizzard continued to wrack the village. Forlo licked his lips and stepped forward.

"We do, Great One," he replied. "I am Barreth Forlo of Coldhope. My companions and I seek your aid."

YES. I HAVE SEEN YOU BEFORE. The wolf's head craned forward, teeth bared. Nostrils flared; frost danced in the air above them. Forlo had the sense that if Tulukaruk—or whatever was now living in his skin—breathed on him, he would freeze solid. *YOU ARE THE ONES CHASING THE STATUE.*

"The Hooded One?" Shedara asked, her voice so soft they could barely hear her words. "You know where it is?"

AND HOW WOULD I KNOW THAT, CHILD OF THE SHADOW-WOOD? The spirit's voice curdled with scorn. *YOU KNOW THE QUESTION YOU MUST ASK.*

"The Wyrm-namer," Eldako spoke. "Ukamiak. We seek him, but know not where he dwells—only that he is in the north."

THE NAMER. . . . The Amaguk drew the word out into a growl. Something popped in the fire, sending a shower of blue cinders billowing toward the ceiling. *YES, I KNOW OF HIM. I SEE MUCH, SON OF THO-KET. I SEE YOU IN THE NAMER'S CAVE, WITH THE BLACK DRAGON'S SCALE. I SEE YOU WITH THE STATUE AS WELL. THIS IS WHAT SHALL BE.*

"Then . . . you will tell us?" Forlo murmured.

I WILL. BUT YOU MUST PROMISE A SERVICE TO ME FIRST.

"What sort of service?" asked Shedara warily.

AVENGE ME. WE AMAGUIK WERE ONCE LIVING THINGS. ONCE, LONG AGO, WE RULED THESE LANDS . . . UNTIL THE DRAGONS CAME AND SLAUGHTERED US ALL, TO CLAIM PANAK AS THEIR OWN. UKAMIAK LED THEM. I DIED BECAUSE OF THE NAMER AND HIS KIN—AND I WAS NOT THE ONLY ONE. ALL OF MY KIND PERISHED IN THOSE DARK DAYS, AND WE LINGER FOR REVENGE. WE REMAIN IN THIS WORLD BECAUSE HE STILL LIVES. I WILL TELL YOU WHERE TO FIND THE NAMER . . . BUT YOU MUST PLEDGE TO SLAY HIM, ONCE YOU HAVE THE KNOWLEDGE YOU SEEK.

Forlo caught his breath. To kill a dragon . . . it seemed impossible, especially one as ancient and powerful as the Wyrm-namer. The others all looked horrified, Eldako more than the rest. The wild elf's people revered Ukamiak, as did the Ice People.

But that was the price, and Forlo knew there would be no negotiating with the spirit-wolf. The hunger for vengeance blazed in Tulukaruk's eyes . . . and eagerness shown in Forlo's as he stepped forward, his head angled back.

"You have our word," he said. "We will do what you

ask. Once we know where the black dragon is, the Namer shall die."

"What?!" Shedara asked.

The Amaguik laughed, and the last of the light vanished from the hut. The spirit-wolf's eyes gleamed hungrily in the darkness. It was not a pleasant sight.

VERY WELL, said the voice. SINCE YOU SUBMIT, I WILL AID YOU. JOURNEY EAST WHEN THE STORM BREAKS. IN NINE DAYS' TIME, YOU WILL COME TO THE MOUNTAINS KNOWN AS THE HOARSPINES. THERE YOU WILL FIND WHAT YOU SEEK, BENEATH THE HIGHEST CRAG, CALLED GREYTOOTH BY MORTALS. THAT IS WHERE THE NAMER DWELLS, WHERE YOU WILL FIND THE MURDERER OF MY KINDRED . . . AND WHERE HIS ACCURSED BONES SHALL LIE UNTIL THE WORLD'S ENDING.

The makau threw back its head and bayed at the roof of the tent. The other Amaguik picked up the call as well, joining so loudly Forlo had to clap his hands over his ears to stop the pain. The fire burst, loosing a huge tongue of flame that started blue, then faded back to white, and finally to familiar orange again. When it was done the light returned, and the spirit was gone. Tulukaruk stood in its place, swaying on his feet, his face old and brown and wrinkled once more.

The shadows fled. Warmth returned. The makau gazed at them, his eyes clouded, then sagged to the floor.

Chapter

15

THE WASTES, LOWER PANAK

The storm broke the next day, leaving blue sky in its wake. Angusuk prepared a sled for the journey across the snows. It was a large vehicle, like a boat on long, whalebone runners, pulled by a pair of nasif—enormous, shaggy-coated deer with sharp antlers, which the folk of Panak tended like sheep or cattle. They gave great strips of smoked nasif meat to Forlo and the others for their voyage, as well as thick hides to keep them warm. To Shedara, the women of the tribe gave a necklace of the animals' bones, intricately carved with images of wolves and spiral patterns. Then the Ice People left them alone, returning to their solemn, silent toil of mourning their dead and digging out from the blizzard.

Tulukaruk remained unconscious until midday, and when he finally woke, he could remember nothing of what the spirit-wolf had said through him. When Eldako told him where they were bound, the makau's childlike face turned grave.

"The Hoarspines," he croaked. "Beware those peaks. The sakalaminuik dwell there also—snow-ogres, they are our people's ancient foes. The snow-ogres are fierce and strong, and friends to none but their own. You will need those blades you wear, if you should cross paths with them."

None of them said anything about the oath the spirit had made them take. There was no need to upset Tulukaruk, they decided, by mentioning they had promised to slay the Wyrm-namer. There was no telling what the Ice People might do if they learned the truth.

"The Namer is ancient, sacred!" Eldako had protested the night before, once the makau's magic had faded from the hut. "To slay him would be like killing the head of a great and powerful church."

"I've done that," Forlo had replied. "These hands took the head of Bishop Ondelos of Thenol. He was an evil man, but many still called him holy. If this Namer is responsible for the deaths of the wolves, perhaps the same could be said about him."

"If," Shedara replied. "It could be a trick by the spirits. How do you know what was said was true?"

Forlo shrugged. "How do we know the Namer's really at this mountain, this Greytooth? All we know is what we've been told. Either we believe the spirit-wolf, or what's the point?"

Shedara made a face but gave no answer. Eldako shook his head—no, there wasn't any other choice. But the elves still didn't like the decision.

Forlo turned to Hult. "What about you? You've been quiet this whole time."

The young barbarian met his gaze, his eyebrows rising. "Have you ever slain a dragon, Forlo? I have—a young wyrm, barely out of its egg. Doing so nearly killed me." He stroked his necklace of dragon teeth, his trophies of that long-ago fight and the one garment he'd kept through their ordeal among the minotaurs. "This Namer is ancient and will be a hundred times more dangerous, a thousand times more cunning. You have taken this oath, so we must try to keep to it, but it may be the death of us."

That was more than enough. The words hung over Forlo like a curse. They didn't speak of their decision again.

They set forth the following morning, climbing aboard the massive sled while the Ice People lashed the nasif to it. Angusuk took the reins: he would make the journey with them, and bring them back . . . if there was anyone to bring back. Most of the clan came out to the village's eastern edge to watch them leave. Even Tulukaruk emerged from his wolf-haunted hut, leaning on his staff and raising a withered hand in farewell. Forlo and the others repeated the gesture; then Angusuk lashed the reins and the sled lurched forward, gliding down a long, shallow slope and leaving Kitaglu behind.

The nasif were surprisingly fast for creatures of their bulk, their broad hooves chewing through the snow, throwing up great plumes that drifted away southward on the wind. The sled itself glided smoothly along, the runners hissing as they slid across the snow-pack. The Ice People's village vanished in minutes, leaving the travelers alone in an ocean of white. The wasteland rose and fell gently as they went, and now and then a few lichen-encrusted rocks poked through, but otherwise it was like being in an endless void, a frozen nothingness gleaming brightly in the sun.

So it went, for eight days and nights. They stopped when the sun went down, Angusuk guiding the nasif to a cluster of rocks so the hulking beasts could feed off the lichen, while he built a peat fire in a small stone urn and used it to melt snow for drinking water. They camped in the sled, never once stepping off its deck, wrapping themselves in furs and chewing on the gamey strips of meat. Sometimes, they told tales or sang. Angusuk tried to teach them cham ka, a complicated game that used dice made from nasif antlers. They all failed to learn the rules—even Forlo, who had mastered most dice games during his time in the legions. The game was just too complex. Finally, Angusuk gave up.

Time crawled. One day bled into the next. It seemed they might just go on forever, damned to spend eternity in this empty, frigid desert. Then, finally, on the ninth morning, they cleared a rise and saw a jagged blue line on the horizon: ice-bound mountains, rising out of the snow-sea. One jutted up among them, a slender needle of rock that was so steep, most of the snow had slid off its sides. The stone beneath was the color of storm clouds.

"Greytooth," Forlo breathed. The others nodded. Wordlessly, Angusuk pulled the reins, aiming the nasif directly at the menacing peak. They glided on.

Hours passed. The sun rose, but did not get very high before sliding down to the west. This far north, there were only a few hours of daylight in the winter, so when nightfall came, the Hoarspine was still several leagues away. Angusuk didn't order the nasif to quit this time, though; they went on through the dusk and dark, as the silver moon rose behind the mountains. Finally, as the bitter wind tried to claw through their furs, the sled came to a stop at the foot of an icy slope. Greytooth soared over them, a menacing finger accusing the heavens. Billows of glittering snow gusted off its highest reaches, trailing for miles into the night.

Angusuk and Eldako exchanged a few words, then the wild elf clapped the other man on the shoulder before coming back to join the rest. "He will remain here with the nasif," he said. "If there are snow-ogres about, they may try to steal them."

"What about us?" Forlo asked, gazing up at the forbidding spire. "We can't climb that. Well, maybe with that spell Shedara used at Kristophan. . . ."

"There is no need," Eldako replied, pointing. "Do you see the base of the spike? The cleft there?"

They all looked, but Forlo shook his head. After a moment, Hult spoke irritably. "I am no elf," said the Uigan. "I cannot see in the dark as well as you."

"I can," Shedara said. "A cave mouth. Looks big enough for a dragon, too. That must be the Namer's lair."

"We'll climb in the morning, then," Forlo said. "If we try going up that slope now, Hult and I will break our necks. One more camp, and tomorrow we find the Namer."

"One more camp," Shedara said. "But not much sleep for any of us, I think."

At that moment a loud howling rose, somewhere up among the rocks—a noise that was almost, but not quite, human. Another voice joined the first, then a third, and finally a whole chorus. The din went on for quite some time, while the nasif rolled their eyes and snorted, kept in place only by Angusuk's soothing voice and his tight hand on the reins. The sled shook as they sought to break free, to find somewhere to run. Finally, the eerie song died away, one voice after another dropping until only echoes remained, bouncing from crag to crag.

Forlo didn't need to ask. None of them did. Those were the voices of the sakalaminuik. The snow-ogres were up there, waiting.

"No," he said. "I don't think we'll be getting any sleep at all."

✦━━━◆✕◆━━━✦

Dawn came, pale and gray, with the promise of snow in the air—though not another storm, according to Angusuk. "We will be well," he said, patting one of the nasif. "We will wait for you."

"Two days," Eldako said. "As we discussed. If we don't return by then, we won't be returning at all. Go back to Kitaglu, and send a messenger south to my father in the Dreaming Green. Tell him of our quest, and that we failed."

"You will not fail," Angusuk said, smiling. "The makau has seen it."

"Of course he has," Shedara muttered.

They climbed down from the sled, but even Eldako's weight broke through the covering crust, plunging him thigh-deep into the loose powder beneath. It took them the better part of an hour to slog the thirty paces to the mountain's foot. One by one they dragged themselves onto the rock and rested, panting and sweating as they fought to get their strength back. Angusuk watched, still smiling, the nasif's reins in his mittened hand.

Glancing up, Eldako sucked a breath through his teeth, but when Forlo looked, he saw nothing. "What was it?" he asked.

"Something there, on the stones," the wild elf replied. "It was watching us, I think. I saw its eyes." He worked quickly, stringing his bow and plucking an arrow from his quiver. "The sakalaminuik await."

"An ambush?" Hult asked, loosening his blade in its scabbard.

"Perhaps," Eldako said.

"I wonder," Shedara said. "If they wanted to attack, they could have done it in the night."

"We hadn't set foot on their territory then," Forlo murmured.

Eldako grunted, giving him a nod. Shedara, however, looked thoughtful. "Listen," she said. "Don't you think it's odd that these creatures live so close to the Namer's lair? I mean, why would he tolerate them?"

"What are you getting at?" Forlo asked.

She looked up again then froze. "Eye of Solis," she whispered. "Look."

Forlo did, and reached at once for his sword. The slope above them had come alive. More than a dozen enormous creatures were squatting on the rocks. Their skin was gray, covered with long, shaggy fur as white as the snow around them. They were long-armed and stooped, their heads squashed onto massive shoulders, flat faced with black, glittering eyes and long, yellow tusks. Some held stone-headed clubs; others hefted small boulders, poised to throw. Forlo had never seen a snow-ogre, hadn't even heard of them before coming to Panak, but he knew he was looking at them right now.

Hult began to draw his weapon. Shedara grabbed his elbow, squeezing tight until he let go. "No," she said. "If we attack, they'll smash us where we stand. Eldako, lower your bow."

The merkitsa had raised the weapon the moment the snow-ogres appeared. Now he frowned, hesitating.

"Do you think you can shoot them all before one of those rocks finds you?" Shedara asked. "Listen. I think the Namer tolerates them for a reason. I think they're his guards."

Forlo looked from her to the wild elf, then up at the sakalaminuik. Slowly, he took his hand off his own sword. "She's right," he said. "They're here to greet intruders. We must show them we mean no harm before we can approach the cave."

Eldako held his stance. His eyes flicked to Forlo, who nodded. At last, with a sigh, he relaxed his pull on the bowstring and pointed the weapon at the ground.

"All right," Forlo said, shrugging off his pack. He kept an eye on the snow-ogres, who watched as he loosened the drawstring and reached inside. "I hope you're right about this, Shedara."

"So do I," she said. "Show it to them, Forlo."

He didn't need to be told. Holding his breath, he hauled the black scale from his pack and held it up for the snow-ogres to see. Then something occurred to him. "Hult," he said, "you can talk to them, in their language. Tell them why we're here."

Hult blinked, then glanced at the jade amulet around his neck and understood. He looked up, hopefully, and found himself uttering a series of grunts and barks, unintelligible to the others, then cocking his head in an inquisitive gesture.

The sakalaminuik started, looking at one another. They had never heard a human speak their tongue before. One shambled forward to lean over the edge of an outcrop and peer at Hult, Forlo, and the elves. He grunted a question of his own.

Hult snarled an answer.

Whatever he said, it satisfied the snow-ogres. Bowing their heavy-browed heads, they put down their clubs and let the boulders fall, harmless, at their feet. Then they parted, flanking what Forlo could see was a path that wended up the mountainside.

"They say we may pass," Hult said. "The Namer awaits within."

Forlo managed a shaky smile, still holding the scale high. "Well, now," he said. "That was easy enough, wasn't it?"

Ice coated the tunnel, thick and rippling, sea-blue and foam-green, reflecting light from outside the mountain. Huge, dripping stalactites hung from the ceiling, poised above stalagmites like so many glistening fangs. In places, they joined into mighty, sparkling columns. Another time, it would have been a sight to marvel at, but Forlo's mind dwelled solely on what lay ahead, in the frozen depths of Greytooth.

The going was slow and treacherous. They had to steady themselves to keep from slipping as they walked, down and down, swords sheathed, arrows tucked safely in their quivers. The snow-ogres followed, making no noise as they shambled along. Every instinct bred into him by decades at war screamed to Forlo that they were dooming themselves by going this way—had already done so when they agreed to walk among the sakalaminuik. There were scores of the creatures following them.

To keep his focus, he held on to the scale. It glistened green and violet in the ice-diffused light, like lamp oil floating on a puddle. His fingers probed its jagged edge, where it had broken away from the dragon, felt the thickness of it, the unbreakable hardness. You could shoot a crossbow at the thing from five paces away and it wouldn't break. This was what they were up against—and what they would face, soon enough. For the dragon who bided in the cavern below was far older than the one who'd taken Essana. And he had sworn to kill it.

Now that he thought of it, that did seem foolish.

"I hear something," Shedara murmured, frost puffing from her mouth.

Eldako nodded. "Breathing. . . ."

Forlo concentrated, listening hard. At first he couldn't detect anything, but a dozen halting paces on, he caught the sound too: a low whooshing, like air passing through some massive bellows. There was something more to it, too—a strange, whistling note buried deep within. Forlo frowned, trying to think what it was and where he had heard something like it before.

"That isn't the breath of something healthy," said Hult. "Once, when I was a boy, Anku Tegin, who was lord of our clan before Chovuk, made me put down a horse with the drowning-sickness. Its lungs were filled with fluid. It could barely lift its head, let alone stand."

Forlo looked at the Uigan, understanding lighting his face. "Yes. That's it. I lost men to something like that, down in the marshes of Thenol. A bad way to die."

"As opposed to all the good ways," Shedara said.

Hult shook his head. "Most are better than drowning in your own mucus."

She looked as if she wanted to argue, but just then the breathing hitched, then stopped for a moment. Then there was another noise, a series of small explosions that made the smaller stalactites break free and rain down in tinkling shards. The dragon was coughing. It went on so long, it seemed it might not end—but it did, and when the fit subsided, the wheezing note in the beast's breathing was louder than ever.

"Who . . . enters . . . my den?" croaked a weak voice from ahead. The words dissolved into another spasm.

Forlo looked at the others. They were all watching him, expectant. He tightened his grip on the scale, then raised his voice to call back. "We come in search of counsel, Ancient One! We seek a name."

"A name . . ." the voice replied. "Long . . . has it been, since . . . anyone . . . came seeking names . . . from me. Come . . . forward. Enter and . . . speak."

Taking a deep breath, Forlo glanced over his shoulder. The sakalaminuik gathered behind them, filling the passage from one side to the other. They watched him with eyes that held no anger, no reproach. No, it was *sorrow* in the snow-ogres' gaze. They were grieving. He knew, then, what was happening here: the Namer was dying. He would not be required to fulfill his oath, would not need to become a dragon-slayer. He could tell from every sound the ancient wyrm made. It probably should have died some time ago . . . days, weeks . . . maybe years. But something had made it want to go on, just a little longer.

He was that something. Him, and the scale.

Exhaling, Forlo strode forward. The others went with him, lost in their own thoughts. The sakalaminuik lumbered behind, making no sound.

The tunnel finally ended, opening into a vast cavern rimed all over with frost. Shafts of light lanced down from above, making the gigantic icicles shimmer. The sound of dripping water was everywhere. The floor dropped away from the tunnel, down a steep, curving slope toward the cavern's bottom. And down below, lying in a trembling heap, was what remained of Ukamiak, the Wyrm-namer.

Looking on the creature, Forlo felt a catch in his own throat. Once, surely, the Namer had been a proud beast, a leviathan of a size unrivalled among its kind. Even now, it stretched fifty paces from snout to tail, and its wings—tattered and peeling with some painful disease—were each thrice the size of the largest sail in the minotaur fleet. One of its horns was broken away, and it was as toothless as the old makau, back in Kitaglu. Its eyes were milky with cataracts. Its muscles were wasted, leaving flesh hanging loosely from its bones. Once, its scales must have been silver, but now they were dark with tarnish, green with illness.

Forlo heard a sound beside him. Glancing over, he saw Shedara was weeping, a hand covering her face. Beside her Eldako stared, his eyes shining with tears. Even Hult had turned pale and was staring at the ceiling.

Shaking his head, Forlo forced himself to gaze upon the wretched creature that was Ukamiak. How long had this creature been here, waiting for one more supplicant to arrive? How much had it endured to last this long?

"Do not . . . sorrow," said the dying dragon. "My time is . . . at hand. At last . . . I will . . . rest."

"You knew of our coming," Forlo murmured. "Something told you to wait. A dream, a vision?"

The pale eyes shifted, gazing up at him. Past him. Through him. The Namer was blind. "Yes," the Namer replied. "A hundred . . . years. Perhaps . . . longer. It is hard . . . to know for . . . certain." He coughed again, and clouds of freezing mist billowed from his crusted nostrils. "But you are . . . here. Give . . . me . . . the scale."

Forlo held out the scale, looking dubiously down the slope toward the dragon. "I don't think I can walk down to you, Ancient One," he said.

"Throw it."

It was hard to let it go. The scale was the one link he had left, the only thing still tying him to his wife. Now he turned it over in his hands, watching the light play across its surface one last time.

"Go on," Shedara said. "Before it's too late."

Ukamiak was fading. Each breath was weaker than the last. Their arrival had brought imminent death to the Namer's cavern. Swallowing, Forlo raised the scale and flung it away. It fell into the gulf of the cave, struck the floor, and slid the rest of the way down, stopping within the dragon's reach. A long, broken talon stretched out and plucked it from the ice.

"My sins are many," breathed the Namer. "I have . . . done ill. But . . . I have paid . . . the price."

His words shifted then, to a different language, the ageless speech of the dragons. It was the language of magic, the first of that kind, from which all mortals had taken their own eldritch tongues. Power seethed in every word, drawn not just from the moons, but from everything—the ice of the cave, the stones beneath, the flesh of dragon and ogre alike. Forlo gritted his teeth as the air around the Namer shimmered with power.

Bit by bit, the magic coalesced. It took a form, long and slender and serpentine . . . and black as the heart of night. It gathered like a shadow above Ukamiak's withered body, coiling and writhing, claws grasping at the air. Venom dripped from its jaws. It was an evil thing, ugly and cruel. Its eyes burned like red coals.

"This is . . . the one you seek," wheezed the Namer. "It is called . . . Sashekul, which . . . is Gloomwing in our . . . speech. Its lair . . . lies on the edge . . . of . . . the Boiling Sea. The valleys of . . . Marak."

"Marak!" Shedara gasped. "Where the kender dwell?"

"Yes," the Namer said. "You will learn . . . more . . . there."

The image began to come apart, bleeding like ink in

water. The black wyrm dissipated, its eyes winking out. Ukamiak the Namer coughed, weakly, one last time.

"It is . . . finished," he gasped.

And was still.

Chapter

16

THE WASTES, LOWER PANAK

The sled glided across the snows in silence, overhung with dark clouds. Snow danced in the air, borne by winds that cut straight through the thickest furs. The nasif trotted tirelessly, snorting frost as they ran. The mountains faded away behind them, forgotten.

It hadn't been what Hult expected. He'd thought there would be fighting, against the ogres and perhaps even the dragon. He hadn't thought it would end so quietly, with the Namer simply lying still, his skull-like head flat upon the ice of the cave. The sakalaminuik had gone down to tend the creature they had worshiped as a god. Their chief had spoken a few grunting words, which he hadn't needed to translate to the others:

"Go now. You have what you need. We mourn."

And they had gone, back up the mountain's throat and to the sled, where Angusuk listened while they told their tale. Then, without a word, he had taken the reins and urged the nasif on, away from the Hoarspine, back along the long white road to Kitaglu. Neither he nor any of the others had spoken a word since.

Hult had thought he knew dragons, from his manhood hunt upon the ice. But the feral cold-drakes he and his

196

friends had stalked and slain were no more like the Namer than dogs were like men. The beast whose death he'd beheld was, he was sure, the only one of its kind, and another would not soon come to Taladas. Perhaps one never would. His death was something momentous, like the fall of an empire . . . or the destruction of a people.

Shedara wept for a while. They left her alone. Eldako stood at the sled's prow, letting the wind buffet his face, bringing tears of a different kind. Forlo sat at the rear, his gaze thoughtful as he stared back toward Greytooth's vanishing shadow. Hult, for his part, prowled from one end of the sled to the other, his hand on his sword, restless. Nine days out, nine days back, and scarcely an hour in between. He longed for a horse under him, the wide expanse of the grasslands sweeping ahead. He wanted war-songs on the air, men laughing and joking, boasting of how many enemies would die on their spears tomorrow—his master, shouting loudest of all.

That life is gone, he reminded himself. His gaze strayed south and stayed there. There, far beyond the horizon, lay Marak. Their next destination: green, steep-walled, misty valleys where the kender dwelled. He knew the little folk from legend, nothing more. None of them had ever been to the place—not Eldako, not Forlo, not even Shedara. None knew what waited for them there—only that the black dragon, Gloomwing, called the valleys home. It would take weeks to reach Marak. Winter would be hard upon Taladas by then.

They spoke that night, at last. Forlo broke the silence, his face looking old in the faint light of the peat fire. The wind moaned across the snows.

"Eldako," he said, "you've done more than enough, bringing us here. When we go back south, if you want to return to your people, I'll understand. No one will hold it against you."

Hult jolted, surprised. He could tell by the weariness in Forlo's voice that the words hurt him badly to speak. He looked at the two of them now, Uigan and merkitsa, his face pinched with anticipation. Shedara's eyes flicked between them all, narrow, watching. They were still red from her tears for the Namer.

Eldako shifted where he sat, his face an unreadable mask. Snow sparkled in his hair. "I will not lie and say I haven't thought long about what you offer," he said. "My heart aches for the Green, for sunlight through leaves and the music of waterfalls. And for the sight of my father as well. He will think me dead by now—word will have reached him of what happened at the Tiderun. He will grieve for me, and it twists my heart to cause him such sorrow. But what you offer, I cannot accept."

"You should," Shedara said, and looked at Hult. "Both of you. Forlo and I each have a stake in this. I'm sworn to destroy the statue, if I have to cross the Abyss to do it. And he must find his wife. But you're both with us for no more reason than chance. I wouldn't ask you to come any farther, any more than I would Angusuk."

"No stake?" Hult asked heatedly. "How can you say that, after all we've gone through? I'm as much a part of this tale as either of you—the people who stole the statue are the same ones who drove my master mad, who drove my people into the jaws of the sea. The memory of the Uigan is my stake in this, and it is no less than yours or Forlo's. If I left you now, it would be abandoning our honor forever. I will not do that. I will see it restored, or die trying."

Quiet settled, the wind and the crackle of the flames the only sounds. Forlo and Shedara studied Hult, long and hard. He stared back. He didn't quite know where the words had come from, but now that he'd said them, it felt like a great burden had lifted from his shoulders. For the first time since before the battle of the Run, he felt proud of himself, that he had a mission in life.

"As for me," Eldako put in, "it is true I have no stake—unless it is the stake all share, and stand to lose, if the Faceless Emperor is freed. But my path is with you, not back to the Green, and you will not be rid of me. Even should you cast me out and shun me, I will follow."

"Why?" Forlo asked.

Eldako shrugged. "That is a human question—why. We merkitsa do not ask why. We follow our instincts, like those that led me to Coldhope when the shadows were about to kill you. Now all my instincts tell me I have a part to play in this, still."

"Then we are one, we four," Hult said. "We go to Marak together."

"And beyond," Shedara replied. "The road won't end there, and we all know it. There's much farther to go before this is done."

The wind groaned. Angusuk, who'd listened to most of the conversation without understanding, bowed his head. Even he could sense the solemnity of the moment. They could all feel what Hult had said—they were bound together. The Wyrm-namer's death had sealed their pact, in a way.

Forlo sighed, a deep and heavy sound, like a stone dropping into a fathomless pool. "All right, then," he said. "We do this together. Marak it is."

He held out his hand, above the fire's guttering flames. There were many small, white scars on the fingers, and a longer one across the heel of his palm: soldier's wounds, little cuts from countless battles. Hult had more than a few of those, himself—and a larger one, too. He extended his own maimed hand. The stumps where his missing fingers had been were healed over, but still the sight made his stomach clench.

"Marak," he said.

Eldako laid his own hand atop Hult's. "Marak, and to the road's ending."

They looked at Shedara. She made a face. "Men and their rituals," she said. "But . . . all right."

She rested her hand on Eldako's. All four sat still, quiet, marking the moment. Something in the fire settled, and cinders rose up around their hands. They stung when they touched Hult's skin, but he didn't pull away. None of them did, until finally Shedara lifted her hand from the others', pushed back from the fire, and lay down.

"Now let's get some sleep," she said. "Like I said, there's still a long way to go."

✦━━━✦━━━✦

The days passed in a white haze. The sled swept on. The snow kept falling, day and night. Somehow, the nasif found their way through the white nothing.

Finally, Angusuk called out. "We are close now!" he said. "Kitaglu lies beyond the ridge."

Hult, who had been dozing at the sled's rear, roused and got to his feet. He nudged awake Forlo, and they went to join Eldako and Shedara, who were watching ahead. Beyond the nasif's bobbing antlers, the ground rose to a crest. Hult wouldn't have recognized the area for the world, but then, none of the others would have known the hillocks that dotted the Tamire as well as he did. Angusuk, on the other hand, was leaning forward, his face lit by eagerness. It made Hult ache a little—he would never again know this feeling, of coming home.

"Something's wrong," Eldako said suddenly. "Where are the Patient Folk?"

Hult blinked, then stared, looking up and down the length of the ridge. There was no sign of the piled-stone statues that protected the Ice People's lands. Now he remembered—

five of them had stood atop this ridge, starkly positioned against the gray sky. He shuddered at the memory. Part of him was glad the Ningasuk were gone—but deep down he knew it was an ill omen, even before Angusuk cried out and started shouting at the nasif, lashing the reins to drive them faster.

Upward the sled climbed, the great deer straining and snorting to get to the top. As they got closer, Hult saw that the Patient Folk weren't actually gone; they had been toppled, reduced to heaps of jumbled rock, scattered down the slope. The sled ran over a couple of these, bucking wildly as it did. It was a miracle the nasif didn't stumble over them and break their legs. Had he been rational, Angusuk would have slowed their pace, but the man was panicking, his eyes wild with fear.

At last, they came to the crest. Angusuk seemed ready to drive the sled right over and down the other side, but before he could lash the nasif again, Shedara reached over and laid a hand on his arm. He looked at her, his eyes wide and white, and for a moment he didn't seem to recognize her. She gazed back, her green eyes shining. It was subtle, but Hult felt the magic around her, a spell being worked.

"Be easy," she told him. "What's happened is done. You won't achieve anything by this."

Angusuk blinked. Then, with an inarticulate sound, he stumbled back. Forlo grabbed the reins and brought the nasif to a halt. The beasts snorted and frothed, pawing at the snow, eager to run again.

Then the wind shifted, and the animals bellowed in fright, their eyes rolling. One reared, and the sled slewed sideways, one of its runners lifting off the ground and nearly pitching them all overboard. Hult staggered, grabbing the vehicle's side to keep from falling over, then recovered himself and jumped out, landing in knee-deep snow. He slogged to the bawling nasif and held up his hand, speaking in the same soothing voice all Uigan learned to use to calm their horses.

"Quiet, old man," he said in his native tongue. "Why do you cry so? All will be well, be still. . . ."

The words didn't matter, only the tone of his voice. But the nasif listened and slowly began to settle down again. Eldako joined him, speaking to the beasts in low grunts and soft bleats—the sounds of forest deer, softer and gentler than the speech of these great snow-beasts. Angusuk made a third, and together they made the animals calm again.

Hult sniffed the wind, trying to pick out the scent that had made the nasif panic, but it was too cold, his nose too runny. He hadn't smelled anything in days. He laid a hand on his sword.

"We should go on foot," he said. "If whatever spooked them gets any stronger, we might not be able to control them again."

"Afoot it is, then," Forlo agreed, climbing down from the sled.

He extended a hand to help Shedara out, and to Hult's surprise she didn't wave him off. They trudged through the snow to join the others. "Angusuk," Shedara said. "Is there an overlook nearby? Somewhere we can watch from out of sight?"

He looked at her a moment, his eyes still glassy from the spell, then nodded, pointing south. "By the Ningasuk," he said. "We can hide among the stones."

So they went, leaving the sled where it was. Eldako untied the nasif's reins, in case they got scared again, but the animals stayed where they were. Giving each of them one last pat, he turned and ran to join the others.

The Patient Folk were utterly destroyed, not a single stone left standing. It looked as if some incredible force had blasted them off their feet, knocking them away from Kitaglu. The nearest one's head lay almost fifty paces away, half buried in the snow, its sightless eyes glaring straight up at the sky. Hult shuddered at the sight, then made his way with the others to where the statue had stood. There, the boulders were jumbled, offering plenty of places for them to hide—or for others to do the same. Hult drew his sword as he approached them; the others followed suit; even Angusuk gripped his club in trembling hands.

Nothing awaited them among the rocks, though. All was still, and now Hult began to understand what had frightened the nasif—and Angusuk. He'd seen Kitaglu; it was a quiet place, but not silent. There had always been the sounds of a living village: children laughing, women singing, the barking of dogs. Now there wasn't a single sound from the hollow below. He'd lived long enough, seen enough Uigan villages wiped out by riders of other tribes—and other tribes' villages destroyed by the Uigan—to understand what it meant. All that was missing were the circling masses of crows and skyfishers above. It was too cold here for that.

A lump formed in his throat as he clambered over the toppled stones. He knew what he was going to see—but still, when he reached the overlook at last and looked down at what lay below, he couldn't help but bare his teeth and pound the heel of his fist against the stones.

Little remained of Kitaglu. The skin-and-snow huts had collapsed, leaving small depressions in the snow where they had stood. The pole with the carved wolves' heads lay on its side, nearly swallowed by the weather. And all throughout the village, scattered like a child's broken toys, lay the half-buried bodies of the Ice People. Men, women, children—all had been killed, many slain from behind as they tried to flee, and left to freeze stiff in the cold.

"There's no blood," murmured Shedara.

"The snow may have covered it," Forlo whispered.

They could all sense it—there was a something about the way everything looked that told them no natural foe had destroyed Kitaglu. Besides the lack of blood, none of the bodies looked to have been killed by anything but keen, slicing blades—no arrows, no crushed skulls, no one torn apart. There were no broken weapons, no bodies of any enemies, no tracks but the Ice People's own.

"We brought death to this place," Shedara said, her voice breaking. "Wherever we go, slaughter follows."

Eldako shook his head. "It is not your fault. You did not choose for the shadows to hunt you. They—"

A horrible sound interrupted him, so close it made Hult jump and whirl, his blade coming up before him. It was a strangled cry, a sound so heartbroken that it made his skin rise in bumps. Only after a moment did he realize the sound came from Angusuk. Shedara's calming spell was wearing off, and watching it happen was like watching the man fall apart. The hunter's face seemed to collapse, his eyes squeezing into blind, tear-filled slits. His mouth opened like a wound. The muscles in his throat jumped as his moan rose into a howl of anguish and rage. Twitching, he rose from where he crouched and started down toward his village.

Shedara tensed to spring after him, but Eldako shook his head. "Let him go," he said. "If you use your magic to deaden him again, it will drive him mad."

"But the shadows—" she began.

"Are long gone. This massacre happened days ago. The depth of the snow should tell you that."

She looked as if she might argue more, but it was too late. The last of the spell had lifted, and Angusuk had broken into a run, stumbling down the slope at breakneck speed. He shouted the names of his family, friends, tribe-mates.

No answer came.

✦━━◇━━✦

They walked among the wreckage. Nothing remained. The clan of the Spirit Wolf was destroyed, though when Angusuk finally stopped digging among the fallen huts, screaming the names of the dead, he admitted some of the hunters appeared to be missing altogether. A handful only, but it was a hopeful sign. All the women and children were dead, but there might be others still alive to carry the memory of his people.

Not the makau, though. Tulukaruk had been murdered as he slept, it seemed, for his body still lay in his anho-ti: He had been killed by a single slash across the throat, from which not a drop of blood had spilled. The look on the mage's frozen face was one of peace, a faint smile curling his lips. Of the Amaguik, his ghost-wolf guardians, there was no sign—although Hult was certain, for a moment, that he heard distant, mournful howling on the wind. Four voices now, not three. He shivered.

Angusuk broke down completely when he beheld the old sorcerer, huddling over Tulukaruk and sobbing for nearly an hour. The others didn't disturb him. Finally, as the sky was beginning to darken, he emerged from the anho-ti, his eyes red. He stripped to the waist, baring his stout, scarred body to the wind, and looked at the others with an expression so pained that Hult had to look away.

"We must burn them," he said. "Tonight. We must do this before my people become Uitayuik."

There was no more discussion than that. The image of the people of Kitaglu, doomed to wander the Panak forever as white-eyed ghosts, was too horrible. Grimly, quietly, they built pyres of peat and what little wood there was in the village. They gathered the bodies, laying them out to burn. The sky was fully dark by the time they were done, the moons and stars still lost behind cloud and snow; they worked by the light of stones that Shedara enchanted to glow, a cold, blue gleam that made even the living look dead. Finally, near midnight, the work was done and Tulukaruk was laid at the top of the highest pyre. Exhausted, they gathered beside the remains, each holding a lit torch. Angusuk, still bare-chested, drew a stone knife and cut a long gash across his body. Then, as the blood trickled down his skin, he uttered a wheezing chant for the dead.

> Go now, my brothers
> My sisters, children and elders
> Go to the north, among the ancestors
> Past the lands of the white worm
> Beyond the frozen seas
> Beyond the spirits of winter.
> Sleep there.
> Sing there, and be glad.
> Know no pain, sorrow, longing,
> For those are the curse of the living.
> We who are left behind.
> Remember us, and call our names
> When our time comes to follow.

With that, he plunged his torch into the central pyre. It took time for the flames to build, but eventually firelight flooded the ruined village, its warmth swallowing Shedara's mage-light. As one, the others lit the remaining pyres. Warmth poured through Kitaglu one last time, melting the snow, thawing the bodies, then setting them aflame. Smoke rose high into the air—and the sky cleared at last.

"Look!" shouted Forlo, pointing north.

Hult whirled, expecting to see more of the shadow-fiends, returning. Instead, he beheld something beautiful, the likes of which he'd never seen before. In the sky, where the clouds had been, strange lights now glowed: red and green and gold, twisting ropes and shimmering curtains, like a rainbow gone mad. There was a sound too, faint but unmistakable: a chiming, as of thousands of tiny bells.

Through his tears, Angusuk smiled. "My people," he whispered. "Rest now. Go. You are free."

They watched the strange lights in the north for hours, until they faded at last, and only stars remained.

Three days later, they returned to the seashore. The elven boat was moored there, waiting for them. Storm and waves had battered it, but it still floated, and its masts remained intact: Nalaran's magic still clung to its hull, protecting it. The dinghy was all right too, standing where they'd left it, above the high-tide mark on the rocky shore.

"Will you join us?" Hult asked Angusuk, as they gazed down from the clifftops. "You are welcome."

The Ice Person stared at the ship, his face thoughtful. He licked his lips, thinking long and hard—then, shook his head.

"I must find the others who still live, the hunters who were away when . . . when it happened." he said. "We clan-brothers must join together. But I will remember you, my friends. I will chant your tale, and it will live on around the song-fires of Panak."

He clasped each of them in turn, pressing his forehead against theirs in farewell. Then he turned and strode to the waiting sled and its nasif. They watched him climb aboard, raise his hand in farewell, and glide away over the snows.

"Well," Shedara said. "Let's be off too, then. Marak awaits."

She started down the slope, toward the sea. Hult glanced back at the frozen wastes, his mouth tightening into a firm line, then followed. He would not return to this place. Twice was enough for one lifetime.

Chapter

17

Akh-tazi, Neron

The elf was a fighter, more than the others. He kicked and screamed as the black dragon set him down. As the yaggol brought him toward the Hooded One, he somehow threw them off, in spite of the cords binding his arms, and he sought to run. His legs were tied, though, and after a few steps he tripped and fell headlong onto the temple roof. His head hit the stone with a ghastly sound, and blood covered his face. He spat out a broken tooth then began to bellow in the birdlike cha'asii tongue.

Essana watched, appalled at how unmoved she felt. How many cha'asii had died before her eyes? Fifty? A hundred? She had no idea. It had become a regular part of her life, as regular as the child's growth inside her. She could scarcely remember a time when she hadn't been forced to watch elves die upon the altar.

"The wretch resists their powers," said the Master. "Interesting. Keeper, inspect him."

Essana glanced at the Keeper, who took pains not to meet her gaze. They had spoken little of late—only when they were alone, and only long enough for her to ask one question, and him to answer.

When?

Not yet. Things are not ready.

She touched the firmness of her belly. It had better be soon.

The Keeper strode to the elf, peeled open one of his eyes to see how hurt he was, then shook his head and began to search his body. After several moments he found what he was looking for: a small talisman of bright green feathers, surrounding a little bauble of gold. The elf had concealed the talisman in his loincloth, sewn it directly into the garment; the Keeper had to slit the cloth with a knife to pull the charm out. He nodded at the yaggol, and they lowered their faces over the elf, the tentacles wrapping around his head. The cha'asii stiffened, gasping as their thoughts forced their way into his mind. The Keeper turned away, studying the talisman as he walked back to the other Brethren. Still he refused to glance Essana's way.

"They grow more cunning at hiding these," he said. "It may be that the yaggol's powers will not be of use to us much longer."

"We must study it," replied the Master, holding out his hand. "Find a way to overcome the spell."

The Keeper hesitated before giving the talisman to the other man. The two of them locked gazes, but Essana couldn't read anything in their bloodshot eyes. Finally the Master snatched it, and stashed it away within his cloak.

"Proceed," he said, gesturing toward the yaggol. The Keeper walked back to his place in the circle.

The hideous things dragged the dazed elf forward and dumped him on the altar. The cha'asii no longer struggled as the Speaker chanted the invocation.

"Hail the Faceless Emperor! Maladar an-Desh, lord of wizards, reaver of cities, the sleeper within the stone!"

"Hail, the Faceless," the Brethren replied.

And then, suddenly, the Keeper was staring not at the sacrifice, but at Essana. His gaze burned into her, and though he stood nowhere near, she shuddered as his voice whispered in her ear.

Be patient. Two days.

That was all. His gaze turned back to the bloodletting. Essana stared at him a moment longer, then looked away as the Slayer stepped forward, his knife flashing toward the elf's waiting throat.

✴━━━✖━━━✴

She dreamed often these days, and not all dark dreams. Increasingly, she dreamed of Barreth. One night, weeks ago, she'd seen him at the helm of a sailing ship, plying waters choked with ice. There were others with him, but they were nameless to her, shadows: she saw only her husband.

Later, she saw him again, aboard a different vessel—a great chariot that slid on blades over endless snow-fields, pulled by two massive deer. He stared ahead, at a line of spiky, ice-covered mountains. Clutched in his hands was a black dragon's scale.

And now, tonight, he was back on the ship again, only this time the vessel was somewhere familiar: the shallows of the Tiderun, heading east on a strong wind. On the shore to the north was a ruined town, burned and broken—Malton, a victim of the Uigan horde. Forlo did not look at the ruined town, however; his eyes were turned south, toward another heap of rubble. Half of Coldhope stood shattered atop its cliff overlooking the Run; the rest, from the Northwatch up, lay scattered in pieces around it, and down in the water below. Crimson words were painted on the parts that remained, in the language of the League.

Traitor. Coward. Regicide.

Regicide? Essana shook her head, refusing to believe it. Barreth was a good man; he would never murder the emperor. But her brow furrowed as she remembered another dream, an older one that had fled from her when

210

she'd woken: her husband, his face pale and spattered with blood, thrusting a sword into something she couldn't see. His eyes were wild, his expression bestial as he twisted the blade back and forth.

"You bastard," he growled, over and over. "You bastard. . . ."

A sound woke her, shredding the dream. She started, sitting up, a hand on her breast. She could feel her heart pounding as the cell door swung open. The Keeper stood there, hooded, flanked by yaggol. He spoke a word to them and they departed, then he stepped inside. The door slid shut again, but darkness didn't fully return. A nimbus of violet light clung to him, just bright enough to see by. He approached her.

Essana blinked. "Has it been two days already?"

"No," the Keeper replied. "Not yet. But I had to make sure you were ready."

"I am," she said at once. "I've been ready from the moment the dragon brought me here."

He nodded. She imagined a human face within the hood, rather than the horror he had made of himself so he could infiltrate the Brethren. She thought that face might be smiling.

"You are a strong woman, Essana," he said, "but there are still the yaggol to consider. Hold out your hand."

Fingers trembling, she did. He reached into the folds of his cloak and produced a talisman of cha'asii make. It wasn't the same as the one he'd taken from the sacrifice: the feathers were iridescent blue, not green, and the bauble in the middle was a bead of dark amber, with what looked like a mantis imprisoned within, but there was no mistaking the aura of enchantment as he placed it in her hand.

"Where did you get this?" she murmured.

"That warrior yesterday was not the first to carry such a token," he replied. "This one I took off a prisoner a fortnight ago. The old woman."

Essana remembered her: an elderly elf with long, silver

211

hair. She hadn't struggled at all. The thought that her salvation had come from a dead woman made bile boil in her throat.

The Keeper caught hold of her hand, made her close her fingers. "She would have died, no matter what," he said. "It was good fortune that I could take the talisman before the others discovered it. When the time comes—and you will know when it does—you must kiss the amber, and place it near your skin. The magic will keep the yaggol from dominating you."

He let go of her. Her hand stayed closed, clenched around the charm. She stared at it.

"When?" she asked.

"In the morning. Now I must go. I have more to do, and little time. We will only have one chance."

She squeezed the amber, smooth and cool. "I'll be ready."

He gazed at her a moment longer, then turned and walked away. The door opened and he was gone. The yaggol peered in, and she shrank back, keeping the talisman hidden from their empty eyes. The door ground shut again.

Essana clutched the amber in her fist. Half the night passed before she could loosen her grip.

She was still awake, what seemed like a thousand years later, when the sound of movement outside her cell roused her. She sat up, cold, sweating, her heart hammering. Legs prickling, she got to her feet.

The door opened. No one came in.

It could be a trick. They could have found out. The Keeper might have been fooling her all this time: part of the ritual, to give her one last burst of hope. The Brethren were that cruel.

There was a thud, and a wet smack, and something slid sideways across the doorway: gray, slimy, many tentacled.

One of her yaggol guards, its bulbous head smashed like a melon, full of pale mucus and ichor. Its eyes stared at her, glassy and dead. Good, she thought.

A shadow stepped over the abomination's corpse. The Keeper. He held a short weapon in his hand, like a hammer with a claw-shaped head. Ropes of white slime dripped off it.

"Come," he said. "Quickly."

She went, stepping over the yaggol's remains as they moved out into the hall. A second creature lay hunched against a wall, the left side of its face torn off, its right arm hanging broken at its side. One leg still twitched.

"A reflex only," the Keeper said. "Just like shellfish when you chop them up for supper."

"Thank you for that," Essana said. "I doubt I'll ever be hungry for seafood again."

He laughed at that—actually laughed, not the weird, croaking noises the Brethren usually made when they were amused. It seemed to surprise him as much as her. He reached to his belt and produced a second weapon, identical to the one in his hand.

"This is a krahd," he said. "A weapon of my people. We use them to kill armored creatures that dwell beneath our islands, called disir. It breaks through their shells very well—or skulls, as you see."

"I do," she said, accepting the weapon. It was heavier than it looked, with most of the weight in the iron head. A good swing would break through just about anything short of dragon hide. She gave it a test swing. "It almost makes me hope we'll find more of them to fight."

"Don't say that," the Keeper replied. "'The foolish wish is the first to be granted,' they say in my homeland. But I understand."

They went, the Keeper leading the way to a narrow flight of stairs, down, quietly, to another hall. Then more stairs. So it went, down and down, until she knew they were no longer above ground. They'd gone too far, and the air had changed—grown even warmer and damper, with the faint scent of earth. Water dripped down the walls over ghastly reliefs and etchings, and pooled on the floor. Insects scuttled across the flagstones, fleeing from their approach. Finally, the stairs ended in a large, low-ceilinged chamber—a cellar, filled with barrels, crates, and sacks. Glowing stones, set into niches in the walls, lit the room.

A shadow moved among the boxes. Essana gasped and raised her krahd—nearly hitting the Keeper in the face with its back end. He stepped away, his own weapon rising, ready to swing or hurl at whatever was out there.

"Ngaaghaj urkh hlauu," he spoke, in a tongue that sounded more like the gurgling of a drowning man than human speech. "Jhoch machauwa haakh."

Silence greeted him. Then, suddenly, a figure rose from behind a row of water casks. It was tall and slender, and its face writhed. Essana's grip on the krahd tightened a little—and again when two more yaggol appeared. The glow of the light-stones made their rubbery flesh glisten.

"Easy," the Keeper murmured. "Let them come closer before you strike. They trust me, remember?"

She nodded, saying nothing. The krahd lowered a little, but she couldn't make herself put it away completely, as he seemed to have done. He raised a hand, wriggling his fingers in greeting. The yaggol did the same in return, only with the cilia where their mouths should be. The nearest one let out a series of wet, questioning burbles that the Keeper answered with a gagging noise of his own.

"What are you saying?" she whispered.

"They want to know why I've brought you here," he said. "I told them it was because of the child you carry. You need specific food to eat, to make sure it stays healthy. They haven't been giving you these things, so the Master bade me bring you here so we could get them ourselves."

She frowned. "Will they believe you?"

"Not for long."

The yaggol glanced at one another, speaking silently by wriggling their tentacles. Essana felt a pulse against her breast, from the talisman. They were trying to breach her mind, and every time the protective magic thwarted them, they grew more agitated.

"Why don't you just use your magic?" she asked. "You must know something that can deal with them."

"Not without telling the Master exactly where we are. He's watching for trouble, always. If anyone casts a spell around the temple, he'll know. And he'll come right for us."

She could sense the yaggol's suspicion growing. "I should warn you, I'm not much of a fighter," she said. "Barreth taught me how to hold a sword, but I'm not very good with one. Or one of these."

"Neither am I," the Keeper replied. "But we don't have to be. The yaggol's power is in their minds. Physically, they're weak. If one comes for you, aim for its head."

"If?" she asked. They were creeping forward now, tentacles flurrying.

He shrugged, producing his krahd. "When."

Then they came, gargling as they charged, claws clutching at the air. The Keeper grabbed Essana's wrist in his free hand, spun, and shoved her away from them, then lashed out with his weapon. It hit the lead yaggol squarely in the side of its head, and the creature let out a horrible hoot as its skull split open. Something slid out and hit the floor with a splat, then the rest of the creature followed, limbs jittering. Bringing the dripping krahd around, the Keeper turned to face the other yaggol—

Only they weren't there. With a ringing, metallic sound, they vanished. Essana blinked at the suddenness of it, then felt a chill in her stomach as the chimes rang again behind her. She whirled, screaming, and the krahd came around in a wild arc that missed everything. The yaggol pounced, and she felt the clamminess of their skin against hers. With another yell, she raised the hammer and brought it down as hard as she could.

There was a noise like a stone dropped into a deep puddle of mud, and one of the monsters hit the ground. It took the krahd with it, the weapon's claws lodged in what remained of the back of its skull. Muck from the wound greased the handle, and it slipped from her grasp as the yaggol flopped to the floor. Lunging, she tried to grab it again. . . .

The last yaggol seized her, bony fingers latching around her arm, then spinning her around so they faced each other. The stench of swamp gas billowed from beneath the tentacles. Their tips reached out, caressing her face, and pulled her closer. She could see what lay beneath them now—an insane, gnashing mass of razor-sharp barbs and bony hooks, surrounding a toothless, sucking maw. Drool dribbled from the hole as it widened, seeking her flesh.

With a yell, the Keeper slammed into the yaggol, knocking it sideways. The creature tried to hold on to her as it stumbled away, and the cups on its tentacles nearly ripped off her face. The Keeper's krahd hacked deep into the flesh between the monster's eyes. The yaggol's head cracked in half, and it fell. Its claws kept plucking at the hem of Essana's garment, long after the rest of it lay still.

She was at the edge of hysteria, and had to fight the urge to shriek. The yaggol were dead. Neither of them was hurt. It was all right. It was all right. . . .

"Move," the Keeper said. "I killed the two up by your cell quick enough that they didn't make a sound. These fellows probably sent out thoughts that warned every one of their kin within two miles."

She nodded, staving off panic. "Which way?"

He said nothing, just hurried down the rows of crates until he came to the far wall. She jogged after, more aware with every step of the extra weight she carried. Her back ached. The child was huge, and not for the first time did she wonder if she would survive giving birth, even if she did make it to safety. She shook her head, irritated at the thought. There were more pressing things to worry about now, weren't there?

Propped against the wall were several enormous kegs, smelling of wine. The Keeper moved down the row, tapping each with his krahd, until one made a hollow noise. Grunting in satisfaction, he grabbed hold of the keg and half lifted, half rolled it aside. Behind yawned a narrow, dark tunnel, dug right into the rich jungle earth. It couldn't have been more than five feet high; both of them would have to stoop. And it was as dark as a dragon's soul.

"What's this?" Essana asked, drawing back. "Where does it lead?"

He turned, fixing her with a hard stare. "The cha'asii dug this passage long ago. They wait on the other side. Now come. I can hear the yaggol."

Concentrating, she found she could hear them too. The sound was faint, the slap of their webbed feet on the stairs down to this cellar, the chittering of their countless, tiny mouth-parts. Only then did she realize she wasn't even armed anymore—stupidly, she'd left her krahd still stuck in the dead creature behind them. Too late to go back: she had to get out of here, now.

Holding her breath, she ducked her head and scurried into the tunnel. The Keeper came behind, rolling the keg back into place. Darkness swallowed them both.

Chapter

18

BENEATH AKH-TAZI, NERON

Essana had thought the dark could no longer make her feel fear. Now, as she crawled behind the Keeper, she learned she'd been wrong. There were different kinds of darkness. Her imprisonment had been cold, bleak and hopeless, but it had also been solid, knowable. Down here, with earth beneath, beside, and above, she was aware of how easily she could die—no, not just die, but be lost forever. It would take only a weakness in the crude shoring timbers above her, or the slightest of tremors in the earth below. She would simply be gone.

Yet there was something even worse: the threat from behind. She waited and waited, as she and the Keeper dragged themselves through the dirt, for the sound of the barrel rolling aside and the gurgling and slithering of the yaggol. She'd barely gotten away from the group in the cellar; here, there was no room for her to fight—and no weapon to fight with, either. She could almost feel their bony fingers closing around her ankles, the cold, wet kiss of their tentacles on her skin. She shuddered.

And felt the first of the aches.

It began more as a twisting feeling that something wasn't right. She fought, trying to find a way to keep the cramp from

218

building, but couldn't stave it off. It gathered, settling in her gut as muscles bunched and something down there stirred.

Oh, no, she thought. Not now. Not here.

It passed quickly, thank the gods, and ahead the Keeper kept going, none the wiser.

"How far?" she grunted, sweating. A shower of dirt poured down on her.

"Soon," he murmured. "This lets out at a secret place, a quarter mile from the temple. Not very far, but they'll still be looking inside, tearing the cellar apart."

"They'll find the keg," she said.

"Yes. But I've put spells of distraction on it. They won't notice it as long as there's anywhere else to look. That should give us a chance—unless one of the Brethren comes to help them."

She nodded. "And if one does? Then what?"

"Then we're in trouble."

"Oh."

They crawled on. The going got harder with every yard. Her knuckles and knees were scraped, bloody. Her shoulders burned. Her back felt ready to snap. But all these little pains faded when the second wave of cramps hit.

Worse than the first, they were intense enough to steal her breath away. She stopped, sucking dusty air through her teeth as she tried to fight through the pain. Her hands clutched her middle. Her belly felt wrong—not as firm as before. Something was moving inside.

No, she thought. No, no, no, no . . .

"Nnnnnnngh," she groaned.

The Keeper finally realized something wasn't right. He stopped, robes rustling as he twisted to look back. Violet light glimmered around him, falling on her as well. His hood had come off, revealing his not-face. With the pain now like a hot iron in her stomach, she barely even noticed.

"What is it?" he asked. "It can't be the child. You're not due for weeks!"

"Tell me all about it," she replied, her teeth grinding.

She rolled onto her side, trying vainly to draw enough air into her lungs. Tears tracked down her face, leaving trails of mud. Finally, the agony began to subside. She lay still, drained, without the strength or will to budge.

"No," the Keeper said, bringing himself around. His hands touched her, first her throat to find the life-beat, then her stomach. His fingers jerked at what he felt there. "This isn't right. This isn't supposed to be—"

He stopped, suddenly pressing the side of his head against her stomach. He had no outward ears—they had gone along with the rest of his face—but the holes in the sides of his head served well enough. He listened, shaking his head.

"What is it?" Essana asked, her voice high with fear. "Damn it, tell me!"

"You're miscarrying!" he snapped back. "The child's dying—and if it does, you'll likely die with it."

It was hot and dank in the tunnel, but Essana felt like she'd been doused with ice water. When she finally found her voice, it was quiet and small. "Help me. Please. There has to be a way."

"Not down here, there isn't," he said. He raised his head and looked up and down the passage. "Shalukh! Of all the times. . . ."

"Keeper!" she cried, her voice breaking. "You have to do something."

A small voice in her head spoke. It sounded like her own, but calmer, older, wiser. *No he doesn't,* it said. *Send him away. Let the child die.*

Another cramp came on, and the world went red, then white. The tunnel, the Keeper—everything vanished in the enveloping pain. She screamed, waiting for the warm wetness that would signal the inevitable.

It didn't come, though; the pain subsided to a dull throb, not quite going away. The world returned. The Keeper was talking, but his voice sounded far away. She choked, wiping blood from her mouth. She'd bitten her tongue.

"What?" she asked.

"I said, as soon as you think you can move again, we've got to go," he replied. "If we get out of here, we can find the cha'asii. Between their healers and me, we might be able to stop this before it's too late. But we have to move fast. Can you do it?"

She didn't think so, but she couldn't tell him that. The next cramp would probably make her lose consciousness. But they had to do this. *Had* to. They'd come too far to give up. She drew a shaky breath and nodded.

"Good," he said. He turned around again, brushing dirt from the wall. The ceiling groaned, sending down showers of grit. "It's only a little way more."

He went on, not looking back. She hated him for it, but she also understood. He was forcing her find her strength, and she found it. Rolling over, she clawed forward again. Her womb never stopped aching. Time became a yawning chasm. They probably crawled only a few hundred more yards, but it could have been all the way back to Coldhope, the way it felt. Near the end, she became aware of a low, rushing sound, up ahead. She tried to see what it was, but there was only blackness, broken by the faint purple glow around the Keeper. She dragged herself on until she bumped into him from behind. He had stopped.

"We're here," he whispered, pressing his hand against a wall of stone before him. He bowed his head, murmuring spidery words, and a low thud shook the tunnel, bringing down dirt all around them.

With a scrape, the stone parted, then swung open. Beyond lay a cave. The air was cool, fresh. It felt better than anything Essana had ever felt as they dragged themselves out of the passage. She lay gasping on the floor. The Keeper bent over her, running his fingers over her middle, then listening again. The rushing noise was much louder.

"There's still time," he said. "Can you stand?"

She shook her head. She could feel another cramp coming: a big one. The fear must have shown in her face. Drawing his hood back over his head, the Keeper bent down and lifted her in his arms. He was stronger than he looked; even Barreth would have had trouble hoisting her while she carried the extra weight of her pregnancy. He turned toward the cave's mouth, and she saw the source of the sound: a waterfall, pouring down beyond the opening. It gleamed ruddy gold, the setting sun bright behind it.

"It's all right," he told her. "The cha'asii will be waiting at the pool below. They'll take us to safety. You'll be better."

From the tone of his voices he didn't quite believe it either, but she nodded, leaning her head against his chest as nausea and pain gathered around her. She wept in anticipation of how bad it was going to be. The waterfall grew louder and louder, deafening her. They stepped out onto a ledge, then started down a path along the cliff face beyond. . . .

And stopped. The Keeper sucked in a breath. "No!" he gasped.

The pain was still growing, not fully bloomed quite yet. She turned her head, looking out past the thundering falls. The water plunged over a precipice some sixty feet high, down a cliff alive with vines and creepers, to a churning pool below. She squinted, trying to make out what had caused the Keeper to panic, and then she saw it: bodies, strewn along the pool's far shore, their blood staining the foaming water pink.

Elves. Cha'asii. Their rescuers.

Around thirty yaggol stood among them. They stared up the slope.

"Oh, gods," she murmured. "Keeper. . . ."

"Did you truly think we didn't know where you were going?" asked a voice, very near.

The Master appeared, stepping out of the shadows where the path descended to the jungle. Two other hooded figures stood with him, along with a dozen more yaggol, their tentacles twisting.

"I found your tunnel weeks ago, traitor," the Master said. "I've known you were a spy even longer, but I chose to humor you, hoping to catch you at your subversion and find out who you were working for. Even I didn't think you'd be so bold as to smuggle our prize out of the temple. Not until the yaggol began to die, anyway."

"Don't come any further!" the Keeper shouted. "I can still rob you of the child. I'll throw her over the edge!"

Essana started, staring at him in shock. "What?"

The Master only laughed. "Go ahead. My magic will catch her before she hits the water."

The Keeper looked down at his fellow Brethren, weighing the truth of the words. He shook his head. "I'm sorry, Essana," he said and set her down on the stone. He turned to face the other Brothers.

"Wait," she breathed. She couldn't move now; the cramp was bending her in half, making bile boil in the back of her mouth. "Tell me . . . one thing, before this is . . . over."

He looked down at her, his hideous eyes shining. "What?"

"Your . . . name."

He hesitated, gazing at her, expressionless. "Azar," he said. "Azar ket-Turang."

She nodded. "Thank you, Azar. For trying."

The Keeper stared a moment longer, then sighed and walked away, down toward the Master and the others. She heard shouting and the clamor of magic and a scream, but she couldn't look. The ache in her belly was too great.

Then the ache burst, and she knew no more.

The flames were everywhere, all around—great red tongues of fire, hundreds of feet high, filling the sky, bathing everything in their ruddy glow. Below, at the foot of the rocky promontory where she stood, magma seethed beneath a thin black crust of hardened stone. Geysers erupted from fissures, hurling bombs of fire high into the air. Smoke choked the air, black and thick. From those terrible clouds a rain of ash fell, fat, gray clots drifting on the baking wind.

The heat would have killed her in an instant, had this been real. But Essana knew it was a dream, a vision consuming her as the Brethren bore her back to the ruined temple. It kept away the real pain of what was happening, the spasms that were trying to purge the child from her womb. Her baby, the one she and Barreth had longed for, the only chance they would ever have of an heir—dying. And she was glad.

They would try to stop the purging. The Faceless would use all their powers to save her son's life—and hers with it. She prayed for them to fail. "Let us die, Mislaxa," she whispered. "We are ready. Do not spare us."

"Speak for yourself, woman."

She stiffened at the sound of the voice behind her. It was familiar, like her husband's, but not. There was none of Barreth's warmth, the fire that had drawn her to him. This voice was cold, flat, scornful. Slowly, she turned.

He looked like Barreth too, but not completely so. He was younger, his hair full and long, his skin a bit darker, closer to her own. He had no beard. But the strong jaw was the same, as was the heaviness of his brow. He wore blue robes that shimmered in the firelight.

Essana's mouth dropped open. When they came, her words were soft, almost inaudible. "My son?"

He smiled, but cheerlessly. His gaze stayed flat, detached. "You seem surprised to see me, Mother," he said. "What, no embrace? No kiss for your beloved firstborn?"

She shook her head; then something in the distance caught her eye. It was the Chaldar, the Tower of Flame, rising like an accusing finger from the sea of lava. Fire bathed its surface, crimson and gold and blue.

"This will be my home," her son said. "No—our home, for I will take you with me. I will remake Taladas as it was—and we will rule, together! I as the emperor who once was, and you as queen-mother! The lesser realms will fall, one by one . . . the Rainwards, the League, the Silvanaes, the ragged tribes of the Tamire. All will bow to us, to Aurim reborn."

She shook her head, tears tracking down her face. They tasted like soot and hot metal. "Not us, child," she murmured. "Never us. You cannot fool me—you are not my son. You are Maladar, and you will not share power. No—I will fight you. I will save my son, even if it means his death . . . and mine."

His smile froze, shattered, falling away. His expression revealed bare hate, glittering like a knife's edge. "You no longer have a choice in that, Essana," he hissed. "Do you think you are the only one I speak to? The child and I have known each other for some time now. He belongs to me now. That is why he rebelled when you tried to flee. Now that the Brethren have reclaimed you, he will be well again. And you will live to see him born."

She stared at him, a cold stone in her heart. She understood now. The Master had found them not because he was clever, but because he had been warned. The child had told Maladar of the plan to escape, and Maladar had told the Brethren. The child had betrayed them. The knowledge drove the strength out of her, and she sank to her knees.

"Oh, gods," she moaned.

The boy looked down, the reptilian smile returning. He drew a dagger of black iron from his belt. She shrank back, but the blade wasn't meant for her. Instead, he set its edge behind his right ear. His eyes burned red, no longer human.

"Blood for the Faceless," he said and began to cut.

Essana woke with a scream, trying to sit upright—but a sudden, wrenching agony in her wrists kept her from rising. She fell back, gasping, sick, weak. There was light here—wherever *here* was: cold, gray light, shining down from a source she couldn't see. She lay upon a table of volcanic glass, cold and hard against her back. Shackles bound her wrists and ankles, the chains taut enough to make her shoulders and hips ache. The only part of her that could move was her head, and now she craned and twisted to see what was around her. The room was small, dark, with a low ceiling and glowing crystals set into the walls. Drapes of purple satin hung to either side of her, sealing off the ends of the room. Behind the one on the left she heard quiet movement; to the right, slow, steady breathing.

Some foolish part of her wanted to call out, to ask who was there. She swallowed the words; she didn't want to draw attention. But it didn't matter: an instant later, she felt a mind touch hers, cold and slippery and inhuman. Yaggol. They had found the talisman—no surprise. She hadn't really tried to hide it. The alien mind slithered around, inspecting her thoughts, then coiled itself, forming words.

She wakes . . .

The movement behind the left-hand curtain stopped. There was a moment's silence. Then the cloth jerked back and the Master strode through. Behind him was a worktable, festooned with glasswork and phials of powders and pickled insects and tentacled things floating in jars of brine. He had been doing something to a beaker that bubbled over an open, blue flame with no obvious source of fuel. Greasy brown smoke flowed over the phial's edges, down onto the tabletop. Two yaggol stood at either end of the table, watching as the leader of the Brethren approached her.

She swore at him, conjuring the vilest oath she could think of. He stopped, taken aback, then shook his head and chuckled.

"My delicate lady of Coldhope," he rasped. "I had begun to wonder if you would ever wake. It has been a week since your pathetic attempt at escape."

She blinked. A week? It seemed like only hours ago that she'd collapsed by the waterfall, the pains of miscarriage overwhelming her. Only hours since the Keeper let out that terrible, agonized shriek and blackness came down.

She looked at her belly. It was round and firm again, even more distended than before. The pain was gone. Essana shut her eyes, letting out a forlorn sigh.

"Yes, the child lives," the Master said. "Though it was a near thing. You came quite close to ruining everything . . . you and that miserable turncoat, the Keeper. It didn't work, though—and now things are far worse for you. You will remain bound like this until it is time for the child to be born. You will only be unchained to attend the sacrifices. We cannot let you try to stop us again."

She said nothing, only glared at him, hate boiling inside.

She wonders about him, said the mind of the yaggol. *The traitor. She wishes to know his fate.*

"Do you?" the Master asked, mocking. "You would learn of your savior? He lives, you know. We decided to leave him alive. Do you wish to see him?"

He lifted his gaze, looking beyond, toward the other side of the room. The other curtain. The breathing. Essana swallowed, shaking her head.

"No," she said, her voice dry. "No, I don't—"

She lies, thought the yaggol. *She yearns for it. The truth.*

The Master laughed, gesturing. "Very well. Look, my lady, and see what remains of the one who would have betrayed us to the Rainward kings."

The curtain pulled back. The breathing grew louder, more rapid. Essana fought the urge to look—and lost. Against all better judgment, she turned . . . and screamed.

They'd hung him from the ceiling, from chains and hooks jabbed deep into his back. After that, they'd started with his limbs: the cutting. Both legs were gone at the knee, both arms at the elbow. Next they'd put out his eyes, and torn out his tongue. Then they'd ripped off his skin, like the Brethren had stripped away their own faces, laying bare bloody sinew and bone. Lastly, they'd cut him open from the base of his throat to the top of his abdomen. The flesh spread wide, like glistening wings. Beneath, she saw the white of his ribs, and within those, his lungs—still pink and twitching, in time with his tormented breathing. Between them, the fist-sized muscle of his heart beat rapidly.

She shut her eyes, looked away—all too late. The sight of the Keeper had burned into her mind, and was all she could see. She began to sob.

The Master laughed and laughed as the curtain swung shut again.

Chapter

19

THE BOILING SEA

Shedara was tired. She'd been tired for days now, taxed by spell after spell, by the moons' power coursing through her, by every moment of waking and sleeping. Relying on magic made her feel weak, irritable, all but useless in the day-to-day work aboard the boat—which Forlo had now dubbed the *Starlight*, after his wife. But the magic was necessary. The alternative to being tired was being dead.

They had sailed back down the coast of Northern Hosk, leaving the Panak behind. When they came to the Run, they'd tacked to port and gone on down its length, taking care not to get too close to any minotaur vessels out on the strait. For Forlo and Hult, it had been a hard journey. At the Run's western end, the signs of the Uigan's defeat still remained: bodies of men and horses, drowned and smashed by the great wave, lying bloated and burst on the rocky shores while crabs and gulls plucked at what flesh remained. There were hundreds of corpses, but Shedara knew it was only a small part of the doom she and Maladar had wrought upon the riders. Thousands more had been swept out to sea, forever lost.

Then they passed the Lost Road: the tower where Forlo had fought Chovuk, which now stood empty, the ravine still torn and muddy from the battle. Beyond lay Malton, a wrecked ghost of a city, its charred walls standing eerily silent, and Coldhope across from it. They kept away from Forlo's old home, bearing north to keep it as far from view as possible. Even so, he stared ever southward, and one morning cried out at the sight of the keep looming in the distance. Following his gaze, Shedara understood why—though it was too far to see anything but dim shapes, there was no mistaking what had happened. Coldhope was shattered, torn down, reduced to rubble. It shouldn't have mattered to him—he could never have returned to his home, even if it were whole—but Forlo was silent and angry for days afterward, just the same.

Finally, they came to the Run's eastern end, and things began to change. The air, which had carried winter's chill, grew warmer. The snow dusting the shores disappeared. Mist clung to the sea's surface, and in the distance, massive, yellow clouds hung above jagged mountains on the distant shore. They had come to Indanalis, the Boiling Sea.

Like the Run, the Sea had been born in the First Destruction. Before that terrible day, it had been a long inlet in Taladas's south shore, running for hundreds of leagues from the jungles of Neron all the way up to the mountains of the Fianawar dwarves. When the rain of fire fell on Aurim, however, and turned that empire into a roiling cauldron of molten rock, the lava flowed outward on all sides. To the north and east, it coursed over land, cooling into sheets of obsidian and badlands of basalt pillars. To the west and south, however, the lava poured into the water—and kept pouring, every day for more than four hundred years. The waters of Indanalis were forever changed: they boiled constantly, giving off noxious steam that poisoned the lands on either shore. Things still lived on the coasts, and in the depths, but the creatures were twisted, corrupted—foul to look at and wracked with pain from the day they were born until their merciful deaths.

This was their road, the quickest way to the valleys of Marak—eight days' sail down the Indanalis, then ashore and through the passes of the Steamwall Mountains, which kept the fertile lands to the west safe from the Sea's fumes. When they crossed into those waters, Shedara's spellcasting began in earnest. Some people, such as the surviving Fianawar, had perfected sailing ships that could survive journeys across the superheated waters, but *Starlight* was not so well protected. So, for the last two nights before they crossed into the Indanalis, Shedara had walked the boat's deck, gouging protective glyphs into the wood with her knife. She made hundreds of carvings, against the terrible heat and unpredictable currents of the Boiling Sea, then—when it was done—drew down the power of Solis and Lunis and bound it into the boat. Enchantment seethed all around them, a shield that kept *Starlight* safe from harm—as long as she renewed the magic every night. If she didn't, they would all die in moments.

Nor was that all. Protecting the boat was one thing, but there were still the people aboard to consider. The fumes of Indanalis were lethal to anyone who breathed them. The bodies of those who did were seldom found, but occasionally an ill-fated ship was found wallowing at the edge of the Sea, crewed by corpses frozen in throes of agony, their faces swollen and blue, dry blood crusted around their ears, eyes, and noses.

So Shedara worked her magic on the four of them as well, every few hours gathering the power to cast spells to protect them when the boat passed through a bank of noxious fog, or when a great bubble of gas rose from the sea floor to the surface. Even so, they all grew sickly and pale, constantly coughing as the vapors burned their lungs. And Shedara grew wearier every day, as the ship hugged the sulfur-crusted coast, riding the scalding waves.

On the seventh night, when she was done with yet another round of spells, she coughed so violently she collapsed, the taste of blood warm on her tongue. Hult and Eldako helped her up—Forlo stayed at the tiller, keeping them on course—and brought her belowdecks, to lie down on her bunk. When she was resting, Hult took his leave, heading back up to help work the sails. Eldako remained, though, wiping sweat from her brow with a cloth. She coughed again, and he blotted red from her lips.

"Thank you," she wheezed.

He nodded. "When we were in Panak, I swore I would give anything to be warm again. I fear I may have prayed too hard."

Shedara's eyes narrowed. She looked at him hard, trying to figure out if he was joking. The merkitsa was hard to read. "Maybe you should pray for clean air," she said. "I don't think too much of that would be bad."

"True," Eldako said, his brow furrowed. "I will ask the ancestors for it. Perhaps Hult can ask Jijin, as well. And you might ask your moon-gods. The more powers we have on our side, the better."

He smiled then, taking her by surprise. And he was holding her hand, too—he'd started by measuring her life-beat on her wrist, but hadn't let go. She looked away, afraid of what she might see in those pale, blue eyes—and what he might see in hers.

She'd always avoided entanglements when she was working—and most of the time when she wasn't. They caused trouble.

"Tell me about Marak," he said.

She blinked. "Hmm?"

"Marak. You have been there, yes?"

"Yes," she said. "Some time ago. Like you, with the Ice People. It's a grim place. The kender used to be a happy people, but the Destruction did terrible things to their valleys. The trees are stunted, the rivers gray with ash. There are earthquakes all the time."

"Yet the kender stayed."

She shrugged. "Where would they go? There are hob-goblins in the mountains north of them and Thenol to the south. And they wouldn't find warm welcome in the League. No, they're trapped there, and it's changed them. They're a gloomy lot, and they don't have much love for outsiders."

"If any remain," Eldako said. "They may all have been changed into shadows."

Shedara hesitated, then shook her head, sighing. "I doubt that. They're good at hiding, and there are more of them than people realize. Still, if we can find a way to stop what's being done to them, we must. We swore to my brother that we'd try."

"Yes. And there are other deaths to avenge, as well."

She was silent, thinking of all the people she'd seen killed by the shadow-fiends. Angusuk's tribe were only the latest in a long line that included many of her own people—her queen included. Yes, there was a reckoning ahead.

She coughed again, but there was no blood this time. The ship heaved and listed to one side, then slowly righted itself. Above, she heard Forlo swearing in the minotaur tongue.

"Another gas bubble," she said.

Eldako nodded. "They could probably use another set of hands up there."

"Go on. I'll be fine down here. Wake me in a few hours, so I can cast the spells again."

He looked worried and might have objected, but thought better of it. Instead, he bent low and kissed her on the forehead. Then he let go her hand and rose, leaving her with her thoughts a mess, lying in the brimstone-stinking dark.

It took a while for her mind to calm enough for sleep.

They had feared, during the whole journey, that they would lose the boat. They all knew it only survived because of Shedara's magic; unlike in the north, they couldn't just leave it moored in the Boiling Sea while they made the trek to Marak. Without it, they would have a long journey ahead, through hostile lands: neither Thenol nor the League would be safe for travel. They could make landfall in the Hulderwood, a tract of ancient forest to the north, but the hulder-folk, a race even older than the elves, were not friendly to outsiders. Still, with so few roads open to them, it was the only way.

On the last day of their sail, however, luck saved them. The sheer cliffs of the Steamwall retreated, leaving real coastline for the first time in days. Here the Sea had retreated a little, leaving a long beach of black sand, scattered with soot and slashed by steaming crevices. Forlo made for land at once, bringing the *Starlight* to shore and running it aground. They furled the sails and tied ropes to the hull so they could haul it out of the boiling water. Even pulling with all their might, it took Forlo, Hult, and Eldako four hours to pull the craft onto land. By the time they were done, they were all exhausted, and Hult was coughing flecks of blood as well.

With a relieved sigh, Shedara let go of the spells that had protected the ship. The air around them seemed to crystallize, then shattered, tinkling pieces vanishing before they hit the sand. She shut her eyes, trying to find her strength.

"We can't stay here," she panted, waving her hand at the yellow fog that hugged the ground. "We'll die. We have to go inland, out of this mist."

None of them replied; none had breath enough to speak. Leaning on one another, staggering like drunkards, they made their way west, away from the bubbling waters. Once they were above the mist, at the edge of the Steamwall, they called a halt and slumped down onto the ash-caked rocks.

"Sorry you stayed with us, Eldako?" Forlo asked.

The merkitsa spread his hands. "I have seen places more terrible than this. I have traveled to the edge of Hith's Cauldron itself, where only gnomes and fire-minions dwell and the land itself melts away. But I am glad to leave this behind us, for now."

Hult nodded, opening his mouth to speak, but he fell into another coughing fit. Forlo pounded on his back until the barbarian shoved him away, shaking his head. Shedara rooted through her pack, looking for her maps.

She didn't have a very good one of these parts—she'd never thought she would come this way when she set out in search of the Hooded One, those many months ago. The map she did have was old and not very detailed. She scratched the back of her neck, studying the chart.

"There," she said, pointing at a line that snaked into the mountains. "This used to be the wash of a river, from the looks . . . probably dried up years ago. We can follow it into the mountains and pick up a larger pass that'll take us out the other side."

They all watched her trace the route through the Steamwall. "It'll be a bit of a climb," Forlo noted. "I don't see anything better, though."

"Not for a hundred miles," agreed Eldako. "Let's just hope the land hasn't changed much."

As if summoned by his words, a quake rumbled the ground. It was just a small temblor, but enough to bring them all to their feet. In the distance, a cascade of broken stone slid down a mountainside, throwing up billowing cinder plumes.

"Well," Shedara said. "Only one way to find out, isn't there?"

They set out inland, following the riverbed. It was hard going, all loose shale and scree, dotted with bigger boulders that had fallen from the heights above. The earthquakes continued every few hours, causing more rockfalls, and at times they had to make their way around hissing fissures that led to hidden depths. But they put the Sea behind them, rising above the worst of its vapors as it vanished from view. For the first time in days, the air began to smell clean again, and no longer burned their eyes and lungs.

"Now . . . can . . . we . . . rest?" Hult gasped.

They looked at one another—tired, pale, weak—reaching a silent agreement. They wouldn't be of much use unless they slept, and the sky was getting dark anyway. Shedara cast about and spied what she was looking for: a dark opening on one slope, with no steam pouring out of it. She pointed, and together the group picked their way among the rocks, up over the shifting gravel to the cave. Drawing their swords, they made a torch and got it lit, then went in.

The cavern was shallow, the ceiling low: as shelter, it wasn't much. But nothing lurked inside, and Shedara, for one, felt she could fall asleep on a mountaintop in a thunderstorm. They made themselves as comfortable as they could, ate a little—they were nearing the last of their provisions—and drank careful sips of water, rationing what they had. Then, at last, they lay down, their cloaks bundled for pillows. It was uncomfortable, almost painful, but Hult was asleep the moment he laid down his head. Forlo snored loudly half a minute later.

Shedara and Eldako stared at each other across the cave. He smiled at her. She tried to smile back, but she couldn't move her mouth anymore. Her eyelids, leaden with fatigue, closed—then flickered open—then closed again. . . .

✦——◼◼——✦

. . . then opened once more, to something prodding her side.

"Hey!" she yelled, snapping wide awake. She pulled back, reaching for her sword, and discovered it was no longer there. Twisting, she got to her feet, her head whipping around—

There were nine of them: little people, barely more than three feet tall. They had elfin features, but their faces were gaunt, wrinkled with premature age. Their long, dark hair was bound up in braids and tassels, threaded with feathers and beads of brightly colored stone. They wore black and gray only, shapeless garments that reminded her, just for an instant, of the shadow-fiends. They stared at her without fear. Three held staffs—one had used his to prod her awake—and the others had bows of pale wood, fitted with pouches on the strings, each holding a heavy, round rock. Hoopaui, the weapons were called. Wielded properly, they could break a man's skull at a hundred paces. The little folk looked ready to do so, at a word from their leader—a lean, graceful female whose face was daubed with streaks of white paint. She looked the four of them up and down, crow's feet deepening around her eyes, one hand resting on the haft of an iron war-axe.

Shedara smiled. The kender had found them.

Chapter

20

MARAK-IN-EXILE, THE STEAMWALLS

His sword was gone. His dagger too. But Forlo had been a fighter all his life, and had even learned a few things from the monks who worshipped the god Manith, who were forbidden from carrying any weapon greater than a walking stick, and so had taught themselves to fight with their bare hands and feet. He was no master of astakha, their art of battle, but he knew a few surprises.

He eyed the kender now as he slowly rose from where he lay, and settled into an easy, relaxed pose, one foot slightly ahead of the other, arms hanging loose at his sides. From there, if the need came, he could drop to a stance the monks called Clutching Griffin, and lay into his enemies. The stone-bows worried him a little, but as long as they didn't shoot him in the face or the knee—or the groin, gods help him—he could probably endure a few hits.

For now, though, he stood still, his eyes flicking to the others. Eldako had settled into a stance of his own, taut as the string of his missing bow. Shedara was eyeing the kender's leader, the woman with the axe. Hult was the most troubled of them all, patting his chest frantically. The amulet Nalaran had given him was gone. Looking around, Forlo saw one of their captors was wearing it, along with four or five other necklaces of various styles—human, hobgoblin, even one blocky thing that had to be of dwarven make.

"Tell him it's all right," Forlo whispered to Eldako. He nodded to Hult, who was on the verge of becoming frantic. "It's just kender. They take things that interest them. We can get it back."

As long as we don't get ourselves killed. . . .

"You should not be here," said the leader of the band, in thickly accented League-speech. "These are Marak lands. Outsiders do not belong."

"Marak lands?" Shedara asked. "But your valleys lie inland, many leagues from here."

The kender exchanged dark looks, a couple of them muttering under their breaths. The one with the axe held up a hand, and they were still. "We dwell here now, in the mountains," she replied. "The valleys are no longer ours."

"I see," Shedara said. "Then the shadows have driven you out completely."

"The shadows? What do you know about them?" the kender exclaimed, startled. Her fellows chattered amongst themselves in a mishmash of languages: elven, minotaur, hobgoblin, dwarven, and three or four human tongues as well. Forlo blocked out the babble—he'd tried to learn kender-speak once, from those of the little folk who liked to follow the Sixth Legion's supply train, searching for interesting items to "borrow" from it. The experience had nearly driven him mad. There didn't seem to be any rules to it at all.

"We have fought them, many times," Shedara said. "They overran my people's woods as well."

"The shadows trouble the Silvanaes?"

Shedara nodded. "They trouble us all. This may have started in your valleys, but it has spread far."

The kender prattled to one another. The leader turned and said something to one of them, an older-looking fellow with close-cropped white hair and a long scar that ran from his temple down to the corner of his jaw; he'd lost half his right ear to the same wound. He stepped forward to face Shedara.

"If you have fought them," he said, "then you will know the answer to this. What do their bodies look like, after they are killed?"

Shedara smiled. "There are none. They dissolve into smoke."

The elder kender regarded her, eyes narrow. Then, finally, he broke into a broad grin.

"You are what you say, then," he said. "Friends to the Marakai. I am Yale Highclover. Once I was an elder of the valley-folk, but now I am an exile, like all who escaped the shadow-blight. This is my daughter, Tanda." He gestured to the woman with the axe, who spoke a word to the archers. Warily, they lowered their hoopaui.

Shedara bowed her head. "I am Shedara, once of Armachnesti. These are my companions—Forlo of Coldhope, Hult of the Tamire, and Eldako from the Dreaming Green. We are exiles too."

"We seek the leader of your people," Forlo interrupted. "We must speak with him."

There was a pause, then the kender broke out laughing. Even Yale chuckled, and shook his head when he saw Forlo's face darken. "I'm sorry," he said. "You must not know our people's ways. We have no leaders—not like the emperor of your League. Shame to hear the new one's dead, by the way. No, we kender take care of our own . . . or did, until the shadows came. I'm the last elder left, the only one who got away when the darkness came . . . so I suppose you'll have to settle for me."

"And me too," put in Tanda. "I'm the one who's in charge of rescuing our people."

"Then are there other survivors?" Shedara asked.

Tanda glanced at her father, who made a grim face and waggled his hand. "A few," he said. "About eight hundred of us fled when the shadows came, but many have left for other lands, and more than a few have died since. The Steamwalls are not a pleasant place. We number maybe half as many now."

"We lose about as many as we save from the shadows," Tanda added. "Perhaps more. Our numbers are dwindling. But we have to keep trying, don't we? Better to die fighting than let our people turn into *them*."

Forlo raised his eyebrows. The kender he'd known had been flighty creatures—not selfish, exactly, but certainly not like these. The Marakai's experiences had changed them, made them more serious. They were like war-orphaned children, grown old before their time. He didn't know how to feel about that: he'd found their curiosity as annoying as any commander might—one had even tried to wander off with his company's battle-standard, once—but seeing them like this, hungry and hunted and even a little grim, only reminded him of all that had changed in the world since the Hooded One had entered his life. Was there anyone in Taladas who hadn't suffered because of the statue and those who had stolen it?

Eldako leaned close to Shedara. "Hult can't understand any of this," he said. "They took the talisman."

He nodded toward the kender with all the necklaces, and Shedara turned back to Yale and Tanda. "We will talk more about this blight," she said. "But before we do, I must ask for our possessions back. Our weapons, and the jade amulet your man is wearing, there."

Father and daughter muttered to each other. After a moment Yale turned back, while Tanda issued several sharp commands to the other kender.

"You must understand," the elder said, "we did not know if you were friend or foe. We took your possessions for our safety, nothing more. We are not thieves."

"Of course," Shedara said, smiling. "We would never accuse you of such a thing."

Forlo suppressed a grin of his own. Kender, as a race, were driven by the need to pick up anything interesting that wasn't nailed down—and to look for a pry-bar for things that were. And they always had an excuse for it. It made them unwelcome in most lands

It took a few minutes, and a certain amount of extra encouragement from Tanda, for the kender to give up everything they'd taken. Eldako made sure to count his arrows before slinging his quiver across his back again. Hult gave the little folk a dirty look when they handed back the amulet, and only relaxed again when he'd slipped it back around his neck. Forlo felt a surprising flash of envy toward Hult—at least now one of them would be able to follow kenderspeak.

"Is that everything? Good," said Yale. "Now, we were speaking about the shadow-blight—"

A call arose, then—an odd noise, halfway between a hoot and a howl. Several of the kender looked toward the cave mouth, and Tanda whispered to her father and went to peer outside. She cupped her hands to her mouth and echoed the call, which came back a moment later. The kender's faces darkened, their hands tightening around their bows.

So serious, Forlo thought again.

"What is it?" Shedara asked.

"Trouble," Yale replied. "We set watchers before we went in here. The fiends come into the mountains every few days, trying to find us. They need us to make more of them, you see. They're—"

"Father!" called Tanda. "We have to go!"

He glanced back at her, then nodded. "I'm sorry," he said and gestured to the other kender, who hurried toward the cave mouth, hoopaui at the ready. "My daughter is right. Come on—we'll take you back to our own caves, where we'll be safe. Or anyhow, I hope we will."

The kender's hiding place was three hours' brisk walk to the southwest, along a path hidden by gray, scraggly brush. They never saw the shadows that were stalking them, but Forlo could feel them—a coldness out there, a sucking hole in the warmth of the winds that scoured the Steamwall. After a while, the feeling got fainter, and the kender's scouts returned. They looked the same as the others, but their faces and hair were smeared white with ash—camouflage enough that even Eldako didn't spot them until they were close.

More scrub covered the cave's entrance; the kender had woven it into a kind of curtain that pulled neatly aside as they approached. More ash-smeared scouts watched them from outcrops and ledges, stones tucked into the pouches of their bows. Tanda hooted to them, and they relaxed a little but kept wary eyes on the visitors, just the same. Forlo kept his hands away from his weapons as he walked by them, and gave them each a nod of respect. The Marakai were a cunning and secretive people; he was used to kender being nothing more than pests. For the first time, he wondered how much he might learn from them.

They entered the cave and stopped. A second curtain blocked their way, this one made of dark felt. It stayed shut until the brush-screen closed behind them, then drew aside, opening into a wide, firelit space full of kender. Hundreds of them filled the cave, all silent, watching as the party strode in. Then the felt curtain pulled closed, and the little folk went back to what they were doing— talking, laughing, cooking, playing flutes and drums. It was something close to carefree, a semblance of what their life must have been like before. There was a sadness lying just beneath the surface of the merriment, though; a knowledge that, for this generation at least, things could never be as they were. Perhaps in the future, the Marakai would know joy without fear again. And then again, perhaps not. Sometimes, a people's scars were too deep. Forlo found himself staring at Hult as he thought about that. The Uigan's scars would never fully heal.

The scouting party dispersed, spreading out through the cave to join their families and friends, leaving Forlo and the others with Yale and his daughter.

"I have never seen so many kender in one place," Eldako said.

"It's a little frightening," Shedara agreed.

"This is nothing beside what it was like before the troubles," Tanda said, shaking her head. "But what you see are all the free Marakai who remain—except the ones on patrol or guard duty, this is virtually every kender who escaped the shadow-plague, and who hasn't turned his back on his people."

Yale glanced at her sharply. "Hush, child. You know we don't speak of such things in front of the others." Tanda bowed her head, chastened, as Yale looked back at Shedara. "For many of the valley-folk, the pain of what happened is still too near. Come—there are deeper caves where we can talk freely."

"Keep your hands on your valuables," Shedara cautioned in a low voice.

They soon discovered how serious she was. Kender congregated around them as they crossed the cave, staring with mournful eyes, occasionally reaching out to touch them. One tried to take Eldako's sword; another reached for Hult's amulet; a third actually managed to get a buckle undone on one of Forlo's boots before Tanda and Yale could shoo him away. By the time they reached a tunnel at the cave's far end, the mass of little folk around them had grown so thick that Tanda had to shove her way through, then stay behind to make sure none followed. Yale led them down a sloping passage toward another cave. The sound of dripping water rose to meet them.

Halfway down the tunnel, Hult suddenly stopped. He sniffed the air, then looked to his left and right and walked over to the passage wall. "Something lived here, before," he said. "Something large. . . ."

He ran his hand over the stone, and Forlo saw what he'd seen: deep furrows gouged into the rock, as if by massive claws. In other places, the stone looked to have melted and run down to the floor in undulating lumps, like candle wax.

"A dragon," Eldako murmured. "This was its lair."

Hult found something lodged in one of the furrows. He bloodied his knuckles prying it loose, then swore under his breath and held it up for all to see. It was a scale, night-black, with an opalescent sheen—identical to the one they had brought to the Namer. Eldako shook his head, looking at the ground.

"Where is he?" asked Forlo at once. He took two steps toward Yale before Shedara caught his arm, stopping him. "The dragon who used to live here. Gloomwing. What happened to him?"

"He is gone," Yale replied, his face creased with disgust. "And good riddance to him. Away to the south, away from us. If only he had gone sooner—but the damage is already done."

"Damage?" Shedara asked. "What do you mean?"

Yale sighed. "It's all part of the same story. Come with me, and I'll tell it to you."

They came to a smaller cavern with a deep pool in its midst, shining in the light of several oil lamps placed around its edges. Its surface rippled as water dripped down from long, sharp stalactites. More furrows marked the floor, as well as scarred and pitted patches of rock—eaten away by Gloomwing's acidic breath. A few more scales lay scattered about as well; Forlo picked up one of them, stared at it in disgust, then threw it out across the water. It dropped into the pool with the faintest splash and sank from sight.

Will this chase never end? Forlo thought. Essana, will I ever see you again, or will I just keep chasing this damned wyrm until I die?

Yale led them to the pool's edge, where the floor was flat and even. A pitcher and several cups sat there; with these, the kender scooped water from the pond and poured some for each of them. They drank—the water tasted refreshingly cold and clear, with a mineral tang that was actually quite pleasant. It was good to have something to wash away the stink of brimstone. Forlo drank deeply, then poured himself a second cup and nursed it while Yale sat down at the water's edge. Tanda came to join them. They all looked to the elder kender, who gathered himself, as if shouldering a heavy burden, and began to speak.

"There was a time," the kender explained, "not so long ago, when our people flourished. Yes, the valleys were dangerous places, and there were enemies all around, but we were safe there. We lived. We thrived. We had peace, even through the Godless Night. But when the Night ended, it all changed.

"I should speak of Gloomwing first, since you already know of him. He lived here, in this very cave, for longer than we can remember. He was othlorx—an outcast wyrm, who rejected the call to war across the sea, almost a hundred years ago. He believed he had a greater purpose than to fight and die for foreign masters. And . . . it feels strange now to say it . . . he was a friend to our people. Often he would fly over the valleys, keeping enemies away. He loved to hunt hobgoblins. He even let some of us speak with him, sometimes. I was one of those fortunate few. He told me he wanted only peace and to be left alone. We believed him. What fools we were."

Tanda leaned close, resting her hand on his arm. "Father. . . ."

"No, child," he said. "It's the truth. We were stupid to trust him. That we live here now is proof enough of that."

"Did he start the shadow-blight?" Shedara asked. "Is he the cause of . . . of all of this?"

Yale was silent a moment, staring into the water. "Not quite. It wasn't directly his doing . . . but yes, he was responsible. One day he came to Marak and summoned the elders to him. He said he had brought someone . . . an ally of his, who would change life for the kender forever. We thought, fools that we were, that he meant the change would be for the better. We had no reason to think otherwise—as I said, Gloomwing had always been our friend.

"But it was all a lie. Gloomwing had no love for the kender—he just thought we might be of use to him, at some point. And we kept enemies away from this cave, I suppose." He smiled, but it quickly faded. "Anyway, we went and met with him, and he introduced us to his ally—a man in a black robe, with a hood that hid his face. He had no name, or none he gave us. He called himself—"

"The Teacher," Hult said.

Yale's eyes widened. "You know him?"

"Yes," Hult replied. "I have met him."

That was all he said—no mention of Chovuk Boyla, or the doom of his people. He did lay a hand on his sword, though, the fingers curling tight about the hilt. Forlo saw the knuckles turn white.

"Well," Yale went on, "that saves some explaining. The Teacher spoke to us of a new life for the kender. He said that, with his help, we wouldn't need to worry about the other races of the world anymore—that we would become stronger than them, and they would leave us untroubled. Most of us believed him—I know I did. I didn't realize until much later that it wasn't his words that made that belief, but magic. He charmed us all into doing his bidding."

Hult bowed his head, his maimed hand rising to pinch

247

the bridge of his nose. "Yes," he murmured. "That is how he works."

"He asked us to gather the clans all in one place—a clearing on the edge of Starshimmer Lake, right in the middle of Marak. We did as he bade, but not all the kender agreed to come. In fact, less than half traveled to the lakeside. My own clan refused, thanks to Tanda—she didn't trust this Teacher, and now I see that she was wiser than me."

"No, Father," she said. "Not wiser. He just didn't use his magic on me."

Yale nodded, giving her a smile, but the pain in his eyes was obvious. He reached out, squeezed her hand. "She even managed to keep me with her, long enough to miss the . . . the ceremony. For that I owe her everything, because when the Marakai gathered at Starshimmer, the Teacher made good on his promise. He cast a spell that would make our enemies fear us. It did make the kender stronger. But it also turned them into shadow-creatures. They became servants to darkness. Their enemies would fear them . . . but they were forced to do his bidding."

"Killers, bound to his will," Shedara said.

"Yes."

"But he didn't get all of you," Forlo added.

Yale shook his head. "Some of us resisted him, tried to keep the shadows from overrunning the valleys. That wasn't very smart, looking back—they were stronger than us, and many kender were caught or killed. Any who were captured, they brought to Starshimmer, where the Teacher made shadows of them too. He comes back often, when the black moon is full, to perform the ritual. The shadows are always looking for more victims. We're safe for now, but one day they'll find these caves. And then . . . then the Marakai will be gone for good."

He stopped, a weight of sorrow in his eyes. Tanda took his hand, clasping it tightly while tears trickled from the corners of his eyes. Forlo let him have his sorrow. His people were dying, doomed to vanish from the world if things continued as they were—and Yale felt responsible. Ensorcelled or not, he and the elders had helped cause Marak's fall. Finally he sucked in a long, shuddering breath and looked up with eyes red with grief.

"As for the dragon . . . he left after the Teacher came. I suppose he felt his work was done. We haven't seen him since. I doubt Gloomwing will ever return to the Steamwalls."

"Do you know where he went?" Forlo asked.

Yale shook his head.

Forlo's face reddened. "Khot," he said.

Hult's eyes were grim. "We have lost the trail, then."

"No," Shedara said. "There's still a way. One who knows."

Eldako smiled, understanding. But Hult frowned. "Who?" he asked.

Forlo looked at Yale and Tanda, then at the Uigan. He knew what the elf meant. "The Teacher," he said. "We'll have to get what we need from him now."

Chapter

21

LAKE STARSHIMMER, MARAK

Hult crouched low, a hand on his sword, watching the shadow-fiends from behind a looming boulder. He hadn't drawn the weapon yet; none of them had. In the twilight, naked steel might catch the dying sunshine. They couldn't afford that until they knew they were safe. Well, safe for now—everything was relative in these parts.

Marak was as the kender had said, a wasted land—not destroyed, but emptied, its villages overgrown by weeds and creepers, swathed with putrid mist. He had not seen a single living soul since they left Gloomwing's cave, except for their own party: him, Forlo, Shedara, and Eldako, with Tanda and half a dozen hoopaui-wielding kender scouts. Yale's daughter had led them through the mountains on safe and hidden paths, four days' hard travel, to the mouth of Bost-Marak, the northernmost of the five valleys that had been her people's home. Down through stunted and twisted forests they'd descended, following a foaming brown river. Now, at last, they had come to the long shores of Starshimmer, gleaming like blood in the gloaming. Here they finally caught sight of the shadow-fiends in what was, for want of a better word, their home.

There were seven or eight of them, maybe more—the way they blended with the darkness, it was hard to get a good count. They gathered near an old fisherman's cabin on the pebbly lakeshore—a crumbling, ivy-choked cottage whose thatch roof had long since fallen in, whose windows were almost all broken, and whose dock had half-collapsed, leaning sideways in the water. The fiends gathered around the dock's base, a vantage that gave them a view of the whole eastern end of the lake.

"Sentry party," Tanda whispered, peering through the woods. "I count ten. That's a lot for around here. Usually they only gather in groups of four or five."

"Could they know we're coming?" Forlo asked.

The kender shook her head. "The way we took was secret. And they'd have sent a pack to stop us if they knew we were here. We never would have made it this far."

"It's the black moon," Shedara said. "It's full tonight."

They all nodded. Hult cast a nervous glance at the sky. He had only heard of Nuvis, Krynn's third moon. Unlike Solis and Lunis, the silver and red orbs, Nuvis wasn't visible, except by marking the stars it eclipsed. It was the source of dark magic; evil would be strong in the world tonight. Strong enough for the Teacher to go about his foul work.

The Teacher. Hult licked his lips at the thought. He hadn't dared hope he would again see the one who'd corrupted his master. Now, the black-robed apparition who'd whispered lies and fed power to Chovuk, all those terrible nights while the horde was riding . . . he was somewhere out there, perhaps gazing upon this very same lake. Hult's blood burned for the chance at vengeance.

But not yet, not right away. They needed the Teacher to reveal his secrets first.

"We can take them," said Eldako, fitting an arrow on his bowstring.

"I know," Tanda said. "I just wanted to make sure

there weren't more, lurking out there somewhere. But they look like they're alone. There aren't many shadows left in Marak, these days. Most have gone away—to the elf-woods, I guess, from what you say." She turned to the other kender, pulling the axe—her chapak—from her belt. "Jaster. Rinn. You're on draw-out duty."

Two of the scouts nodded, grinning, then rose from where they crouched and started down toward the lake, moving with the appearance of stealth but making just enough sound to hear them go. Hult smiled, recognizing the tactic. His people had used this strategy often against the rival Kazar: sending out a small group to lure the enemy, then pulling them straight into a greater force and springing the trap. He glanced at the others and saw that they, too, understood. Forlo was nodding, and Eldako had pulled his bowstring halfway back to his cheek. Shedara's eyes were shut, her lips moving soundlessly. Hult felt a shift in the air, the elf's magic beginning to stir. He tightened his grip on his blade and watched around the edge of the rock as the kender stole toward the lake—then froze, staring at the cabin. The shadows had spotted them.

The kender ran, the shadows streaming behind them. Jaster and Rinn had huge grins on their faces as they pelted back uphill toward the boulder: in spite of everything, in spite of all their suffering, kender were kender. This was fun for them.

The shadows poured after them, terrible and silent, now five steps away, now four, now three. . . .

"Down!" Tanda yelled, leaping up onto the boulder. She raised her axe. "Hoopaui!"

At her command, Jaster and Rinn threw themselves flat on the needle-strewn ground. At the same time, the other four kender leaped up, raised their stone-bows, and let fly. Eldako did the same. Three of the shadows ripped apart, and the other seven stopped, just for a moment—long enough for Jaster and Rinn to scramble for safety. Shedara jumped up next, stretching a hand out toward the shadows. She spoke a single word, and three bolts of white fire sizzled through the air, blasting one of the remaining shadows in the face. It tore to shreds.

"Now! Blades, go!" Tanda shouted.

Hult didn't need to be told. As soon as the missiles leaped from Shedara's fingers, he yanked his sword from its scabbard and charged. Forlo was right behind him, and Eldako, too. Tanda leaped down from the rock with her axe held high. Shedara and the other kender came last.

The shadows shrank back, understanding too late that they'd been fooled. Hult hit them first, swinging his sword around in a wide arc; it just missed one of the creatures. A second parried the same stroke with one of its sickle-bladed knives. Hult shoved hard, pushing the shadow back—then had to duck as another blade whistled toward him. He felt it brush the bristly hair on top of his head.

Then Forlo was there, his own sword hacking down, and the shadow cried out and vanished. Hult heard other shrieks as Eldako and Tanda laid in with their own weapons. Then he twisted and spun, his blade slicing low, through the ankles of the shadow who'd parried him. The creature howled and collapsed, then dissolved as he drove his sword through the emptiness where its heart had once been.

He heard a shout and whirled to see Forlo beset by another shadow. He leaped at it, sword humming through the air. It took off the top of the monster's head, trailing darkness behind.

And just like that, it was over. One of the kender lay on the ground, groaning—Hult saw it was Rinn. A shadow's knife had sliced his arm open, and the bloodless wound was already blackening around the edges. Eldako whispered with Tanda briefly and gave her herbs for Rinn's wound. She, in turn, passed them to Jaster, who set about making the healing poultice.

"Come on," she said, beckoning. "You can see from here."

Tanda led them down to the lake, where the water lapped at the shore. The dock creaked; a half-drowned boat sat low in the water, thudding against one of the pilings. Another lay hull-side-up on the shore. Tanda pointed out across the lake, toward the far side, maybe three miles away. Hult shaded his eyes: the last sliver of sun was just now vanishing behind the hills. Above, the first stars flickered in the purple sky.

Across the water, several large fires burned in a broad clearing, sending black smoke curling high over the lake. In their midst stood a small ziggurat of red stone. More flames burned on the platform at its top. Shapes moved around it, like a seething tide.

Shadow-fiends. Hundreds of them.

"That's the place," Tanda murmured. "They're getting ready for the ritual again."

"Do you think they heard anything?" Shedara asked.

The kender shook her head. "The chanting would drown out anything that carried across the lake. Listen—you can hear it from here."

And they did. Concentrating, Hult heard a low, droning noise, in a language he could not speak, even with the amulet—but which he recognized just the same. It was the same speech he'd heard coming from Chovuk's yurt, on those awful nights while the Boyla fell deeper and deeper under the Teacher's sway. He felt a stab of regret—why hadn't he stopped this? He'd known something foul was happening in the tent in that seemingly long-ago time . . . why hadn't he forced his way in and put an end to it?

He shook his head. He'd thought at the time that he was doing his duty by not questioning his master. Now he had an opportunity to undo his mistake.

"We're already late," Tanda said, her brow wrinkling. "It'll take us hours to get around the lake. The rite may be done by the time we get there."

They were silent, looking out across the water. Behind them, Rinn moaned in pain as Jaster daubed salve on his arm. They would have to leave him here, continue with one fewer. At least no one had died. . . .

"We could cross the water," Eldako said, nodding at the beached rowboat. "It would be quicker."

Tanda shook her head. "They'd see us coming."

Hult turned, looking at Shedara. So did Forlo and Eldako. One of her eyebrows rose. "I think," she said, "I might be able to do something about that."

✳━━━✳✳━━━✳

The boat slid across the lake in silence, leaving almost no wake behind it. The oars dipped into the water gently, raising only the smallest ripples, which were soon swallowed by chop whipped up by the wind. No one who wasn't looking for it would have noticed any sign of its passing.

No one spoke, for fear of being heard. There was no need, anyway: they had worked out the plan on the shore, before Shedara cast the spell of invisibility. They watched the far shore, growing nearer with every stroke. The ziggurat shone like a beacon in a sea of darkness, the shadows moving around it in a circle. The fires atop it leaped higher, cold, blue flames that made Hult's scalp prickle to look at them. The sounds of many low, chanting voices—so dark and somber, it seemed impossible the creatures they belonged to had once been kender—carried across Starshimmer's surface. There were too many of the creatures to fight. If they landed and tried to take the ziggurat, it would end badly.

"You'll need a diversion," Tanda had said, standing by the ruined dock. "We're good at that, my people. If we attack from the flank, they'll come for us. It should draw enough of them away, for you to do what you need to."

"Six? Against that many?" Forlo had asked. "They'll cut you to pieces."

The kender had only smiled, shaking her head. "Just like a soldier—thinking the only way to fight is head-on. We'll hit them, then fade away. Pick 'em off one by one. Keep moving, never let them get a clear shot at us—or figure out how many of us there are. We've done this before; trust me."

The shore was close. Forlo and Hult—who had been working the oars the whole way across—pulled to the left, turning the boat. There was an outcrop of stone, crowded with moss and pines, five hundred paces from the ziggurat. They made for the rock, shipping the oars so the boat coasted up to bump against it. Eldako caught the rock and held them steady as the kender clambered out, one by one.

"Remember," Shedara whispered. "The first shot you loose—"

"We'll be visible again," Tanda finished, flashing a quick grin. She hopped out, landing nimbly on the shore. "We know, don't worry. We won't let them get a good look at us. Wait for my signal."

They nodded. No one wished anybody luck. It seemed a bad idea, somehow, to do so. Perhaps it was the black moon, hanging fat in the east. Hult glanced that way, at the jagged teeth of the Steamwalls. Above the peaks, he imagined he could actually see Nuvis, an ebon disc like a hole in the sky. He could certainly sense its power, which gave the air an unnatural chill and made his mouth run dry. He swallowed, then brought his oar back down as Eldako pushed them away from the rock. The boat came about, and he caught a glimpse of the kender hoisting themselves up the stone and slipping away into the forest.

They glided along the shore, back toward the ziggurat. The magical fires roared even higher now, writhing pillars twenty feet tall, their color shifting slowly to green. They gave no smoke, made no sound. The boat drew within thirty paces of the foul structure—close enough that when he glanced over his shoulder, Hult could see small figures clustered at its pinnacle, bound and gagged and blindfolded, but still squirming and struggling, trying to get free.

Kender.

A bubble of hate formed inside him. He'd known only a few kender before coming to Marak, and had found them to be pests in the best of circumstances. But the sight of the little folk, helplessly awaiting their fate, made him furious. His fists tightened around the oar; it was all he could do to keep pace with Forlo, rather than trying to drive the boat forward, as fast as it could go.

Fifteen paces from shore, they lifted the paddles out of the water again. The shadows were thick, a thriving mass always in motion, murmuring in the tongue of dark magic. They raised their sickles, waving them in the air like so many scorpions' stingers. Now and again, one threw back his head and screeched at the stars, a sound that could have been agony or rapture—or possibly both. They laughed, mocking the kender's struggles, the same struggles they themselves had surely put up before the Teacher ruined them.

And then, all at once, they fell still. A hush descended on the clearing, broken only by the creaking of trees and the splash of water upon the rocks. The fiends' swirling ceased, and they parted as a figure moved among them, toward the stairs carved into the ziggurat's side. Hult saw him, and the hate bubble inside him swelled. The Teacher had come.

He had seen the black-cloaked man only twice before—once, briefly, in the Dreaming Green, and again in Chovuk's yurt, the night before the slaughter at the Run. Still, he had no doubt it was the same man. There was an aura about him.

He climbed the steps slowly, rising above the shadows. They bowed, prostrating themselves upon the ground. He ignored them, rising to the top of the ziggurat and walking to the center of its roof. The captive kender shrank back, whimpering through their gags. A soft radiance gathered around him, a putrid turquoise, the color of corruption. The flame-pillars at the ziggurat's corners were the same ghastly hue. It drained the color from the world; in that light, the kender looked pallid, gray, already dead.

"Where's that damned diversion?" muttered Forlo, his hands tight around his oar. He looked like Hult felt: tense, ready to leap into battle now, the odds be damned.

Shedara touched his shoulder. "Be patient."

And when he starts killing the kender? Hult thought. Or whatever it is he does to them? How patient should we be then?

He didn't say anything, though. He only watched, eyes burning, as the Teacher raised his hands to the black moon. The fingers began to move, weaving through the air with disturbing grace, the gestures of magic. He spoke spidery words, the same ones the shadows had been chanting. His voice was deep and resonant, carrying an unmistakable sneer. Hult knew it well. The aura around the Teacher grew brighter, and he bent down and seized one of the kender by the arm. The poor creature whimpered as he wrenched it up into the air.

Eldako already had an arrow nocked; now, his face pale and stony, he pulled his bowstring back to his ear. Shedara shook her head, mouthing *wait*. For a moment, it seemed he might not listen, but finally he relaxed his grip on the string.

Hult knew the kender in the Teacher's grasp was doomed, that they would have to watch him meet his fate, unable to help without throwing their own lives away. That knowledge made it no easier. As they looked on, the Teacher placed his free hand over the wriggling creature's face. The kender's struggles grew frantic—then ceased, his entire body going slack. The air around him grew hazy, like he was wreathed in black smoke, swirling around and around his small, limp form. His flesh, already wan in the witch-light, began to wrinkle and wither, stretching thin over his bones and skull.

Hult made a low, animal sound. Shedara glared at him, eyes glittering.

"Not yet!" she breathed. "Wait for the signal . . . and remember, we need that bastard alive."

Hult said nothing, his lips curling into a snarl.

Shedara shook him. "Hey! Do you understand?"

He blinked at her, then came back to himself. He nodded, and she let him go. Atop the ziggurat, the Teacher dropped the wasted kender, who fell to the stones in a boneless heap . . . then twitched and rose, darkness swelling around him, his bonds falling away. A quiet sigh rose from the congregation of shadow-fiends as their newest kin started down the steps to join them. Nodding in satisfaction, the Teacher bent to reach for another kender.

Then, at last, they heard it: a soft, hooting noise, from the direction of the outcrop where they'd left Tanda. A commotion, too—shadow-fiends shrieking their death-cries as the first stones rained down on them. In moments, the gathering dissolved into chaos, dark forms streaming away into the night. Oblivious, lost in the rapture of the ritual, the Teacher lifted the second kender from the ziggurat's roof.

Hult and Forlo exchanged glances, then looked at Shedara and Eldako. The elves nodded. It was time.

His hate bubble bursting, Hult began to row.

Chapter

22

LAKE STARSHIMMER, MARAK

They were still five paces from shore when Hult leaped out of the boat, ripping his sword from his scabbard as he vaulted over the side. Eldako tried to grab him, but the Uigan was too quick, and the next thing they knew he was splashing through knee-deep water, his face red with rage as he slogged toward land. With him gone from his oar, the boat began to slew sideways, out of control. Forlo let go of his own paddle and jumped out too, leaving it unmanned to coast the rest of the way, crunching at a slant onto the stony beach.

The shadow-fiends didn't see them as Hult hurled himself toward them: their attention was either on the commotion caused by Tanda and the other kender or on the Teacher atop the ziggurat. Forlo followed on the barbarian's heels, his own sword ringing clear of its sheath. Uncertain, the creatures turned to face this new threat. Shedara cursed and jumped down onto the beach, a throwing dagger in each hand. Eldako rose where he stood, steadying himself as the grounded boat shifted beneath his weight, then drew back and loosed an arrow at the fiends.

The shaft tore through shadow-stuff. There was a howl and one of the creatures faded away.

The merkitsa drew a second arrow, sighting down its length. He was visible now, and the fiends charged, sickles slicing through the air, pointed teeth bared—right into the path of Hult and Forlo.

They laid into the shadows like a pair of farmers scything a field of millet. Swords rose and fell, then rose again, trailing wisps of blackness. Shrieks of the damned filled the air, and shredded shadows erupted all around them, leaving a smoky haze in their wake. They drove straight through the shadows' midst, bound for the ziggurat, where the cloaked figure of the Teacher stared down at them, his face inscrutable in the shade of his hood. The sorcerer dropped the kender he'd picked up and walked to the edge of the pyramid's roof to look down at the sword-wielding maniacs who were streaming toward him.

He began to chant. His hands danced. He extended a finger. Forlo saw it but couldn't do anything to stop it—could only keep hewing at the shadows, cutting them apart as they surged and boiled around him.

"Shedara?" he shouted. "Eldako!"

The warning wasn't necessary; the wild elf had already seen. With a yell, he let go a shot, straight at the Teacher. The shaft was aimed at his knee, rather than any vital part . . . enough to bring him down without killing him. But the Teacher saw the attack coming. He barked a sharp word, and the arrow burst into flame, burning away in an instant. All that hit him, when it was done, was a puff of white ash that powdered the hem of his robe.

The hooded head rose toward the boat. The hands followed. A spear of white-hot flame flared from the Teacher's fingertips and screeched through the air, over Forlo's head. The boat exploded in a gout of fire and burning splinters that peppered the ground like hail. Forlo risked a glance over his shoulder and saw Eldako lying on the rocks, his arms covering his head as scraps of smoldering wood came down all around him.

The Teacher's fingertips danced as he spoke the words of another spell. Forlo had to fight the urge to fling his sword at the sorcerer: it might save the merkitsa's life, but the blade was the only thing keeping the shadows from ripping him apart. He clenched his teeth, preparing for Eldako's death-cry.

It never came. Instead, the Teacher let out a howl, and one leg gave way beneath him, buckling. He stumbled and barely kept himself from falling down the ziggurat's steps. Forlo craned his neck, looking to see what had happened, and caught sight of the hilt of a knife, sticking out of the back of the Teacher's thigh.

Shedara.

She was there now, on top of the pyramid with him—had taken advantage of the shadows' attention on Forlo and Hult to skirt around and climb the ziggurat from behind. Now she stalked forward, drawing her shortsword as the Teacher spun to face her. The black moon's power seethed around the sorcerer, and he shaped it with an incantation that twisted in Forlo's mind like brambles. His hand came up again, and with a crack a bolt of green lightning flashed toward Shedara.

She dropped her sword, bringing her own palm around just before the bolt could strike, and shouted a counter-spell. The lightning struck her hand and erupted in a storm of sparks that fell, harmlessly, to the ground—but the effort was taxing, and she gritted her teeth to hold back the Teacher's magic. Finally, with a yell, she lost control and the bolt burst into a storm of flaring energy, blowing her back over the pyramid's edge, down the stairs, out of sight.

The Teacher watched her fall, satisfied, then his knee gave out and he fell onto one side with a shout. After that, Forlo lost track of what was going on up there: the shadows were thickening around him, knives spinning in deadly circles. He snapped his sword left and right, quick, precise.

Two patches of darkness vanished, but many more advanced. Hult was pressed against him now, a whirlwind of steel and Uigan curses, killing and killing again.

Then Eldako was there too, battered and bloodied by the boat's destruction but still fighting hard, in the dancing style of his people. He came in low, his long, slender sword whipping around and down, catching a shadow across its neck. The shadow-fiend ripped apart, and Eldako ducked and rolled to thrust the blade straight through another's gut. Forlo let out a whoop of joy as the merkitsa carved his way to them: the third blade was all they needed to break the wall of shadows between them and the ziggurat. Hult leaped through the breach, bounding up the stairs with a roar of fury. The Teacher was waiting, and stabbed a finger at the Uigan. With a flash, a dart of magic launched and plunged deep into Hult's left shoulder. The smell of burning flesh hit Forlo, fierce and sharp.

But the wound didn't even slow Hult down. Too angry to know he was hurt, he leaped up the last few steps, to the ziggurat's roof. Stunned by his ferocity, the Teacher tried to back away, but his leg gave out and he stumbled again. He raised a hand, fingers tensing to unleash another spell. Hult bellowed, hacking down with his sword. The sorcerer's arm came off at the elbow and fell over the edge of the pyramid, flopping halfway down the stairs to lay still.

The Teacher screamed, clutching the stump where the limb had been. Blood poured over the stones as he collapsed. The remaining shadows hesitated at the sound, turning to look—giving Forlo and Eldako time to cut them to pieces. They looked up at Hult as the Teacher tried to scuttle away. The Uigan's face was a mask of vengeful madness as he strode forward, sword held high.

"No!" Forlo shouted, running up the stairs. Eldako was charging up behind him, and both of them knew they wouldn't be able to make it in time. His face twisted into a crazed grin, Hult brought the sword down. . . .

A second blade appeared out of nowhere, blocking it with a crash. Hult staggered back, startled, and looked to see Shedara. Pale and shaking, she shoved him away from the Teacher.

"No!" she said. "We need him alive."

He stared, dazed, not comprehending. Forlo made it to the top and stood with her, putting himself between Hult and the Teacher. Eldako did the same. When the Teacher tried to drag himself farther away, though, the wild elf turned and held his blade at the sorcerer's throat.

"Oh, no," he said. "You're not going anywhere."

"He has to die!" Hult said through clenched teeth.

Forlo shook his head. "He has to *talk*. I haven't come all this way to lose Essana because you want quick justice for your people."

"And I want the Hooded One," Shedara added.

For a moment everyone was still, and Forlo thought they might come to blows. But in the end, the madness lifted from Hult's eyes, and he let his sword drop. It clattered down onto the ziggurat's roof.

Forlo looked around. Eldako still had his blade at the Teacher's throat. The surviving kender lay where they had been throughout the fight, bound and gagged. He pointed at them with his sword.

"Come on," he said. "Let's get the little folk free—and then get out of here. There are still a lot of shadows out there. We need to get away before they regroup. And keep a close eye on the Teacher. He may still have some tricks."

"Don't worry," Eldako said with a cold smile. "If he makes a move, the other arm comes off. And after that, the legs."

The Teacher glared up at him, his hood still hiding his face. Forlo thought about ripping that mask, off but decided to let that wait for later. Instead, he followed Shedara and Hult, in a hurry to set the kender free.

Tanda and her warriors found them an hour later, in a ravine not far from the fisherman's house. Forlo and Eldako met them with swords drawn, but stood down when they called out with their hooting signal. The rescued kender, unbound and gathered in a miserable cluster as far from the Teacher as possible, perked up and looked curiously toward the path as Tanda's group made their way down to join the group. There were only four of the six left. One of the missing was Jaster.

"The others?" Forlo asked.

Tanda shook her head, her expression grim.

They took a moment, after the kender had all introduced themselves to one another and sorted out whose possessions were most likely to be whose, to mourn those who had died. Then Tanda posted her three remaining warriors as guards around the camp, and they turned their attention to their prisoner.

Eldako had managed to get the stump of the Teacher's arm to stop bleeding, tying a bandage up near his shoulder during a pause as they'd fled around the edge of the lake. The sorcerer was delirious, though, drifting in and out of shock.

Grimacing, Shedara pulled back the man's hood. Tanda cried out in horror at the grisly skull-mask that glared back at them. Forlo felt his stomach turn at the sight, even now. Eldako muttered something Elvish under his breath.

Hult bent down, a dagger glinting in his hand. He set its tip against the Teacher's left cheek. The blade made a sickening *click* against the exposed bone.

"You remember me," he said. "Don't you?"

The Teacher didn't answer; only stared, his eyes ablaze with hate.

Hult moved the dagger up, slowly, until the tip was a finger's breadth from the Teacher's eye. "Don't you?" he asked again, an edge of steel creeping into his voice. "You've seen me before, with Chovuk Boyla."

With an effort, the Teacher swallowed. With the dagger so close, his nod was almost imperceptible.

"Good," Hult said. The blade didn't waver. "Then you know I am Uigan. Because of your meddling, my people rode to their deaths. We horse-folk take vengeance seriously. It is a cleansing rite for us. I would like nothing more than to make you scream before you die."

The blade flicked, serpent-quick. The Teacher tried to draw back, but wasn't quick enough. The jab was aimed just wide of his eye, though, and left the orb untouched. Instead, it cut a small nick out of the bony bridge of his nose. He hissed between his teeth, resentment blazing in eyes—but fear, too.

Hult flashed an evil smile, then pulled back and motioned to Shedara and Forlo. "Ask him what you will. I'll be here if he needs . . . encouragement."

They all nodded. They had scripted this part, working it out while the Teacher was slipping in and out of consciousness. Now Shedara sat closer to the Teacher, resting a hand on his good shoulder. Forlo crouched down on the other side, his swarthy face stern.

"You serve Maladar the Faceless," he said. "You're part of some cult. You bred the shadows to help you steal the Hooded One and to spread chaos to cover your tracks. True?"

The Teacher only glared at him. Shedara shook her head.

"Hult?" she asked.

Smiling, the young barbarian stepped forward, balled his hand into a fist and punched the Teacher in the leg—right where the throwing-knife had struck him. The sorcerer cried out, writhing, his stump waving in a pathetic effort to clutch the wound. Hult hit him again, and a third time; then Shedara held up a hand.

Forlo grabbed the skull-face, his lip curling at the feel of it against his fingertips. He wrenched it around, made the Teacher look at him. The sorcerer's eyes had dulled a little.

"He'll do that again when we ask," Shedara said, her voice carefully devoid of emotion. "And if he gets tired, Forlo here will take over. And then maybe the kender would like a chance as well. We all have scores to settle with you—especially me. You tried to kill me, didn't you? In the Necklace, and again at Coldhope."

The Teacher shook his head. His voice, when it came, was weak and scratchy. "That was not me," he gasped. "That was the Slayer. It is not my role to murder for the Brethren."

"No," Tanda said. "It's your role to destroy. To corrupt. To enslave our people and turn them into . . . into. . . ."

Forlo shook his head at the kender. "Easy, Tanda. He'll answer for those crimes. But he must talk first." He turned back to the Teacher. "These Brethren . . . how many of you are there?"

"There were six . . . six of us," the Teacher answered. "But now there are five. The Keeper betrayed us, tried to help the prisoner escape before her child could come. But he failed, and he paid the price."

Forlo stiffened. The world around him sharpened, as if a veil had lifted. His heart beat quickly. "Prisoner?" he asked. "Essana? You have her still?"

The Teacher's eyes flicked to him, sparkling with cruel humor. If his face were capable of it, Forlo knew the man would be smiling. They locked gazes for a long moment; then the Teacher turned away.

Forlo reacted without hesitating, before any of the others could react. Snarling, he ripped his dagger from its sheath, reversed the blade, and hammered the pommel into the Teacher's face. There was an awful chorus of snapping sounds as the blow broke half the man's teeth . . . and his jaw besides. He raised the knife again, but Eldako and Hult caught his arm and pulled him back. Forlo struggled, but Eldako pressed a spot on the inside of his elbow and his hand went slack. The dagger fell into the dirt.

The Teacher lay gasping, his jaw askew, splinters of teeth dropping from his mouth. His head drooped. Shedara shook him, trying to rouse him, but his head lolled and he didn't wake. "Damn it!" she growled. "We were so close!"

Forlo shook his head, breathing hard, his face red with anger. "Don't lecture me!" he snapped. "If it were your brother instead of Essana, and he gave you that look, you'd have done the same."

"I think I'd have more brains than that," she shot back. "If he dies, your wife dies with him. And your child. Now stay back and let me finish this, if I can."

She leaned forward, touching her fingertips to the Teacher's throat, feeling for the life-beat. A moment passed; she shook her head and shut her eyes.

"Is it bad?" Eldako asked.

She gave him a look. "As opposed to good?"

"I mean, are we losing him?"

"Not yet," she said. "But I don't know if he'll come around again before he dies . . . and he probably won't be able to talk if he does. Not with his mouth all in pieces."

"Khot," Forlo swore, then turned away, angry at himself.

"What now, then?" Tanda asked. "Is there anything you can do?"

They all looked at Shedara, who hesitated, then nodded. "My magic," she said. "I can search his mind. I was hoping to avoid that—reading the thoughts of a man like this is never pleasant. But it may be all we have left."

"Do it, then," Eldako said.

She nodded, then closed her eyes, turning her face up to the heavens. The red moon was high and waxing; the silver was almost new, and had set shortly after sunset. She calmed herself, the lines of worry fading from her face, then lifted her hands and began to chant in the sorcerers' tongue.

Forlo watched the power gather around her. He held his breath as she drew in the magic, shaped it, made it into something she could use . . . then she reached down and touched her left hand to the Teacher's glistening forehead. She shuddered, opening her eyes, and Forlo caught his breath. They had rolled back, showing only white. Her mouth dropped open.

"You . . ." she said, in a voice not her own. It was deep and sonorous, what must have been the Teacher's before his mutilation. "You are too late. The woman will bear her child. Maladar will have his prize. You cannot stop it."

Forlo went cold, like the winds of the Panak had suddenly blown over him. "No," he breathed.

Shedara twitched, a spasm contorting her features, and then she spoke again, this time in her own voice. "You're a liar, Teacher," she said. "There's still time. You know it . . . I can feel that you are lying. You must tell us where she is. Where they all are . . . Essana, the Hooded One, the rest of your Brethren."

Her eyes rolled back again, her voice shifting once more. "No," she said. "I will not. I have taken an oath of secrecy, and I will not break it."

She bowed her head. "Then I'll make you," her own voice said.

Her face contorted then, lined with pain, her upper lip peeling back in a defiant snarl. She swayed on her feet for a moment, then dropped to her knees with a groan. Eldako took a step forward to help her, but stopped when she looked up again. Forlo could see the two minds warring on her face, the Teacher fighting as she delved into his mind, forcing her way deeper. She snarled and grunted, then finally threw her head back and bellowed in rage and defeat—and let go of the Teacher, falling back and lying still on the leaf-cluttered earth.

Eldako went to her, as did Tanda. Together they helped her sit up and held her, trembling, her eyes squeezed shut.

Tears leaked between the lids, on down her cheeks. Forlo crouched in front of her.

"What happened?" he asked. "Do you remember?"

She shuddered, opening her eyes. They were red and swollen, filled with pain. For a moment she didn't seem to recognize any of them—then she came back to herself and pushed them gently away. Hult drew close. They all waited while she fought to recover herself.

"Shedara," Eldako murmured. "What did you see?"

She looked at them again, pain deep in her eyes. She sighed. "I saw a temple . . . a ruined place, like the pyramid across the lake . . . only bigger, and black. It was surrounded by dark trees, as far as the eye could see. The Emerald Sea." She made a face, as if she'd just swallowed something bitter. "Neron. They're in Neron."

No one spoke. The wind sighed through the pines. Then the Teacher made a sound—a grating noise, deep in his throat. Forlo turned to look, and understood. The man was dying.

"We're losing him," he said.

Shedara shrugged. "We have what we need."

"Let me end it, then," Hult said and drew his sword.

They exchanged glances, then looked at Tanda. The Teacher had wronged her people every bit as much as he'd hurt the Uigan. But the kender only shook her head, waving them away.

"I want no part of this," she said. "I don't have the stomach for it." With that, she turned and walked back to the other kender.

Forlo watched her go, the look on her face burning into his mind. Pity. Revulsion. One for the Teacher, the other for them. They'd turned into monsters, in her eyes. The kender wanted noble heroes to save them, but they'd gotten cruel avengers. He shook his head at what they'd become, here, tonight . . . but it wasn't as if they'd had a choice. This was how it had to happen, if they were to get what they needed to save Essana.

Wasn't it?

Hult gave the rest of them a look—half question, half challenge. Forlo didn't know what the boy's reaction would be if any of them told him not to do it. He didn't have to find out, though: Eldako gave him a slow nod, then Shedara. Forlo followed suit and stepped back. A predatory smile darkened Hult's face.

He stepped forward, to where the Teacher lay. He raised his sword to his lips. "For you, my people," he whispered. "For you, my master. Let justice be done."

Shedara turned away. So, to his own surprise, did Forlo.

The blade rose.

And fell.

The Teacher's head rolled away.

Chapter

23

Akh-tazi, Neron

She lay still. She couldn't remember what it felt like
to move. What it was not to be in pain, tormented by
the grinding of shackles against skin, against bone. By the
clenching spasms that seized her back. Lying there, Essana
thought she might have gone mad—but the fact that she
wondered at all must mean she was still sane—mustn't it?

How long had she lain here? How long had her only companion been a single yaggol, who always sat in the room, just
far enough behind her that she could feel his presence but
not see him, no matter how hard she tried to look? He was
always there, his cold thoughts caressing her own. He only
budged to feed—tasteless gruel and warm water—or exam-
ine her, make sure the child was still healthy.

The child. She had been pregnant too long. She knew
this. How many months had it been? Ten? Eleven? The
swell of her belly was monstrous—no. Use another word,
any word but that. Huge. Enormous. She felt her son kick:
it hurt her. He might have been the size of a toddler, by the
weight inside her. When would he come? Why hadn't he
come yet? What was he waiting for?

The worst part, though, was the curtain, and what it
concealed. He was still there. The flayed remains of Azar

272

the Keeper still hung behind the arras: impaled, mutilated, alive. She could hear the wet sucking of his breath, the rattle of the chains from which the Brethren had hung him. Now and then he moaned, and sometimes he cried, quiet sobs of agony. He would stay there until the child came. They needed a sacrifice to Maladar. With every gasp, the Keeper paid the price for betrayal—and she paid along with him.

Days passed; weeks. The child grew stronger. She weakened. Azar's suffering never ceased. And then, one day—night? morning? who knew the difference anymore?— she heard a new sound.

It started out as a faint clamor in the distance—shouting, the ring of steel. A horn blew, somewhere in the temple's depths. She stirred, her head lolling. The yaggol was up as well, tentacles twitching, translucent lids flicking across empty eyes as it moved to stand before the door. She felt its mind leave hers, questing elsewhere, seeking answers. As it became distracted, the noise got louder, the voices more distinct. Men . . . and minotaurs.

Essana caught her breath. For the first time in weeks, she fought against her bonds, ignoring the pain as she ripped off scabs from previous struggles. She had to rise, had to be ready. . . .

BE STILL, came the yaggol's slippery voice, thrusting deep into her mind. She fell back as if a massive hand were pushing her down and stayed there, gnashing her teeth, unable to move.

The horn blew again, and her heart leaped at the sound. It was a zharka, a dragon's horn made to sound the calls of the Imperial Legions. And this call she knew. She'd heard it many times, these long years. It was the call of the Sixth.

My love, she thought. *You've come . . . you've come for me. . . .*

BE STILL!

The yaggol's thoughts nearly knocked her unconscious. She groaned, blackness swimming before her eyes, crimson stars exploding. She shoved back, gathering her hatred of the inhuman creature, but it did no good. She was defenseless against its power.

Then, with a thud, something hit the door, drawing the yaggol's attention away. She turned her head toward the noise—just in time to hear a second crash and see the blade of a battle-axe hack through the wood. It stayed there for an instant, then rocked back and forth before disappearing again. Someone outside bellowed and struck a third blow, even harder than before.

The door shattered, splinters flying. Essana shut her eyes and mouth as the fragments peppered her. Then there was a clatter of armor, and she looked again to see two figures in the doorway, lit orange from behind by gathering flames. One was a bull-man, tall and broad, one she knew. Grath, her husband's friend. He bared a fang-filled grin as he swept in, axe whirling, and lopped off the top of the yaggol's head. Milky ichor spattered the wall, and the thing's mind vanished as it flopped, jerking, to the ground.

She barely saw any of this, though; her eyes were on the other figure who strode into the room, sword streaked with white blood, eyes wild with vengeance.

Barreth.

She struggled all the harder, trying to reach him, heedless of the blood running down her arms and legs. He ran to her in three bounding steps, ripping the gag from her mouth and crushing her lips with his. She tasted his tears: he was laughing and crying all at once, and now so was she, even as Grath came up with his great axe and sheared the shackles away from the plinth.

Shards of obsidian flew as the minotaur chopped her free. She tried to stand but didn't have the strength; Barreth set down his sword and lifted her with ease. He kissed her again.

"You came," she croaked.

He smiled. "What did you expect? I looked for you a long time, Starlight. A long time. But I'm here now, and I'm getting you out—"

There was a sound, like a snap. Barreth blinked, confused—then his face changed, creasing with pain. He stumbled.

"Starlight . . . ?" he asked.

Then he fell. She went with him, landing on top of him. There was blood everywhere—all of it coming from a deep gash in his back. The Master stood above them, a dripping dagger in his hand.

"No!" Essana cried.

Grath roared with anger, swinging his axe in a wide arc. But the Master flung out his arm, pointing a single finger, and a ray of gray light shot forth, striking the minotaur full in the face. Grath froze, glowed for an instant like a star had exploded within him, then collapsed into fine dust that spilled all over the floor.

Barreth was trying to move, to get back up. But his legs wouldn't move, and blood was leaking from his mouth. It pulsed from the wound, less of it with every heartbeat. Weeping, Essana heaved herself up off her dying husband, grabbed the edge of the table—the sharp, chipped obsidian cutting her hands—and heaved herself to her feet, facing the Master.

He glared at her from the depths of his hood, and laughed. Then he flung his dagger down, impaling Barreth neatly through the throat. Essana watched, grief-torn, as her husband's back arched, one last time . . . and relaxed.

She gathered all her rage and spat in the Master's face. He only laughed.

"Thought you could escape, did you?" he asked. "No, lady. Not even in your dreams."

It came to her, then—she was not awake. This was a fantasy, not something real. Barreth wasn't really dead—or, at least, wasn't dead here, now. There was no rescue.

And the Brethren, with the yaggol's help, wouldn't even let her think about salvation. She leaped at the Master—and slipped in Barreth's blood.

With a shriek, she fell . . . .

. . . and awoke to terrible pain, and dampness, and a faint, meaty smell that filled her nostrils. It was her smell, her own. She stiffened, feeling cold all over, and lifted her head enough to look down and see brownish fluid seeping across the surface of the table.

"Oh, gods," she groaned, leaning back. "No. . . ."

Just a heartbeat later, the first clenching pain grasped her, tightening like a serpent around her middle. It was worse, so much worse, than she'd felt in the tunnel, when she and the Keeper had tried to flee the temple. She yelled, beating her fists against the table as the life within her stirred.

The day had arrived. Her water was broken. The child was coming at last.

Wind whipped her; rain soaked her. Lightning flared bright, stinging her eyes. The crash of thunder made her cries of agony seem horribly small. Essana knew the storm was not just a coincidence; either the Brethren had summoned it, or some greater power had willed it to come. It was a part of this, part of the rite, as much as every elf the Faceless had bled here, on the temple's roof.

When they brought her up here, two short hours ago, the sky had been clear blue, with not a cloud in sight, the midday sun beating down hot and sultry on this accursed land, where winter never came. The clouds hadn't appeared until the Brethren were all gathered—only four now, with

276

the Keeper's betrayal revealed. Another of their number, the Teacher, was said to have been killed in a land far away. Though they didn't say who had slain him, she said a silent prayer that it had been Barreth. There had to be justice somewhere in the world.

She had expected the Master to be furious that he'd lost another of his circle, but he'd only shrugged as if it were no matter. Perhaps it wasn't; Azar had told her that the Teacher's role had been to make shadows of the kender and set the empires of Taladas against one another. With the birth at hand, the Faceless had less need for him. His death was no great blow.

The storm had arisen with sudden violence, boiling up in the north like clouds of silt from the sea floor. In less than a quarter of an hour, the day had gone from bright to gruesome green-black, then opened up with rain and lightning and scouring gales. Essana lay bolted to the altar, turning her head every few breaths to cough up the rain water that poured into her nose and mouth, trying to fight back the spasms that ripped through her insides.

The statue loomed above her, its hood thrown back, water streaming down its ruined face. Its eyes flared like torches with every lightning flash. She could sense the presence within, eager and yearning. The Hooded One hungered for life inside her, hated her for being in the way. That only made her resist all the more—but it was a losing battle, and she knew it. The child would come, whether she wanted it or not . . . and that was the worst part, her own body betraying her, this corruption of what should have been the happiest moment of her life. She punched the altar as another contraction tore through her. Thunder roared.

Oh, Mislaxa, she thought. Take my son. Let him be stillborn. Don't leave him to this. . . .

The Master laughed, leaning forward. His hood, too, was thrown back—as were those of the Slayer, the Watcher, and the Speaker. They had crowded close to her; the dragon,

Gloomwing, was perched behind them, staring with curled lip at what—to a creature born of an egg—was an ungodly, gruesome sight.

"Pointless prayers," said the Master. "The Hand of Healing does not hear you. No gods do. You belong to Maladar, my lady—to the Faceless Emperor, and no other. Your son will live—and I will cut him from you if you fight much longer!"

He raised his hand. In it was a long, curved knife of obsidian. The raindrops that struck the blade hissed, boiling away into puffs of steam. He displayed it above her swollen belly, turning it so light sparkled on its edge.

Essana pictured herself rising, ripping the manacles from the altar and smashing in the Master's skull. Revulsion exploded within her, but when the next contraction came, she went with it, pushing with all her might. Something happened: a new pain, sharper. The Brethren looked down, eyes gleaming as lightning struck the top of a neighboring pyramid, splitting it in half and showering red-hot stone into the jungle below.

"He comes," said the Speaker.

"He comes," the others echoed.

He comes . . . said another voice, dark and grim and brimming with evil. Essana cringed. She sobbed, then choked and had to spit out water again. Thunder pounded.

The pain struck again. She howled at the black, churning sky.

The Master moved in. The pain grew so hot, so fierce, she thought she would burn up from inside . . . and then the hurt vanished, replaced by an awful, yawning emptiness. The Faceless Brethren stirred, murmuring.

Trapped within the statue, Maladar began to laugh. *How beautiful!* the hateful voice rumbled, and lightning flashed in response.

A shudder shook Essana's body, and she looked down to see the Master lift her son. The boy was huge, the largest baby she had ever seen, pink and wizened and smeared with blood—but he was beautiful. The loveliest thing she had ever seen.

The Master reached to the child's mouth and cleared it. The baby began to squall as all newborns do. Nodding, the Master produced the knife and cut the umbilical cord. Then he held it up before the Hooded One, naked to the storm.

"Behold thy flesh, Sleeper Within the Stone," the Speaker intoned.

The Brethren stirred. "Behold thy flesh."

How beautiful, Maladar said again. *How beautiful I will be.*

"No!" screamed Essana, straining against her bonds, cutting her wrists and ankles anew. "He isn't yours! Give him to me! Let me hold him!"

They stared at her, their skinless faces unreadable. She might have been an interesting insect, caught but soon to be discarded. One by one, they turned and walked away. Only the Master remained, holding the baby close to him, sheltering him among his thick robes. He watched, eyes burning, as she wept until all her strength was gone. The child shrieked on.

"Please," Essana sobbed. "Let me touch him. . . ."

Had she hoped for mercy? She wondered, in the lightless days to come, why she would expect such a thing. The Master gave no compassion, of course—only turned, and nodded over her shoulder. Two yaggol came forward, their cold thoughts molesting her mind.

"Take her back to her cell. Leave her with the traitor," he said, looking straight into her eyes. "This part is finished, milady, but the rite continues. We have need of you still, before the end."

With that, he whirled and was gone. Essana did not get a second look at her son before she was swept away.

Chapter

24

THOUSAND-SPIRE BAY, NERON

I am dreaming, Forlo thought. This is not real.

He was asleep in the hold of their boat, moored in an island's shadow, a few miles from the coast of the Neron jungle. Part of him, dimly, could sense the world around him: the gentle rock of his hammock as the ship bobbed on the current flowing out of the Indanalis; the silver moonlight washing down through the open hatch; the stifling humidity that made the air feel like a warm, damp blanket. At the same time, though, there were other sensations, and they felt just as real. Perhaps more.

He saw the Faceless atop their ziggurat. He saw the black dragon perched nearby, and the Hooded One, set there as the focus of some ritual, its cowl thrown back to reveal the horrible face beneath. He saw nightmare creatures with bulging skulls and waving tentacles instead of mouths. And he saw an altar . . . with his wife chained to it, screaming amidst thunder and rain. She was in pain, her face pale, her lip bleeding where she had bitten it in her throes. For a horrible moment, he thought the Faceless were killing her, but then he realized it was something else. Even before the one called the Master moved in, before the final spasms began, he knew what was happening.

His Starlight was giving birth.

"No," he groaned. He wanted to reach out to her. But he had no body in this dream and could only watch as the Master crouched down and prized something red and screaming from Essana's body. "No. . . ."

The Master held up Forlo's son, showing it to the statue. The boy was huge, and he howled like one of the bauvan, the ghost-women who haunted old battlefields, forever searching for their dead lovers. Rain poured down on him, washing the blood from his skin. His little arms and legs moved feebly, trying to wave away the water and noise and whatever foulness surrounded the Hooded One. Then the Master turned and strode away, taking the child with him. The tentacled things seized Essana, undid her shackles. She lay upon the altar, sobbing and robbed of strength. Forlo groaned in his sleep, afraid, mourning her, sure she was about to die. Lying in his bunk, he fumbled at his belt, where his sword should be. But still he could do nothing as the creatures lifted her dazed and exhausted form and dragged it away. He tried to follow but couldn't move. Soon they were gone, vanished into the night. He didn't know where.

The dragon remained: Gloomwing, who had stolen his life away while he was fighting the Uigan horde. The wyrm slithered on the temple roof, spreading its dark wings and throwing back its head to screech at the heavens. Its eyes glinted like rubies, catching the flare of lightning in their smoldering glow. Then, serpent-quick, they flicked in Forlo's direction and froze. There was a deep cruelty in those eyes, and mockery too. He realized, with a shudder, that the dragon could see him. The beast was looking right at him, right now.

Words formed in his brain. The voice was cold, unstirred by human emotion. It knew only malice, greed, and spite.

You followed my track, Gloomwing said, its gaze still locked with Forlo's. *You have done much to hinder us . . . but*

*it makes no difference. The child is born. The ritual proceeds.
In days, it will be over, and your son will belong to Maladar.
Forever.*

You have lost, human.

You are too late.

※━━━━◇◇━━━━※

He woke with a yelp, disoriented, panicking, and nearly
fell from his bunk as he struggled to get up. When he finally
found his feet, his heart thundering, Forlo saw Hult watching him from his own berth, his eyes questioning. The
Uigan made as if to rise, but Forlo raised a hand, shaking his
head. Now, more than ever, he needed to be alone.

He glanced at Eldako. The merkitsa lay motionless in
his bunk, but Forlo knew he was awake, waiting for a word
to be spoken or an untoward sound before he stirred. Forlo
gave him neither, but stole to the ladder, shirtless and sweat-
soaked, and climbed up onto the ship's deck.

There was a breeze; it cooled him a little, but not much.
The weather down here, in the southernmost reaches of
Taladas, was hot and sultry even in the depths of winter.
He had been down here once before, accompanying his
legion to the fisherman's kingdom of Syldar, and it had
been torment then. Both he and Grath had joked that if
they were ever asked to come back, they'd desert their
posts instead, and take their chances with the headsman
if it came to it.

A lot I knew, Forlo thought, walking softly across the
deck to look to the west. *I've cheated the headsman, and
here I am again.*

From Marak, they had returned to the kender in their
hidden cave. The little folk had greeted them as conquering
heroes for defeating the Teacher, but Forlo hadn't felt like
a victor. He knew a long road still lay ahead, and they had
set out again the next morning. Tanda and her warriors

accompanied them back to the Boiling Sea and helped push the boat into the water. Protected by Shedara's magic once more, they had left the kender behind and made south and east, following the jagged curve of the Steamwalls for another ten days—until, finally, they reached the end of the strait and glided out into an open bay, leaving behind volcanoes and brimstone and superheated waters. This was the Thousand Spires, a scattering of tall, rocky islands covered in exotic trees. To the west lay the Blackwater Glade, which covered the southern fiefs of Thenol; ahead were Syldar and its fisheries, where men worshiped shark-gods and an order of dark warriors from across the sea, who called themselves the Knights of Neraka, kept the dark and impregnable outpost of New Jelek.

None of that concerned Forlo. All that mattered was the land to the east, the mass of thick, tangled jungle swaying in the wind, just this side of the horizon. This was the Emerald Sea of Neron—an ancient land, unexplored except along the coasts. Countless stories were told about what lay in the interior, almost all ending in madness and blood.

They had first sighted Neron late yesterday, dark against the setting sun. Tomorrow they would go ashore, in search of the temples Shedara had seen in the Teacher's mind. They would walk into the teeth of all those evil tales, and only the kender of Marak would know where they'd gone.

Forlo went to the rail and leaned out, looking at the jungle. In the distance, a storm hung over the land, alive with lightning but too far away to hear the thunder. He shivered at the sight, knowing it was the same storm that had been raging in his dream.

Starlight, he thought, I'm coming. Just hold on. Hold out. . . .

You are too late, whispered the dragon in his mind.

He bowed his head, his hands balling into fists, and slammed them into the rail. Then he struck it again, and again, and again. When he was done, his knuckles were bloody and torn. He stuck them in his mouth and sucked out splinters, glaring at the storm—so close, but so far away.

"Nice punching," Shedara said. She had crept up beside him while he was lost in thought.

He blinked, then shook his head and turned away. "Leave me alone," he said. "I don't want to talk now."

"Too bad," she replied, taking hold of his shoulder and forcing him to face her. "I know what happened, Barreth. Your son was born tonight."

Forlo stared at her, his eyes narrowing. "How? Have you been spying on my mind?"

She rolled her eyes. "Don't think so highly of yourself," she said. "I had the same dream, that's all. I have a bond to the Hooded One, just as you do with your wife. There's a lot of power hanging over that jungle tonight . . . enough that it drew us both in." She frowned, looking troubled. "A lot of power."

"Did you hear the dragon too?" he asked. "It told me we were too late."

"I heard it," she answered. "It didn't exactly fill me with glee, if that's what you're asking. But . . . well, it's a dragon, Barreth. It could have been lying. What better way to hamper us, than to make us think there's no chance of stopping them in time?"

He frowned, turning the idea over in his mind. It sounded like wishful thinking . . . but then again, there might be something to it. What made him think Gloomwing was telling the truth? Nothing, except his own pessimism. He'd suspected, ever since Kristophan, that he wouldn't reach Essana in time. He glanced at the jungle again and shook his head.

"Look, I'm not saying things are good," Shedara said. "The child came. That can't bode well. Soon they'll try to free Maladar from the statue. But that didn't happen tonight, and it probably won't for some time yet. The babe's probably still too fragile for . . . for what they mean to do with it. We still have a chance."

"A chance . . ." he said dully.

She shook him, losing her temper. "Yes, damn it, a chance! That's all we've ever had. It's more than you thought you had when you rode to battle against the horde. Wake up, Barreth . . . or give up, if that's what you want to do!" She drew one of her daggers and handed it to him. "Your choice."

She turned and walked away, her boots thunking against the deck. He watched her disappear down the hatch, back into the hold. Then he turned to watch the storm. Essana was out there, under the clouds somewhere. His son too . . . two lives now, separate. They both needed him.

He looked down at the dagger, its edge glittering with starlight. He turned it this way and that . . . then raised it and buried its tip in the ship's rail. It was still quivering as he whirled and stomped away to find what sleep he could before morning.

* * *

The coast loomed ahead, the jungle dark and thick and still. On the shore was a narrow beach, overhung with leaning palm trees, then nothing but a riot of green, alive with strange cries and shrieks. A large blue bird, with a crest of crimson feathers, broke free of the foliage with a keening cry and soared out over the water; a moment later, a bright green serpent with leathery wings shot out as fast as an arrow and caught the bird in its gaping jaws. With a scream and a flurry of sapphire feathers, the flying snake jerked its prey out of the air and vanished once again among the trees.

"Lovely," muttered Forlo, steering as Hult guided from the bow. He glared at the forest and shivered, trying not to think about what lay ahead. At least the storm was gone—either dissipated or moved away to the east before dawn.

Shedara stepped close to him, hauling on a halyard to trim the mainsail. She met his gaze and grinned.

"You could have given me back the dagger," she said. "It took me ten minutes to pry it loose from the gunwale."

Forlo chuckled. "Thanks for the talk."

She shrugged, then they both glanced ahead as Hult raised his hand. "Tack starboard!" the Uigan shouted. "Shallows ahead!"

Shedara moved on, guiding the sail as Forlo leaned on the rudder. Eldako went to help her. The boat leaned to the right, booms swinging, then shuddered as the keel scraped the sandy bottom and slid free again. Hult waved, signaling all clear, and Forlo smiled. Over the weeks, the four of them had gotten quite good at piloting the ship together. For a moment, with the wind blowing strange scents from the shore and the waves slapping the vessel's hull, he managed to forget his worries. For the first time since—well, he couldn't remember—he managed a laugh.

And then the jungle exploded.

There was no warning, no sign anything was amiss. One moment they were gliding along, angling toward the coast with less than a hundred paces between them and dry land; the next, a deafening roar filled the air, accompanied by the sound of shattering trees as an enormous bulk hurtled out of the forest.

An enormous black bulk.

"Aiya! Dragon!" yelled Hult, falling back from his vantage, one hand fumbling for his sword. Over by the larboard rail, Eldako strung his bow and slid an arrow from his quiver. Shedara dropped her halyard and drew her knives.

"Khot!" Forlo swore, hauling on the rudder, trying to pull away from Gloomwing as the beast barreled right at them. The boat shuddered as the keel struck sand again—and then, with a noise like a gale, the dragon howled overhead.

As it passed, its hind claws wrapped around the mainmast, yanking the boat wildly to the side. The top ten feet of the spar snapped and came away, then the sail tore from the rigging, fluttering behind the wyrm. The ship listed wildly, and Forlo fell to the deck, hanging on to the wheel to keep from sliding down the deck. A moment later things began to right themselves, and in the distance Gloomwing let go of his prize, the ruined mast and sail splashing down into the water as he tilted his wings and wheeled in a great arc, intent on a second pass.

Eldako loosed a shot, but it glanced off the dragon's snout, breaking in half and spinning away. Undeterred, the wild elf reached for a second shaft. Shedara spun, grabbing him and yelling something. Forlo's eyes were fast on Gloomwing, whose wings pumped as he swept toward them, raising spray from the ocean's surface. The dragon rose, claws clutching the air, jaws dropping open to reveal teeth that could tear a man in half with no effort at all. It was horrible and beautiful all at the same time, and Forlo found he could only gape in awe at the majestic creature, soaring higher and higher, then turning its snaky neck to stare directly at him. The monster's gaze made him feel small, insignificant. He was an insect, a stain begging to be cleansed from the world. How could he pursue such a godlike being? How dare he believe that he could thwart it? How—

"Barreth!" Shedara shouted in his ear. "Wake up! Snap out of it!"

Forlo blinked, momentarily angry at her for disturbing his thoughts—but then the glamour Gloomwing had cast over him lifted, and a cold revulsion took its place. He'd let the beast catch him, fascinate him. If not for Shedara, it would have held him with its gaze until it killed him.

"What—" he began.

"No time!" she yelled, pulling him toward the rail. Looking past the snapped and dangling rigging, he could see that the dragon was now beginning to dive, its mouth gaping wide. "It's going to breathe! Go!"

He stumbled after her, glancing down the deck. Hult and Eldako were already gone—overboard, he presumed, trying to get away from approaching death. He looked up and saw something green and steaming boil up Gloomwing's throat, a bubbling bile that poured from its mouth with an awful, vomiting sound. A pungent reek struck him, like vinegar but far more potent; it made his lungs burn, his eyes water. Acid, he thought as the fluid rained down on the boat's deck, raising huge billows of yellow fumes. It ate through wood, metal, everything, right down to the hull and the water beneath. Ropes and sails fell away, smoldering.

They were at the rail now. Searing droplets spattered them, making Shedara grunt in pain and his own armor hiss as the acid tried to eat through. "Jump!" the elf yelled.

They leaped together, as more and more sizzling slime sprayed the ship. The deck collapsed; seawater boiled up through the ruined hull, and for just an instant, as he was falling through air down to the sea, he saw the whole boat split in half and begin to sink. The dragon thundered by overhead.

Then a hunk of flying wood, flung free of the wreckage, struck him in the side of the head. The sun got very bright; then everything vanished in gray mist. He was gone by the time he hit the water.

Chapter

25

THOUSAND-SPIRE BAY, NERON

Shedara hit the water hard, sucked in a mouthful, and barely managed to swallow before it could go into her lungs. Drops of green slime spattered the surface above as she plunged to the sandy bottom, pieces of the boat sinking beside her. A huge, dark shadow swept overhead as Gloomwing shot past the wreckage of the *Starlight*.

The dragon would come around again soon, aiming for another pass—coming in low to pluck them out of the water, one by one. She'd watched a wyrm do it once, from a safe distance: a hungry blue who had devoured half a clan of mer-folk as they tried to flee the shallows where she'd trapped them. That would be her fate, and her friends', if Shedara didn't move quickly.

The first step, as was often the case, was magic. A quick gesture and a muffled word sent a blizzard of bubbles rising through the brine, and she felt a change run through her, down deep in her body. Shutting her eyes to fight back the wave of panic that always came with this spell, she forced herself to suck in another gulp of water—and this time, let it fill her lungs. For a moment there was the terrible sensation of smothering . . . then it disappeared, and she was breathing the water as easily as air.

Without the need to surface again, she cast about in search of the others. Eldako and Hult were nowhere to be seen—but then, they'd abandoned the ship first. Hult still couldn't swim, but the merkitsa was as strong a swimmer as she knew. She had to trust that they'd already made it to shore because. . . .

Forlo was bad off, lying face-up in the sand, pinned by a torn hunk of the boat's hull, which had come down on top of him. Pink streamers of blood ran from his temple and nostrils; he was very pale, his lips turning blue. Already drowning. She swam for him, tiny silver fish darting away from her.

A sudden darkness from above was all the warning she got, but it was enough. On instinct, she dove deep, flattening herself against the sea floor as Gloomwing's jaws plunged into the water. He ripped a furrow through the waves, fangs snapping as he sought prey. All he got, though, were a few of the silver fish; he passed by Shedara, tossing her crazily in his wake, then pulled up and out again. She saw his shadow recede as she lunged for Forlo again.

The wood trapping him wasn't hard to shift under water; she got it off with one great shove, then grabbed his arm and pulled him away. He was far from light, with his mail and sword weighing him down, but fear gave her strength, particularly when she glanced up to see Gloomwing finish wheeling about and start to dive again. She didn't make for shore; there wasn't time, so instead they went deeper, to where the acid-scorched bulk of the ship was settling, even now, into the sand. There were two large pieces, one of which lay upside-down, enough to give some semblance of shelter. Dragging Forlo, she ducked into a pocket just as Gloomwing hit the water again.

Shedara held Forlo tight to keep him from drifting away, watching the water above grow dark as night. Gritting her teeth, she listened to the roar of the black wyrm approaching. The slab of hull above her shuddered with the impact, slid a few paces, then shattered, pieces flying everywhere. It had served its purpose, though: the dragon was past them again, its shriek of frustration barely audible from twenty feet deep.

They were still alive—that was the good news. The bad was there was nowhere else to hide. The other half of the hull lay facing upward: a feeding bowl for the wyrm, nothing more. She had no choice left but to flee—so she did, one arm wrapped around Forlo's chest as she swam madly toward shallower water.

Never make it, said a voice in her head. Not with this extra weight. Leave him—he's probably already drowned, anyway.

Shut up, she answered. He comes with me.

To her left, Gloomwing rose again, pulling away from the surface and starting to round about, one more time. Shedara clenched her teeth, uttering curse after curse as she swam on. She could see the jungle, shimmering up above the water. She'd once followed a mirage in the desert for an entire day before realizing it wasn't real; this seemed every bit as false.

Look, she thought. I don't know what gods might be listening right now, but anything you can do . . . anything at all. . . .

The dragon dove, its fanged mouth raking the water, heading straight toward her. She shut her eyes, awaiting the pain. Death would be quick, at least. One quick snap. . . .

Instead there was a shriek, and Gloomwing jerked and turned aside, one wingtip dragging through the water, slicing all the way down to the bottom, throwing up a storm of sediment that swept over her, blinding her. She shut her mouth just in time—breathing water was one thing, getting a lungful of silt something else—and held Forlo tight as the wake buffeted her again.

Then everything was still again, and she didn't know where the dragon was. She didn't waste any time looking for him; instead she swam as hard as she could, wondering which god had answered her prayers. She hoped it was one she liked.

The shallows came fast, and she sputtered as she burst up out of the water, vomiting brine, then yelled for help when her lungs cleared. Hult was there, sprinting down the beach, sand flying behind him. He got to her as she tried to haul Forlo up onto land, his face questioning. Shedara shook her head, then waved toward the trees.

"I don't know. Just get him in there."

It was hard, even with two of them, but together they dragged Forlo ashore, then lifted him and staggered down the beach. As they went, she caught sight of Eldako—standing at the water's edge, bow in hand, staring out across the water. Gloomwing was fighting to stay aloft, three arrows lodged in the joint where his left wing connected with his body.

Not a god after all, then. She grinned.

Then she looked back toward the jungle and nearly dropped Forlo in shock.

There were faces among the trees—small, painted faces beneath wild manes of bright hair, threaded with feathers and beads. Each held a weapon—a small bow of wood and horn, or a long blowgun, or a slender spear hooked into a throwing stick. One met her gaze and put a finger to his lips—a graceful gesture. None of them made a sound.

Elves. She'd heard the legends, that a race akin to hers dwelt in the jungles of Neron—an ancient people called the cha'asii. Unlike the merkitsa, however, she'd never seen them—not until now. Now she shivered as they watched her with wide eyes, so dark they seemed to be almost all pupil. They parted to let her pass, and she and Hult laid Forlo down, just inside the tree line.

He wasn't breathing. Tilting his head back, she balled her fists together and pumped his chest, his chain mail digging painfully into her flesh. After a few hard shoves, she bent over him and breathed into his mouth, forcing in air.

The cha'asii watched her for a moment, then turned to peer out toward the water again. She glanced that way too and felt a twinge of terror: Gloomwing had got control back, and was wheeling for another attack. Now he turned toward Eldako, who stood ready, waiting. The dragon swept in over the sparkling water.

The merkitsa's quiver was empty. He dropped his bow and drew his sword.

"What in the blue Abyss is he doing?" Shedara exclaimed, starting to rise. But she couldn't leave Forlo. Not now. Every moment counted.

Her stomach clenching, she breathed into Forlo's mouth again, and again, and again, thinking, *come on*. Hult touched her arm.

"Eldako baits the beast," the Uigan said. "My people did it this way, sometimes, when we hunted griffin or steppe-tiger. One man rides out alone, to draw in the enemy. That man must have courage that will not fail."

Shedara glanced at the cha'asii standing ready. There were perhaps fifty of them in all. They lifted their blow-guns, drew back their bowstrings, and waited. Gloomwing came on, jaws open wide, sharp teeth glistening.

She bent over Forlo and breathed, one more time. At last he reacted, choking at first, then coughing up a great gout of water and vomit, all over her legs.

"The dragon?" he gasped.

"Being dealt with," she said, turning to watch. "Lie still."

Gloomwing, evidently, was not very intelligent—not as dragons went, anyway. And he was hungry and hurt, which made him stupider. He saw Eldako, and he saw prey. The merkitsa didn't balk, didn't flinch as the dragon bore down on him—only stood, sword low at his side, waiting. Shedara couldn't see his face, but she imagined a grim smile.

Looking back, in the days to come, she knew that was the moment she finally fell in love with him.

The dragon came in low, skimming over the floating stub of mast that was all that remained of their boat. He drew a furious breath, and the tang of acid stung Shedara's nose. A cold feeling came over her.

"Eldako!" she cried.

Gloomwing spat a sizzling spray of slime. It hit the merkitsa head-on. He fell, vanishing into the surf.

At the same moment, the cha'asii leaped out of the trees, taking aim at the wyrm. The satisfied leer that had begun to light the dragon's eyes disappeared, replaced with shock. Madly, he pumped his wings, trying to pull up, but the arrows in his shoulder hampered him. Silently, the jungle elves let fly.

The dragon screamed. One of his eyes was pierced; the roof of his mouth too. His wings were tatters. Riddled with darts and spears, he tried to bank, lost control, and slammed into the trees not thirty paces from where Shedara stood. The crash of splintering wood and shattering bones filled the air, followed by a shriek of agony. The earth shook.

Then Gloomwing was silent, and there was only the crashing of the waves.

She combed through the breakers for what seemed like forever, while Hult stayed with Forlo, and the cha'asii went after the fallen dragon. She waded out into the water until she was hip-deep, picking her way through the driftwood that had been their boat, walking a quarter mile one way, then just as far the other. The sky turned red, then began to darken, the stars glinting above—a firmament almost completely different than the one that hung above Panak, so many leagues away. She could barely remember what it had been like, to be so cold for so long, to have gone without seeing anything green for weeks. She wondered, as she searched the churning water, what had become of Angusuk and the other survivors of his tribe. Anything not to think about what she didn't want to.

Quietly, she began to cry.

She saw it, every time she closed her eyes—Eldako standing tall and still, goading Gloomwing on, giving the jungle elves the chance they needed to bring the great beast down. Had he forgotten the wyrm's breath, that deadly spittle that had eaten through their ship? Had he thought he could dodge it, when the time came? Either way, Shedara cursed him for a fool.

It was senseless. Eldako had a part to play in their hunt for Essana and the Hooded One. But she couldn't bring herself to believe it was to die here, on the Neroni coast. Helping defeat the dragon was a noble goal, but . . . it didn't feel right for him to be dead. She slogged on through the brine, refusing to give up.

Finally, she heard someone yelling her name and looked back toward shore. It was almost full night, twilight's ruddy glow fading in the west. Her elf-sight picked out the warm figures of Hult and Forlo, the two humans standing at the water's edge, trying to find her in the gloom. They called again—her name only. Not Eldako's.

She felt a new rush of tears at that, then wiped them away with a growl. She raised her hand to them. "Over here!"

Still weak from his near-drowning, Forlo stayed where he was, but Hult waded out until the water foamed around his knees. Behind him, small blue lights glimmered at the edge of the trees: the cha'asii had gathered solemnly, were watching.

Shedara walked shoreward, started to speak, then caught herself and coughed as her voice broke. She shook her head angrily and tried again.

"How is he?" she asked, nodding at Forlo.

Hult spread his hands. "He was dead, almost. Now he isn't—thanks to you. Considering that, he is well. A night's rest, and he'll be fine, mostly."

"Good," she said, glancing out at the waves again. "And the dragon?"

"Dead, though he was still breathing when the elves found him. They cut off his head. They mean to take it back to their village, to use as a totem. They think it will protect them against the akitu-shai."

"The what?"

"Crawling Maws, in their tongue." Hult's hand strayed to the amulet, hanging flat against his broad chest. "Creatures that serve the Faceless. They abduct the cha'asii and kill them."

Shedara nodded, anger roiling in her breast. "Blood sacrifice. To Maladar."

"Yes."

"Will they help us?"

Hult shrugged. "I don't see why not. Will you come out of the water? It's getting late. If you haven't found—"

She raised a hand. "Don't say his name."

The Uigan started, hurt, then turned away and walked back inland, toward Forlo. She watched him go, then gazed back out at the sea, trying to accept what she'd been refusing to consider: Eldako was gone. It still didn't seem right . . . but death seldom did. Shuddering, she turned and strode back up to the beach. Hult and Forlo stood near something that lay half-buried in the sand. She bent to pick it up, and felt her eyes burn when she uncovered it. Eldako's bow.

She unstrung it, relieving the tension on its limbs. Then, holding it gently, she turned back toward the ocean and stared, long and hard. The red moon was low over the jungle now; it made the water glisten like blood.

A hand touched her shoulder. She tried to shake it off, but Forlo refused to let go. Shedara turned to face him, and gasped to see the man's face. It was sallow, his cheeks sunken, his eyes dull and tired. He looked twice his age.

"I'm sorry," he said. "I can't believe it either. He's the only reason we're still alive. It's not the first time, either."

He bowed his head.

Hult held something out. It glistened in his hand. "I took this from Gloomwing's body. You should have it. I already have one of my own, as does Forlo. Perhaps, one day, one of us might travel to the Dreaming Green. If we do, we should give it to Tho-ket and tell him tales of his son."

She took the object from him. It was long and black, pointed, slightly curved. A talon. Gloomwing's. She squeezed it tight in her hand.

"Damn it," she murmured.

A voice called out from the trees in a language she didn't know. She saw the cha'asii standing there.

"They say we must go," Hult told her. "It isn't safe here. The Maws come at night."

Shedara wanted to tell them all to go rot in the Abyss. She'd leave when she was ready. There were still places she hadn't looked—a spot to the south in particular, where the coast got rocky and there were many nooks and sockets to be explored. In her heart, though, she knew better. Eldako was lost—the riptide had probably carried him out to sea. She bowed her head and sighed.

"All right, then," she said and turned to walk toward the jungle. Hult and Forlo left her alone, following silently a few paces behind. Now they were three.

Chapter

26

KE-CHA-YAT, NERON

The cha'asii lived in the trees—huge, gnarled trees that rose a hundred feet and more above the jungle's fern-carpeted floor. Up there, among the broad, green leaves and dangling, golden blossoms, the elves had built platforms from wind-fallen wood, webbed with bridges of woven reeds, all of it camouflaged to be invisible from below. Hult and the others didn't even know they had arrived at the village of Ke-cha-yat until a vine ladder dropped down from the boughs above, and the cha'asii began to climb.

None of the elves had said a word since they left the coast, some three hours ago. Night had fallen hard: even with the moons out, the Emerald Sea of Neron was a dark place, lit only by occasional shafts of silver and crimson through the foliage. The cha'asii carried lamps to light their way, globes of milky crystal in which glowing moths fluttered, battering against the insides as they fought vainly to escape. The moths gave off an eerie blue radiance that drained the color from people's faces, making everyone look like ghosts. That, and the elves' utter silence—no twigs broke beneath their feet, no branches rustled as they passed—gave Hult the feeling that he had left the mortal world.

He climbed after the cha'asii, going up easily, rung by rung. Shedara came behind, then Forlo, still weak from his near-drowning but stubbornly pushing on, keeping pace. Hult looked down past the man, half expecting to see Eldako, but of course the merkitsa wasn't there. It was strange to think he was gone. It had been too sudden. Hult felt the claw he'd taken from Gloomwing, now hanging on the same cord as the jade amulet, and said a prayer for the wild elf's spirit. It was a sacrilege—according to the Uigan elders, elves were devils, with no souls to voyage on to Jijin's hunting halls—but he didn't care. Eldako had been a friend, and no god who refused a prayer for a friend was worth worshiping.

The climb was long and tiring. He was breathing hard when he reached the top. Ke-cha-yat was a large village, its huts woven from fronds and grass, lashed to the platforms and reinforced with more deadwood. Moth lamps hung from creepers above the walkways, looping from tree to tree. But something wasn't right here—nearly half the huts were dark, their lamps snuffed out, their ceilings bowed inward, reinforcing sticks poking out like bones. Something had emptied the village. Hult's people had been raiders, and he knew the signs. Ke-cha-yat looked like a Kazar encampment after the Uigan had ridden through.

The akitu-shai had been busy, it seemed—but it hadn't been a completely one-sided war. Severed heads stood impaled on stakes in front of many of the remaining huts: they were brown and withered, their eyes sewn shut, and they definitely weren't human. The shapes were wrong, too bulbous, and there was no sign of hair, noses or ears. Tentacles, dried to leather by whatever preserving rituals the elves employed, hung from where the creatures' mouths should be. These were the Crawling Maws, then, ones the cha'asii had managed to slay.

Now the last of the party were coming up the ladder, and with them they brought their latest trophy. Hauling on cords of jute, they dragged up the dragon's head, laying it upon the wooden platform. Gloomwing had seemed majestic in life, but now, his face pierced by arrows and spears, one of his eyes burst, the wyrm looked pathetic. Still, Hult couldn't go so far as to feel sorry for the beast—not when it had led them on such a long chase and taken Eldako from them at the end.

Word spread through the village of what the party had brought back. Huts emptied, small, nearly naked figures climbing down from higher platforms, scurrying across the bridges, swinging over chasms on vines. They stared at Hult, Forlo, and Shedara with wide eyes, and some clenched their fists and bared their teeth in what looked like warding gestures. They were all armed, every single adult—whether it was a spear, a hatchet, or a long, obsidian knife.

There were bows and blowguns as well, and after what had happened to Gloomwing, Hult and the others kept their hands away from their weapons, just in case. Within moments, almost two hundred elves had gathered around them and the dragon's head. They made no sound, only stared with wondering eyes at these giants in their midst. Even Hult, who was the shortest of the three, towered over the cha'asii by more than a head. It was like being surrounded by tiny spirits.

At the rear of the crowd, movement caught his eye. Someone was moving through the mass, elves parting to let her pass, their eyes cast downward. It was the oldest elf he had ever seen, the only one he had ever beheld who actually showed true age. She was even tinier than her kin, stooped and withered, wrinkled skin hanging loose on her bones. She moved haltingly, hobbling with every step, her joints so stiff she could barely move. A fan-shaped crest of waving feathers—all of them pure white—loomed above her head, and a cloak of the same covered her shoulders. Her face was lined with age and dusted pale with chalk. Her eyes were clear, icy blue—the only part of her that didn't look ancient.

Veiled elf maids flanked her, holding her elbows to keep her upright as she tottered up to Hult.

"I am Yu-shan," she said in a voice like the croak of a raven. "Grandmother to our people. I speak for them."

Nalaran's amulet pulsed against Hult's breast. He nodded, then bowed. Behind him, Shedara and Forlo followed suit. "I am honored, Grandmother. Among my people, the elder-women are revered. It is good to see the cha'asii are as civilized."

Yu-shan smiled. Unlike the crones of the Uigan, she still had all her teeth. The crinkles in her face deepened even more.

"A flatterer, this one!" she said to one of her handmaidens. "You be careful when he is near, child. We do not want any man-children being born."

The handmaiden flushed behind her veil, lowering her gaze. Hult felt his own face redden.

"You may trust me, wise one," he said. "I took an oath to remain chaste."

"What a waste," the Grandmother said, looking him up and down. "You would have many strong sons, I ken. But no matter. Important things have happened, I hear. The black wyrm is slain, and you have come. Yes, it is as was foretold."

Hult shivered, thinking of the makau of the Ice People and his spirit-wolves. "You knew we were coming as well?"

The old elf nodded. "Grandmother knows all," she replied. "Grandmother sees all. Your coming was prophesied, long ago. Well before you were born, or any of your friends. The leaves whispered of your coming—two men-folk and two of our kind, with the head of a dragon as tribute. You are to save our people from the akitu-shai . . . only. . . ." She stopped, peering at the others. Her brow furrowed. "Where is the fourth? The second of our kin?"

Hult felt a spasm of grief. "He is lost, Grandmother. Eldako fell to the dragon."

Yu-shan stared at him, fear widening her eyes. "No," she said. "It is not possible. The spirits spoke of four, not three! Three is an ill number. The fourth must come—without him, we cannot prevail."

"Eldako is dead, wise one," Hult insisted.

"And the body? You saw his corpse?"

He frowned. "Well . . . no, but. . . ."

"Ah!" Yu-shan grinned, her eyes lighting. She snapped her fingers. "You should not have left him, if he fared so badly that you thought him slain. Bad luck, bad luck. Now it falls to me. I must find him. We must, together. Come."

She turned and, her handmaidens guiding her, hobbled quickly away. Hult took a step to follow, bewildered by what the ancient elf had said, but Shedara caught his arm, stopping him. He turned, staring at her, then saw the confusion on her face. He and Yu-shan had been speaking the cha'asii tongue. The others had understood only one word they'd spoken: Eldako's name.

"What's going on?" Shedara whispered.

He told her. She slapped him, then turned on Forlo.

"You made me leave!" she shouted at them both. "You told me there was no hope. Now we're told he's alive?"

Hult looked away, his cheek burning where she'd hit him. Forlo shook his head.

"How were we to know?" he asked. "You saw what happened to him, Shedara. How could he survive that?"

She glared at him, then turned and walked away, following the Grandmother and her attendants. The cha'asii parted to let her pass. Hult stayed behind a moment with Forlo. They traded glances, sharing the same thought: how could Eldako still be alive? And if he lived, what was left of him? Wouldn't death be better?

Shaking his head, Forlo walked after Shedara. Hult went last of all, his thoughts as dark as the jungle below.

The Grandmother's hut was higher than the rest of the village, rising up among the topmost branches of the trees, dappled with moonlight that broke through the leaves. Many dried heads surrounded it, both Crawling Maws and other monsters Hult didn't recognize: a great cat with a third eye in the middle of its forehead, a snake with curling horns, and something that looked to be equal parts ogre and bat. Gloomwing's head would soon join the others, a crowning trophy among Yu-shan's collection, the enemies of the cha'asii brought low.

The hut itself was long and low, the near end covered by a blanket of grasses that served as a door. Branches of twisted wood stuck out of the top like spines. Its sides crawled with the glowing moths that lit the rest of Ke-cha-yat—free, not trapped in crystal globes, their cold shimmer making a mosaic that illuminated the platform as bright as day. The glow rippled as Hult watched, the moths spreading their wings to flit from one point to another.

The platform was a circle some twenty paces across, with no rail around its edges; glancing over the side, Hult felt overcome by dizziness. They were so high, he couldn't see the ground: just fluttering leaves and bridges and huts, down and down into shadow. It felt as if, if he fell over, he would plunge forever through the moth-lit trees. Catching his breath, he stepped back, turning toward the hut.

The Grandmother stood alone, quietly watching them. As Hult watched, moths rose from the walls and alighted on her headdress and cloak. Their light made her seem swathed in stars. She gazed at him with her pale eyes, then at Forlo and Shedara, beckoning them closer. As she did, Hult noticed something he hadn't seen before—a bowl-shaped depression in the platform's midst, perhaps two paces across and lined with multicolored seashells. Yu-shan hobbled to its edge and held her hand over the bowl. She spoke a word, and the familiar shimmer of magic poured down. When it was done, the bowl was filled to the brim with clear water. Hult and the others drew near, surrounding the pool.

"There's no reflection," Forlo said, peering in.

"It's for scrying," Shedara explained. "The Voice had something like this, in my homeland." She looked over at the old elf. "This is to search for Eldako."

The Grandmother eased herself down to sit by the pool's edge, waving Forlo and Hult away when they stepped forward to help her. She smiled at them, then gestured to the pool's edge.

"Sit," she said. "I will need your memories of him to know exactly what it is I seek. Do you have a token of his? Something he carried, that you took when you thought him dead?"

Shedara and Forlo looked at Hult, not understanding. He translated, and Shedara nodded, unslinging Eldako's bow from her back. She had refused to leave it by the seaside, and now she held it out to the Grandmother, its wood gleaming in the light of moths and moons.

Yu-shan shook her head. "I cannot accept this," she said. "It is a weapon of great power. The spell will unbind its magic, destroy it. Have you nothing else?"

Hult repeated her words. Shedara shook her head and offered the bow again. "It is all there is," she said. "He will understand."

Regretfully, the Grandmother accepted the bow. She ran her hands over its curves, whispering to it as if apologizing. Then, with a wistful sigh, she laid it on the water. The bow floated out, drifting into the pool's midst.

"Sit," she said again. "We will begin."

They did as she bade and shut their eyes, each remembering Eldako as Yu-shan began to chant. Hult thought of the first time he'd met the merkitsa, deep in the Dreaming Green. He remembered how Eldako had killed Hoch and

Sugai, the rebellious lords who had sought to usurp Chovuk on the eve of battle—shooting them from a distance Hult still couldn't credit, his arrows seeming to descend from the heavens. He thought of the wild elf rescuing them at Coldhope and again in Kristophan . . . of his solemn face as the Wyrm-namer died, and the song of his bowstring at Starshimmer Lake. Last, he saw him standing on the shore, his arrows spent, waiting without fear as Gloomwing skimmed toward him over the waves.

Sorcery surged around him, blasting him from all sides like a whirlwind. There was a flash of light, and he opened his eyes to see white flames leap from the surface of the pool—flames filled with faces, appearing and disappearing too quickly to recognize. The bow caught fire and vanished amid the inferno. Across the burning water, the Grandmother's head snapped in his direction, her eyes rolling back in her head. She pointed a finger and spoke in a shrill, brittle wail.

"Hold to your thoughts! Remember him! Remember, or the spell will fail!"

Terrified, Hult shut his eyes again, summoning the memories where he'd left them. He watched Eldako lower his bow, let it drop into the sand. Drawing his blade, the merkitsa walked forward into the water. Waves lapped around his shins, foaming. His eyes never left the black dragon, shrieking in like death itself, his mouth gaping wide, filled with glistening fangs. Acid boiled up the monster's throat.

"No," Hult groaned as he found himself running forward. This confused him for a moment: he hadn't done this before. He had stayed with Forlo, back where beach met jungle. Now, though, his feet flew across the sand as he hurried to help his friend.

The spell had taken hold. He felt its claws sinking into him, burrowing in his mind as the Grandmother searched his memories. He fought the urge to resist, letting the magic work its way deeper and deeper as he sprinted to Eldako's side.

"Get out!" he cried as the dragon came soaring closer. "Get away from here!"

The wild elf didn't notice him. His gaze was fast on Gloomwing, so close now Hult could count the dragon's teeth. Hult grabbed for Eldako, but his hands didn't reach him. The spell could not change what had happened; it only let him see things better, closer. He wondered, briefly, if that was so good an idea—then the dragon made the terrible, vomiting roar he recalled, and he looked up in time to see sizzling green slime fly through the air and splatter the merkitsa.

"Eldako!" he shouted. He heard Shedara cry out as well. Only Forlo, who hadn't beheld this moment, and so had no memory of it, remained silent.

An awful smell hit him then, and Hult knew it came from the wild elf. The acid ate through Eldako's beetle-shell breastplate, burned away his tunic, seared his flesh. Greasy, yellow fumes rose from him. Eldako opened his mouth to cry out but could only make a retching sound—then leaped forward, hurling himself into the water and vanishing from sight.

Leaped. Did not fall.

Wracked with despair. Hult dove after him. Every instinct told him this was suicide—he was no swimmer—but the magic compelled him. Panic whitened his mind as he plunged into the surf; when it cleared again he was under water, following Eldako as the tide dragged him away. The acid had stopped eating the elf, but Hult caught glimpses of the damage it had done—armor and clothing in tatters, skin bubbled and blackened, hair scorched away—as the merkitsa tumbled over and over, helpless, unconscious. Above the water, the wyrm's shadow passed overhead, and he heard a muted roar—Gloomwing's cry as the cha'asii loosed their deadly volley. A few moments later came the crash as the dying dragon plowed into the forest.

Then, all was quiet. Eldako's body kept drifting, pulled by current and tide. Hult glided after, more flying than swimming, no longer troubled by thoughts of drowning. He felt the Grandmother's mind touching his, driving him on. He wondered if she was doing the same with Shedara, or even Forlo. She probably was. If it came to it, he could break the spell simply by opening his eyes.

Minute after minute crept by. The water darkened as twilight settled into night. Still Eldako drifted, limp as a dead man, the current bearing him along. Finally, ahead, something loomed close—something large and solid. Hult pulled up and burst through the surface of the water to see craggy coastline—the same rocks Shedara had wanted to search when he and Forlo had convinced her to stop. Shame burned in his heart as he watched the wild elf's charred body break the surface and slam against the rocks. He groped impotently toward his friend as a wave pinned him against the stones—wanted to help him but couldn't. What he was watching was already done, though no one had been around to see it until now.

The wave receded, leaving Eldako bobbing in the shallows. A moment later, however, another swell came in, larger than the last. This time it broke over the rocks, pushing the merkitsa with it. Hult lost sight of what was happening and searched frantically as the foaming breaker drained away—and finally saw his friend, sprawled at the edge of a tidal pool, surrounded by starfish and urchins.

Then he saw the miracle: Eldako stirred, gave a great, wracking cough, and vomited sea water onto the stones. When he was done, he lay groaning, huddled in a heap until another wave broke over the rocks and shoved him deeper into shore, smacking and bumping against the stones. He clung to the rocks, whimpering in pain as the surge tried to pull him back out to sea.

It was too dark to see just what the acid had done to him. For that, Hult was thankful. He didn't sound right, though—his breathing had a reedy wheeze. Eldako lay gasping, groaning—then gathered enough strength to crawl, scraping his way over the rocks, away from the pounding surf. When he finally collapsed again, he'd made it almost to the trees. The waves kept bursting against the stones behind him.

He lay there a long time, face-down in the dark. Hult felt hours pass. The stars wheeled across the night sky; clouds formed and tore apart; the moons glided westward. Eldako remained still, near death or sleeping.

Then, finally, something happened. Midnight had come and gone, though dawn was still hours away. There was movement in the blackness, but it wasn't Eldako; three shadowy figures slipped out of the trees. Hult moved toward them to get a better look and felt horror crawl over his skin. The creatures were man-shaped, clad in pale robes, with slimy skin like the flesh of something that had crawled up from the bottom of the sea. One was pale violet, another bilious green, and the third the yellow-gray of disease. Their heads he recognized, for he had seen them already, dark and shriveled on stakes all over Ke-cha-yat. Alive they were even more horrible, their eyes white and empty, their mouth-tentacles writhing as though they had minds of their own.

The Crawling Maws had come.

The akitu-shai hesitated, looking at one another, and Hult had the sense of silent conversation, unspoken thoughts buzzing through the air. A conclusion reached, they strode forward, moving among the rocks toward Eldako. Spindly, alien hands reached out, clutching for the merkitsa . . . then stopped, the creatures straightening and glancing at one another in wordless communion. Then, to Hult's amazement, they turned and looked straight at him.

LEAVE! shouted three voices in his mind, so loud he cried out, and opened his eyes.

The spell broke.The flames that covered the pool flickered out, leaving no sign of Eldako's bow—not even ashes. Hult held still, trembling at the memory of the Maws. Forlo sat across the pool from him, pale and confused; he hadn't shared the vision. Shedara had, though, and she bowed her head, her shoulders shaking. Tears shone on her cheeks.

"So it is," said the Grandmother. "The akitu-shai have him. We must get him back, if you are to succeed at your task."

Hult rose. "I will go. It is partly my fault that they have him."

Yu-shan nodded.

Hult explained things to the others, and Forlo offered to help as well. Shedara remained quiet, staring into the emptiness of the pool as the water vanished from within.

"And you, girl?" asked the Grandmother. "What will you do?"

Shedara looked up, her face creased with anguish. Her eyes were fierce, though—so much so it was Yu-shan who glanced away, flushing beneath her stare.

Chapter

27

THE EMERALD SEA, NERON

He awoke.

Eldako hadn't expected to live—at best, he thought he'd find himself among his ancestors in the gods' hunting grounds, as the shamans said happened to the dead. Drawing breath, after what he'd been through, came as a surprise.

It also came as a relief, for it would have been a bad death, a foolish death. The merkitsa believed their spirits returned to the world after a time in the afterlife, and their place in things was determined by how they died. Standing out in the open, daring a dragon to attack him—then misjudging and not getting out of the way before it unleashed its deadly breath—was a stupidity that would make him certain to come back as a cockroach or a goblin. It would mean a downward turn of fortune's great wheel, and Eldako was glad he didn't have to face that.

Not yet, anyway. He could already sense a wrongness to things, even drifting at the edge of consciousness. He was hardly safe. An awful smell, like rotting fish, hung heavy in the air—and there was something even worse. A slimy feeling, sliding through his mind. He was not alone in his own head.

He opened his eyes, or tried to. That was the first inkling he had of how bad his wounds were. He'd felt a brief but incredible flare of pain when the acid struck, in that moment before he'd hurled himself into the sea. Luckily, the water had washed away the dragon's breath, sparing his life. But the vision in his right eye was cloudy, as if someone had covered it with gossamer. He guessed it would never be clear again.

His left eye wouldn't open at all. After a moment, he understood why. It was gone.

Nor did the rest of his face feel right—the flesh on the whole left side, from scalp to jaw, felt taut and ill-fitting. His face stung worse than the harshest sunburn he'd ever had. He knew what he must look like and felt a surge of revulsion: the dragon's acid had seared and melted his skin, leaving it misshapen and hairless, his left eye an empty, staring socket. He realized, with no small amount of regret, that he would never be able to shoot a bow properly again.

His arm felt equally maimed, and the left side of his chest as well. Only his right leg had escaped Gloomwing's spittle. He would be hideous to look upon and probably a poor fighter as well. He was ruined, a broken semblance of what he'd been. A lesser man would have given up and died on the spot, but Eldako was a prince of his people and one of the finest warriors of the Dreaming Green. He thrust aside self-pity and concentrated on surviving whatever was next.

He tried to sit up, but couldn't. Tried to raise his head, but failed at that as well. He didn't have a broken back, for he could twitch his toes and fingers, nor did he feel anything binding him. It felt as if someone lay on top of him, physically holding him down. But there was no one there, not that he could see.

He was alone, staring up at a dark canopy of branches. His hearing was almost as bad as his sight—the acid had taken his left ear as well—but he could make out the sound of movement and a soft, wet noise he didn't recognize. He gritted his teeth, the most he could do with his mouth—the invisible hand was holding his jaw shut as well—and pushed as hard as he could against whatever was restraining him.

It wakes, said a voice inside him.

Eldako startled, then felt the slithering in his mind again, probing at thought and memory. He tried to block it out but didn't know how. It slipped about like an eel, twisting and flopping whenever he tried to grasp it. He understood, then, why he couldn't move. His captors had hold of his mind.

He fought even harder, struggling to wrest back control of his thoughts. There was a white flash, like a star exploding in his head, followed by a wave of pain and nausea. He groaned, nearly blacking out, and forced himself to remain calm. Only when his thoughts were tranquil again did the agony abate, leaving him exhausted and shivering on the jungle floor.

Strong, said a second voice, as toneless as the first. *Not like the cha'asii.*

Yes, said the first speaker. *Strong.*

A good catch, agreed a third. *Better than any since the woman came.*

The Brethren will be pleased, noted the second.

More movement, to his right. Figures slunk into view . . . four of them, or more. In his near-blindness, it was hard to tell. They were oily creatures, with flesh like something left over in a fisherman's net, tentacles squirming on their faces. And the eyes . . . the empty, white eyes. . . .

Crawling Maws. He'd heard Hult mention them, back on the beach. And from what had been said, the Maws were in league with the people they sought, the Faceless. Their minds rooted through his own, as supple as the cilia covering their mouths. They touched every notion that came to him.

312

It knows of us.

And the woman.

There were others with it. They seek the Hooded One.

It is as the Master said. When the child is born, our enemies will come.

Yes....

Eldako swallowed. He knew what he had to do. If they could read his mind, he had to keep them away from . . . certain things, or the others would be in jeopardy. There was no overcoming them, not this many, but he could build walls. Block off his thoughts. He shut his eyes again, not pushing back, but simply keeping his mind blank, as empty as a summer sky.

It was harder than it seemed. They knew what he was doing before he even started, and used his own mind against him. They dredged up painful memories: the death of his mother, battles he'd lost, his own regret that he would likely never see the Green again. Those moments played out as if they were fresh, happening all over again. He bit his lip, focusing on nothing, and the recollections tore to wisps and faded away.

They tried other things. He'd accidentally given them the simplest visions of his companions, and now he saw them again, hurt, dying—their blood pouring down the steps of a great black pyramid somewhere deep in these woods. But it wasn't his companions, not really; there were obvious differences. Shedara's hair, not quite right. Hult, half a head taller than Forlo. Forlo's face untroubled by thoughts of Essana. It wasn't his friends, but imposters, half-formed creations of his mind and the Maws'. Again he thought of emptiness, and the vision vanished.

The alien minds stilled, and Eldako let himself smile. He had played a game with the other children of his clan, when he was just a boy, trying to be the last of his group to think of a golden dragon. It was a game he usually won—not by actively thinking of other things, but by thinking of nothing at all. He used that discipline now, knowing the Maws had relented only for the moment—another attack would come.

When it did, it didn't matter how prepared he was—they overwhelmed him all the same. The Maws all hit him at the same time, six different minds pounding at his own, their thought-voices as loud as if they were shouting in his ear. He choked, his scarred face twisting as he tried to shut the voices out, but it was no good. Bit by bit, the Maws wore away at the nothingness. It tattered and tore, leaving bare his thoughts. More flashes of white pain followed, and Eldako had to fight back the urge to vomit. Tears slid from his good eye, down into his hair. He bit his tongue, tasted blood. . . .

The images came. Hult and Chovuk, held captive by his clan. His father, agreeing to send him with the Uigan. The Tiger's horde, sweeping across the Tiderun, only to be consumed by the sudden, voracious wave. Shadow-fiends at Coldhope, and in Armach-nesti. The emperor of the minotaurs, dying. Panak. The Wyrm-namer. The kender. The Teacher's headless corpse. Gloomwing, bearing down on him, his jaws yawning wide. . . .

"No!" Eldako cried, his back arching as the Crawling Maws ripped his mind wide open.

Without warning, four of the six voices vanished—one suddenly, with a cry of pain, the other three silently pulling out, distracted by something nearby. He heard the thrum of bowstrings, and the ring of steel. Voices, too. Many were strange, speaking a birdlike language he didn't know. Three he recognized, however. Three were his friends.

Stop them! shouted one of the Maws that remained in his brain.

They are everywhere, said another. *The cha'asii—*

Humans, also. They are too strong. They are protected. I can slow them, but—

Eldako fought the Maws as best he could, pushing back against the invisible hands that held him down. He couldn't

314

shake them off—not entirely—but he got back some control over his own body, enough to roll over and look toward the commotion. As he did, a head spun past, turning end over end, twitching tentacles spreading wide. It trailed ropes of white blood that spattered the ferns. One of the Maws collapsed where it had been standing, falling first to its knees, then sideways onto the ground. Behind the toppling body, he saw Hult, whipping his sword around as he finished the killing stroke. The Uigan's tattooed face was twisted into a look of disgust, spattered with pale ichor. He let out a ferocious battle cry, then staggered back as one of the other monsters pointed at him. One hand flew to his head, his mouth gaping in pain. The Maw twitched his tentacles, and Hult flew backward into a tree.

Then Forlo was there, cursing in the minotaur tongue as he raised his sword above Hult's tormentor. The Maw whirled, extending a bony finger, but Forlo's sword snapped around, taking the creature's arm off at the elbow. A hideous shriek filled Eldako's head, pain seeping from the maimed creature's mind into his own. He grunted, trying to stem the agony.

The prisoner! cried the Maw's mind-voice. *They have come for him. Get him out, before—*

Forlo brought his sword down again, on top of the Maw's bulbous head. Its skull shattered like an egg, scattering slime in all directions. The monster sat down hard, its legs jerking as the last echoes of life faded from its body.

The Maw's companions had heard its death-cry, and now their bony hands grabbed Eldako and hauled him to his feet. Their thoughts bored into his mind, forming a compulsion he tried to resist. He couldn't, though; together, the two creatures were too strong.

RUN.

Eldako had been a fine runner, before. Now, though, he was tired and in pain, and he didn't want to follow the Maws' orders anyway. He moved like a string-puppet, jerking about and lurching away from Forlo and Hult. The Maws fell in beside him, one cold hand on each of his arms, coaxing him, cajoling him, forcing him to obey. When he got his coordination back, he began to gather speed. Behind, Forlo and Hult were yelling, their swords singing against unseen foes. The cha'asii loosed volley after volley at the Maws.

Another cry tore through his mind, and one of the voices left his head. His captors' numbers were dwindling—but he was sprinting faster, the shakiness leaving his stride. Running hurt him, hurt deeply, but he couldn't stop, couldn't disobey the commands. The Maws filled his brain, drove out all thoughts but those aimed at flight. They drove him on, faster, leaving the fight behind. Eldako had the horrible feeling that, no matter how much his body protested, no matter what damage it did, they would keep driving him.

They would break him, if it came to it. He kept trying to fight, but the creatures were too strong. He might tear the soles of his feet to ribbons, snap an ankle, rip muscles and snap tendons, and still he would keep fleeing, driven by their cold, passionless thoughts.

A shadow rose in front of them, a dozen paces away. The Maws flinched in surprise, trying to change Eldako's course, but too late. In a single, fluid motion, the figure drew something from its belt, cocked back its arm, and threw.

The knife whistled as it spun through the air. It struck the Maw to Eldako's right, plunging deep into one of its staring eyes. The creature made a wild, gibbering sound in his brain, then it stumbled and fell, its claws ripping bloody furrows in his arm as it lost its grip. Its mind slipped away from his—

And then there was only one. And Eldako felt stronger.

With a roar of pent-up fury, Eldako shoved the final Maw's thoughts out of his brain. It squealed and struggled, but he got rid of it just the same. He didn't waste a moment, coming to a halt in mid stride, then spinning and hammering the edge of his good hand into the creature's tentacled mouth. The Maw made a wet, pulpy sound, and he grabbed hold of the quivering cilia and slammed the monster into the trunk of a tree. Tiny, awful, needlelike things bit at his hand—the creature's jaws, or teeth, or whatever nightmare lay beneath the tentacles.

He barely noticed. His anger was too great. Still bellowing, he pounded the Maw against the tree, again and again until the back of its head was a white, seeping ruin. The fiend went limp, all save its tentacles, which squirmed in his torn and bloody hand. Finally he let go, and the creature crumpled in a heap and lay still.

Silence returned to the jungle. The battle was over. Eldako turned, his arm slick to the elbow, and stared at the shadow who had saved him. Shedara stepped forward, moonlight softening her face.

It did no such favors for his own, by the way she bit her lip. The horror in her eyes told him all he needed to know. She hesitated. He held out his dripping hand, the one he'd used to slaughter the Maw.

"I am the same person as before," he said. "You needn't fear me."

Shame colored her face. Shaking her head, she stepped forward and cupped her hand to his cheek—the unscarred one, he noticed. At least it was something.

"I thought . . . I thought you were dead," she whispered.

"So did I."

He tried to smile, but his lips wouldn't obey. There was pain all over, in his face, his missing eye, his blistered arm: the Maws' control over him had been holding back the full agony of his condition. Now, as the frenzy of the fight drained away, he found himself collapsing, the strength going out of his legs. Shedara caught him, helped lower him down. She bent over him, forcing herself to look at him. He could tell it wasn't easy. This was what he loved about her, though—she was brave and had a stubborn streak a

Fianawar dwarf would have envied. Trembling, she leaned in close and kissed his swollen, acid-ravaged lips.

"It's all right now," she told him. "I'm here."

Chapter

28

THE TEMPLE OF AKH-TAZI, NERON

The Keeper was finally dying. Essana could hear it happening, a change in his rasping breath, a weakening in the rattle of the chains from which his broken body hung. She heard him gurgle, a nasty wet sound he made when he forgot he could no longer speak. He sucked in a breath, let it out in a wet hiss . . . and was silent.

She lay in the dark, bound by shackles, her hands resting on the loose skin of her belly, where the baby had been. "Azar?" she whispered.

He replied with a groan and another weak, reedy breath. The chains clattered. Essana sighed and shut her eyes—death would come for the Keeper, but at its own pace. The Brethren wanted him to linger; their magic held him here.

The hours drifted by. Azar stopped breathing again and again, and each time she prayed to Mislaxa—take him, take him, finally free him from his pain—but as with her son, the goddess never answered. Every time, just when she began to hope, the breathing started again. He whimpered with frustration: he was trying to die, but it wasn't enough. He was as trapped as she was.

No, that wasn't right. He might be in constant agony, unable to move, speak, or see, but they'd done far worse to her. He hadn't carried another life for month upon month, only to have it wrested away at the moment of birth. He hadn't begged and screamed to see his child, only to be pummeled into silence by the yaggol's unfeeling minds. He didn't have to live, day after day, with the knowledge that something terrible was happening to his son . . . something he had no power to stop. The Keeper couldn't know that kind of anguish. Essana would have traded it for pain a hundred times worse than what he was enduring.

They had left her after the birth, spent and weak, drifting in and out of fever. They had not returned to the cell—not with food, not with water. She could sense the yaggol's thoughts, lurking at the edge of her own, observing without caring. But the Brethren didn't come. For all she knew, they had gone on to the Burning Sea, with her son and the Hooded One—but she didn't think so. There was more to be done. She and the Keeper both had a part to play, still.

Finally, after the gods knew how long, she heard movement outside. Essana raised her head as the door creaked open and cold light spilled across the floor. She stared, waiting for a black-cloaked figure to enter—the Master or one of his brothers. But the one who stepped into view was not one of the Faceless.

This figure wore no hood; just a simple cassock of colorless linen. He was short, too—no taller than a kender. With the light from the hall behind it, she couldn't make out any features—only that he was very thin, with long hair spilling down over his shoulders. But there was something in his bearing as he stepped through the doorway that was weirdly familiar. It was as if she were watching Barreth decades ago, as . . .

As a six-year-old boy.

Essana sat up, feeling cold all over. Ignoring the pain as the manacles tore at her wrists, she tried to reach out toward the figure, wanting to cry out his name. But she'd never given him a name. She'd never had the chance.

"My son!" she breathed.

The boy stepped back, afraid. Later, she would reflect on how frightening she must have seemed—a dirty, blood-smeared apparition, pale and gaunt, chained to the floor. To this child, who likely didn't even know the word "mother," she would be a more horrifying sight than the yaggol and the Faceless.

Now, though, his reaction made her heart ache. She reached out her hands. "Please, it's all right. I won't hurt you. . . ."

He shook his head, shrank back into the doorway. She begged him with her eyes. No. Don't leave me alone here. . . .

Then he was gone, out the door again, feet pattering down the hall, the door left ajar behind him. Essana stared at the empty opening, eyes stinging, too parched for tears. She hadn't even gotten a good look at his face. All she had were questions.

How had he grown so old? She hadn't given birth more than a few weeks ago, by her reckoning. The Brethren had done something, made him age faster.

She bowed her head, defeated. "You bastards," she breathed. "You're robbing him of his childhood. Stealing his life."

"Perceptive," said a voice from the door, thick with disdain.

Looking up, she saw him. The Master stood where her son had been, peering down at her, hands folded in his sleeves. Two yaggol lurked behind him. She felt their minds slither over hers, ready to defile her at a gesture from their lord.

"We have no use for children, you see," he said. "The Faceless Emperor will not enter this world in a brat's body. Our magic will keep aging him until he is grown . . . perhaps twenty years old.

"Of course, his wits will still be those of a babe, but that is little matter." The cloaked shoulders rose and fell. "He is a vessel only—the mind doesn't matter at all. Once Maladar emerges from the statue, the body will be his. And with the power of the Faceless Emperor, the boy will stop aging altogether. He may lose his childhood, but neither will he know old age. You should be glad, my lady—your son will live forever."

He bowed slightly and turned to go. Essana watched, a chasm yawning in her belly, too stunned to reply. As he laid his hand upon the door, though, he turned and glanced back at her, eyes flashing from the depths of his cowl.

"A pity that you will not be around much longer to watch him grow."

She lunged—and was met with a white-hot explosion, deep in her brain. She flopped down again, retching, her insides a twisting knot. The yaggol regarded her through the entrance, their tentacles waving; then the door thudded shut again. Darkness filled the room.

She stared toward the doorway, wishing the boy would come back—that she could behold her son again. But that time had passed. The next time she saw him, he would be older. She would never know him as a child.

Sleep came, in time. Even in dreams, her son never showed his face.

More time passed. It seemed like days. The Keeper slid toward death repeatedly, only to revive before the gods could claim him. His groans were the only human contact Essana had. She felt her sanity fraying, her thoughts dwelling on the child, wanting to hear his voice, hold him in her arms . . . everything the Brethren had denied her. She dreamed he might return to her, pity her, try to set her free.

It was folly. Her son wouldn't know pity. With the Master for a father, he would learn only cruelty, deceit, wickedness—and that hurt worse than anything. When the Faceless were done with him, her son would be as evil as they were.

And then Maladar would take him, and he wouldn't be anything. He would be gone, swallowed up, like the flame of a candle thrown into a bonfire. She could do nothing to stop it. She even gave up praying. Either she was beyond the gods' power or they simply didn't care. It came to the same thing.

In time, the door opened again. Essana tried to turn toward the opening. She could barely move now, her muscles atrophied by hunger, her mind fuzzy with thirst. The deprivation would have killed most by now, even the strongest minotaur; only the Brethren's magic held her here. After several excruciating attempts, she managed to face the door. She hoped it would be the boy again, but it wasn't. Six yaggol stood there, and with them was one of the Faceless, the Watcher. He stepped in, the tentacled aberrations crowding around him.

"What is it?" she asked. "What more do you want?"

The Watcher shook his head. "Not you, my lady. Not this time."

He pointed across the room, toward the curtain. Four of the yaggol walked to where the Keeper hung. The others kept their eyes on Essana, ready to seize her mind. She fought to keep her thoughts calm, not to give them a reason.

"What are you going to do with him?" she asked.

"What should have been done long ago," the Watcher answered. "He will pay the price for his treachery."

She watched him walk up to the curtain. With a swift jerk, he ripped the fabric down.

Essana cried out, trying to turn away. She was too weak, however, and though she squeezed her eyes shut, it was too late. The image of what hung in that alcove had burned into her mind. She knew she would see it for the rest of her life—however long that was.

The Keeper had rotted. His skinless flesh had mummified, pulling taut and shrinking to a black husk over his skeleton. Here and there it had split, laying bare his bones. Tarry sludge dripped from the sockets of his eyes, from the stumps of his hands and feet. His fate was monstrous, even worse than what the death-priests of Thenol inflicted on their enemies.

"Azar," she wept. "Oh, gods, Azar, I'm sorry. It's my fault—"

BE SILENT, spoke the yaggol, and she was. She didn't open her eyes, only listened to the wheezing as the Watcher regarded the shriveled thing the Keeper had become.

"You held the key to glory," the Watcher said. "All the power of Old Aurim was in your grasp—and you threw it away. Why? Not for the woman, I'm sure—no one would be that stupid. It was for some memory of virtue, wasn't it? Some vestige of nobility.

"I can sense your mind through the yaggol, Azar of Suluk. I understand now—you were never one of us. Oh, the Rainward Kings were clever, to send you into our ranks. They can cling to that cleverness when their palaces and fiefdoms burn. Perhaps, once Maladar forges his new empire, he will give me the ruins to govern.

"But you, you who were called Keeper, who were second among us, next to the Master himself . . . now your part in this saga must end. The Brethren await. The Slayer's knife is sharpened. You will be the last to die upon the altar before the final ritual. Your blood will bring forth the Emperor. Ironic, is it not? Your death, accomplishing the very thing you swore to—"

Even when it was done, Essana wasn't quite sure how it happened. She didn't see it, but she heard it all—the sudden gasp from the Watcher, putting an end to his gloating. The two screams that followed—one tongueless and filled with rage; the other rising and rising, breaking in pain. A hideous, wet crunch, stopping the second scream.

Spattering—blood, warm on her face. A body falling to the floor.

She opened her eyes.

It shouldn't have been possible: the Keeper was a ruin of a man, and four yaggol surrounded him, their minds locked with his. Unprotected by the cha'asii's magic, he shouldn't have been able to budge, much less cast a spell. And yet, drawing on some awesome reserve, he had. The proof was the Watcher's corpse, sprawled backward on the ground. The head was a pulpy mass, crushed like a walnut in a man's fist. Bits of blood and brain flecked the walls.

It was Azar's last act of defiance. Now the yaggol moved in, an instant too late, and the hanging mummy went limp, its strength gone. They seized him and tore him down from the chains, the hooks ripping through his flesh as he tumbled to the floor. Bones broke, but he didn't notice. He had lost consciousness. Essana hoped, as they dragged him from the cell, that he would never, ever regain it.

They brought her along too, as she knew they would. She had witnessed every other sacrifice atop the temple, since the dragon bore her here. This would be no exception.

Mist, bloodied by Lunis, blanketed the jungle as the yaggol dragged her up the steps to where the remaining Brethren awaited. They were three, now: with the Watcher's body cooling in her cell, only the Master, the Slayer, and the Speaker remained. Nor was there any sign of Gloomwing, which was strange; he had been present for every bloodletting before.

She wondered about that—but not for long, for there was another figure on the rooftop, and the sight of him stole her breath away. Her son stood next to the Master—no longer dressed in the cassock he'd worn earlier, but clad in black, a hood covering his head. She felt a spike of panic, wondering if the Brethren had cut off his face—then calmed down when she saw the brown arc of his chin beneath the cowl.

He was taller, dwarf-height . . . perhaps eight or nine years old, still aging fast. In less than a month, at this rate, he would be grown. And then. . . .

She shuddered, her eyes flicking toward the altar. Azar lay upon it, looking like a thousand-year-old corpse dug out of a bog. She would never have believed he was still alive, but his limbs twitched and shivered upon the stone. Above him loomed the Hooded One. Maladar's hunger hung about the statue, like the tingling before a thunderstorm. He wanted the Keeper's life, more than any of the elves the Brethren had brought him.

"Bring her," beckoned the Master.

The yaggol shoved Essana forward—and toward her son. She stared at the boy, but his gaze fastened on the Hooded One and the pathetic thing on the altar. She wanted to rush to him, to call out to him, but the yaggol prevented her, forcing her thoughts away. She turned instead to face the Master.

"Another of your Brothers is dead," she said. "And where is your pet wyrm? You're running out of allies."

The Master regarded her from the depths of his hood. There was hate in his gaze, of course, but something else as well: a glimmer of fear. He, too, had expected Gloomwing to be here for this important ritual. The Master didn't know what had happened to the dragon, any more than she did.

"Don't let's compare allies, milady," he said. "You're about to lose the last of yours."

"You lie. There is my husband."

"Lord Forlo will not save you. I doubt he even knows where you are."

She regarded him, eyes narrowing. "Oh? Then why are you afraid?"

The Speaker and the Slayer glanced at each other, surprised. The Master glowered, then nodded to the yaggol. Essana had an instant to brace herself before a blast of nausea drove her to her knees. She heaved, trying to vomit, but her stomach was empty.

"This is the last rite you will observe, Essana of Coldhope," the Master said. "But not the last you shall attend. When the time comes, when the vessel is ready to accept the Faceless Emperor . . . then it will be your turn to lie upon the altar. Your blood will flow in his name." He started to turn away, then looked back at her, his voice sharp and vicious. "And it will not be the Slayer who wields the knife."

Essana stared at him, at the child by his side. The Master laid a gloved hand on the boy's shoulder and led him away.

She stayed where she was, unable to move, as the terrible ritual began. Her mind dark with horror, she watched the Brethren gather by the altar, chanting orisons in Maladar's name. Her son didn't join in, but the boy watched in fascination as the Slayer strode to the Keeper's side, the long knife glittering in his hand. A light rain began to fall; clouds swallowed the red moon.

"Come forth, Great One," proclaimed the Speaker. "Your time is at hand. Accept this offering; let it give you strength. Come forth, lord of Taladas, emperor of us all."

"Blood for the Faceless," declared the Master. "Blood for Maladar!"

The Keeper didn't struggle; the yaggol's minds gripped him tight. He lay as placid as a lamb as the Slayer raised his blade to the statue then laid it against his throat. He made no sound as the edge drew across, parting flesh, scraping bone. Essana wept as the blood flowed free. She watched Azar die.

The Slayer gathered his blood in the skull bowl and poured it at the statue's feet, as he had done so often before. This time, however, there was a difference—a blurring around the Hooded One that made her want to rub her eyes. Power seethed atop the temple, making the air swelter. Sparks burst in the air. The Slayer stepped back, and as one the Brethren bowed their heads.

And Maladar an-Desh, the Faceless Emperor, the Sleeper in the Stone, came forth.

It was only a shade of the man, a pale ghost in the exact image of the statue, bound to the black stone by ropes of gray mist, yet it was him. There was no doubting it, no mistaking the evil that poured from that spectral figure. Beside him, even the Master seemed insipid, a feeble mockery of his malevolence.

"I am risen," he spoke in a voice that rolled like distant thunder. "Now I hearken to your call, my faithful. But you are fewer than I expected. What of the rest?"

The Faceless glanced at one another, uneasy. "The Keeper lies before you, Great One," said the Master. "He betrayed us, and death on the altar was his reward—but he murdered the Watcher before we could kill him. The Teacher died at the hands of our enemies, in the vales of Marak. As for the wyrm . . . his fate we do not know. He flew forth some weeks ago and never returned. I fear he has been slain."

"A pity," the specter said, with a dismissive wave of his hand. "But you three are enough for what remains. Have you the vessel?"

The Master leaned down, speaking softly to the boy, who stepped forward. For the first time, Essana heard her son speak, and his voice wrenched her heart. The tone was flat, devoid of feeling. He had a Rainwards accent, like the rest of the Brethren.

"I am the Taker. My body shall be yours."

Maladar gazed down on the boy, his eyes flashing, then rounded on the Brethren. "A child? I cannot dwell in one so young. My power would rip him apart!"

"He will not be a child then," the Master said. "He will

be grown, worthy of your presence. His father was a mighty warrior. There is strength in him."

"Hmmm," the Emperor mused. He wasn't convinced, but finally he nodded. "What you say had best be true. I shall be wroth if I cannot use him. Now, what of the sacrifice? Whose blood shall he spill at my feet?"

The Faceless parted, and the ghost's eyes fell upon Essana.

"His mother," said the Master. "Newly rid of him. She gave birth but five-and-twenty days ago and pines for him still."

At this, Maladar seemed impressed. He nodded, his eyes glinting. "That *is* cruel," he said. "You impress me, my thralls. The grief she feels when the blade bites will make me all the stronger. I can almost taste her life."

"I am glad you approve, Great One," said the Master. "The day will come soon. When the black moon is full, two weeks hence, we shall gather here again, and the deed shall be done."

Essana slumped, burying her face in her hands. Two weeks. Barreth, she thought, oh gods, where are you?

Chapter

29

KE-CHA-YAT, NERON

Eldako nearly died, in spite of everything. Forlo had never seen a man so badly hurt, who still somehow managed to survive—not in more than two decades in the Imperial Legions, fighting hobgoblins and the Thenolite dead. The shock of the elf's wounds alone would have been enough to kill most soldiers—and then there was his maltreatment by the Maws, and the difficult journey back to the cha'asii tree town. And always, there was the threat of his wounds rotting. Forlo had been in lands like these; you could die of black-blood from a cut while shaving, much less burns over a third of your body. But Eldako lived, through three nights of fever in the Grandmother's hut, while the ancient elf chanted over him, made him drink sour tea, and burned pungent leaves to her ancestors.

Finally, on the third morning, the fever broke. He lay quiet and still, no longer raving about tentacled horrors in the dark . . . no longer dreaming of being back in his home in the Green, hunting hill-bear with his father. He was here again, now again, his remaining eye no longer glazed with delirium. Shedara sat by his side; she'd barely been away from him since they'd brought him back. She held his good hand as Forlo entered the sick hut and perched on the edge of the merkitsa's spruce-bough bed. Hult arrived soon after. He stayed standing. Yu-shan, the ancient crone, bowed her silver head and departed, leaving them alone.

"I did not think we four would be together again," Eldako said. His voice was slurred and rough, its beauty stolen by the dragon's acid. "Yet here we are, almost at the end."

"Almost," Shedara said, squeezing his hand.

She smiled, but there was a deep sorrow in her eyes. Forlo understood why. He and Essana had looked at each other that way, just before he rode out to face Chovuk's horde. There was love between these two, but it was love without hope. They all knew Eldako's time in the world was precious.

"The cha'asii will help us," she went on. "They've hated the Maws since the eldest days. They'll do what they can to fight them—and their new masters."

Forlo nodded as she spoke. They had spoken to the Grandmother while Eldako hovered at death's brink. They'd learned the history. Once, the akitu-shai had enslaved the elves, forcing them to build a great empire in these woods, until the cha'asii learned how to break the power of the Maws' thoughts. Great wars were fought, and the empire crumbled as both sides nearly wiped each other out. This was many thousands of years before the First Destruction, in the days when Forlo's ancestors had been barbarians, no more civilized than the Uigan. Since then, elf and Maw had lived among the ruins alongside one another, under an uneasy truce broken by skirmishes and murder.

That had changed two summers ago, with the dragon's coming. Gloomwing had not long been in Neron before he started attacking the elves—always small villages and hunting parties, never war bands who could put up a fight. He had killed many cha'asii, but other elves simply went missing.

Finally, a warrior of the elves, one of Yu-shan's sons named Te-kesh-ke, managed to track the wyrm, back through miles of jungle, to a valley where several old temples stood—monuments of the Maws' old empire, crumbling and engulfed by the jungle. From a distance, hidden among the taller tree tops, Te-kesh-ke had watched as Gloomwing brought his prisoners to the sacrificial altar atop the tallest pyramid, an edifice the elves called Akh-tazi.

At this point in the tale, Yu-shan's face grew dark and troubled. "My people . . ." she said, tears shining in her eyes. "There were men there—not elves, but humans, from what land I do not know. They laid my people on the altar and bled them to death. Strong cha'asii died, screaming, at the hands of men without pity . . . or faces."

"The Teacher and his brothers," Shedara had said.

"A thousand plagues upon them," the Grandmother replied. "There were six in those days; they are fewer now. But I will say more of that later."

Things had gone on like that, for years, according to Yu-shan. Every few weeks, Gloomwing would return, slaughtering scores of elves each time, then carrying the survivors east to the temple. Te-kesh-ke put together a war band with the intent of assailing the temple and putting an end to the dark rites, but when the elves marched on Akh-tazi, they found that the Maws were in league with the men there. Te-kesh-ke died on the temple steps, along with all but three of his warriors. These returned to Ke-cha-yat to tell of the slaughter. Since then, there had been three other assaults, but none had succeeded. Between the men's magic and the Maws' powers, the cha'asii had been defeated again and again.

Finally, in the autumn, something new happened. Gloomwing vanished for more than a month, and the elves had dared to think he was gone for good . . . but one night, not long after the three moons rose full together, he had returned from the north, bearing two things.

"A statue," Shedara had murmured.

Forlo had glanced at her, nodding. "And a woman."

This surprised the Grandmother only for a moment. They had already told her their tales, what had brought them here. She went on with hers.

After the dragon's return, his attacks grew more daring and frequent. Gloomwing kidnapped more and more elves, and the Brethren cut their throats and offered blood to the statue while they forced the woman to watch. The winter rains came, and still this went on, while the woman . . . Essana . . . grew larger and larger with the child she carried. Dozens more cha'asii perished on the altar, victims of the Faceless.

Then, one night when the winds blew cold from the north, one of the hooded men came to Ke-cha-yat. He appeared out of nowhere in the middle of the town and demanded to speak with the cha'asii's leader. The tribe's warriors balked, but in the end Yu-shan came down from her hut. He called himself the Keeper and asked their help. He knew they had charms that could block the fell thoughts of the Maws, whom he called yaggol. He had one with him, and asked for another—and for help. He was a spy, and he meant to help the woman escape. If he didn't, the Brethren would take the baby and kill her afterward.

This made the Grandmother angry, for the Keeper had allowed many elves to die. What made the woman's life more important?

"Not her," the Keeper had explained. "The child. They will use it to free a powerful evil from the statue, so it can walk the living world again. I cannot let that happen. They must be stopped."

Hearing all this, Forlo had risen, feeling ill and dizzy, and left to walk alone around Ke-cha-yat. Hult tried to follow, but Shedara warned him not to, so Forlo wandered the town, his eyes turning east toward the temple.

The Keeper's rescue attempt had ended in dismal

failure, according to Yu-shan, and he himself had disappeared. Essana remained at Akh-tazi, and the sacrifices continued . . . until one night, not long before Forlo and the others reached the Neroni coast. There was a terrible storm that night. Forlo, having returned to listen to the Grandmother as she concluded her tale, remembered seeing that storm in the distance, remembered that night well.

The night his son was born.

He was too late. Essana might well be dead by now, their child lost. He rued every lost day since they left Coldhope, especially his captivity in Kristophan. If he could have slain Rekhaz again, he would have done it gladly.

The storm night was the last of the sacrifices, Yu-shan said. The next day, Gloomwing had come to the coast, to investigate the strange boat there, and the cha'asii had had their revenge at last. The dragon's skull hung from the branches before Yu-shan's hut now, glaring down over the town. His death had avenged thousands of elves . . . but the grief remained . . . and the loss. It would always be there, as long as the cha'asii lived here.

"So they will aid us?" Eldako murmured. "They will help us against these Crawling Maws?"

"They'll help," Shedara said. "And they've given us these."

She reached to her neck and pulled out a talisman, made of crimson feathers and turquoise, carved with whorls and zigzags. Hult showed his; jade, like Nalaran's amulet, with white feathers. As Forlo produced his own, blood-red jasper and black plumage, Shedara produced a fourth. It was glistening opal, ringed with feathers as yellow as gold. A crack ran through its center. Eldako managed something like a smile as she slid the leather thong over his head.

"Broken," he said. "Like me."

"But still powerful," Shedara said, settling it between his collarbones. "They'll protect us from the Maws, keep their minds out of ours. We wore them when we rescued you."

Eldako looked at the opal, then up at her. "When do we leave?"

Now, Forlo wanted to say. We should have left long ago. My wife, my son . . . and the statue too—if all isn't lost yet, it will be soon.

He kept his silence, though. He'd already resolved to head east alone if there were any more delays. He caught Eldako watching him. The understanding in the merkitsa's good eye haunted him. The wild elf knew exactly what he was thinking. There was shame on his ravaged face. Rescuing him might have cost them more time than they could afford to lose.

"I am ready now," Eldako said and started pushing himself up.

Shedara blocked him, forcing him back down. "No, you're not," she said. "You still need rest. Besides, it's sunset now. The cha'asii won't leave until tomorrow."

"The morning, then," Eldako said. "First light, we set forth. I will keep pace with you, I promise."

"We know you will," Hult said. He bowed his head, his hair hanging down almost far enough to cover his eyes. There were streaks of gray in it, though he was the youngest of them all; the road had been hard. "And if you have trouble keeping up, I will carry you."

"My thanks," Eldako said. "You are all better friends than I have ever known. I would be dead if not for you."

"Don't be foolish," Shedara said. "You'd be back in the Dreaming Green if it weren't for us. Certainly not down here. You owe us nothing."

She bent down and kissed his forehead, heedless of the puckered scars on his skin. At that gesture, Hult leaned forward and laid a hand on Eldako's shoulder. Forlo followed suit, touching the merkitsa's knee.

Eldako looked at them all, smiling.

Dawn found the tree town already awake, dusty green-gold light lancing through the trees onto platforms and bridges alive with activity. A band of nearly a hundred cha'asii—nearly every able-bodied adult left in Ke-cha-yat—had gathered in the main square, beneath the Grandmother's hut. They were clad in leather breechclouts and feathered headdresses, silver armbands and disk-shaped earrings, their faces painted to resemble jungle cats and serpents. They wore bows and quivers of long arrows, blowguns and sheaths of poison-tipped darts, spears and clubs edged with obsidian, and shields of woven bamboo.

A phalanx of minotaur warriors, properly kitted and well rested, could have chewed through them in minutes, Forlo thought as he looked out over the war band—but appearances were deceiving. He had fought in the jungle before; warriors there didn't fight face-to-face, or with what the League's soldiers considered a code of honor. And the jungle itself took its toll, through heat and sickness. Steel armor was a liability, not a help. Heavy weapons got snagged in trees and brush. Men fell into sand-water and sank forever or forgot to check their boots and died screaming when scorpions stung them. He'd seen entire divisions fall to enemies they never even glimpsed. That had been in Syldar, a hundred leagues away, but he had no reason to doubt the fierceness of the cha'asii.

Each of them also wore one more protection: a talisman matching the ones Yu-shan had given to him and his friends. These were the last such charms left in Ke-cha-yat; either the elves would defeat the Maws, or they would vanish from Neron altogether.

"It feels strange," said Hult. The Uigan stood by his side, one hand on his sword, the other touching his twin amulets, Nalaran's and Yu-shan's. "To have a horde again."

"Not exactly the riders of the Tamire, though," Forlo said wryly.

The barbarian shrugged. "The horses would have had trouble with this terrain, anyway."

Forlo clapped the young man's shoulder. "At least we're on the same side this time."

"The right side," Hult agreed. "We will pray for victory, each to our own gods. With luck, someone will hear us this time. I look forward to meeting your wife, my friend."

Your people would have killed Essana if they'd caught her, Forlo thought grimly. They'd have thrown her from the walls of Coldhope or chased her on their horses until one speared her on his lance. But he kept that idea to himself.

Instead, he turned at a sound behind him and bowed his head. Eldako was limping down from his sick hut, Shedara holding his arm. The wild elf was in constant pain, his face creased with the effort of moving at all. With his burns, he looked like a wax sculpture, left too close to a fire. The cha'asii fell silent, signing circles in the air to ward against whatever devils might still hang over him.

Forlo shook his head. This was foolish. The merkitsa would only slow them down. He was in no condition to fight. But Shedara would not to leave without him, and the elf refused to be left behind. And Yu-shan insisted that they must be four.

Forlo glanced to the east, out through the treetops. Even from the town's highest vantage, the temple of Akh-tazi was too far away to be seen, beyond the horizon, and two horizons beyond that, according to the elves. That made a hundred leagues of hard travel through the jungle. Even with the cha'asii to guide them, it would be almost a fortnight before they reached their destination.

Please, he thought. Starlight, just stay alive long enough for me to reach you. . . .

"Your wife still lives, my friend," Eldako said as he

hobbled up to them. "I don't know how I know—perhaps I felt her mind through the Crawling Maws, while they held me captive—but I am sure of it. She lives and yearns for you."

Forlo felt tears rush to his eyes and blinked them away. He nodded, making an inarticulate sound in reply.

Above, something stirred. They turned to watch as the Grandmother emerged from her hut, clad in a cloak of shimmering green scales, a plume of snow-white feathers rising high above her head. Her women supported her as she started down the stairs. The cha'asii fell silent, touching their lips in reverence, then parting to let her pass. She approached a dais in the platform's midst. Her attendants helped her step up onto the platform, but did not follow. Alone, as fragile as bird bones, she tottered to the center of the dais. Her people looked on, silent.

"A time of reckoning has come to the Emerald Sea," she spoke, sweeping her hand to encompass all the jungle. "For twenty generations of our people, we have held the truce with our enemies. Even through the Destruction and the Second, we held the peace and did not fight the akitu-shai.

"That time is now ended. The peace was broken with Gloomwing's coming, and again with the Faceless. Now all rests on you, my children. The Maws must be destroyed, and their masters with them, just as you defeated the dragon himself."

All eyes on the platform rose to the giant skull that loomed high above Yu-shan's platform. It leered down at them, glistening white, dull black sockets where red eyes had smoldered. The cha'asii beamed. So did Eldako. He hadn't seen what remained of Gloomwing until now, and his pleasure at seeing the wyrm's remains was as plain as the scars on his face.

"Let my blessing, and your ancestors', be upon you all," Yu-shan spoke. "Their spirits will guide you to victory. The plague of the Maws will be ended, and at last, these forests will be ours . . . and ours alone."

"Victory!" cried the elves. "Glory to the wood-folk! Death to the mind-killers!"

Spears punched the air. Fists rose. Feet stamped. Somewhere, unseen hands pounded on drums. The cha'asii settled into a hopping dance, shouting victory over and over. All through it, they kept their gaze on Yu-shan, adoring her.

The Grandmother raised her hands. The air trembled, and even Shedara shied back. The power the old crone drew down was tremendous, almost as much as Forlo had felt when the wall of water obliterated Chovuk's horde. It filled the air, making it sluggish, like the damp that ruled the jungle below. And, like the damp, it could not be contained forever. It had to burst forth, had to rain.

The power revealed itself first as a golden flare, high above the Grandmother's head, then blossomed outward, forming a glowing nimbus that spread through all of Ke-cha-yat. It crackled and sizzled, giving off waves of heat. Forlo felt the hairs on his arms and neck stand erect as it flowed above him, and Hult bit the heel of his hand, an automatic gesture to ward against evil.

Finally the wave of power stopped, shifting and shimmering, rumbling like faraway thunder. They all stared up at the glowing sky—and the storm broke.

Golden motes exploded from the aura, pouring down on the cha'asii. The motes flickered as they fell, leaving trails of yellow flame, but they didn't burn when they struck the elves. Instead they burst with a chorus of loud snaps, their glow persisting in the air, leaving blue ghosts behind when Forlo blinked. He felt a few strike him, then many more. He expected a jolt, pain, something—but there was only a moment's warmth and a stranger feeling, a tightening in his muscles that increased with every touch. He shivered, feeling energy flow into him, strength he'd never had before.

Glancing over, he saw Hult flex his arm in wonderment, and Shedara nod in approval. Even Eldako looked sturdier, standing tall and proud despite his ghastly wounds.

The last golden raindrops fell. The nimbus disappeared. The cha'asii returned their gaze to Yu-shan.

"You are mighty, my people," she said. "The power of the ancestors lies in your bones. Go, now—to Akh-tazi, and let none stop you!"

The elves cheered, raising their spears again. Invigorated by the Grandmother's spell, Forlo cheered with them, hope overcoming his despair.

Starlight, he thought, I'm coming at last.

Chapter

30

The Emerald Sea, Neron

Left on their own, Hult knew he and the others would be lost within a day. The jungles were unlike any place he had ever known, even more frightening than the Dreaming Green. Having lived most of his life on the open, golden grasses of the Tamire, he found the riot of greenery and closeness of the trees as alien as the bottom of the ocean. Nowhere he looked could he see more than a dozen paces ahead—usually much less. In places the growth became so thick, they had to use swords to cut through the tough vines, creepers, and shrubbery that clawed and scratched at their flesh. The air felt thick, so heavy with water it was hard to breathe, and the frequent, violent rain showers did nothing to relieve the relentless heat.

The nights were even worse. The cha'asii slept soundly, but this was their home. The rest of the group found only skittish rest, constantly jumping at growls and shuddering moans from the dark. When dawn came, they were still tired from the night before. Fortunately, these strange woods provided even for that: the cha'asii gave them leaves from a black-barked tree and told them to chew. Hult was leery at first, particularly at the bitter taste, but once he started, he found new energy flowing into him. The leaves, which the elves called ulashu, reminded him of the yarta root his people ate before battle. But yarta only worked for so many days before a rider became immune to its effects. Hult hoped the ulashu were more potent, because he didn't think he would sleep through a single night while he was in the Emerald Sea.

The war band moved at a slog, sometimes traveling so slowly it seemed not to make any progress at all. Distances a rider could have devoured in an hour on the Tamire took a whole day to cover. The ground rose into steep, rocky hills, slick with rotting leaves, or dove into gorges where white rivers thundered; these they had to cross by felling trees and inching across the moss-covered trunks. Even worse were the lowest depressions of the land, where the ground grew so boggy it felt as if they might fall in and drown. Indeed, one time Forlo got stuck in a pit of mud that tried to suck him under; it took Hult, Shedara, and three cha'asii hauling on a vine to haul him out again. The air was thick with biting flies, glistening blue and violet in the sunlight—and they were only the least of the jungle's nuisances. There were also spiders the size of small dogs, scorpions with red skulls on their shells, massive black jungle cats that had to be driven away with much shouting and clashing of spears, and snakes so large Hult could scarcely believe his eyes. Once, he saw a serpent that had to be thirty paces long, which had pulled a deer up onto a low-hanging branch and was swallowing the animal whole.

Twelve days passed. Hult had no idea where they were anymore. It seemed this accursed wood might go on forever. Sooner or later, the jungle would defeat them. And it would take Eldako first.

Even with the strengthening spell Yu-shan had cast, the wild elf was suffering. Eldako started each morning walking on his own, but by midday he began to stagger, and sunset found him leaning hard on one of his friends—usually Shedara, but Hult and Forlo helped as well. His face was pale beneath its war paint, and though he refused to speak a word of complaint, they could all tell how much his wounds pained him.

"Why is he even with us?" Hult murmured to Forlo on the twelfth evening, watching while Shedara helped the merkitsa swallow water from a hollow gourd. "He can't shoot a bow. He can lift a sword, but we both know he can't fight. We should never have brought him on this journey."

Forlo nodded then sighed. "I know. I think the same thing every time he stumbles. But he thinks he still has a part to play—and the Grandmother seemed to agree." He flinched and looked away into the night when Eldako's scarred face turned toward them. "Maybe he's wrong about that . . . but who's going to tell him? We didn't let him come along. He chose to. And as long as he's not slowing us down too much, I'll respect that."

Hult grunted. "Can he still feel your woman's mind?" he asked. "Is she still alive?"

"He hasn't said. And I haven't asked."

They were close now; they could all feel it. In two days they would come to Akh-tazi—the elves had told them as much, reading whatever invisible clues they used to tell where they were in this nightmare land. The only thing that kept Forlo going was the belief that his wife still lived. He couldn't risk knowing the truth now; if he was wrong, he would fall apart.

Hult had never met Essana of Coldhope. After all this time with her husband, though, he knew she must be a remarkable woman. He hoped he would have the chance to know her. He said nothing of this to Forlo, though—only clapped his friend's shoulder and lay down, staring at the branches above and waiting for sleep that wouldn't come.

They had just stopped for a rest at midday the next day when several elves, who had gone on to scout ahead, stepped suddenly out of the bushes and spoke in hushed tones with Le-nekh, the warrior in charge of the band. There was a great deal of gesturing, but Hult couldn't hear more than the occasional word.

One, however was akitu-shai.

"Trouble?" he asked Le-nekh when the scouts had finished. "Are there Maws near?"

The elf looked at him, his painted face stern. "Very near. Akh-tazi is only two valleys away. We are in their land now. A party stands in our way. And . . . they are not alone."

"What is it?" Forlo asked, a hand on his sword. "One of the Faceless?"

"No. Vaka-te-nok. The Mouth Beneath the Earth."

The others exchanged glances. Forlo shook his head, and Shedara shrugged. Eldako, however, caught his breath. "This Vaka," he said. "Is it a large beast, black, with many tentacles around a great, snapping beak? Does it wait for its prey beneath the leaves?"

"They dwell in your woods as well, I see," Le-nekh said. "They are abominations, bred by the Maws in ancient times. There must have been akitu-shai in the north, once."

Eldako nodded. "Long gone, if so. The Vaka are called winlesh in our land. They are hard to kill. But if you know where one is, it should be easy to avoid. They do not move on their own, after all."

The cha'asii exchanged glances. Le-nekh scowled.

"Perhaps not in your land," he said. "Here, though . . . where the earth is soft. . . ."

"Can't we go around?" Shedara asked. "There must be a way."

Le-nekh shook his head. "Not for many days' journey. A ravine lies between here and Akh-tazi. It is a hundred miles long, and too broad for trees to cross. The only way is the Bridge of Tears. That is where the Maws and the Vaka await."

"Then we have no choice," Forlo said, loosening his blade in its scabbard. "The black moon is nearly full. Maladar is coming."

"There will be no more secrecy, if we fight," Hult said. "If what Eldako believes is true, the Maws' minds all touch one another. If they see us coming, the Faceless will know."

"Then let them know," Forlo said. "Let them fear us."

Shedara held up a hand. "Hang on. We might not be able to hide the fact that we're coming, but we can keep them from finding out how many we are." She turned to the scouts. "How many Maws were there?"

They spoke with each other, whispering and gesturing, then one waggled his hand. "Eight, maybe ten. No more than that."

"Ten," Eldako said. "If I could still shoot. . . ."

"Shooting or no, we can handle ten," Forlo said, cutting him off. "They're easy to kill, if their minds can't reach us. And as for this Vaka—"

"Leave that to me," Shedara said, flexing her hands. She looked at the others, eyebrows raised. "Well? Shall we?"

<hr />

The Bridge of Tears was a span of black stone, a single crumbling arch webbed with tough vines that, to Hult's eyes, seemed to be the only thing keeping it from tumbling down into the chasm below. Greenery grew right up to the canyon's edge, then began again on the far side, trees leaning out over the abyss to grasp at sunlight. Mist and the sound of raging water rose out of the ravine. The river that plunged through the cut was ferocious, nothing but white foam battering jagged rocks.

There were, in fact, nine Maws guarding the span.

They stood in groups of three, one on the bridge, the others to either side. They peered this way and that, each group maintaining an eerie rhythm that left no direction unobserved, even for a moment. Their tentacles writhed in silent communion. Hult's lip curled at the sight of the creatures—so different, so alien from anything he'd ever seen.

"Where's this Vaka?" whispered Forlo, crouched in the brush beside him. They were far enough back that leaves and shadows hid them from view, and the cha'asii talismans kept their minds out of the monsters' reach.

"I think it was there," Shedara replied, pointing at a spot near the rightmost group of Maws. The black earth there was broken, churned like a freshly dug grave. But there was no sign of the creature the elves had spoken of.

Eldako coughed, his good eye darting this way and that. "It could be anywhere, if the ones in these lands burrow to hunt, rather than waiting for prey."

They all glanced down. Hult drew his sword, feeling ill.

"You've seen these things," he said. "Is there any sign before they attack?"

The merkitsa shook his head. "Not much. The ground will tremble a little, then heave and burst. It happens in an instant."

"Great," Forlo said, sliding his own weapon from its scabbard. His eyes fixed on the soil at his feet.

"Don't worry about the Vaka," Shedara said. "I said I'd deal with it. You handle the Maws."

Hult nodded, glancing back toward the bridge. "We could rush them," he said. "Take them by surprise. They won't put up much of a fight."

"But we'll draw the Vaka right to us," Eldako said, then glanced at Shedara. "I'm sorry. I can't not think about it. I saw one of those things kill half a hunting party once before we brought it down. It ripped them limb from limb."

Forlo licked his lips. "Push through to the bridge, in that case. It can get under us on solid ground, but there we'll be safe."

"Safe?" Hult repeated. "Trapped on that thing, surrounded by the Maws?"

"You just said they won't put up much of a fight."

"Keep your voices down," hissed Shedara.

"Forlo is right," Eldako said. "When my people fight the winlesh, we always try to put stone under our feet. The bridge will keep us from harm."

Hult looked at the wild elf, then at Forlo, then back at Eldako again. He was outnumbered, but couldn't shake the bad feeling the bridge gave him. In the end, he shrugged.

"All right," Forlo said. A cunning smile curled his lips. He was a man born for battle. Hult understood—he was the same way. "On three. One—"

The ground beneath them trembled.

"Go!" Eldako yelled, leaping out of cover. He grabbed Shedara's arm to drag her away. "It has come! Go!"

They hurled themselves forward just in time. Behind, there was a thump as the soil flew up; great clots of it struck Hult in the back as he ran, and finer powder rained down all around, pattering into the underbrush. Then there was a massive, furious screech, and something whipped by, just over Hult's head. He glanced up, and his mind went blank: it was a long, black tentacle, as thick as his leg and covered in bony barbs like thorns. A sharp, white hook protruded from the end. He ducked, stumbled, somehow kept his balance, and kept running.

More tentacles lashed the air. They jumped, twisted, ducked—and suddenly Forlo was gone, yanked off his feet with a yell and hauled into the air. Hult whirled, his sword whipping around. It slit open a tentacle, exposing bulging gray flesh beneath. Ichor sprayed, stinking like rotten meat. The limb lashed at him, and he cut it again, catching it closer to the tip. Two twitching, rubbery feet of it flopped down among the ferns, and the stump jerked away, slime spurting from the wound. Somewhere behind it, the horrible screech rang out again.

I made it angry, Hult thought with satisfaction.

"Khot!" shouted a voice above him. "Rut with your mother, you stinking whore-son!"

Hult glanced up. Forlo dangled among the treetops, held aloft by a tentacle that had curled around his legs. Somehow, he'd held on to his blade, and was hewing the air wildly, trying to cut through the Vaka. It wasn't working. Gritting his teeth, Hult started forward.

Shedara flung out an arm, hitting him in the chest and shoving him back. "Let me handle it, I said!" she yelled. "Deal with the Maws!"

Hult was about to argue when a pair of tentacles shot toward them out of the churning earth. Shedara pointed, shouting in the language of magic, and a bolt of white lightning arrowed from her fingertip, searing through one and blackening the second. The Vaka howled, pulling the limbs back into the soil.

"Go!" Shedara yelled. "Help Eldako!"

With a glance, Hult saw that the merkitsa had run ahead without them, awkward-gaited from his wound, but holding his sword high as he charged the Crawling Maws. Hult swallowed hard and turned and ran as Shedara blasted another of the Vaka's tentacles.

It was easy to catch up to Eldako, slowed as he was by his burns. They hit the first group of Maws side by side, blades carving the air in unison. Two pallid heads came free, whirling away. Two slimy bodies crumpled to the ground. The third leaped back, eyes narrowing, gill-like slits opening on either side of its bulbous skull. Hult felt a weird, shivery sensation, like claws scrabbling at the edge of his mind, and he knew the Maw was trying to break through the magic of the talisman.

Hult stopped it by ramming his sword through its gut. Gargling, the thing groped at the blade, then went limp. Hult swung the weapon, flinging the dead creature off; it flopped near the chasm's edge, rolled, and vanished into nothingness.

The other six Maws were regrouping, drawing hooked blades, somewhere between knives and swords in length. Hult and Eldako barreled onto the bridge. The Maws milled about in disarray, then followed them onto the span. Eldako killed one, hewing off its sword arm and then hacking deep into its face. Brains spattered them.

Cilia waving, the Maws backed away, leaving Hult and Eldako standing back-to-back. Behind them, there was a peal of thunder, a flash, and a scream. Hult saw Shedara pull Forlo away from the smoldering remains of a tentacle, ripped out and blackened at its root. Of the rest of the Vaka, there was no more sign.

Then the Maws made their move. They came on in perfect coordination now, their minds linked together. Hult could sense their thoughts, cold and gruesome. Their swords danced; he parried and nearly had his weapon wrenched from his grasp as a Maw twisted its blade's hooked tip around it. With a grunt, he stepped back, then punched the Maw in the face with his free hand. Its flesh was soft and spongy, absorbing the blow as its mouth-tentacles shot out and wrapped around his wrist.

He howled as tiny hooks dug into his flesh, anchoring the creature's grip, then he kicked another Maw in the stomach as it tried to stab him. The creature folded up, dropping to its knees. Meanwhile, the one that had hold of him swung a blow of its own, cutting his leg just above the knee.

Pain bloomed, somewhere in the back of his mind, but he thrust the sensation aside and swept his sword in low. It sliced into the Maw's side. The creature squealed, knees buckling, and dropped its sword as the life ebbed from its body. It nearly dragged Hult down with it, but he brought his sword around as the tentacles pulled taut and cut them off in a mass. Spinning, he aimed another kick at the Maw he'd winded, hit it in the neck, and knocked it off the bridge.

His side of the bridge clear, he tore the severed tentacles from his wrist and turned to see that Eldako had killed one of the Maws on his side. Now only two remained—and Forlo was attacking them from behind. He drove his sword through one Maw's back, then reversed the stroke and hit the second between the eyes with the pommel. The creature stumbled back and toppled into the canyon.

Shedara was there too, standing on the bridge, looking back the way they'd come. Her fingers curled and uncurled, sparks dancing between their tips.

"What happened?" Eldako asked, cringing with pain. He'd been cut too, a bloody furrow running half the length of his forearm. "Is the Vaka dead?"

She shook her head. "I don't think so. I fried it, and it let Forlo go, but then it disappeared, down into the dirt. Hard thing to kill."

"At least we're safe here," Hult said. "You were right about that, Forlo. As long as we stay—"

Before he could finish the thought, though, a geyser erupted right at the bridge's end, spraying them with dirt. Five tentacles burst out of the soil at once . . . then wrapped around the span and heaved. The bridge shuddered, driving Eldako to his knees and sending Hult stumbling toward its edge. Forlo caught his arm before he could fall into the misty fissure and hauled him back.

"It's going to rip the whole bridge out!" Forlo yelled. "Do something!"

"Not yet," Shedara said, squaring her stance as the bridge shuddered again. She backed away from the creature, lips moving, hands held out before her. Hult glanced behind him, at the far end, and knew they couldn't make it to safe ground before the span toppled into the chasm.

"If not now, when?" Forlo muttered, his mouth twisting.

The tentacles tightened their grasp, shaking the bridge again. Shedara tensed, her fingers curling . . . then relaxed, shaking her head. "It's no good. I can't kill it if I can't see it. We've got to bring it up out of the ground."

"How?" Hult asked, grabbing Forlo as the other man stumbled.

"Cut it!" Eldako said, fighting to regain his footing. "Make it angry! That's how my people do it!"

Hult and Forlo needed no more goading. Together they lunged, pushing past Shedara and driving their swords into the Vaka's limbs. They stabbed, hewed, and hacked, sending ichor spurting in all directions—and with a bellow, the creature heaved itself up out of the ground.

Its body was shaped like one of the Maws' heads, but much, much larger—a bloated, black bag of flesh with two tiny, yellow eyes and a snapping beak in the midst of its mangled and blackened tentacles. Hult stood transfixed, appalled by the sight, and by the hideous stench billowing from its jaws. It mewled like a hungry baby.

"Get down, damn it!" Shedara yelled. "Move!"

Forlo knocked Hult down then leaped back, out of the way. Thunder roared, deafening them, and every hair on Hult's body stood up as a lance of lightning seared the air, right above his back. He shut his eyes. The darkness flashed red. The Vaka screamed . . . and then there was a spluttering, exploding noise, and the sound of wet things falling from the sky. Something rank and slimy slapped his cheek, making him retch.

Hult opened his eyes and beheld the carnage. The Vaka's remains lay ruptured and smoking at the end of the bridge. Shedara's lightning had hit it square in the beak and blown it apart, throwing innards all over the place. Gray sludge dripped from the bridge and ran in rivulets over the cliff's edge. The reek of burned flesh made his eyes water. The tentacles wrapped around the span had gone slack and unwound as he watched, to slide down over the abyss. Their weight made the whole creature pitch forward, and he stared in disgusted silence as it finally slipped over the edge and disappeared into the fog.

"Khot," Forlo swore.

Hult rolled over, looking up at Shedara. She smiled at him, wiping slime from her face. "See?" she asked. "I told you I'd take care of it."

Chapter

31

Akh-tazi, Neron

Silence. Pure. Complete.

Essana had thought it was quiet in the cell before, but she hadn't realized just how much noise her tormented cellmate made. Now, with Azar gone—his ruined body bled dry and burned upon the altar—the small noises he made had gone with him. She was alone, in a way she had never been before. Even before the Keeper became her ally, she'd had the life inside her to give her hope. Now, though, there was only emptiness—in the cell, in her womb, in her heart.

Her son had never known her. And now, with the black moon high and fat above the temple—she could feel its power, though she had never beheld it before—the time was nigh. Her turn to die. And her own child would wield the blade.

Kill me, Mislaxa, she prayed. Kill me, Sargas. Kill me, you gods of the Uigan. Whoever might be listening . . . if my life is the key to freeing this faceless monster . . . kill me now, and save the world the suffering he would cause.

A sound from the door interrupted her misery. Essana turned her head—she no longer had the strength to raise it; hunger and despair had weakened her too much—and saw a crack of pale light, then darkness again as the portal shut. Whispering footsteps: human, not yaggol. A quiet cough. She squinted, trying to see.

"They say you gave me birth," whispered a voice. "They tell me you are my mother. Is this the truth?"

Essana caught her breath. She wanted to raise her arm, touch the face so close to hers, just out of sight. But she couldn't. Her eyes burned: for lack of water, she could no longer make tears.

"I am," she croaked. "You are my son. Mine . . . and Barreth's."

"My father," said the voice in the dark. A bitterness there. "They have told me about him as well. How he rode off to battle and left you alone while you were carrying me."

She shook her head. "It wasn't like that. He went to protect—"

The boy snorted—only, by the sound of him, he was a boy no longer. He would appear sixteen now, at the rate he'd been aging. Perhaps eighteen. Her son, only weeks old . . . a grown man now. She shuddered.

"The man abandoned you," he said. "He abandoned me. I will hear no more."

"Why have you come, then?" she shot back, surprised by her sudden anger. "Just to torment me? Or did the Brethren send you for a reason?"

He was quiet a time, stung by her bitterness. When he spoke again, his voice sounded flatter, farther away. "They did not send me," he murmured. "I came on my own. The Brethren do not know I am here."

Oh, Essana thought, but they do. They always know.

"Then speak," she said, "and have done."

Again, the silence. She had snapped the last words; she couldn't help herself. Here he was, her own offspring, and he hadn't shown any concern for her condition, though she knew she was a horror to behold. He hadn't offered to save her. No, he would soon cut her throat because the Faceless told him to. He had no right to be stung by her tone. No right at all.

"I am grown," he said. "I am a man. And yet . . . I have no name. The Brethren call me the Taker, but that is what I shall do. It is not who I am."

"And you wish me to name you," she said, understanding. "You wish something to call yourself, in these last hours before Maladar takes you."

"You are my mother. It is your place."

And who taught you that? she wondered. Anger boiled inside her—this was some sick game, some diversion by the Master. The boy didn't know he was being manipulated . . . this visit was meant to hurt him . . . or her. Probably both. She thought of just telling him to leave . . . but no, she couldn't. The need to do this small thing, to play some part in her own child's life, was too great.

"Your father and I spoke of this, when we learned I was pregnant," she said. "It is the custom of our people to name children after dead family and friends. We chose my own father's name, if you proved to be a son. Varyan Forlo, future Baron of Coldhope."

"Varyan," he said, tasting the name.

"But," she added, "I will not give you that name."

Another pause. "No? Why not?"

"Coldhope is lost, so you will not be its heir. You speak ill of your father, so I will not name you after mine. There is another name, one more fitting."

"Speak it, then. Give it to me."

"Azar."

He snorted. "After the Keeper? You would give me a traitor's name?"

"I give you the name of one who tried to save me," she said. "Of a man who sacrificed all in the hope of stopping this darkness. The Keeper was a good man. Perhaps, with his name, some part of that goodness will pass to you."

She could feel him glaring at her, the fury in his eyes. She smiled. The Brethren would be displeased at this: they would want no reminder of the Keeper. The Master, in particular, would be infuriated.

"I do not accept this name," he said.

She shrugged. "All the same, it is yours. You can change it if you like, but other names are fleeting. This one shall remain with you always, your mother-name. When you stand before the gods, at your life's ending, it is the one you must give them. Azar Forlo, son of Barreth."

"And you will give them yours," he said, "much sooner than that."

There was a ring of steel, a sudden movement. Essana felt a blade press against her throat, its edge dimpling her flesh.

"I will use this blade," he said. "I will stand before you as you lie upon the altar. And I will send you to your vaunted gods."

"Why wait?" she whispered through gritted teeth. She let none of her fear show through her voice. "Do it now."

One last time, he was silent. Then, with a frustrated snarl, he withdrew the blade and strode away. The door opened again, the crack of light spilling through. In the glow, she saw his face. He looked older than she'd thought possible. Twenty or more, now. Hate had twisted his features, made them ugly.

"Your time will come, Mother," he said. "As it will for my father, when he comes."

She blinked, her mouth opening. "Barreth? He's coming?"

"Did you not know?" He smiled, an expression of sheer cruelty, devoid of mirth. "A yaggol patrol sighted him, the day before yesterday. Him, and several others. They are coming for you, Mother. But the Faceless are ready. They will capture my father, and bring him to the sacrifice. He will watch as I kill you."

Finally, after all this time, after all her suffering, this news was too much to bear. Essana screamed and screamed.

Her only answer was the door booming shut and her son's retreating footsteps, lost in her cries.

***

It was a calm night, cloudless, the air hot and still. The sky over the temple was a riot of stars—more than Essana could ever remember seeing, as if someone had tried to paint the heavens and didn't know when to quit. Solis and Lunis were nowhere to be seen, but an eerie luminance bathed the jungle nonetheless: a light whose hue she couldn't quite name. It wasn't blue or violet, or even gray. It made everything seem weirdly vibrant, but the colors were all wrong. The ocean of leaves surrounding the temple were yellow. Her own skin was tinted green. The flames that leaped from the braziers were almost white. The weird colors of the night made her shiver, gooseflesh rising on her arms.

She looked up and saw.

Nuvis was supposed to be invisible, a hole in the sky marked by the League's seers and astronomers, not by its form, but by the stars it blocked out. Priests of the evil gods and wizards devoted to darkness were said to be able to behold Nuvis as clearly as its red and silver cousins. It lit the world of the dead, an emblem of the Thenolite armies. But common folk, those untouched by shadow, simply could not see the third moon.

Yet there it was, risen above the jungle: a disk of purest black, but with many colors swirling within: purple, and crimson, and midnight blue. She saw craters and seas on its surface, forming what looked like a dour, glowering face. An aura shone around it, snaking out in all directions like ink in water. Nuvis was alive, seething, its magic dancing in the night air.

"Yes," said a voice like grinding stones, from the far side of the rooftop. "My power is strong here. It surrounds this place. You can see Nuvis, just as all in Aurim could see it when I ruled. And all Taladas will see it, in time, once I am reborn."

Essana tore her attention from the black moon, forcing herself to look at the statue and the specter floating above the altar. Maladar's shade was unchanged: pale, as insubstantial as mist, bound to the Hooded One by ropes of silver fog. His face was more horrible than any of the Brethren, a carved and charred mass of gnarled flesh, with patches of skull showing through. His eyes gleamed with the green-brown of rotting meat. Her heart sank at the sight of him.

"I do not fear you," she said defiantly.

"You lie," he answered. "I can smell your dread, Essana of Coldhope. It hangs thick in the air. You know your fate, and it terrifies you, but you try not to show it. You are a strong woman. In another time, I would have made you one of my wives."

She raised her head. "In another time, I would have poisoned you while you slept."

Maladar laughed. "Many have tried. I flayed their skin and left them spitted on stakes atop the tallest towers of my palace, for the skyfishers to take. My courtiers made a game of it—who would lose his eyes first, whose liver they would take. Quite a few lingered for days before the end. Once, I skewered every slave I owned because one was caught approaching my bedchamber with a knife. . . ." He fell silent, lost for a moment in thought, then waved his hand. "But this is no time for pleasant memories. Not now. Bring her to me, my servants."

The Slayer and the Speaker stood to either side of her, flanked in turn by yaggol, whose minds were lodged like splinters into hers. Bowing, the Brethren dragged Essana forward, toward Maladar. Every step was torment, forced upon her by her captors: she could never have walked on her own, in her weakened state, but the yaggol's thoughts compelled her. They approached the altar, the bloodstained slab where the Keeper and countless elves had died.

"Look at me, girl."

She didn't want to, but it didn't matter. Her gaze rose, inexorably, to the gruesome ghost above her. And yes, she felt fear. A kender would have felt it.

"He is out there," Maladar said. "Your husband. He is coming, as the Taker told you. He will watch you die, and I will feast on his rage, his anguish. They will only increase my power. A pity, a cruel irony—to have searched half of Taladas for you, only to lose you again as soon as he's found you. It will tear him apart."

"Barreth won't let me die," Essana growled. "He'll find a way."

Maladar shrugged, then looked over her shoulder. "Ah, the prodigy and his mentor. Now the ceremony can begin."

Essana tried to turn, stumbled, and only caught herself at the yaggol's command. Jerkily, like a puppet, she righted herself and raised her gaze to the top of the stair. There, lit by Nuvis, stood the Master and her son.

"Your mother awaits you, boy," Maladar hissed. He relished this cruelty. Here was a man who had known malice so long, it had become his only desire. "Have you the blade that will open her veins?"

The boy was older than even a few hours ago. Another year of his life, maybe two, had passed. "I do, my lord," he said, drawing a curved knife, identical to the ones the Faceless carried. It glistened in Nuvis's shifting light.

"Good," said the specter. "Come, then. We had best be ready when your father arrives."

Fight them, Essana told herself, as the Slayer and the Speaker took hold of her arms and dragged her backward. You have to resist. You must fight!

But she could barely hold her head up on her own, and the yaggol wouldn't let her do anything, even if she could. Grinding her teeth, she let the Brethren lay her down upon the altar. They slid chains around her wrists and ankles, though they were of little need. Her head hung a little over the slab's edge, settling into a niche so that her throat lay bare, exposed. Maladar hovered above her, his eyes agleam with hunger. Nuvis shone behind him.

Footsteps. The Master drew near, her son at his side.

"You have given us much trouble," he said, his bloodshot eyes afire with scorn. "Now see how much your struggles avail you."

She ignored him, her gaze fixed upon her son. "Azar," she breathed. "Please. . . ."

But he shook his head, raising the knife in salute to Maladar. "I am the Taker," he declared, "and your life is mine."

Chapter

32

The Emerald Sea, Neron

The going was hard for Eldako. He ate little and slept less. The pain was with him always, every mile they journeyed through the jungle. He told the others he could feel the end coming: his people called it tsaris ni'vask, "the gathering twilight." Most of the heroes in merkitsa folklore felt their end coming: struggling toward a final goal while one's life ebbed away was a common theme in wild elf tales. It was nothing to be ashamed of, and Eldako did not complain. Watching Shedara, though, Forlo knew it was hurting her to lose him by stages. She was pale, her mood brittle. At times, at night, when she thought the others weren't watching, she sat up and stared at the moons with shining eyes.

Forlo understood her grief, what it was to fear losing what you loved. With every day of their journey through the jungle, he feared he would know it too well, soon enough.

The black moon grew fatter every night. Forlo grew anxious, trying to forge ahead through the brush too quickly. Twice now, Hult had had to pull him out of sucking death mires. The cha'asii, for their part, were unperturbed by their steady pace. The vale they sought was soon coming. The temple lay ahead.

And then, at dawn after yet another sleepless night, they saw their destination, at last. Eldako did not—his dragon-ruined eyesight, once eagle-keen, made it impossible for him to make out anything at all beyond a few dozen paces—but he heard the others murmur and asked Shedara to describe it.

"Beyond the next rise," she said. "Pyramids, seven of them. Only the tops are visible above the mist. All gleaming black—but there's something atop the tallest. Something that . . . shines." She squinted, then shuddered. "Solis, have mercy. I think it's Maladar."

"The statue?" Forlo asked. He didn't have elf eyes. He didn't see what she saw.

She shook her head. "No. I glimpsed him before. When he conjured the flood to destroy the horde . . . he stepped out of the statue, for a time. A ghost. He glowed, but the light was pale . . . cold. The same light shines atop Akh-tazi."

"Ah," Eldako said. "That is a good omen."

"Good?" she replied, looking at the wild elf as if he were mad.

Eldako shrugged. "He is awakened, but still just a shade. He hasn't come into his full power yet."

They tried not to let Forlo hear, tried to keep their voices down. He heard anyway. He knew they were afraid for him, for what fear and pain and worry were doing to him. He'd seen his reflection just this morning, in a pool near where they'd camped. He'd barely recognized the man he'd become: ashen, sunken-cheeked, deep shadows under his eyes. Now he stared across the last miles, at the hovering ghost, the evil thing that would take his child's body. His hands opened, closed, opened, closed. His whole body was tense, like a hunting hound with a scent thick in its nostrils, straining to be let loose upon its quarry.

Hult leaned close. "Soon," he said. "Be easy, my friend. Your wife lives. Your child is unclaimed. There's still time to save them. And time to avenge."

The end of their journey was near, and that knowledge seemed to give Eldako new energy. That day, as they crossed down into the last valley, wending slowly down a steep slope, then along the bank of a wide, swift river to a cascade of waterfalls, where the water was shallow enough to ford, then back up an almost vertical bluff on the far side, the pain of his wounds seemed to fall away.

"I wish I had my bow," he said as they neared the top of the ridge.

"I'm sorry," Hult replied. "If we hadn't burned it. . . ."

"You never would have found me. I know. And I suppose it wouldn't matter in the least if I did have it." The wild elf flexed his ruined arm, the puckered skin glistening. "I know I haven't the strength to pull or the sight to aim. This is my companion now." He touched the sword sheathed at his side.

Finally, nothing lay between them and the temple. The tallest pyramid loomed huge against the ruddy blur of sunset, the faintest flicker at its top. They stared at it, quiet, solemn.

Eldako's face was peaceful now, with the end of their quest in sight at last. Forlo knew that look, had seen it on the faces of men who faced battles they knew would claim their lives. Not fear anymore, not anger—just calm acceptance. Serenity. Shedara must have felt some of what was in his mind, for her eyes glistened when she looked at him. Her hand slid into his. Neither of them spoke a word, only held each other with their gaze, Eldako nodding. A farewell.

After a while, she leaned in close to kiss him. Forlo turned away.

A commotion rose among the cha'asii, much frantic gesturing and chattering. Hult answered them, then glanced over his shoulder. His eyes widened.

"The moon," he said in a hoarse voice. "It rises."

They all turned and saw Nuvis in its dark glory. The black moon hung above the trees, visible, its dark aura bleeding away into the bruise-colored sky. Hult bit the heel of his hand to ward off evil. Shedara's grip on Eldako's hand tightened.

"Merciful Astar," she breathed. "I've never felt the dark moon this strong."

Forlo turned, looking back at the temple, almost frantic. Essana. He could almost hear her voice, crying out to him. Wondering where he was. "We've got to go," he said. "We're almost out of time."

Eldako nodded. "Yes," he said. "Let's end this for good."

Together, the cha'asii as silent as shadows on either side of them, they started down toward Akh-tazi.

The plan was simple. The night before, they'd gathered around a guttering cook-fire, over which roasted the carcass of a large jungle snake. The cha'asii knew the land around the temple well, knew the ways in, the terrain, and even where the Maws tended to post guards. They had sent out new scouts every two weeks. Unfortunately, the word from the most recent party was not good.

"There is only one approach now," Le-nekh explained. "Only one way to attack—we go up the hill from the south and push on up the steps to the top of the temple. All other ways are barred. Bridges cut, Vaka on the prowl . . . but the south . . . there is still a path that is clear."

"Then it's got to be a trap," Shedara noted. "These Faceless are too smart to leave one direction clear, out of many. They'll be waiting for us."

The cha'asii nodded, the feathers in his hair bobbing. "Yes. Many akitu-shai will be waiting."

"So what?" Hult asked. "If there is one way, there is one way. We cannot turn back."

Forlo shook his head. "Surely there must be a secret

passage. There always is, in case the temple were overrun and the priests inside had to flee."

The cha'asii exchanged glum looks. A log popped in the fire, dousing the sizzling snake in golden cinders. "There was such a way," Le-nekh said. "We had hoped to use it ourselves . . . but now it is shut. The Keeper used it, when he tried to rescue the woman. The dark ones hold it now. It will be trapped, guarded, or sealed. Perhaps all three."

"Khot," Forlo said.

"South it is, then," Shedara said. "And just the four of us will go."

"What?" asked Le-nekh.

"What?" asked Hult.

Eldako smiled, understanding. "Like we did with Gloomwing."

"We're the bait," Forlo agreed. "The Maws won't know the rest of you are coming. You wait in hiding. We lure them out, and you fill them with arrows."

"And if you see any men in black robes, shoot them first," Hult added.

And so they went, down into the valley of Akh-tazi, the temple rising before them on its low, steep hill. Skyfishers circled above, expecting blood. Maladar's unholy glow rose into the starry night sky. Nuvis was a dark eye, watching them, unblinking. They circled the tor, pushing through the jungle until they came at last to a path leading up its southern face. There they stopped, gazing up. Eldako licked his cracked and peeling lips.

They had a plan, knew it well. But Forlo, a veteran fighter, knew that a plan was often the first casualty of the battle.

No matter. Separating from the cha'asii, who crept along behind, they began to climb the hill.

There were things in the underbrush, near the pyramid's base. Horrifying faces hewn from dark, porous rock, webbed with ivy and tiny red flowers. None was even vaguely human: at best, they resembled the Crawling Maws, all bulbous skulls and tentacled mouths. Others were stranger still—a scaly head, featureless save for a single eye above a fanged mouth; something that looked like a giant brain with a beak like the Vaka's; an amorphous mass of claws and feelers and jagged fangs.

These were old idols, things once venerated by the akitu-shai. Maybe they were real gods, Erestem and Hith and Sargas, and all the other dark beings that dwelt beyond the curtain of the world. Maybe they were monsters that crawled up out of the Abyss, in times before elf or man walked the face of Krynn. Maybe they were born of the Maws' imagination alone, false idols to whom they sacrificed blood and burned flesh. Whatever, they belonged to the jungle now. Vines completely covered some, and others lay in crumbled heaps, pulled apart by growing things. In time, the rest would join them. It might take a thousand lives of men, but nature would bring these dark things to ruin.

It heartened Forlo, somewhat, as the four of them stepped out of the trees, to stand at the foot of the tall, steep flight of steps that led up Akh-tazi's side. The glow of Maladar's specter washed over the edge of the temple's roof, mingling with Nuvis's weird, black light. And there, waiting for them, were the Maws.

There were scores of them—a hundred or more. They swarmed down the steps, tentacles thrashing—some empty-handed, some holding hooked blades. Their mouth parts gnashed and hissed, making a sound like a pit of scorpions. Their eyes gleamed ice-blue in the putrid moon glow, devoid of emotion.

As they chittered down the stairs, Forlo felt their minds push against his, scrabbling like rats against the barrier of cha'asii magic. None could get through, but the clawing sensation made him want to scratch at his temples. They tried to form words in his mind, tell him what to do, wrest control of his body. And, worse, some part of him wanted to let them. They were ancient, beyond any other creatures in Taladas. They knew secrets no one else did—even now, in their degenerated form, so far from their onetime glory. They would share these with him: all he had to do was take off the talisman, cast it away, yield himself to them.

It was so simple. He reached for the feathered amulet. . . .

"No," Shedara said, reaching out and grabbing his hand.

He looked at her, not recognizing her face. She was only an obstacle, trying to thwart him. She had to be stopped, had to be dealt with. He tried to pull away.

"No!" she yelled again, gripping his hand so tightly the bones ground together. "They'll destroy you. They'll crush your thoughts and make a puppet of your empty flesh. And then I'll have to kill you!"

Forlo blinked. The yammering voices at the edge of his mind receded. Calm came over him. He shuddered at what he'd almost done, lowered his gaze.

"Thank you," he said. "Something must have gotten through the magic."

She shrugged. "I don't think the cha'asii made these amulets with this many Maws in mind."

Forlo glanced toward the steps. The writhing mass of creatures was halfway down, their pace slow, deliberate. He drew his sword. Hult's blade was already bared, and now the others followed suit. There was strain on all their faces—tensed jaws and sweat-drenched brows from fighting off the Maws' invasive thoughts. They would have to watch each other, these next few moments, and carefully. Forlo had nearly fallen; the others could do the same.

"Come on!" he yelled, brandishing his sword at the akitu-shai. "Cowards! Quit skulking and attack us!"

The Maws hesitated, glaring down at them with their

cold eyes. Then their tentacles tensed, rising and arching like talons, and a chorus of shrill screeches split the air, driving like a rusty spike into his skull. Hult replied with a Uigan battle cry. Forlo roared in the minotaur tongue. Eldako joined in, skirling like a hunting hawk. Shedara shouted profanities, clashing her sword and dagger together.

The Maws charged.

They came on much faster than Forlo expected. The creatures practically dove down the stairs, leaping down three or four steps at a time, landing on the soft earth like panthers, then springing forward, claws and knives extended. He brought his sword around, almost too late, and killed two with a single blow. White slime spattered his face, got in his mouth, tasting of rotten meat. He spat it out, cursing, and swept the blade back, taking off the left side of a Maw's head. The creature staggered on its feet, the mealy remains of its brain dribbling from the wound, then dropped to his knees. He kicked it in the face, felt the rest of that ghastly head burst, and sent it sprawling back into the press.

Shedara and Eldako and Hult hewed all around them, hacking off limbs and tentacles, stabbing eyes and hearts, slaying one Maw after another. Each of them killed eight, ten, twelve of the creatures, and still they kept coming, beginning to push the four of them back toward the trees and the demonic, creeper-swathed heads. Sharp fingers raked Forlo's skin. Tentacles flailed, dripping mucus. To his right, a bellow of incoherent fury told him the monsters had seized Hult. Eldako followed a moment later. Forlo knew he would be next: with her short fighting knives, Shedara would hold them off the longest. It was nearly over. He threw back his head and screamed at the jungle.

"Now!" he shouted. "For your ancestors, for your people, do it now or never!"

There was silence. Forlo counted slowly to five, then

dove flat, tackling several akitu-shai in the process. A blade bit into his arm, and he lost hold of his sword.

The jungle came alive. Hidden among trees and ferns, the cha'asii surged forward. A storm of arrows and blowgun darts and thrown spears flew before them, slamming into the Maws. The monsters squealed in surprise, then rage, then mounting panic. They were tricked, outnumbered, already beaten. Some at the rear tried to turn and flee, scurrying back up to Maladar and the Brethren. None made it; they all crumpled, their bodies tumbling down the side of the temple, skulls splitting open as they fell, leaving the stairs greased with pallid jelly.

Forlo flew into a rage, hammering the nearest Maw with the edge of his hand, catching it in the side of the head and staving it in. The creature folded up at once, the life smashed out of it. He shoved back to his feet, fists and feet hammering into one Maw after another. The others did the same, Hult brawling while Eldako and Shedara fought with their blades. In what seemed like no time, the last of the akitu-shai lay dead or dying, tentacles still twitching.

Le-nekh appeared again, jabbing a dying Maw with the tip of a spear. The creature shrieked, clutching at the weapon. He thrust it deeper, and the monster died thrashing. "That was a good fight," the cha'asii said, his face shining "We will surround the temple. No akitu-shai will trouble you now."

"Thank you," Hult said, then turned toward the body-strewn stairs. "Come on. We're almost there. It's almost done."

So is Eldako, Forlo thought glumly. The wild elf had been stabbed and cut in the melee. With his new wounds, he appeared near death, only stubbornness keeping him on his feet. It would be over for him soon. I may win back my family, he thought, but lose a friend.

The merkitsa turned to Le-nekh. "Give me your bow," he said.

The cha'asii glanced at Shedara, who shook her head. "Eldako, you can't shoot anymore."

But he insisted, holding out his good hand. "I still have it in me," he said, "for a little more."

Le-nekh nodded and handed the weapon to him. He shook his head as the cha'asii began to shrug off his quiver.

"Just one arrow," he said. "I won't have the strength for a second."

Solemn, the jungle elf drew out a single shaft. He clasped it between his palms for a moment, his lips moving silently. "I have prayed to the jaguar and the wood-serpent," he said. "And to my ancestors. May it fly true."

"Thank you, my friend," Eldako said and took it.

Then they turned to the temple.

Forlo could sense them up there: Essana, his son. And others, too. The Faceless and Maladar. It would end here, one way or another.

They climbed.

Chapter

33

AKH-TAZI, NERON

The black moon loomed too large, too close. Shedara knew it was wrong—as a moon-thief, she'd called on all three moons for her spells and could see Nuvis as well as any evil mage. It was the nearest and smallest of the three—the pupil, when they all conjoined to form a staring eye. But the disc that hung overhead tonight was huge, easily three or four times its normal size. And she had never seen it shed so much light—certainly it had never before been visible to non-wizards.

She had no doubt that this phenomenon was because of Maladar. Had it been like this during his reign, back in the heights of Aurim? No wonder his power, and his people's suffering, had been so great: he'd found a way to call down not just the black moon's power, but the black moon itself. Evil throbbed in the air.

She looked to the top of the stair, so long and steep her legs had begun to burn only halfway up. Maladar's sickly-pale light shimmered and wavered: he knew they were here. The Maws were destroyed. Nothing stood between them now. She thought she could sense something new from the temple's roof. Doubt? No.

It was fear.

Beside her, Eldako stumbled, his bad leg giving out. She grabbed him—a broken neck waiting to happen—and with her other hand seized a vine that clung to the stones. They hung there like that, together, then she hauled him back to her.

"Easy," she said. "We don't want to lose you."

But I'm going to, soon, she thought. He was beginning to succumb to his many wounds. They had both known, when they set up from Ke-cha-yat, that he would not return from this quest. The full truth of that hit her only now.

But I love him, she thought. In the old tales, that would be enough for a miracle. Yet there were other old tales, tragedies, ending in woe and death for all.

Up they climbed, Eldako leaning on her, breathing hard, fading. She looked up toward the others, wanting to call out for them to slow down, but she didn't have the breath. Hult and Forlo had charged on ahead, almost to the top now. They wouldn't have waited anyway. Desperation drove Forlo. Death might have stopped him, but not much else. As she watched, he leaped up to the top of the flight.

"Starlight!" he cried.

"Barreth, no!" screamed a woman's voice, one Shedara barely recognized. Suffering had broken it, making it old and shrill.

There was a white flash, so bright that, for a moment, Shedara couldn't see anything else. She shut her eyes with a curse, bright blotches of color bursting against her eyelids, then willed herself to open them again. Looking up, she expected Forlo and Hult to be gone, burned to ashes. The Brethren were powerful sorcerers.

Her two companions were still there, though, still whole and unhurt—albeit frozen where they stood, held in mid stride by a swirling storm of magic. She thought furiously, delving into her own mind and trying to find the incantation to counter the spell. In time she gave up: she just didn't have it.

The cruelty of the Faceless hit her then. They'd wanted Forlo to reach the top. They wanted him to watch what happened next . . . what they did to his wife . . . what became of his child. Only when it was over would they kill him.

That Hult still lived was more of a surprise—but then, the same spell had trapped them both. They could slaughter him, too, at their leisure.

"Where are the others?" rasped an awful, grating voice. It had to be the Master, the Brethren's leader. Just the sound of him made Shedara's spine hurt. "The shadows said there were elves with you, a pair of them. Where are they?"

Shedara crouched lower, pulling Eldako down. Be smart, she thought, staring at Forlo. Lie. Say we're dead—the Maws killed us, or the Vaka.

It wasn't Forlo who betrayed them, though. Nor was it Hult. Instead, it was a booming voice, the voice of a man from whom even the tiniest slivers of humanity had been stripped away. She had heard it before, in the caves beneath Coldhope.

"They are near," said Maladar the Faceless. "They wait on the stairs, to see what happens next."

Shedara glared up at the flickering, dead glow. Hate smoldered in her heart.

"Ah, of course," the Master replied. "Then let us show them."

There was another flash, and Hult collapsed. There was no warning, nothing they could do. He just crumpled without making a sound. Dead? Alive? Shedara couldn't tell. Eldako made a growling noise, deep in his throat. She laid a hand on his wrist as he edged up another step.

"Don't," she warned. "It's what they want. You can't help him now, either way—"

Her voice broke. Of all the others, the Uigan had been most distant from her. But to see him fall like this, after such a long, brave journey, broke her heart every bit as much as when she'd thought Eldako slain by the dragon.

"If they have killed him," Eldako murmured, his face blank with cold hate, "they will know regret."

Shedara nodded, then looked up again at Forlo still frozen and Hult a huddled shadow against the stars. The Brethren wouldn't do the same to Forlo—the more she thought about it, the more she understood his importance here. His anger at what they were going to do to his wife and son would catalyze Maladar's magic, make the black moon's power even stronger. She bared her teeth, angry for not thinking of it sooner.

If Forlo hadn't come. . . .

She shook her head, dismissing the thought. It would have been easier to hold back the tides than to keep him from this place.

"Our turn now!" she called loudly. "Do you hear me, Maladar? We're at the game's end, and we have one move left. But you don't know what it is, do you?"

"It matters not," boomed the Faceless Emperor. "Whatever you do, I will counter it. I promise I will make your deaths quick."

She laughed back, mocking him, knowing it would infuriate him. "Promise? What good is the word of the lord of lies, a man who killed entire cities out of spite? I'll cut my own throat before I throw myself on your mercy."

"Well said," Maladar replied, laughing now. The sound seemed to rime the air with frost. "A fine idea. Perhaps I will *make* you cut your own throat, when all this is done. It would be a fitting end for you, elf. You can use a piece of the Hooded One to do it. Obsidian is sharper than the finest dwarf steel, after all.

"But as you say, this is the endgame. Make your move— but do it quickly. Your time is running out, for when Nuvis is at its height, my hour shall have come."

All was silent then, except for Forlo's desperate grunts as he tried to free himself from the Brethren's spell—and the faint, soft sound of Essana weeping. That noise, more than anything—even what they'd done to Hult—set Shedara's will. She turned to Eldako, saw the same look in his eyes that must be in her own.

"I have a spell," she whispered. "It will protect you from their magic—but not for long."

"Long enough for one arrow?" he asked.

She nodded. "Can you make the shot? As you are?"

"I think so. Isn't that why I'm here?" he said wryly. His good eye caught Nuvis's light, shining.

Shedara swallowed. "All right, then."

The power of the silver and red moons was sluggish. It wouldn't be enough. But there was more than enough magic in the air. Her eyes flicked to the heavens, then she shut them and started drawing down from Nuvis.

The magic sickened her, coursing through her veins like poison. She'd used the black moon's power before, and it was never a comfortable feeling, but it was much worse now, as if Maladar's own presence made Nuvis even more foul. Perhaps it did.

Inky threads trailed from her fingertips, drifting to spool around and around Eldako. He shuddered as they touched him, their dark power causing him physical pain. But this was needed. As she chanted the words to seal the spell, Shedara hoped it would be enough to resist the Brethren. There wouldn't be a second chance.

At last the spell ended. The threads broke away from her, and her hands fell still. The queasiness lingered, like nausea after a bad meal. She fought the urge to retch, swallowing it down instead. Eldako watched her, his body enmeshed in magic, and there was sympathy on what remained on his face.

I must look like the Abyss, she thought, *if he's pitying me.*

Slowly, the threads wove themselves into his red, puckered flesh. He shuddered, his good eye rolling over white—then recovered again. He looked no different than before the spell—but he was smiling now, breathing easier than he had in days.

"I can feel it working in me," he said, and fitted the arrow onto his bow. "I'm ready."

She nodded. "Come on."

They climbed, up toward where Forlo stood, still frozen . . . and where Hult lay. She could see now that the Uigan wasn't dead—he was beginning to stir a little, groaning—and she offered a silent word of thanks to Jijin, the riders' god. Then she was up on the temple's pinnacle beside them, Eldako rising up behind her.

Three of the Brethren remained. One held his hands outstretched, weaving back and forth, fingers dancing—spinning the magic that kept Forlo still. Another was pulling Nuvis's power in, ready to cast another spell. This was the one who had struck down Hult. The third stood back, watching, and Shedara knew he was the leader of the cult. The Master.

Behind them, Essana lay upon the altar. A fourth man stood over her with a blade in his hand. Seeing his face, Shedara had to blink: he looked just like Forlo, but twenty years younger. Was this his son? But he was all grown. . . .

And there, floating above the scene, lashed to the Hooded One by ropes of silver light, was Maladar. His ghost had grown in size and power. He looked more real—more solid. His eyes gleamed with vicious joy amid the skinless ruin of his face.

The one who weaved the holding spell spotted her and Eldako. He gathered the energies he wielded into one hand, freeing the other to point at the elves.

"Cover your eyes!" Shedara cried, shutting her own. "Don't look—"

A blaze of light silenced her. She hoped Eldako had protected himself in time. No magic in the world could help him make his shot if he were blind. She looked again, feeling the sting, and was unsurprised to find she couldn't move any other part of her body. She could blink, and breathe, and swallow. That was it—every other muscle refused to budge. The paralyzing spell had hold of her.

Dear gods, she thought, let this work.

Then, out of the corner of her eye, she saw Eldako step forward and raise his bow, nocking his lone arrow and pulling it back. His arm shook from the weight of the draw. As he did, the other Faceless pointed a long finger at him and spoke a sharp word. There was a roar of thunder, and an arc of blue lightning leaped away from the sorcerer. It was a blast powerful enough to blow Eldako right off the temple roof—but Shedara's enchantment flared to life as it struck, blazing around Eldako and absorbing the shock. The lightning bolt burst into a shower of harmless sparks.

The Brethren stared, horrified. "Master . . ." stammered the one who'd thrown the lightning.

Eldako loosed.

The arrow flashed across the distance to the Brethren in a heartbeat, to strike the one who cast the holding spells. It hit him square in the eye.

"Speaker!" cried the lightning-thrower, reaching out. But it was too late. The head of the one called the Speaker snapped back, so that the feathered shaft stuck straight up in the air. His arms flew wide, the strands of his spells leaping from his hands and fading to mist. Without a sound, he toppled over backward, dead.

Eldako let his bow drop. He collapsed. The lightning-thrower—the Slayer—stepped back, alarmed, as the holding spell dissipated. Shedara caught her breath, stifled a groan. Every muscle in her body felt cramped, but she could move again.

So could Forlo. With a shout of inchoate rage, he leaped forward, sword held high. He charged straight toward his wife, but the Slayer moved to block his way. The sorcerer raised a hand, muttering spidery words to summon another lightning bolt. Forlo had no protection cast upon him. The lightning would strike before he could get near anything. He would die within sight of his wife.

A knife dropped out of Shedana's wrist-sheath, into her waiting hand. Pinching its blade, she cocked her arm back and threw. The blade whizzed through the air and struck the Slayer—not a killing blow, nor even one that did much harm. But it clipped the Faceless on the shoulder, throwing him off-balance. He flung out his arms to steady himself—and lost control of the lightning spell before he could cast it. Black mist floated away from him, Nuvis's power dissipating.

"Bitch!" the Slayer shouted at her.

Shedara smiled. "Damn right."

The Slayer drew a long, curved blade from his belt, raising it in time to block Forlo's first sword stroke. Shedara could tell right away he wasn't a proper warrior, though, and Forlo knew it too. Laying on with all his stored-up anger and frustration, he swept aside the dagger that had murdered countless cha'asii, then spun his sword in a tight arc and took the Slayer's arm off at the elbow. The Faceless screamed, a sound that trailed away into a choking gurgle as Forlo rammed his sword deep into his stomach. Blood burst everywhere, and the Slayer fell.

Forlo pulled out his sword—

And found himself face-to-face with the Master.

"It ends here," said the lord of the Brethren.

A bony hand reached out, touching Forlo's brow. There was a gentleness to the motion, but Forlo shrieked in pain and fell to his knees. He stayed there a moment, trying to resist, then collapsed into a twitching, howling heap.

Shedara started toward him, but the Master raised a hand without even glancing at her, and strands of spider-web flew like white, fluttering bats, binding her to the temple's roof. Furious, she tried to pull free, but couldn't. The gossamer was as strong as steel, holding her fast. She swore, trapped by the simplest of spells.

"Now," said the Master, his eyes still fixed on Forlo, who huddled at his feet, weeping and thrashing in agony amidst the growing pool of the Slayer's blood. "You will watch, my friend. Soon Nuvis will be at its greatest height. Do you see your child there? He is the Taker, the vessel, foretold by prophecy. He will cut your wife . . . his own mother. Her blood will fuel Maladar's strength, and he will enter the boy's body, crush the soul inside and make the flesh his own, to reign over the world anew. And you . . . you will watch it all—"

"No!"

The Master turned to look. Shedara did too, and caught her breath. Somehow, miraculously, Eldako was back on his feet, even running now, the threads of the protective spell sparking around him, unraveling fast. The Master pointed, a ray of gray light lancing from his finger.

It hit Eldako full on. His breastplate shattered, his sword crumbling in his hand. But the protective spell held, and though he staggered a little, he kept on coming. The Master rose, stepping back from Forlo, fear in his eyes. Above, Maladar watched, uncaring, as the greatest of his disciples sought to flee.

But there was nowhere to go. Eldako hit the Master hard, knocking the wind out of his body, then grabbing him around the waist and hurtling onward, past the altar, past them all.

Shedara gasped, tears leaping to her eyes. She knew what was about to happen . . . but the webs still held her fast. She couldn't move. "No!" she shouted.

Yelling a wild merkitsa war cry, still clutching the panicking Master, Eldako leaped off the rooftop.

Forlo saw what Eldako did, as if from a deep hole in the earth. The wild elf charged across the temple, scooping up the Master as he ran. His whole body still riddled with pain from the spell the leader of the Faceless had cast on him, Forlo managed to push himself up onto his elbows and open his mouth in a wordless shout as the two hurtled off the edge the roof. Shedara yanked an arm free of her webs and extended it toward Eldako and shouted spidery words, a spell that could save his life, the magic she'd used at Coldhope, what seemed like years ago.

But it was too late. A heartbeat later, he was gone.

The Master bellowed as he fell. There was a terrible, final sound—a thud, a crunch. Then all was silent. Shedara stared, wide eyed, her hand still pointing as the spell died on her lips. Truly, this time, the merkitsa was dead—but the last of the Faceless Brethren had perished with him.

Forlo groaned, shuddering, and began to push himself back to his feet. Across the rooftop, he saw Hult doing the same. The Uigan's face was pale, his mouth hanging open. Forlo wiped blood from his mouth and nose, staggered to where his sword lay, bent to pick it up, lurched back upright and turned to face the altar.

The boy—too old to be his son, but with a pang Forlo noted the resemblance—stood over Essana. A long, wickedly curving dagger gleamed in his hand, reflecting both the black light of Nuvis and the ghostly glow from above. Hanging over them all, the specter of Maladar stared down, his ruined face inscrutable.

The Faceless Emperor glared at them, at him, in silence. Then, instead of fury, he began to laugh. Magic flashed from his eyes, and Forlo went down again, his sword clattering from his hand. The pain returned, as strong as before. It turned his blood to liquid fire, made frost of his flesh, filled his mind with white lightning. His back arched, his fingers clutching like claws at the sky.

"You think you have won," the ghost said, its voice seeming to rise from the roots of Akh-tazi. "You have gained nothing. The Brethren served their purpose. Now the Taker will serve his."

Forlo's eyes flicked to the boy—no, he corrected himself, a young man, older-seeming than Hult. His son gazed up at Maladar, eyes shining with purpose, fanaticism, adoration. He lifted the knife, pressed its edge to his lips, then drew it sharply down against himself, splitting flesh. Blood poured down his chin, increasing as he smiled, tearing the wounds open even more.

"An offering for thee, Sleeper," he declared. He raised the blade, turning to salute the Hooded One, then looked back down at the body on the altar, the flesh that had carried him, given him birth.

"Hult!" called Shedara. "Come here. Cut me loose. Quickly!"

Forlo saw her in the corner of his vision: halfway out of the magical cocoon, the strands of webbing crumbling as she writhed against them. Hult raced to her, swung his sword, and clove it open. Together they managed to haul her out—then both turned to face Maladar. He hovered before them, eyes ablaze with blue flame, and spoke a word that sounded like the buzzing of ten thousand wasps.

The ground shook, leaped, fell, and both Shedara and Hult slammed down, the wind knocked out of them. Hult's sword skipped away. The rooftop beneath them cracked, and hands of black stone burst out, grabbing them by ankle and wrist. The obsidian's sharp edges sliced into their flesh, and blood flowed.

"Stupid elf," Maladar said. "You may have awoken me, but you cannot defeat me now. Nuvis fuels my strength!"

"Nuvis fuels our strength," echoed Forlo's son.

Essana wept uncontrollably, her eyes dark with despair. She looked up at the young man with the dagger and shook her head, just slightly. She had no more strength than that. The Faceless had wrecked her.

Forlo glared up at Maladar, towering over him, strips of flesh hanging from what had been his face, and felt neither awe nor fear. Only loathing.

"I will kill you," Hult shouted behind him. "By Jijin and all my ancestors, when this is done, you will be dead by my hand!"

The dead emperor laughed again. "You will never rise from where you lie, Uigan. You will join your Boyla in the Abyss."

"The moon," groaned Shedara. "The black moon. . . ."

Forlo saw. It had reached its zenith, its power pouring down upon the world. He wondered what people in other lands must be thinking now, confronted with such an awful sight. Or could they see it at all? Were they far enough from Maladar's power that the night sky looked normal to them? Were they sleeping soundly in the League and on the Tamire, unaware of what was about to happen? He ground his teeth, trying to fight, but every movement brought fresh agony.

"You gods-damned caitiff," he panted. "You fatherless troll-get. . . ."

Maladar paid him no mind. He turned his back, facing the Hooded One. The strands of magic that bound him to it glowed brightly, throwing off arcs of white energy. The statue seemed to swell, bulging as the wards that held him to it began to weaken.

"By blood was I bound," said the specter. "By blood I shall be loosed."

"By blood," spoke the Taker, holding the dagger poised, gripped in both hands. "So shall it be."

No.

The magic that held him didn't weaken, not in the slightest. Even breathing hurt horribly. But as the blade rose above Essana, Forlo found hidden strength, a well he'd never tapped before. He thrust the agony aside, sat up, rose to his feet. Blood filled his mouth. It poured from his nose. He could even feel it trickling warmly from his ears. Maladar's spell was slowly killing him.

Starlight, he thought, I'm coming.

The world shrank around him—jungle, temple, his friends all vanished. Even Maladar disappeared. All that remained were the altar, his wife, and the monster that was his son. He staggered forward, leaving his sword where it lay. He'd forgotten he even had a sword; he didn't even know the *word* sword.

Behind him, he heard voices yelling, a man and a woman shouting a name. Forlo. He wondered who that was. Every step was a shuddering ordeal, but he kept going. Kept . . . going. Kept. Going.

"Come forth, O highest, lord of all lands beneath the sun," intoned his son. He didn't look up, his attention focused on Essana alone. "Let thy wrath be kindled anew. Let thy vengeance cleanse the paltry empires that have arisen in thy absence. Let the people know, by their suffering, of how thou wert wronged. Come forth, and reign over the world, supreme and forever."

The dagger came down.

Forlo was still three paces away. He roared and hurled himself forward, flinging himself on top of his wife. The blade struck flesh, ground against bone.

The pain went away.

Hult stared, horrified. Forlo lay still atop the altar. The Taker gaped at him, flabbergasted, then stumbled back. The dagger was lodged deep in Forlo's back.

No. First Eldako; now this. Jijin, he thought, it isn't supposed to be this way. It is too much! Beside him, Shedara made a heartbroken sound.

Then something started to happen. Blackness bloomed up from the altar, enveloped the statue. The silvery bonds that led to the ghost darkened, became oily, cancerous.

"What?" Maladar asked, stunned. He flung up a hand, trying to reach the Hooded One, to stop whatever had begun deep within the stone. "NO!"

Too late, Hult thought. A wild and vicious joy leapt within him. Too late!

The statue burst.

It didn't shatter, crumble, or explode: it bulged, then split open like an over-filled waterskin, the stone peeling aside to reveal a core of blazing, violet light. Hult squinted, throwing up an arm to shield his eyes as the magic that had kept Maladar trapped inside for a thousand years flared bright, then poured out in a silent wave. It washed over Forlo and Essana and their son, then struck Hult and Shedara. He expected it to be burning hot, but instead it was freezing, colder even than the storms of Panak. It sent him staggering back as it blew past, moving on out over the jungle, stirring the leaves of the trees, leaving them brown and frost-rimed in its wake. When he turned to look at the Hooded One again, only a stub of black rock remained, greasy smoke curling upward from its cracked, pockmarked surface.

"The magic," Shedara breathed. "It's gone."

Hult nodded. Even he could feel it. Maladar had vanished as well, the moment the wave touched him. He hadn't even had time to scream—he had simply disappeared.

"Is that it?" he whispered. "Is it done?"

Shedara looked around, frowning. "I don't sense him," she said. "But . . . well . . . do you think it could be that easy?"

"No," Hult said, and pushed against the obsidian hands that held him. They cracked apart, their own enchantments broken. Shedara did the same, and in a moment they were both on their feet, swords in hand, turning to face the altar.

Forlo lay there, motionless, sprawled on top of his wife. The boy had stepped back, eyes wide and mouth open. The knife was still in Forlo's back.

Forlo had his victory, had rescued the one thing he held dear in this world.

But the cost . . . oh, the cost.

A tear spilled down Hult's cheek as he and Shedara walked toward the altar. Essana had lost consciousness. She might be dead, but Hult didn't think so. Even the gods couldn't be so cruel, could they? And then there was the son . . . the young man with blood on his hands, now staring as if he didn't know how it got there.

Hult raised his sword, pointed it at the one who had called himself the Taker. "I should kill you where you stand," he said, his voice shaking with rage. "You have murdered your own father. There is no greater crime than kin-slaying."

"I . . . I didn't mean to," said the boy. "He got in the way."

"Of your attempt to sacrifice your mother!" Hult shot back, moving forward. The young man stepped back, tripped over the hem of his robes, fell. Hult moved in quickly, laying the edge of his blade against the Taker's throat. "I say it again—you are a dog. If I struck off your head now, no man would call it unjust."

He paused, turning the blade. The fear in the boy's eyes ran deep as the flesh of his neck creased. A thin trickle of blood ran down the sword's edge. Then Hult turned his head, spat on the Hooded One's remains, and lifted the weapon away.

"But not now," he said. He pointed his maimed hand at the boy. "Do not rise. Do not move. Speak no word until I tell you. Do you understand?"

Confused, frightened, the boy nodded. *He is only a babe*, Hult thought, *without the poison the Brethren poured in his ears, without Maladar to goad him.*

"He's breathing," said Shedara.

He turned, looking toward her. She was bent over Forlo, one hand on his throat, bending low to put her ear by his mouth. "His life-beat," she said. "It's . . . still strong. He has a knife jammed in his lung, but he sounds completely healthy. . . ."

Hult felt something, then . . . a low thrumming, like the beating of a heart. The sound came from above. He looked up and felt cold all over. Nuvis hadn't retreated with the Hooded One destroyed; it was as huge as ever . . . maybe even larger, its gangrenous light shining brighter than before. Scalp prickling, he grabbed Shedara's arm and pulled. She resisted, giving him an incredulous look.

"What are you doing?"

"The moon!" he shouted, pointing with his chin. "Maladar isn't gone at all! Get back now!"

She glanced up, turning pale. Beside her, Forlo stirred. Shedara let out a startled yell, then jumped back, a throwing knife dropping into her hand. Hult's sword came up, quivering.

"No," Shedara gasped. "Oh, no . . ."

Groaning, Forlo rolled over, then sat up. His eyes were dark, bleary, like a man who'd just woken from a deep sleep. The being who looked out of them, however, was no longer Forlo. Hult recognized the cruelty in that gaze, the inhumanity, the evil.

A cold, reptilian smile spread across Forlo's face. "Yes," he said, and the voice was Maladar's. "You know what has happened here. The wards are broken. I am free. And I have a body . . . not the one I intended, but a body just the same. And your grief fuels my strength, as I had hoped his might."

He reached back, clawed at the dagger's hilt, yanked it free. No blood spilled from the wound, nor was there any on the blade as he dropped it at his feet.

"You have won nothing," said Maladar with malicious glee. He stepped away from the altar, from Essana lying there, mercifully unconscious. "The Brethren's purpose is fulfilled. This day, my reign begins anew."

"Not if I have anything to say about it," Shedara said, and threw her dagger.

The man who had been Forlo held up a finger. The blade burst into flame, then burned in midair like it was made of paper, until it was no more than a cloud of white ash.

"You don't," he said, sweeping the air with his hand.

Shedara reeled as if he'd punched her, stumbling back, then crashing to the ground. Her head smacked against the stone, and she lay still.

Anger boiled inside Hult. The tip of his sword rose another inch—then it, too, caught fire and burned away to nothing, leaving his hand dark with soot. He clenched his fists, glowering at the thing that dwelt inside his friend's flesh.

"Oh, how boring," said Maladar, and waved his hand again.

It was like a hammer had struck him. The world spun around Hult, full of exploding stars. He sat down, hard. Maladar looked down on him, still smiling.

"I would kill you," he said, "but there are fates crueler

than death. Live, Hult, son of Holar. You could not save Chovuk Boyla, and you could not save Forlo of Coldhope. Live, knowing your ancestors have turned their backs on you."

Hult could only sit there, dazed, while Forlo-Maladar shut his eyes and raised high his hands. Flames poured down from them, red and gold, washing over his body. He laughed and laughed, a sound that knew nothing of mirth. There was a flare of light as the fire consumed him . . . then he was gone, and all was dark.

Hult looked up. The black moon had receded again, invisible in the night sky. Burying his face in his hands, he lay back on the temple roof.

Chapter

35

AKH-TAZI, NERON

They buried Eldako, son of Tho-ket, in the rich, dark earth of the jungle, not far from where he'd died. The cha'asii sang over his grave, a rhythmic tune accompanied by a stomping dance, a warrior's chant. They struck arrows against their bowstrings, the soft thrumming sending the merkitsa to his rest.

When the song was done, Hult came forward. His face looked less alive than the stone visages looming out of the trees. In his hands he held a single arrow, cracked in the middle and caked with blood—the same shaft that had slain the Speaker.

"I feared elves, once," Hult said. "My people and his did not know each other, and the elders told terrible tales of those who dwelt in the Dreaming Green. When I went there with my master, I thought it a land of ghosts and demons. I did not expect to leave the place alive. The last thing I expected to find there was a friend.

"Eldako saved my life many times. I cannot count them now, with the grief so near. We were sword-brothers, he and I, both missing our homes but bound to this quest. Now, for him, the tale is done. If there is any justice in this world, if Jijin and the elven gods truly are kind, I will live to bring word of him back to the Tamire and the Green, so his people and mine may both sing of his bravery."

He held up the arrow. His hands trembled.

"Eldako was many things—a warrior, a healer, a prince—but of them all he was proudest of his bow-craft. There was no better archer in all the Tamire—perhaps all of Taladas. This was the last arrow he ever loosed. A killing shot. With it, and with his own life, he slew two of the last three of the Faceless. He did all he could to give us victory . . . and if we have failed, it is not—" He stopped, his voice cracking. "It . . . was not his fault."

He raised the arrow to his lips, kissed the fletching, then thrust it down, point-first, into the wild elf's grave.

"Farewell, my brother," he said. "There is good hunting where you are now."

As he moved away from the grave, Shedara came forward to take his place. She wept openly, making no effort to hide her sorrow, her mouth an ugly grimace.

"I bear no gifts," she said. "I make no speeches. I'm not going to stand here, bawling over his grave either. He wouldn't have approved."

Hult chuckled, nodding. Shedara glanced at him, then turned to look back at the grave.

"I loved Eldako. Our love was late in coming . . . too late. I only knew myself when I thought him lost, on the shores of this land. It was a gift that I could spend time with him after that, even crippled as he was. For those few days I loved him openly, and he loved me. I haven't known that sort of love before. I don't think . . . I don't think I will again."

She bowed her head, a hand coming up to pinch the bridge of her nose. Her shoulders shook.

"I just wish . . . I wish we could have done better for you," she said, and drew a shuddering breath. "I wish we'd. . . ."

That was all. She stood silent a while longer, covering her eyes, her free hand balled into a fist. Then, shaking her head, she turned and strode away, into the trees. Hult watched her go but didn't follow.

Essana watched too.

She was still alive, in part, because of Eldako's sacrifice, but she felt neither glad nor sorrowful. She felt nothing at all. Everything was dull, numb. So she watched from where she sat, on the bottom of the temple stair, while one by one the cha'asii came forward and thrust their own arrows into the wild elf's grave. And then the funeral was done.

There wasn't to be a second.

They had talked long and hard about what to do about Barreth Forlo. Shedara considered him dead, and though he didn't say it, Essana knew Hult thought so as well. Those two should know. They had seen the dagger pierce him, seen his stillness in the moments before the Hooded One exploded. Essana had not; she'd passed out, her strength finally failing her in those last moments. When she'd woken, it had been over. Maladar was gone, and her husband too.

Shedara had told her what happened: Forlo was dead. The only thing that animated his body was the soul of the Faceless Emperor, who had taken residence in his flesh.

But Essana didn't—wouldn't—believe it. She would allow no funeral for him, not until she felt certain he was gone. The "killing" knife had had no blood on it. There was still a chance, and she wouldn't give that up, no matter what. She'd believed in him, and he'd come for her as she'd hoped. She'd keep believing.

Movement behind her made her stiffen. She turned and looked, still weary but no longer paralyzed now that her captors were all dead, their spells lifted. She didn't need to see, though: it was clear who it was. She knew the sounds of his footfalls.

Azar wouldn't look at her, not in the eye. She didn't blame him. The guilt over what he'd almost done to her—and what he had done to his father—must be over-whelming. And the horror of what Maladar had meant to do to him. . . .

He came down the steps and sat beside her. He gazed at the grave, his young-old eyes glistening. "Pretty words. Who was he, again?" he asked.

"A friend of your father's," Essana replied. "An elf."

Azar pursed his lips as the last of the cha'asii planted their arrows. "I know he . . . died trying to save you. From me."

She looked across at him. His face was dark, tormented. Her heart, already broken many times over, gave a little wrench. "From them," she said. "From what they made you do."

He shrugged, turning away.

"I should have died," he said. "It should be me they're burying."

Yes! Essana thought. It should be. But she swallowed those thoughts, born of grief and spite. "It wasn't your fault," she said instead. "If the Master had meant for me to wield the knife, I would have had no more choice than you. And you didn't know better. You never had a chance to."

She held out her hand. It was feeble, bony, and spotted—an old woman's hand. She didn't think she would ever look or feel young again. It hovered over her son's shoulder for a long moment, trembling, then she forced herself to touch him, to try to give him comfort.

He shrank back as if burned, hissing between his teeth. "Please, don't."

She could have pulled away, left him here in his torment, then. A large part of her wanted to. But instead she shifted closer, put her arm around him, drew him closer. He stiff-ened, as she'd known he would—then, all at once, the fight went out of him and he sagged against her, put his own arms around her, buried his face in her neck.

"I'm sorry," he moaned.

"I know, child," she said and held him close, cradling him. "I know."

Daylight bathed the Emerald Sea. It seemed a less terrifying place now, teeming with life, almost serene. With the Brethren and the yaggol and the black wyrm gone, perhaps it was. The cha'asii, at least, saw what had happened as a victory. But Hult and Shedara were grim and quiet as they looked out from the temple's rooftop. They gazed north, over the rippling, mist-shrouded carpet of trees, toward a distant, purple line of mountains. Birds and flying serpents broke out of the canopy, darted through open air, and dove back again. Somewhere in the distance, a waterfall roared.

Shedara held a slim, jagged chunk of stone: a piece of the Hooded One. She squeezed it until its sharp edges dug into her palms.

"He's out there," she murmured. "Somewhere. I can feel it."

Hult nodded, thoughtful. He wore a new sword on his hip—the same blade Forlo had carried when they attacked the temple. "Wherever he went, we don't have much time," he said. "If he isn't stopped. . . ."

Essana stepped up behind them. Azar was holding her up, helping her walk. "The Burning Sea," she said. "They're going to where Old Aurim used to be, at the center of the fire. They're going to raise the Chaldar."

Hult blinked at her, startled, and Shedara turned pale. "How do you know?" the elf asked.

"I saw it," Essana replied. "In a vision, when Maladar's mind touched mine. I saw the Chaldar, risen anew. He had taken it over, raised new armies of flame . . . armies to lay waste to Taladas. He's not going to forge his empire again. He's going to destroy everything and rule over the ashes."

Shedara sighed, a hand going to her forehead. She turned

to look at Hult, who looked ill. "Armies of flame . . . how can we beat that? We don't even have any allies. The minotaurs certainly won't listen, and my people and yours are too few."

"There are other places," Essana said.

"Oh, yes," Shedara shot back. "Thenol, Syldar . . . or maybe we can gather what's left of the Ice People and the kender. 'Oh, we know your people are almost all dead, and what's left might not survive, but . . . would you mind coming with us to the Burning Sea?'"

Essana shook her head, undeterred. "There are still the Rainwards."

Hult rubbed a bruise on his face. "The Rainwarders don't deal with foreigners," he said. "They will not help us."

"Yes, they will," Essana said.

"What makes you say that?" Shedara asked, her brows knitting.

Essana glanced up at Azar. Then she looked out, across the sun-washed jungle, at the mountains beyond. "Let me tell you how my son got his name."

Epilogue

THE ASHEN SHORE

The roar of flames was deafening, the ruddy glare too bright to look at without pain. Stinking, yellow smoke hung in the air, so thick that every breath scorched. There was no relief, no respite. Those who ventured to these lands without magic to protect them died quickly—the only question was, of what? Poison, suffocation, burning . . . it was a race to see which would kill a man first.

Maladar feared none of these sorry fates. He had his magic, spells woven so tightly about him that he didn't need to breathe. He felt no hunger, no thirst, no weariness, no pain. He felt only hate, a golden-glowing coal of it, buried deep inside. He nurtured the hate, fanned it, made it grow.

He stood upon a beach, at the edge of a vast and roiling sea, ringed with roaring volcanoes. The beach was not sand, but soot and ash, black and white mingling into great, gray dunes. And the sea was not water, but molten stone, a wound in the earth so deep that in four centuries it had not healed. Left alone, it never would. Maladar had learned of the Burning Sea from the Brethren. It sat at the heart of Taladas, its heat and fumes so powerful that much of the continent remained unlivable. It had been like this since the First Destruction, when a massive ball of burning rock, ten miles across, had struck the city of Aurim. It had slain hundreds of thousands, and unleashed plagues and earthquakes that killed millions more. Entire nations vanished, and the survivors became nomads, settling in realms far away . . . the League, the Rainwards, and elsewhere. The world had never been the same.

This was mine once, Maladar thought as he gazed across the churning ocean. *From here, I ruled the greatest empire Krynn has ever known—even greater than Istar across the sea. Gone now . . . burned away, lost. The fools let it fall into ruin.*

"I could have stopped it," he uttered with absolute certainty. "I could have smashed the moon of fire that fell upon my palace. I could have prevented the Destruction, and all the suffering that followed. But I was trapped in that thrice-damned statue, lost to the ages."

"No more, though," whispered a voice to his right. "Now you are free."

Another man might have been surprised—frightened, even—to see what was coming toward him, walking through the ashes without leaving a single footprint behind. It was not a man, that much was certain; it had the barest shape of one, but mostly looked like an empty cloak of tattered gray cloth, surmounted by a hood where two red eyes smoldered. But more terrible was the aura that surrounded it, the sensation of formidable power. For all his might, all his arcane knowledge, Maladar nearly fell to his knees before the awe and terror that radiated from that wraithlike figure.

Nearly . . . but did not. Instead he folded his arms across his chest, the sensation strange after all these years. He had gotten used to his prison of stone; a body of human flesh took some getting used to again.

Maladar an-Desh knelt before no one. Not even a god.

"You came," he said. "I had some doubt."

The cloaked shape bowed—not a mocking gesture, as it might have used with a more insolent being, but respectful, grave. "Oh?" it asked, in a voice like a scorpion skittering over bones. "And why would you have doubt?"

"Rumors I have heard," Maladar answered. "Some say the heavens are troubled these days. That there is strife among the gods. Already one has died."

"Erestem, yes," the shape hissed. "And her counterpart, the platinum dragon, has lost his powers. Others may follow, before matters are settled. But that is not our concern. Not here, not today."

"No, Lord Hith. It is not."

Hith, god of lies, looked him up and down. "You have a new body."

"I do," Maladar agreed, uncrossing Barreth Forlo's arms. He eyed his hands, the scarred palms and callused fingers. "Not the one I wanted, though. It is . . . older. Not as agile."

"It will suffice," the god said. "Before long, you will have your pick of younger bodies, and you can give this one to the fire." The glowing eyes shifted, looking around. "I cannot help but notice that you are here alone. Where are your disciples?"

Maladar felt a flash of anger. "You know well enough. Surely you watched as they fell, one by one . . . the last three at the final hour."

"I did," Hith allowed. "A pity none survived. Their fear when they met me would have been . . . pleasing."

Maladar shrugged. The Faceless Brethren meant nothing to him anymore, now that he was free. They had served their purpose.

"So, then," Hith pressed. "One leg of your journey ends; another begins."

"With you to guide me," Maladar declared. "If you still wish this, that is."

The god looked at him, the hood cocking sideways. "And why should I not? I yearn for power, as much as you do. While my brothers and sisters quarrel, I will take what

I can. Taladas is in disarray, ready to fall. Even the minotaurs' empire has collapsed into chaos. None remain who can stand against you."

"There are the Rainwards," Maladar said. "One from those lands came very near to thwarting us."

"You speak of the Keeper, Azar. I have his soul now, you will be glad to know. The torments I have shown him!" Hith laughed, a rusty, grinding noise. "The Rainwards will be dealt with. You are not my only agent in this world."

Maladar raised an eyebrow, but asked no more questions. "Well, then," he said. "Show me my road."

The god bowed again, an empty, flapping sleeve extending to point across the sea. Maladar's eyes followed the gesture, noting where the lava there began to roll and churn. Something was rising from its depths: something long and broad. After a time, it broke the surface: a bridge of rough iron, glowing golden from the heat. He watched as it cooled to amber, then to red. Its near end shifted, sliding up onto the beach. It extended away from the shore, out across the Burning Sea, until it vanished in the lethal haze.

"This is your road. It will lead you where you must go," said Hith.

"To the Chaldar?" Maladar asked. "The tower of flame?"

Hith neither nodded nor shook his head. The red eyes glinted with amusement. "It will lead you where you must go."

A noise arose, a loud blustering like a whirlwind. As Maladar watched, the god's shapeless cloak folded in on itself, crumpling into a smaller and smaller bundle, then vanishing altogether. Ash puffed up from the beach where he had stood, then slowly settled.

Annoyance gnawed at Maladar. Hith was vexing, but his power was necessary . . . for now, anyway. He could not have crossed the Burning Sea otherwise: even his own magic couldn't give him the power to walk a hundred leagues and more across molten rock. But this bridge—cooled to black now, its surface gnarled and pitted by the fire—would serve him. He started toward it—then stopped, a voice in his ears.

Help me, it begged, small and alone and afraid. Starlight? Hult? Shedara?

Maladar listened to its pleas with a smile. He cared nothing for the suffering of Barreth Forlo. The man had traveled half the world to attack him. He was paying the price now, trapped and helpless in his own body. None could hear the voice but Maladar, and so he let it whine. It amused him.

Chuckling, he stepped onto the bridge. He half expected it to vanish like smoke as soon as he was over the lava—Hith was a capricious god—but it was solid, firm beneath his feet. He gazed down its length, into the smoke, yearning to see what lay beyond.

Then he began to walk.

GLOSSARY

<u>Geographic terms and place names:</u>

Akh-tazi: A ruined temple in Neron, thousands of years old.

Armach-nesti: A small elven kingdom, home to the Silvanaes.

Aurim: A vast empire that covered much of Taladas, smashed in the First Destruction.

Chaldar: A tower of solid flame that once stood in the midst of Hitehkel.

The Dreaming Green: A forest north of the Tamire, home to the merkitsa elves.

Greytooth: The tallest of the Hoarspine mountains.

Hitehkel: A sea of molten rock at the center of Taladas, where Aurim stood before the Destruction. Also called Hith's Cauldron.

The Hoarspine: A line of sharp, icy mountains that cut through the Panak Wastes.

Hosk: The western half of Taladas, divided by the Tiderun into northern and southern parts.

The Imperial League: An empire of minotaurs and humans that covers much of Southern Hosk.

Indanalis: The Boiling Sea, a long channel of super-heated water between Southern Hosk and Hith's Cauldron.

Marak: Several valleys in the central Steamwalls, home to clans of kender.

Neron: A little-known jungle land in the southeast of Taladas.

Panak: A frozen wasteland in the north of Taladas.

Rainward Isles: A piece of Aurim that survived the Destruction, now home to kingdoms of refugees.

Starshimmer: A lake in the heart of the Marak valleys.

Steamwalls: A range of volcanic mountains in the east of Southern Hosk, on the Indanalis coast.

Suluk: A kingdom of the Rainward Isles.

Syldar: An island in the southwest of Taladas, home to fishermen and bloodthirsty tribes.

Taladas: A continent on the northern hemisphere of the world of Krynn.

The Tamire: A vast stretch of grasslands and steppes, covering much of Northern Hosk.

Thenol: A human realm in Southern Hosk, ruled by evil priests and necromancers.

Tiderun: A shallow strait running east-west across the middle of Hosk. Also called the Run.

People and Cultures:

Amaruik: A clan of Ice People who take the Spirit Wolf as their totem beast.

Anho-ti: The snow lodge of a makau, the heart of an Ice People village.

Astakha: A martial art perfected by Manithite monks.

Boyla: The prince of the Uigan, the highest lord of all the Tamire.

Cha'asii: A small, reclusive race of aboriginal elves in the jungles of Neron.

Cham ka: A complicated dice game of the Ice People.

Chapak: A battle-axe used by the kender.

Fianawar: A hardy race of dwarves who dwell among the Steamwall mountains.

Heerikil: A Silvanaes term for non-elves.

Hoopaui: A kender bow, used to hurl rocks instead of arrows.

Hosk'i imou merkitsa: Clans of barbaric elves native to the Dreaming Green. Also simply known as the merkitsa.

Hulder: A mysterious, elf-like people once common in Hosk, now almost never seen.

Ice People: Tribes of humans who rove across the Panak Wastes.

Ishka: A large, pulpy fruit from Syldar; sweet and yellow when ripe, but very sour when still green.

Kazar: A nation of barbarians native to the Tamire, all but exterminated by the Uigan.

Khot: A minotaur obscenity, often used by soldiers.

Krahd: A clawed hammer, used by the folk of the Rainward Isles.

Makau: A shaman and sorcerer, the leader of an Ice People tribe.

Ningasuk: Stone statues erected by the Ice People to ward against the Uitayuik. Also called the Patient Folk.

Shalukh: A curse-word in the tongue of the Rainwards.

Shivis: A boardgame popular in the Imperial League, also used by the minotaurs as a tactical tool.

Shuk: A curved Uigan saber.

Silvanaes: An elf people of Southern Hosk, descended from survivors of an ill-fated expedition from Ansalon.

Tegin: A Uigan clan-lord, answerable only to the Boyla.

Tenach: A warrior sworn to protect and serve a Uigan lord.

Uigan: A powerful people of horse-riding nomads, native to the Tamire.

Ulashu: The leaves of a Neroni tree, chewed by the cha'asii for stamina.

Yagrut: A Uigan profanity.

Yarta: A root chewed by the Uigan to give energy.

Yakuk: A dragon-bone totem, in the shape of a beast, that stands in the middle of an Ice People village.

Zharka: A minotaur war trumpet, made from a dragon's horn.

Creatures:

Abaqua: A primitive race of ogres from Northern Hosk.

Akitu-shai: The cha'asii name for the yaggol. Also called Crawling Maws.

Amaguik: The spirit of a makau, appearing as a half-wolf, half-man.

Bauvan: A ghostly woman who roams old battlefields, searching for her slain husband.

Disir: A race of thickly armored savages who dwell beneath the Rainwards.

Horax: A huge, many-legged worm with a thick carapace and razor-sharp mandibles.

Huraj: The Uigan name for the horax.

Nasif: Giant, sharp-antlered deer herded by the Ice People.

Othlorx: Outcast dragons of Taladas who refused to join the Dark Queen in her war on Ansalon.

Sakalaminuik: Shaggy snow-ogres native to the Hoarspine.

Skrit: An enormous, flea-like creature of the Tamire, with an impenetrable shell.

Skyfisher: A large, ugly carrion bird, usually found among ruins and on battlefields.

Tan-amat: The merkitsa name for a hippogriff.

Uitayuik: White-eyed specters of men who died in the blizzards of Panak.

Vaka-te-nok: A burrowing creature with many tentacles, found in the jungles of Neron.

Winlesh: The merkitsa name for a Vaka-te-nok.

Yaggol: An ancient, degenerate race of Neron. They have bulbous, hairless heads and masses of tentacles where their mouths should be, and can also force their way into people's thoughts.

Gods and Moons:

Astar: The god of the elves, a hunter and bowman.

Erestem: The Queen of Darkness, now slain.

Gilona: The goddess of knowledge and learning.

Hith: A god of deceit.

Jijin: The god of the Uigan, a warrior and protector.

Jolith: A human war god, revered in the League.

Lunis: The red moon, called Lunitari in Ansalon.

Manith: A god of contemplation.

Mislaxa: A healing goddess known across Taladas.

Morgash: A god of sickness and decay.

Nuvis: The black moon, called Nuitari in Ansalon.

Sargas: The warrior god of the minotaurs.

Solis: The silver moon, called Solinari in Ansalon.

Zai: A goddess of the sea and storms.

History:

Dread Winter: The troubled times immediately prior to the Second Destruction, when much of Taladas was covered in snow and ice.

First Destruction: Taladan term for the Cataclysm, when the gods rained fire upon Krynn. Also called the Great Destruction.

Godless Night: The years after the Second Destruction, during which both gods and magic vanished from the face of Krynn.

Second Destruction: The Second Cataclysm, caused by the Chaos War.

A NEW TRILOGY FROM MARGARET WEIS & TRACY HICKMAN

THE DARK CHRONICLES
Dragons of the Dwarven Depths
Volume One

Tanis, Tasslehoff, Riverwind and Raistlin
are trapped as refugees in Thorbardin, as the
draconian army closes in on the dwarven
kingdom. To save his homeland, Flint begins a
search for the Hammer of Kharas.

Available July 2006

For more information visit **www.wizards.com**

DRAGONLANCE, WIZARDS OF THE COAST and their respective logos are
trademarks of Wizards of the Coast, Inc. in the U.S.A. and other countries.

© 2006 Wizards of the Coast

ENTER THE NEW WORLD OF

THE DREAMING DARK TRILOGY

By Keith Baker

A hundred years of war...

Kingdoms lie shattered, armies are broken, and an entire
country has been laid to waste. Now an uneasy
peace settles on the land.

Into Sharn come four battle-hardened soldiers. Tired of
blood, weary of killing, they only want a place to call home.

The shadowed City of Towers has other plans...

THE CITY OF TOWERS
Volume One

THE SHATTERED LAND
Volume Two

THE GATES OF NIGHT
Volume Three
DECEMBER 2006

For more information visit **www.wizards.com**

EBERRON, WIZARDS OF THE COAST and their respective logos are trademarks of
Wizards of the Coast, Inc. in the U.S.A. and other countries. © 2006 Wizards of the Coast

ENTER THE NEW WORLD OF

THE WAR-TORN

After a hundred years of fighting the war is now over, and the people of Eberron pray it will be the Last War. An uneasy peace settles over the continent of Khorvaire.

But what of the soldiers, warriors, nobles, spies, healers, clerics, and wizards whose lives were forever changed by the decades of war? What does a world without war hold for those who have known nothing but violence? What fate lies for these, the war-torn?

THE CRIMSON TALISMAN

BOOK 1

Adrian Cole

Erethindel, the fabled Crimson Talisman. Long sought by the forces of darkness. Long guarded in secret by one family. Now the secret has been revealed, and only one young man can keep it safe.

THE ORB OF XORIAT

BOOK 2

Edward Bolme

The last time Xoriat, the Realm of Madness, touched the world, years of warfare and death erupted. A new portal to the Realm of Madness has been found — a fabled orb, long thought lost. Now it has been stolen.

IN THE CLAWS OF THE TIGER

BOOK 3

James Wyatt

BLOOD AND HONOR

BOOK 4

Graeme Davis

For more information visit **www.wizards.com**

EBERRON, WIZARDS OF THE COAST and their respective logos are trademarks of Wizards of the Coast, Inc. in the U.S.A. and other countries. © 2006 Wizards of the Coast

THE YEAR OF ROGUE DRAGONS
BY RICHARD LEE BYERS

Dragons across Faerûn begin to slip into madness, bringing all of the
world to the edge of cataclysm. The Year of Rogue Dragons has come.

THE RAGE
Renegade dragon hunter Dorn has devoted his entire life to killing
dragons. As every dragon across Faerûn begins to slip into madness,
civilization's only hope may lie in the last alliance Dorn and his
fellow hunters would ever accept.

THE RITE
Rampaging dragons appear in more places every day. But all the
dragons have to do to avoid the madness is trade their
immortal souls for an eternity of undeath.

THE RUIN
May 2006

For more information visit **www.wizards.com**

FORGOTTEN REALMS, WIZARDS OF THE COAST and their respective logos
are trademarks of Wizards of the Coast, Inc. in the U.S.A. and other countries.
© 2006 Wizards of the Coast